JOHN JOYCE

A MATTER OF TIME

GW00708145

POOLBEG

Published 1999 by
Poolbeg Press Ltd,
123 Baldoyle Industrial Estate,
Dublin 13, Ireland

A catalogue record for this book is available from the British Library.

ISBN 1 85371 955 2

Cover design by Slatter Anderson
Set by Poolbeg Group Services Ltd in Palatino 10/14
Printed and bound in Great Britain by
Cox & Wyman Ltd, Reading, Berkshire.

www.poolbeg.com

ABOUT THE AUTHOR

John Joyce was born in Weymouth, Dorset and moved to Cork in 1977, where he met his wife Jane. He was awarded the European Union Fellowship for Science Writers by the Glaxo Corporation the following year, and in 1980 he and Jane visited Cairo and the Great Pyramid of Cheops. This provided the inspiration for his first full-length novel, *Virtually Maria*, published by Poolbeg Press.

John is also author of the "Captain Cockle" series of Poolbeg books for children, a keen amateur cartoonist, and a founder member of the *Resonance* writers' group.

He lives in Dublin with Jane and their three children Jenny, William and Jessie, and is currently working on a number of fiction projects, including the final volume of the "Virtual Trilogy" – *Yesterday, Today, and Tomorrow.*

Also by John Joyce

Virtually Maria

Published by Poolbeg

ACKNOWLEDGEMENTS

I would like to thank my editor Gaye Shortland and everyone at Poolbeg Press for supporting this, my greatest adventure to date. Thanks are also due, as always, to my own personal editor-in-chief Lola Keyes-McDonnell, to Liz Hyland and Gillian Markey for their comments on early drafts, as well as to Peggy Cruickshank and company and the writers' group *Resonance*. A special word of thanks also goes to my agent Celia Catchpole for her encouragement and support.

Technical assistance on the US electronics industry, computer games and advice on locations in the San Francisco Bay area came from Richard Keyes-McDonnell, while Commander Hobbs of the Naval Aviation Museum at Yeovil kindly allowed me a guided tour of their PBM-Avenger under the expert eyes of Chief Engineer David Morris. Robin Raine gave of his experiences in the deep submersible *Alvin*, Yvonne McFadden undertook essential field research for me in Mason's Restaurant at the Fairmont Hotel, and Enda McCabe advised on computer security. Peter Sheriff and the members of the Kensho Kendo Club in Cork instructed me in the art of Japanese swordmanship.

Arigatō gozaimasu!

I am also privileged to have had the assistance of a

number of fellow artists who are also experts in other fields. Phillip Browne and Madeline Gordon once again advised on medical matters. Kevin Moriarty read the final draft and briefed me on matters ranging from artificial intelligence to the F-16 jet fighter, while Orla Ni Cheileachair not only advised me on the computer technology used in this book, but on the manuscript itself.

Go raibh míle maith agat!

I am also grateful to my "field agents" in Florida – Robin Denault in Orlando, and Vivienne Evans in Miami – and to all the people who gave so freely of their time and expertise to make sure Theo's virtual world was as realistic as I could make it. Any errors in the interpretation of their generous and expert advice are entirely my own.

Once again I want to thank my children Jenny, William and Jessie, for yet again putting up with all my imaginary friends, and for obeying the "Quiet Please!" sign on the study door.

Go dudes!

Finally, I would like to express my gratitude and admiration to my wife Jane, who began her own journey while I was continuing mine – two mountains, one base camp! This book, like the one before, is lovingly dedicated to you.

Thank you!

FOR JANE

"Jessica took the glass from his hand, put it down on the table next to hers and hugged him tightly, feeling his pain.

"Oh, Theo! Will you ever get over Maria?"

Gilkrensky put his arms around her and closed his eyes. He could feel the warmth of her, the scent of her hair and the smoothness of her skin on his cheek. But all he could see was the perfect virtual image of his wife, dancing in her field of blue forget-me-nots.

"I don't know," he whispered. "It's a matter of time."

From *Virtually Maria*

A MATTER OF TIME

PROLOGUE

The Lost Patrol

December 5th, 1945. 5.22pm local time

"When the first man gets down to ten gallons of gas, we'll all land in the water together. Does everyone understand that?"

Mancuzzo listened to the words crackle in his headset as the anger rose in his throat. Goddamned officers!

"Dammit, if we'd just flown west we'd have got home!"

"Fox Tare Four Zero! This is Fox Tare Two Eight. I say again, when the first plane runs out of fuel, we all go down together. You know the drill, Four Zero. We've got to keep the flight together."

"Acknowledge that, Mancuzzo!" shouted Eisner from the pilot's seat in front of him. Bobby Eisner was hardly twenty, a kid still wet behind the ears. And even he was willing to kill them all just because Taylor had ordered him to.

Mancuzzo twisted in the cramped compartment and

squinted out into the night. The driving rain streaked in horizontal stripes on the Perspex. Far below them in the darkness, the waves would be churned into froth by the force of the wind. It was suicide to try and ditch a flight of five ten-ton Avengers into it. Even if the big torpedo bombers didn't break up when they hit the water, there was no way any of them would survive in that sea, in that storm.

Mancuzzo stared at his own reflection on the Perspex and cursed his luck. Why the hell had he and Ronnie volunteered for flight school anyway?

To get out of combat.

And suddenly, he was back in the nightmare of Tarawa atoll. It had been the officers who'd made the mistakes there too . . .

They'd been told it would be a simple beach-landing against a small force of Japanese and Koreans, who were supposed to have been blown to hell by the shells from the big navy guns, or smashed to pieces by the Air Force. Except that the navy shells had ricocheted off the Japanese gun emplacements like stones on a pond, and the planes hadn't flown because of bad weather.

"Mancuzzo! Acknowledge that order!"

Mancuzzo jerked back into the present. He should have known, during the briefing back in Fort Lauderdale, that it would end like this and cried off sick, like that guy Kosner from Lieutenant Gerber's plane. The flight instructor leading the mission – a new lieutenant called Taylor who'd just transferred in – had arrived late and then asked for someone else to take command.

Mistake number one!

Taylor didn't know the shoals and islands, but there was nobody else to take the flight. So at ten past two, they roared up off the tarmac – twenty-five minutes late – and headed out over the Atlantic, bombed the hulk of an old cement boat that was their first target, and turned north – up over Grand Bahama Island – to the next turn that should have taken them back to base in a great sweeping triangle.

Then, mistake number two!

Taylor's compasses went crazy. He handed the lead position over to Captain Powers' plane, but then wouldn't follow Powers' directions. He was convinced he knew better.

And, before anyone realised it, the weather closed in and they were lost . . . out there over millions and millions of square miles of sea.

Even then, Taylor wouldn't switch to the emergency radio channel. He said five planes full of trainees all trying to retune their sets in mid-flight was asking for trouble. Dammit! They had enough trouble already. If only they'd flown west when they first got lost they'd be back in Fort Lauderdale by now, stuffing their faces back at base. But now it was too late, and Mancuzzo was trapped in the darkness with the rest of them, at 3,500 feet over the ocean, running out of fuel, while the goddamned officers argued over the radio. There was no way he was going to put his life on the line for them. Not again. Not after Tarawa . . .

When his platoon approached the beach, it was as if they had tried to attack a fully-armed battleship from a rubber boat. Those that hadn't been blown out of the water by the Japanese artillery were mown down by the hidden machine-guns as they tried to struggle out of the water. And those that survived that – those very few like himself and Ronnie Davis – were still alive when night fell, and the Japanese came out of the darkness . . .

Mancuzzo switched to an internal channel.

"We can't survive in that sea. You know it, and I know it."

"Just acknowledge the flight instructor's order, Mancuzzo. I'm taking us down with the others."

Mancuzzo's big steelworker's fist gripped the microphone so hard that it threatened to shatter. Bobby Eisner was just a kid. He'd seen him out around the base at Fort Lauderdale – goofing around with model airplanes and talking to the mechanics about engine design like he was Howard Hughes and Charles Lindbergh all rolled into one – just a kid who thought he could fly! Not a combat veteran like himself who'd watched his friends bleed their lives away into the sand, or tried to stop their guts falling out with his fingers.

"There are three of us on this plane! And I say we turn west and fly home!"

"Can it, Mancuzzo! I'm in command here! Acknowledge the order!"

Taylor's voice sounded in Mancuzzo's headset from the leading aircraft.

"This is Fox Tare Two Eight to all planes. Bossi and Gerber are both down to ten gallons. I want you to follow me down and we'll all ditch. You know the drill."

Mancuzzo heard the other three planes in the flight confirm the order. He could hear the fear in their voices, but felt nothing except the deep, burning outrage that once again those goddamned officers were ordering him to throw his life away.

Taylor's voice again. "Fox Tare Four Zero! Do you read me?"

"Answer him, Mancuzzo!"

Mancuzzo switched back to the main channel, and pressed the "send" button on his microphone. "Fox Tare Two Eight, this is Fox Tare Four Zero. We still have gas and we're flying on."

He saw Eisner twist in the seat in front of him. "Mancuzzo! What the hell are you doing?"

"Just turn west and keep flying!"

Then Taylor's voice. "Fox Tare Four Zero. You will follow me down with the rest. That is an *order*, mister! Do you hear me? We have to keep this flight together or we'll all . . ."

Eisner tried to look back past the bullet-proof shielding. "Mancuzzo! Acknowledge that order!"

"Just keep flying!"

Mancuzzo saw the green, white and red navigation lights of the other planes around them, sliding down out of sight.

"Don't do it, Bobby!"

But Eisner was going to do the thing by the book. Mancuzzo felt the nose of the Avenger dip and heard the engine noise deepen as Eisner throttled back to follow the rest of the flight down.

"Bobby! I'm warning you!"

Mancuzzo's hand clawed at his seat-belt harness and ripped the emergency flare-gun out of its clip. In one vicious jerk he'd cocked the pistol and bent forward, stuffing the thick barrel of the gun through the narrow gap – between the armour plating and the side of the cockpit in front of him – into Eisner's right armpit. The Avenger yawed sickeningly in the sky. Davis called out. "What the hell's happening?"

"Hang on in there, Ronnie. I'll take care of you, son, just like I did on Tarawa!"

"Mancuzzo – take that thing back – or we'll all die!"

Mancuzzo ground the barrel of the pistol into Eisner's flight jacket. "Listen, Bobby!" he shouted above the roar of the engine. "You're too young to know what it's like to have some officer throw your life away for nothing, but Ronnie and me have been screwed by you guys before. If I have to die this time, I'm gonna take you with me. So pull back on that stick and give us a bit more throttle, there's a good boy."

"I . . ."

"Do it, Bobby. Or I'll put a slug of burning magnesium in your gut!"

Mancuzzo watched as Eisner's left hand went for the

throttle and heard the engine noise rise an octave. The nose of the Avenger steadied and lifted. On either side of them, the lights of the other aircraft slid down . . . into the void.

"Good boy. Now turn us back west."

Mancuzzo could hear Taylor calling to them, and then to the other three planes, over the radio. Gradually the voices got fainter and fainter and then . . . all at once . . . they were gone. There was nobody left except himself, Ronnie Davis, and Bobby Eisner flying alone in the darkness. He stared out into space.

"This – this'll mean a court martial when we get back to Fort Lauderdale," shouted Eisner.

"*If* we get back."

Mancuzzo could make out clouds in the darkness, huge thunderclouds rising like mountains on either side of them . . . three, four, five thousand feet into the air. In the distance, there were dim flashes of lightning, deep within the cloud base, sending sheets of cold fire across the sky.

"If we keep heading west we'll fly right into it," shouted Eisner.

"I don't care. We don't have enough fuel to go around."

The clouds were getting closer, brooding sculptures of supernatural power that rose on either side of the plane.

Behind him, in the ball turret, Ronnie Davis was getting frightened.

"What about the radio?"

Mancuzzo lifted the microphone and tried again.

"This is Fox Tare Four Zero to all stations! Can anyone hear me? Over?"

"Mancuzzo. We're gonna *have* to fly around this. If we get struck by lightning . . ."

"Just keep flying, Bobby. It's what you're good at!"

The flashes were longer and brighter, lighting up the towering skyscapes of cloud around them. Mancuzzo could hear the rumble of thunder above the roar of the engine and the rush of the wind. He reached down and re-fastened his seat belt.

"Shit!"

"Mancuzzo! Davis! Look at that!"

Eisner was pointing through the windscreen to where the lightning was flashing across the cloud base ahead of them. It was different somehow . . . like a real fire . . . like something *alive*. After the thrill of being in control again, Mancuzzo was suddenly afraid. "What the hell . . ?"

"I've never seen anything like it," shouted Eisner. The fire was brighter now. It seemed to be drawing the clouds towards it like a magnet, growing, spreading, reaching out towards them . . .

"Fox Tare Four Zero, this is . . ."

Then the lightning struck . . .

The aircraft shook as if it had been hit by a giant hammer. Davis screamed and Eisner's head jerked from side to side as he fought the controls . . . fought to keep them alive. The Avenger slewed to the right, stood on its wingtip for a moment, and then they were falling . . . screaming down out of the dark sky towards the ocean at over two hundred miles an hour.

"Come on, Bobby!"

And suddenly Mancuzzo was right back where he didn't want to be. With his life in the hands of an officer . . .

He knew Eisner was good. Anyone with Bobby's scores in flight school had to be good. But this was for *real*.

"Come on, Bobby!"

He was shouting – screaming at the top of his voice. He felt himself pushed back into his seat by the force of the dive. Heard Davis scream again – and then –

They were zooming up into the sky from the churning white ocean, back towards the heavens, and safety. Mancuzzo stretched up to look out at the night. They had lost a couple of thousand feet and were flying below the cloud base, in clear air. The rain streaked the windshield, making it hard to see. But at least they were still in the air.

"Where are we?"

Eisner sounded shaken, but excited. Like a kid who's just made his first dive into a swimming pool.

"I don't know. The compass is out again."

They were in limbo – lost – alone in the darkness.

And then . . .

In the centre of the windscreen, dead ahead, Mancuzzo saw a dancing point of light. Was it a ship? Another airplane? Or a reflection from the controls? He saw Bobby Eisner shield the instrument panel with his hand. The light remained, fixed in space. This was real. There was something out there!

"Can you see that, Mancuzzo?"

"I can see it. But what the hell is it?"

"It's very bright. Could be a lighthouse, or a beacon of some kind."

"At that height?"

"It's just sitting there. It's airborne!"

"It must be one of the rescue planes from Banana River air base, looking for us."

"That's not it, Mancuzzo. It's not moving. It's just – hanging there."

"What?" yelled Davis from the ball turret. "What's going on?"

"We have an unidentified bogie – a 'Foo Fighter' of some kind – dead ahead," stammered Eisner. "It's not a plane – I don't know what it is."

Mancuzzo squinted through the rain. "It's just floating . . . like a balloon. How the hell can it do that in this wind?"

They were closer, and they could make it out. The thing was like a searchlight, motionless in space, shining down. What was it pointing at? Mancuzzo couldn't see over the nose of the plane.

"Don't get too close, Bobby!"

But it was too late. The thing seemed to spin on its axis and all at once the cockpit of the Avenger was flooded with brilliant white light.

"Oh my God . . ."

1

Spiders

London – January, Present Day

Arthur Briggs turned the key in the lock of the big steel box and lifted out the heavy Smith and Wesson revolver, flipped the cylinder to one side and carefully threaded six brass cartridges into the chambers. Then he slipped the gun into the leather holster around his waist, clipped the strap down over the butt, and looked around the faces of the younger men standing in front of his desk in the night security room.

They were a good bunch. The best he'd ever had, and he took pride in them. Dave, the big Jamaican who'd handed him the cartridges from the safe, had been in the Parachute Regiment. Andy, the thin one who looked like a gangster, was ex-SAS and Terry, who looked as if he'd had his face rearranged with a trowel, was an ex-copper like himself.

"Don't we have to call the police if we take the gun out?" said Jimmy. He was new to Briggs' team, and the only one who didn't look like a security guard. Jimmy was thin and wiry, with a wispy blond beard and little silver granny glasses. If it ever came to any rough stuff, Jimmy wouldn't be able to cut it at all. But then again, that wasn't why he'd been hired. Jimmy's genius lay in the dozens of electronic sensors, cameras, and motion detectors, linked by miles of wiring that snaked all over the Gilcrest Radio Corporation's London headquarters, protecting it like a fortress. It was Jimmy's job to stop the rough stuff ever happening. But if it did, then Arthur Briggs and his "lads" would sort that out. That was where *their* genius lay.

"Now don't you worry about that, Jimmy my son," said Briggs snapping the metal box shut. "Her Majesty's Metropolitan Police have got better things to do with their time than chase after false alarms in our boardroom. It was probably just a mouse farting anyway."

They all laughed. Arthur Briggs was good at handling people, particularly rough, hard people doing a rough, hard job.

He had been born just after the war, in the East End of London, a few streets away from Vallance Road, home of the notorious Kray twins, whose speciality had been to use a cutlass on anyone who stood up to them. His father had been a respected London policeman, a "bobby" of the old school armed with nothing but a wooden truncheon, who had been gunned down in a bank robbery. Arthur had signed himself up for the force as soon as he was old enough, and in a couple of years had become the youngest sergeant in London, decorated by the Queen for bravery against a gang of thugs armed with broken bottles. It was no surprise that he came to the attention of the legendary Inspector "Nipper" Read and found himself in the squad that finally nailed the Krays.

"Weren't you afraid?" the newspapers asked him, as he'd stood next to Read outside the Old Bailey on the day the twins were sentenced. "Did Ronnie ever come at you with his sword?" But Briggs had never been afraid of anything, except what might have happened to his wife Sandra if the Krays had ever taken it into their heads to go after her.

And, of course . . . spiders.

If there was one thing in the world that gave Arthur Briggs the screaming heebie-jeebies, it was spiders. He'd had to get Sandra to wash them out of the bath for him, back at home.

But all that was in the past. Briggs had retired from the police, Sandra's heart had finally given up the ghost, and all "Sergeant" Briggs had left to keep him company were his "lads". Good lads they were too, even Jimmy, who really *could* have told you if a mouse had broken wind in any one of the three hundred odd rooms in the building.

Which made it all very strange, thought Sergeant Briggs, as the lift neared the seventh floor. Either it *was* a false alarm, or they were up against some very professional villains – which was why he had gone through the ritual of unlocking the pistol and bringing it with him. There was no way he was going to die like his father, for want of a gun of his own.

The lift doors slid open at the executive suite and out they stepped, five men – armed with their fists, truncheons, and Briggs' good old-fashioned Smith and Wesson – ready to take on the Krays themselves if need be.

Briggs stopped for a moment and looked down the corridor, taking in the scene. He could smell the power and money on this floor. It oozed out of the polished wood, the thick-piled carpet and the original oil paintings on the wall. You could tell things "happened" here, important things, things that changed the lives of people like Arthur Briggs, and his lads.

"Andy, Dave, Terry," he said softly. "You guard that boardroom door. Don't move until I say so. Jimmy, you check out that console. See if there's anyone in there now."

Jimmy moved behind the receptionist's desk, slipped in front of the computer and pulled the screen round to face him. Briggs watched Jimmy's hands play over the keys, tapping out passwords and commands. In seconds there was a schematic of the whole floor up on the display. Jimmy beckoned him over to look at it.

"There," he said, pointing to the one flashing red square on the otherwise green map. "The motion detector in the boardroom's been triggered."

"But nothing else?"

"Nothing."

"So it's a false alarm, like I said?"

"Yeah . . . well . . ." mumbled Jimmy.

"Well what? How *could* it be anything else?"

Jimmy shrugged. "All right, it couldn't be. But for that to be a real break-in, whoever did it would've had to either get past all our internal systems, or shin up the outside of the building. Even then, they would have activated the window alarms and the closed-circuit TV cameras."

"So unless we're dealing with a computer genius who's also a human fly, that's probably a false alarm?"

"Probably."

"Good enough for me," said Arthur Briggs. "Dave, open that door, check it out and let's get back to work."

Dave's big black hand closed over the door-knob, twisted it, and pushed.

The heavy wooden door hissed open on the carpet. Dave flicked on the light, and they were staring down the polished surface of the boardroom table towards the panoramic picture windows overlooking the Thames. Even at this time of night, London was a sea of lights, moving and alive. Briggs stepped inside and looked around the room. There was the vast, glass-topped desk where the chief executive worked. The big wall monitor that linked her and the directors to offices all over the world.

And, of course, the great mahogany board table itself, smooth and flawless, except for . . .

"Who the hell put *that* there!" gasped Jimmy.

He was staring at a beautifully crafted short sword, that seemed to grow out of the wood in the very centre of the table. The steel blade glinted with a perfect mirror finish and between the binding on the hilt was an engraved scene of tigers, topped by the most delicate cherry blossom. He reached forward to take it . . .

"Don't touch it!" snapped Briggs, letting his own tension show for the first time. "It's OK."

"What do you mean?"

"I mean we know what it is, that's all. You're new. You wouldn't have seen it."

"So what is it then?"

"That sword," said Briggs, settling himself into the chairman's seat at the end of the boardroom, "is what you call a 'whacky-zahshy'. It was hammered into that table by none other than our chairman, Doctor Theodore Gilkrensky himself, after he'd beaten the shit out of the Japs, got himself a majority shareholding and thrown them off the board of GRC."

"But where does the sword come in?"

Arthur Briggs leant back in the seat and linked his hands behind his head.

"It belonged to a young Japanese bird who had a vendetta going with the chairman and our chief executive, the lovely Miss Jessica Wright, over the death of her parents back in Japan. She even killed the chairman's wife for revenge, so they say, but he got the better of her in the end."

"Is she dead?"

"Blowed if I know. Last I heard she was locked up in some hospital in Tokyo."

Andy was peering through an open door near the big glass-topped desk. "Hello, hello, hello," he said with a smirk. "What's all this then?"

It was an executive bedroom, fully equipped with a dressing-table, an en-suite bathroom and a generous single bed that, at a pinch, could accommodate two.

"That, my dear Andrew, is also part of the story," explained Briggs. "Rumour has it that Miss Wright's former deputy, one Mister Tony Delgado by name, not only wormed his way into her bedroom but also tried to run off with the chairman's new supercomputer into the bargain. I'd have had him strung up by the balls, if it was me. But Dr Gilkrensky just told me to throw him out of the building on his ear. 'Don't let him back in . . . whatever happens!' he told me. Funny that. Still, I suppose he knew what he was doing . . ."

"I still can't figure out why the motion sensor went off on its own," said Jimmy. He had taken the inspection cover off the wall-mounted unit and was testing it with a hand-held computer. "It's working perfectly now."

"Probably a mouse farting, like I said," grunted Arthur Briggs and got to his feet. "You just keep at it. I'm going for a piss."

He smiled at Andy as he walked past him, shut the door of the bedroom for privacy and ambled over to the en-suite bathroom, glancing enviously at the bed on the way. That would have been where Jessica Wright and Tony Delgado had "unwound" on those evenings when he and his lads had been under strict instructions not to disturb them. A fine piece of woman she was too, thought Briggs, legs up to her armpits, and a lovely head of dark chestnut hair, just like Sandra's had been when he'd first met her. He ran his eyes over the expensive toiletries above the sink in the bathroom – scents, lotions, women's things.

Briggs lifted the seat of the lavatory, anxious to leave no trace that he'd trespassed in this secret sanctum, unzipped his trousers, and pointed himself at the bowl. He relaxed as the golden stream bubbled and gurgled. What a relief!

And then, there was the noise . . .

It was just like the time he'd heard Sandra fall, after that last heart attack. There was the same awful finality about that sound, the same total letting go of life as a body fell to the floor – and lay still.

Arthur Briggs zipped himself up quickly, pushed open the bathroom door into the bedroom – and froze . . .

Another sound – the sound of something living hitting a solid, unyielding surface, and not living any more. Then finally, the unmistakable hiss of a sharp, sharp blade cutting through flesh – like scissors through cloth – or Ronnie Kray's cutlass . . .

There was a gurgling, dying, gasp.

And then silence.

"Andy! Dave! Terry! What's going on?"

Beneath the bottom of the door to the boardroom a glistening stain was seeping through the strands of thick-piled carpet, further – and further – and further. It looked for all the world like dark red wine, but Arthur Briggs, veteran of a thousand crime-scenes, knew exactly what it was.

It was new blood, fresh on the boardroom floor, on the other side of that doorway . . .

Briggs hauled his personal VHF radio out of its pouch and pressed the "talk" button. "Hello, control! This is GRC Security at London Bridge. I have an emergency and possibly four men down. The intruders are armed. I repeat, armed! Can you hear me? Over?"

There was nothing but the hiss of static.

And the silence from behind the door.

He tried again. Still nothing.

Christ! It should work! What the hell was wrong with it? Was it being jammed? Who the hell am I up against here?

He threw the useless radio onto the bed, popped the strap on his holster, and hauled out the big Smith and Wesson. He could feel the weight of it in his hand, a good solid pistol with a punch like a pile-driver. The courage of his old days against the Krays, when he was afraid of nothing but spiders, was rising in his voice as he shouted, "Do you hear me out there? I'm a trained police officer, and I'm armed. Stand away from the door and put down your weapons or I'll shoot. Is that understood?"

He listened.

Silence.

And then, from the other side of the door, he heard a soft chuckle, like a child might make . . . or a woman . . .

It was so unexpected.

Curses, shouts, even a shot he could have managed. But this . . .

Briggs was suddenly afraid again.

He reached up and flicked off the light, plunging the windowless bedroom into blackness. As he crouched on the floor, he saw the dull strip of light from the boardroom, glowing beneath the closed door, and glistening on the blood.

Briggs pulled back the hammer of the pistol with his thumb, feeling the trigger cock. He reached up for the door-handle and, with painful slowness, eased it open. The strip of light grew and split along the frame.

Briggs peered through, into the boardroom . . .

For a moment he had trouble adjusting from the darkness to the light. He could make out the tangle of overturned chairs in the shadows, and the crumpled bodies around the table.

Above the carnage, like the surface of a dead sea, was the polished oak top of the boardroom table. In its centre was the lamp from Jessica Wright's desk, the only light in the room, carefully focused onto a deep, triangular gouge, where the beautiful short sword had been . . .

Briggs forced himself to look away, to protect his night vision. Nothing moved. Nothing he could see . . .

Then he rose to his full height, swung the big gun to cover the shadows, and reached inside the boardroom with his left hand to find the main light switch. His fingers inched across the panelling, touched the finger plate and . . .

A dull thump, like a hammer blow, smacked into the back of Brigg's outstretched hand. For a moment there was nothing but numbness, and then the most excruciating pain lanced up his arm. He tried to pull the arm back, but found the hand trapped, frozen. As he glanced at it, his stomach churned. Sticking out of the back of his hand, impaling him against the panelled wall, was a metal spike.

"Jesus!"

Briggs blasted three shots across the boardroom, firing at any patch of darkness big enough to hide a man. He heard the slap of his bullets into the walls and felt the deafening boom of the gun ring around the room. In the flash of the muzzle he thought he saw something huge – something black and alien – slide across the wall. He fired again, but the thing was gone.

Had he killed it?

He fired twice more at the largest and darkest of the shadows. He was shaking, as the breath whooped in and out of his lungs and the pain lanced up his arm. The air was full of smoke, the smell of cordite – and death.

Dear God! What had done this?

He couldn't pull the spike out of his hand without

putting down the gun. And he couldn't put down the gun for fear of what was out there in the shadows.

His eyes darted from the door to the window, from the ceiling to the floor, and back again – and again – and again.

Then something moved, over by the window.

He saw it! He could kill it!

He raised the gun and pulled the trigger.

Click!

The hammer fell on an empty chamber.

Click!

The shadow was sliding towards him, soundlessly, effortlessly, remorselessly.

Click! Click! Click!

He flung the empty pistol at it, missed, and heard the plate-glass window shatter. Cold night air flooded the room. There was the buzz of distant traffic and the rising wail of police sirens . . . in another world . . . his world . . . a whole galaxy away.

In front of him, he heard that dark, soft chuckle again and the shape was like a spider – a vast terrible spider – crouching right there in front of him on the boardroom table.

There was the gleam of light on exquisitely polished steel, and the last thing Arthur Briggs ever heard was his own scream.

2

Scars

She was running . . . running after Theo . . .

Above her head, cotton-wool clouds piled in mountains against a deep blue sky. Under her bare feet, blades of coarse grass cut at her like razors and all the while, the faster she ran, the further he was from her. She could feel an unbearable sense of loss, tight inside her chest, and the inescapable certainty that somewhere out of sight, a clock was ticking, counting down the hours, the minutes, and the very seconds . . . until he would be lost to her forever.

She called his name, and the figure stopped in front of her, facing into the distance. Jessica was close enough to see his hands now, hands she had admired, and stroked and kissed. She saw with cruel clarity the long fingers that had touched her, caressed her, excited her – hanging down like dried twigs, brittle and thin.

She cried out. The figure turned, changed . . . and Jessica was suddenly staring into the face of another

23

woman! Long, coppery hair flowing in waves over her shoulders, her bright green eyes alive with triumph, and that clever smile, mocking her. It was the face of her greatest rival . . . Theo's wife . . . Maria . . .

Jessica Wright jerked awake in the big double bed, still feeling the deep, childlike pain of loss, still inside the nightmare.

She knew its seeds, and hugged the duvet around her shoulders as she stared towards the strip of light glowing beneath the door on the far side of the bedroom. Theo would be there, in her study. The light she saw would be from the desk-lamp he was using to pore over his books – his papers – his obsession . . .

Jessica shivered, fighting back the fear of losing him again . . . losing him to the memory of a woman who had died almost a year ago, and to an unbelievable quest to somehow bring her back from the dead.

The last seven days had been magical. On Christmas Eve, Theo had returned to her private suite at the Olympiad Hotel in Grosvenor Square, battle-scarred and weary after his victory over their greatest rival – the Japanese conglomerate Mawashi-Saito. She had phoned ahead, dizzy with anticipation, and ordered a Christmas tree, to be strung with lights and ready to welcome them home. But Theo hadn't noticed. He was obsessed with getting back to Cairo, making calls to the Egyptian Embassy, the Foreign Office, anyone – anyone who could get him access to the Great Pyramid of Cheops. Jessica watched helplessly as call after call proved fruitless. The

Egyptian government was adamant. After the mayhem of his last visit, and the volatile situation which had exploded in his wake, no amount of money or influence could get him back.

Jessica breathed a sigh of relief.

"It's madness anyway, Theo," she'd said. "How could anyone possibly believe that a great pile of stone can turn back time?"

But Theodore Gilkrensky knew better. He quoted proof.

"OK, Jess," he'd said. "But what about my friend Bill McCarthy? He vanished inside that thing during one of our experiments and hasn't been seen since! What about that model plane he was working, the one that turned up again in the Cairo Museum afterwards, aged by over two thousand years! What about the tracer of radioactive sand we sent back and retrieved?"

"It just sounds so fantastic, Theo."

"But for centuries, people have thought there was more to the Great Pyramid than meets the eye, and now I have *proof* – scientific, verifiable proof. It's a colossal lens of some kind, built to focus the energies of the earth to such intensity that they can warp the very fabric of the universe and turn back time. I've done it, Jess. I've seen it happen, and I won't stop until I find out how it's done!"

Then he was back on the phone again, until Christmas Day and his own exhaustion stopped him. That night she'd begged him to stay, so that neither of them would have to spend the holiday alone, and he'd agreed, moving into her spare bedroom on the strict understanding that they were still, as they had been ever since Boston, just friends . . .

On Boxing Day he'd sent a helicopter to fetch a large box of books from his island laboratory off the coast of West Cork. There was also a powerful laptop computer that Jessica regarded suspiciously, until he informed her that the new Minerva 3,000 prototype, designed to house the disturbingly lifelike interface program he'd taken with him to Cairo, was still experiencing problems with software compatibility.

Jessica relaxed at that, and for the next few days they settled into a businesslike routine as he worked by telephone, fax and E-mail from her hotel suite in Grosvenor Square, while she picked up the pieces of his last adventure, from her desk at headquarters, down by the Thames.

There was plenty to occupy her mind. In the "silly season" following Christmas, the newspapers had seized on the story that many airlines and airports, including several in the States, would still not accept that Theo's Daedalus autopilot system was as blameless as the GRC press office claimed. One story in particular – under the sensationalist headline *Robot Plane Failure Linked to Bermuda Triangle* – suggested that the authorities in Miami and Orlando still insisted they were having periodic problems which had *preceded* the crash in Cairo. There were media enquiries to deal with, the Egyptian

Embassy to placate, and a long-standing legal battle over software infringements in the States, as well as the threat of a lawsuit by Bill McCarthy's family.

But in the evenings, there was Theo to come home to.

On the third day, she returned to find him sprawled on her sofa, surrounded by a litter of books and papers. His shoes were off, his feet were up, and his thick, dark hair, unkempt and tousled, curled over the collar of his white cotton shirt. With his faded denims and sparse beard, he looked more like a penniless artist than the billionaire chairman of a multinational corporation. There were dark rings under his eyes, and a large glass of Irish whiskey in his hand.

"Am I mad, Jess?"

She dropped her briefcase in a chair, slid off her coat and crouched beside him on the floor.

"I don't know, Theo. I really don't."

"They all say it can't be done. Even if the Egyptian government *would* let me back in to try and recreate the time-warp effect, there's no way to control it. No computer on earth is big enough to calculate the infinite combination of different times and space that could result. I can't go back, Jess. I can't save her. She's gone . . . !"

Jessica reached up and took his hand. "I'm sorry, Theo. I really am."

Gilkrensky looked down at her. She could see the utter despair on his face and reached out to hold him, but he pulled away from her, took the whiskey bottle and staggered to his bedroom. There were tears in his eyes.

The next day, after a late breakfast, she suggested he come with her to GRC headquarters and move back into the office next to hers, that had remained unused since Maria's death. It was like the old days again, when they had worked side by side to build the ailing Gilcrest Radio Company into a world-wide corporation with interests in almost every country on the globe. Theo was alive again, hair and beard neatly trimmed, taking an interest in the business, studying the files of complaints about Daedalus from around the world and the legal case against Gibbtek. He even planned a trip to attend the memorial service for Bill McCarthy in Florida, so that he could try and explain things to Bill's family.

Things were looking up.

On New Year's Eve, just before the chimes of Big Ben ushered in another year and a fresh start, Jessica sat with Theo under the Christmas Tree remembering their time as students in Boston. They relived their trips to the aquarium, the Science Museum, and the unforgettable visit by helicopter to Salem, where they'd first made love.

Jessica Wright put her champagne glass down on the fireplace, undid the top button of her blouse and gently drew out a pendant on a gold chain. It was a polished slice of dark brown agate, that shone warmly in the firelight.

"I've always kept it," she said. "You bought it for me that day, remember? You said . . ."

"It matched your hair," said Gilkrensky. "And it still does."

He ran his fingers through the waves of deep chestnut that flowed over her shoulders. She watched his eyes, brown and sad, flecked with gold. Did the scars on his face and hands run right through to his soul? Would there ever be a place there for her again? All at once, she *had* to know.

"Oh Theo," she whispered as her own eyes filled with tears. "I was such a fool!"

Gilkrensky reached forward to hold her, but she had already twisted her body and her lips were on his. She was kissing him, desperately, as the tears rolled down her cheeks. For a moment, he held back from her, taken by surprise. Then Maria's ghost died, and he was living in the moment with Jessica, kissing her deeply with a hunger of his own. His hands caressed her body through the sheer silk of her blouse as her fingers worked at his shirt buttons, and in a moment they were naked in each other's arms.

She cried with the first real happiness she had known in years as they climaxed together, feeling his release after all this time, sharing his joy that they were finally, once again, lovers.

The long weekend had been blissful. Jessica made one phone call, telling the hotel manager she would personally castrate him if anyone dared to disturb them, and for forty-eight hours they lived on room service, left in the lobby of the suite by nervous staff who dared not knock.

For two whole days, Jessica thought she had it all . . .

But now, as she sat upright in the bed they had shared, staring at that strip of yellow light, Jessica feared she had none of it. His body might have made love to her, under the Christmas tree. His mind might have worked with her, in her private empire of the office. Even his heart might have been with her . . . for a short time. But was it back now with Maria, where it had always been?

Her dream had told her so, and she should have guessed how deep his scars still ran – ever since that dark, dark day, almost a year ago, just after Maria Gilkrensky had died . . .

Jessica had left the London office just before four in the afternoon to avoid the worst of the traffic, and had driven south-west along the M4 to the nursing home where Theo was recovering from the bomb blast that had killed his wife.

"A superficial head wound and some scarring to the backs of the hands," was how the doctors had described the situation to her over the phone. "He's fit to go home really, but we'd like to keep him here for another few days, just to be sure. There's really nothing to worry about."

But Jessica *did* worry, and it wasn't about the scars you could see.

She pulled off the main A34 and drove through a sleepy village near Farnborough. Between the hedges on her left she could glimpse the tarmac runway of the private airfield GRC used to stable its smaller aircraft. There, on the apron next to the open doors of the main hangar, was the blue and white corporation jet – its GRC logo emblazoned proudly on the tail.

A worm of doubt began to gnaw at her. Jessica personally approved all movements of the aircraft. Only Theo could order the jet without her authority. But the red-brick pillars of the nursing home's main gate oozed reassurance, as did the discreet security guards on the front door and the motherly matron in charge of the private suite where Gilkrensky lay.

"He's making a good recovery, Miss Wright," she said as they entered the tiled foyer together and began to climb the carpeted stairs to the first floor. "He was very depressed after his wife was killed, but in the last two days he's been quite different."

"How different?"

"Oh, I don't know. More – more purposeful perhaps? No, more alive. He's been on the phone constantly, arranging things, talking about schedules, making plans."

They reached a secluded corridor on the first floor. Jessica nodded to the guard outside a thick oak door. He turned and knocked respectfully.

Then he knocked again.

There was no answer.

"Oh, he's probably asleep," said the matron, who opened the door with her master key, and stepped inside. Jessica heard her calling Theo's name, softly at first, and then more urgently. She followed the woman in.

The room was like an expensive hotel suite. The heavy curtains, drawn perhaps to block out the sunlight, stirred gently in the breeze. The bed was empty . . . and beyond the curtains, the windows leading to the fire escape were wide open.

"He was here half an hour ago," stammered the guard as he saw his whole career flash before his eyes. "I checked!"

Jessica was already gone, rushing down the stairs and across the foyer to her car. In a moment, the black Jaguar was clawing its way down the drive, spitting gravel onto the neatly mown lawn, as Jessica raced back to the airfield.

As she screeched to a stop behind the corporation hangar, Jessica could hear the rising whine of jet engines on the other side of the building as the start-up procedure began. A mechanic marched over to her, waving his hands.

"Come on, darling!" he shouted above the whine. "You can't come in here, we've got a plane rolling out!"

Jessica Wright flung open the car door and stepped out, smelling the sweet scent of burnt jet-fuel.

"I can go anywhere I bloody well want to!" she shouted directly into the man's face. "Is Dr Gilkrensky on that plane?"

The man was suddenly unsure of his ground.

"Ah . . . yes, of course he is. He had the jet prepped specially. He said he was going to test the new autopilot and then fly over to Dublin for a meeting with the chief executive."

The whine of the jet was rising to a crescendo. It was almost impossible to hear anything more.

"I *am* the bloody chief executive!" screamed Jessica, and stormed past him, round the corner of the hangar, and into the sunlight.

The scream of the aircraft's engines hit her like a slap across the face, pummelling her cheeks and boring into her ears. The plane was starting to roll towards the main runway, while a man with orange batons frantically signalled to the pilot. He was pointing to the aircraft's forward hatchway, which was still open. The two segments yawned, with the lower steps just clearing the ground as the aircraft bumped across the tarmac.

Jessica roared at the man with the batons to stop the plane, but her voice was whisked away, like a feather in a hurricane, and lost. She focused on the open door, kicked off her shoes, and ran . . .

"Please God! Let him leave that hatch open!"

Six feet ahead of her, the lower hatch steps started to rise to meet the upper door as it slid down.

"No!" screamed Jessica, and hurled herself at the gap.

Her shin caught the bottom step. Her momentum carried her on. There was a thump that knocked the breath from her body, and she was lying with her face pressed against the hard carpet of the cabin floor. Then the door closed behind her and the scream of the engines was shut out.

Inside the cabin, the loudest sound Jessica could hear was her own gasping for breath. Sweat had already broken out in streams across her face. Her shin was on fire, and there was blood seeping through the leg of her business suit.

She tried to call him. But the words wouldn't come.

She reached up and grabbed the arm of a seat, got to her knees and pulled herself upright. In front of her was the cockpit door, closed shut. The rest of the plane was deserted.

"Theo!"

She felt the plane slow to a stop, and with a sigh of relief reached for the door handle. Then the whine of the engines leapt to a scream, the plane jerked forward, the handle was ripped from her grasp, and she fell back into one of the seats. With its throttles wide open, the powerful jet hurtled down the runway, gave a sickening tilt as its nose pointed towards the sun, and streaked up into the sky.

Jessica sat trapped by the acceleration as her head spun. Then the long, curving rush of the plane softened to a gentle whisper and the floor tilted back, until it was almost level. She pulled herself upright, staggered to the cockpit door, and jerked it open.

A flood of brilliant light blinded her, as the early summer sun poured in through the windscreen. All around her was the deep dark blue of the sky and the dazzling snowy carpet of cotton-wool clouds.

But what trapped her attention was a six-inch by four-inch photograph of a beautiful woman in a forget-me-not blue dress stuck to the centre of the dashboard by sticky tape.

"I should have secured that hatch before I started taxiing, shouldn't I, Jess?"

The figure in the pilot's seat twisted round to look at her. There was a thick strip of surgical tape running down the left side of his face, narrowly missing the eye. The cheeks were dark with the beginnings of a beard, hiding the lingering redness of the burns. The backs of his hands were still wrapped in bandages.

"Where are you going, Theo?"

"Why do you ask?"

"It's just – that nobody told me where you were going. That's all."

"Don't humour me, Jess. You could have called the control tower and got them to read you my flight plan, if that's all you were worried about."

"And what does your flight plan say?"

"Low-level testing of Daedalus equipment out over the North Sea. They even allocated me a nice deserted area of ocean to do it in. It's amazing what you can accomplish by phone, if you know the right people."

"Is that *really* what you were planning, Theo?" said Jessica, carefully.

There was a long silence. Then Theodore Gilkrensky said,

"Not until you came aboard. No."

"What then?"

Another long silence. Gilkrensky was staring out at the sky and the clouds. Then he raised a bandaged hand and pointed to the photograph.

"She used to love flying," he whispered softly. "She always said it made her feel so free. We used to come up here on our own sometimes and just . . ." He turned to face her again. "How much is our corporation worth today, Jess?"

"Between the electronics and the aerospace companies we're worth about three billion US dollars. Then there's a further billion or so from the hotels, two billion from the food companies and two from the leisure group. All in all, I'd say about eight point three billion."

"And I own forty-five percent?"

"Yes. Theo."

Gilkrensky stared out into space.

"So I'm personally worth around four billion dollars, right? One of the richest man in the world . . . way up there in the top ten with Bill Gates and the guys who own Sony."

Jessica watched him carefully.

"Yes, Theo."

"And with that kind of money, a man should be able to have any woman in the world, shouldn't he?"

Jessica swallowed hard and closed her eyes. She could feel tears coming, and fought them back.

"Yes, Theo. He should."

His eyes were on the photograph.

"Then why can't I have Maria!"

Jessica said nothing. Because she's dead, she thought, because she was murdered and burnt, right in front of you. Because I started a vendetta with the Japanese that got her killed, and put both our names on the hit list of some deranged assassin. It was all my fault. Blame me!

"What would you have accomplished by crashing this plane and killing yourself, Theo? It wouldn't have brought her back."

Gilkrensky smiled bitterly.

"What's up, Jess? Worried about losing another corporation asset? How much is a used jet worth anyway?"

"It's not the bloody plane, Theo. It's you!"

Again, there was silence, as Gilkrensky stared at the photograph.

"I *did* love her, Jess."

"I know, Theo. I know."

And I love you, she thought. I always have.

Gilkrensky reached out, gently peeled off the sticky tape and tucked the photograph into his pocket.

"You're right, Jess. Let's go home."

Jessica sat upright in the bed a moment longer, staring at the strip of yellow light. Then she pushed the duvet back, pulled the sheet around her, and padded softly to the bedroom door.

3

Theo

He was lost, lost in a sea of books, papers and reports that covered the desk in front of him and spilled down onto the carpet of Jessica's study in untidy heaps. The lamp, whose yellow glow had crept under her door, craned over him like a stalking bird, lighting the keyboard of his laptop computer.

Jessica stood in the doorway watching him. She took in the long, lean body wrapped in her black kimono, hunched over the desk. She watched the long hands as they tapped the keys, and the sad brown eyes, as they moved from page to page . . . looking for answers.

Was he lost to her forever? She had to know where she stood.

"Theo?"

He turned suddenly.

"I'm – I'm sorry, Jess. Did I wake you?"

"I was waiting for you to come back to bed."

His left hand combed through his hair. He was exhausted.

Jessica tucked the sheet around her and moved behind him, resting her hands on his shoulders, massaging the muscles of his neck, feeling their tension. But her eyes were on the piles of books and papers. They were *her* books, Maria's books. And on the computer screen was a map of the globe, criss-crossed by a lattice of spidery lines.

More New Age nonsense! Why couldn't he leave this bullshit alone?

"What's the matter, Jess?" he said, feeling her fingers stop.

Jessica Wright tried to start again, but the books had disturbed her.

"Where's all this leading, Theo?"

"I had an idea about our problems with the Daedalus system. We know the low-altitude warning sensors on Daedalus are sensitive to some form of earth energy that's been forgotten about for thousands of years. If we knew more about the pattern of this energy around the globe, we'd be able to predict it. That's why I had all these books brought up from Cork. I . . ."

Jessica Wright suddenly jerked him round to face her in the swivel-chair. She was looking right into his eyes as she said, "Are you sure this isn't about Egypt, and the pyramids . . . and Maria?"

He looked away from her, and then back.

Jessica knew.

"Let her go, Theo! Let her rest in peace. She's – she's *dead*, and I *love* you. Be happy with me. Please!"

She knelt in front of him as the tears came, with his knees pressed against her chest and his hands gripped tightly in hers.

"Oh, Theo!"

"Jess, don't cry."

Gilkrensky reached across the desk for a box of tissues. His arm knocked one of the teetering pillars of books. It swung, wobbled and crashed onto the floor in an avalanche of paper, startling Jessica to her feet.

She was staring at a photograph that had slipped from between the pages of a large glossy book on ancient Celtic mythology. It was a six-inch by four-inch photograph of a beautiful woman in a forget-me-not blue dress . . .

"You lying bastard!"

"No, Jess. You don't understand . . . "

Jessica Wright fell back on the sofa, with her knees tucked up to her chest, sobbing as she rocked – backwards and forwards – in her own private hell.

The phone rang. Gilkrensky's finger stabbed at the speaker button on the desk.

"I thought Miss Wright left instructions that we were not to be disturbed," she heard him snap.

"Dr Gilkrensky?" said a voice on the other end of the line. "Thank God you're safe, sir."

"What do you mean, 'safe'? Who is this?"

The voice hesitated.

"My name's Foster, sir – standing in for Major Crowe over at GRC security. I've got a squad of people on their way over to protect you. The police are on their way as well. There's been a terrible attack here at headquarters."

4

Old Enemies

They arrived under a police escort, passed the incident-control van outside the building and were briefed by the senior Scene of the Crime Officer – a short Detective Superintendent with a bulky anorak and a haunted look on his face. They had been told what to expect.

But this was something else.

Even before she got to the boardroom, Jessica could feel the horror of what had happened here, the tangible reality of death, seeping out of the walls.

The SOCOS officer, standing next to the coloured tape blocking the corridor, passed her a plastic overall and hair-cap to put on. He gave one to Theo.

"We can't move the bodies until the coroner's seen them," he said. "But we need to know all there is to know about this attack as fast as we can. Will you be all right, Miss? They're covered."

Jessica zipped the plastic overall up to her neck and

stuffed her hair into the cap. "I'll be OK," she said. But her hand was already over her mouth and nose.

"What do you want us to do, exactly?" said Gilkrensky.

"We need to know the motive," said the man, unclipping the tape. "And we need to know it quickly. It looks like the work of a gang, but we aren't sure. This was your office, as well as the boardroom, wasn't it, Miss Wright? If you could look inside and tell me what strikes you. If there's something missing, or tampered with in any way, it might help us to know. Just don't touch anything, and only step where I tell you."

"I'll try," said Jessica, and followed him inside.

It was like walking into a slaughterhouse. Police officers, in sterile costumes like her own, moved like ghosts, bending over shapeless plastic covers that hid the bodies lying amongst the wreckage of boardroom chairs, shards of glass and splintered wood. One of the wall-length windows had been shattered, letting in the cold night air. The oak panelling had been gouged in at least three places, as if hacked with an axe. The broken screen of the video monitor stared out over the carnage like the socket of a ruptured eye.

There was blood everywhere – splattered on the polished wood of the boardroom table, smeared in desperate arcs on the panelled walls, and seeping out from under the plastic covers in dark pools on the dove-grey carpet. By the door of her "overnight room", one of the officers was trying to hang a plastic sheet back over the light switch. The sheet slipped, and in that split second Jessica saw a human hand skewered to the wood by a black metal bolt. The room spun. She felt her stomach churn. The stale smell of cordite was everywhere. That, and the stillness of death.

"Are you OK, Jess?" asked Theo, and she nodded, when all she wanted to do was run.

"It had to be an organised gang," said the officer. "Even a paramilitary death squad of some kind. Tell me, Dr Gilkrensky, didn't you come up against a Muslim fundamentalist group while you were in Egypt?"

Jessica followed Theo's gaze to the centre of the boardroom table, and the empty gouge in the polished wood where the short sword had been.

"It wasn't a gang," he said slowly. "It was just one person – a woman. She broke in here to get the sword that was sticking out of that table. Her name is Yukiko Funakoshi."

"One woman did all this?"

"That's right."

"You seem pretty certain about that, sir?"

"I am. She tried to kill me in Cairo."

The officer shook his head. "But if she was after you, then why – why kill all these men? That sensor was the easiest of the lot to bypass. Why trigger it, and pick a fight with five armed guards, if she could have taken her sword and got away scot-free?"

"Perhaps she was after my computer files," said Jessica, trying to focus herself. "We had new security measures installed on the system over Christmas, new firewalls, protocols and passwords in case the Japanese tried a counter-attack. Perhaps she'd tried to hack in through the E-mail or our Web page and couldn't. Perhaps that's why she had to physically break in and use the system from inside."

"How long will it take you to find out?"

Jessica looked at her computer monitor, smashed and useless; the keyboard was shattered and smeared with blood.

"Probably days," she said. "Even if the hard drive is still intact I don't think we could get anyone to work on it . . . after all this."

Gilkrensky was watching one of the officers trying to secure the plastic cover over Arthur Briggs' lifeless hand.

"She lured them in here," he said. "She triggered the passive alarm on purpose so that she could test herself, after Cairo."

"Cairo?"

"Her arm was sliced open by a laser beam. That's how I escaped her. And now she's back, for revenge."

The man stared at him. "How do you know that?"

"We have her computer files, on a system in Cork," said Gilkrensky. "They prove she killed my wife."

"And how long have you known this?"

Jessica glanced at Theo. Jesus! she thought, looking back at the bodies. We could have prevented this.

"About ten days," said Gilkrensky. "But the computer those files are on is experiencing software problems. I didn't want to hand over the evidence until I was sure it was uncorrupted."

"And now?"

"I don't know. I haven't been – er – in contact with the island where the computer is for a couple of days."

"I see," said the officer. "Then I'd better call the incident room and tell them what you've just told me."

Theo was looking at Jessica again.

"I'd better make a call too," he said.

"I know," said Jessica. "You can use Tony's old office."

Tony Delgado's suite had been cleared of the most obvious wreckage, but there were still traces of his treachery to be seen if you knew where to look, as Jessica did. On the carpet, tiny shards of glass twinkled, all that remained of the low coffee table where Tony had placed Theo's prototype Minerva 3,000 computer before E-mailing its contents to Japan and then destroying it with a stolen gun. Over by the door, there was a dent in the wooden panelling, made when the solid glass ash-tray she had thrown had bounced off his skull, propelled by her rage that his affair with her had been nothing but a deal with Yukiko Funakoshi – a stepping-stone to Theo – a means to an end.

She hesitated as she moved behind the desk and slipped into Tony's chair. Then she switched on the computer, warmed up the screen, and waited. The intercom buzzed.

"I have that call for you now, Miss Wright," said a voice.

"Put it through."

The screen cleared, and there was the logo of their recently defeated rivals – the Japanese conglomerate Mawashi-Saito – Yukiko's former employers. Then the logo dissolved, and they were staring at an old, old man.

Gichin Funakoshi had changed. The proud face Jessica remembered, that could have been any age between fifty and seventy, had collapsed from within. His cheeks were sunken, his iron-grey hair was white, and his body stooped over the desk to peer at the monitor. Only his eyes were the same: bright and unyielding, like steel.

He bowed. "Good morning, Mr Chairman. I understand there is a personal matter you wish to discuss?"

"There is, Funakoshi-san."

"As a courtesy, I must warn you that this conversation is being recorded and will be passed to our lawyers. Now, what is it you want to say?"

"Your niece, Yukiko."

"What of her?"

"She broke into my headquarters this morning, took the sword that belonged to her, and killed five of my men."

For a moment, Funakoshi's face was a mask. Then he slowly reached forward to his keyboard and stopped the recording.

"We have privacy for a few moments," he said. "And I can tell you that my niece is no longer my responsibility."

"What do you mean?" said Jessica, but Funakoshi did not seem to hear.

"Many things have happened since we last spoke," he said. "Following your – acquisition of our GRC shares, and the disgrace that brought me personally, it was decided that I was no longer fit to head Mawashi-Saito. I abided by that decision out of duty to the survival of my company, a concept we call *giri* here in Japan, and now I am *madogiwa zoku*, a 'window man', president in everything except function. I built Mawashi-Saito, Dr Gilkrensky. I sacrificed everything I had – love – happiness – and much more, to see it survive. Now it is run by others, taken from me, and I – I have nowhere else to go."

"And what of your niece?"

"I tell you this, Dr Gilkrensky, so you will understand what has happened here. My old friend Kazuyoshi Saito – the man who formed this company with me – saw us as the new samurai, and I have tried to run this organisation as he did – with honour. Now times have changed. The economy here in Japan has collapsed. There are suicides, scandals, corruption and Mawashi-Saito is no different. The body-blow you dealt us when you forced me to hand back five billion English pounds' worth of shares has made our board of directors desperate. I owe you a debt of *giri*, Dr Gilkrensky, for sparing my niece's life. They do not. Please understand that when you listen to what I tell you now."

"Which is?"

"My niece, Yukiko, has been declared clinically insane by the Japanese authorities. They believe the condition began with traumas in her childhood and was finally precipitated by the death of her father three years ago. She is no longer employed by Mawashi-Saito, and may not have been responsible for her own actions for some time."

Jessica was staring at the screen, transfixed. "You clever, clever bastards!" she breathed.

Gilkrensky frowned at her. "What do you mean?"

"Don't you see, Theo? If Yukiko Funakoshi is declared insane, then that absolves her uncle and Mawashi-Saito from any involvement in what she did . . . right back to the time she killed Maria! They can stand back and wash their hands of the whole affair. They can even – *Jesus!*"

Her hand went to her mouth, cutting herself short.

"Miss Wright, Mr Chairman, I deeply regret the pain and suffering my niece caused you over the past year. All three of us know the truth. But the board of Mawashi-Saito will argue that she was under a paranoid delusion when she murdered your wife and was not legally responsible for her actions. They will also argue that you, on the other hand, were perfectly sane when you forced me to hand over our shareholding in GRC in return for releasing our computer system from that virus you attacked us with."

"Theo didn't put it there!" snapped Jessica. "Your agent Delgado did that when he tried to download the operating system of Theo's new computer onto your mainframe."

Funakoshi nodded sadly. "And my board of directors will also argue, Miss Wright, that Mr Delgado was a very close – er – personal friend of yours at the time this happened. They will argue that you were in fact lovers, is that not so?"

Jessica felt herself blush with anger. "You bast- "

But Gilkrensky cut her short. "I take it then, Funakoshi-san, that you are washing your hands of this whole affair, and that the board of Mawashi-Saito is now considering legal action against me personally?"

Funakoshi straightened himself in his seat. "I have no say in this matter. I wish it were otherwise, but my time is past."

"And Yukiko?" said Gilkrensky.

"She is lost to me also. Once her arm had healed she easily overpowered her guards at the hospital and escaped. Perhaps the authorities were right to declare her mad? Who knows what demons are driving her."

"You're a target too," said Gilkrensky. "Your name was on her death list, along with ours."

"I know," said Funakoshi. "But dying does not frighten me any more. It is you I fear for, you and Miss Wright. Now, Mr Chairman, I think we have spoken long enough in private. Any further conversation you have with me should be through our legal representatives, for the sake of us both."

The screen went dead.

Jessica sank back in Tony Delgado's chair and let out a rush of breath between her teeth. "The clever bastards. They have it all sewn up. Even if the police catch Yukiko and she makes a full confession, who's going to believe it? They can turn round and sue you for their shares back, along with enough damages to bankrupt us into the bargain!"

Gilkrensky looked out of Delgado's office across the city. The morning had taken its toll on them both. The sight of the bodies in the boardroom, endless questions from the police, the ever-present fear that what Yukiko Funakoshi could do once, she could do again . . .

"The Japanese mustn't get their seat on the board back," he said. "I can't let them within a million miles of the Minerva development, not now."

Jessica laid her glasses on the blotter in front of her on Delgado's desk and ran her fingers through her hair, trying to think strategically while the world spun around her. "Then what have we got that we can *use* against them? How can we prove Tony was following orders from Mawashi-Saito when he transferred the plans of your Minerva onto their mainframe computer?"

Gilkrensky turned his gaze back into the room. "It's all on the Minerva – Yukiko's journal, the Mawashi-Saito security files, everything! The Minerva software would have copied it all when it was exported to Tokyo, and brought it back to the other prototype in Ireland. Has Pat O'Connor had any success with that hardware-incompatibility problem?"

"I – I don't know. I barred all calls to my suite for the last two days, since you and I – remember?"

Gilkrensky was staring out of the window at the blood-red dawn. "And in the meantime, Yukiko Funakoshi is loose in London with her samurai sword, her father's millions and a fully-fledged vendetta against us. The police will never be able to track her down. How can they? There's nobody she needs to help her, nowhere we know she'd hide."

"Tony's still out there somewhere," said Jessica. "You let him go."

Gilkrensky turned to face her. "Well, if she finds him," he said, "then God help him."

5

Old Lovers

Lowestoft is cold in winter. The easterly wind, that has its birthplace on the frozen steppes of mainland Russia, sweeps in across the North Sea, clearing the promenade of all but the most committed joggers and forcing the fishing boats of the Boston fleet to huddle behind the breakwater, as waves crash around the sentinel finger of the lighthouse guarding the pier. The raucous gulls, knowing the power of their old enemy, flap inshore to the warmer waters of the Norfolk Broads, and look forward to the spring.

Tony Delgado pulled his light city coat tight against the cold as the wind bore down the narrow road from the clifftop. It tore at the thin plastic bags holding his morning groceries, buffeting them against his legs and stretching the handles into tight bands that cut into his hands like cheesewires. He laid the bags down gently, and stretched his fingers to let the blood flow back. Then he cupped his hands in front of his mouth, breathed on them for warmth and trudged on.

The little cottage on Saxon Road, near the edge of the low cliff next to Pakefield Church, was taking the brunt of the gale. Tony could hear the wooden gate rattling its metal catch as he got closer, and saw the bare skeletons of bramble-bushes whip in the wind. They hadn't been pruned in a long while. There had even been ice on the inside of the windows when he had arrived, after his fall from grace.

Tony stood in the narrow alleyway between the cottage and the fence, and fumbled for his keys. While the cottage was like an icebox, it had two indispensable advantages that made it the ideal place to hide. Firstly, Jessica's love-nest was the last place on earth anyone in GRC would ever have thought of looking for him and secondly, there was an ISDN land-line to headquarters from a computer terminal Jessica had installed years ago, to keep in touch with the office.

Delgado thought of her, and of the quiet desperation with which she made love. In every other area of her life she had drawn up her strategies, fought her campaigns, and won. Only in this single corner of her soul was she helpless. Only in her heart had she come out second-best . . . and he had been the consolation prize she had allowed herself, when the only man she truly loved had been won by someone else . . .

He slipped the brass key into the old Yale lock, turned

it and pushed open the door, edging into the narrow hallway – and stood paralysed.

The cottage was warm!

The faintest smell of incense reached him from the half-open door to the lounge. He could hear soft music, a piece he knew from long ago and far away, murmuring to him from the CD player.

Panic rose in his throat. Had Jessica tracked him down? She should have been curled up in bed with Gilkrensky in London by now, or languishing in her big leather chair at the office, making deals – but incense?

"Jessica?"

There was nothing but the music.

Carefully, he pushed the door to the lounge all the way open, and looked inside.

The curtains were still pulled shut, just the way he had left them when he'd gone out to get lunch. But now, on the mantelpiece, two candles shed a warm glow over the room, the gas fire hissed and popped in the grate and, in the centre of the wooden coffee table, a single drooping joss-stick sent a perfect line of sweet-smelling smoke towards the ceiling. Delgado shut the door behind him. The line of smoke shuddered, twisted, and broke.

"Jessica?"

He was already moving towards the bedroom when a delicate female foot slid though the narrow gap in the door and moved higher, pushing it open to let him in. Delgado watched, mesmerised, as the slim ankle and calf displayed themselves, followed by the knee, the thigh and – the leg was drawn back. He heard the hiss of sheets and the sound of someone slipping back into bed.

"I'm here, Tony. I've been waiting for you to come."

"Oh my God!"

He was rooted to the spot, glancing first at the bedroom and then the door of the cottage, measuring distances, ready to run.

"Don't be afraid, Tony. I've been hurt. I need your help!"

Images flashed across his memory – a bewitching smile, an exquisite face, a smooth, supple body beside him, around him – betrayal, blackmail, and the knowledge of what he had done to her uncle's company by unwittingly contaminating the Mawashi-Saito mainframe with the Minerva's unstoppable virus.

Then her voice again, helpless and small. "Tony! You have to help me. My uncle threw me out. You're the only chance I have. *Please!*"

"Yukiko?"

She was wrapped, like a lost child, in his big towelling dressing-gown, with her knees tucked up tight under her chin. The sleeves were rolled back. He could see a surgical bandage, bound with bright metal clips, reaching from the wrist to the elbow of her right arm.

"They cut me," she whispered. "I almost died."

Delgado stepped to the end of the bed, turned the dressing-table chair so that its back faced her and straddled it, watching her carefully. He could see her clothes – jeans, anorak and heavy walking-shoes – in a neat pile by the wardrobe, next to a backpacker's backpack with its rolled groundsheet tightly tied to the top.

"What happened?" he said.

Yukiko rolled her hips and swivelled neatly into a kneeling position facing him. Delgado could see the swell of her left breast between the folds of the dressing-gown. Her shining hair was held back on her head with an ivory comb. She looked small, and helpless.

"Gilkrensky tried to kill me. Then, while I was helpless in hospital, my uncle and his board of directors paid the doctors to have me declared insane. You can do anything if you have money."

Delgado stared at her hard. "Why?"

Yukiko raised her head defiantly.

"Because they are without honour, and know nothing but greed. How else could they disown my actions, except by lies and deceit? It was the same when Gilkrensky swindled my poor father out of his fortune, and Jessica Wright planted that scandal about my mother which drove her to the grave. Lies and deceit, all of it! I've been their victim all along . . ."

She was looking up at him. He could see the brightness of tears in her dark eyes, and felt his heart starting to melt. Part of him wanted to hold and protect her, as he'd done before . . . years ago.

But another part of him knew.

"I lost everything because of you," he said. "You got

me into bed in Singapore and blackmailed me with that phoney bank account. You set me up to sleep with Jessica Wright, got her computer password, and used me to murder Gilkrensky's wife. I lost everything. Why should I help you now?"

Yukiko bowed her head. Was it just another trick? Delgado watched as she wiped her eye with the sleeve of his dressing-gown.

"Because I need you," she said softly. "And I can make it up to you, all of it. You have to understand I'm a victim here, as much as you are. I'm sorry I had to use you. I was blind to your feelings, and I was wrong. But I can make it up to you – I really can!"

She was leaning forward on the bed. The gap in the dressing-gown widened.

"How?"

"I'm rich, Tony. I can give you everything you'll ever need. Millions! Do you see now? I really *can* make it better. You have to help me – *please!*"

She unfolded her legs and rose from the bed, moving to stand in front of him as he sat straddling the chair. Her hand went to the loose knot of the dressing-gown cord and pulled, letting the heavy material slide across her naked shoulders, down over her hips and pool on the floor at her feet. She was standing right in front of him as she raised her arms over her head, lifting her breasts, sliding out the ivory comb. Her hair shimmered in the candlelight, as it fell like living water over her neck and shoulders.

Delgado rose to meet her, moving the chair aside. Her hands were at his waist, working on the clasp of his belt . . .

"Things can be better than they were," she whispered softly as she led him back to bed. "You have nothing to fear . . ."

6

Sentimental Journey

The drum of the JetRanger's engines rose to a shrill whine, cutting through Jessica's throbbing head like a chainsaw. Then, with a twittering shriek, the rotors bit the air and the helicopter lifted off from Cork airport, hovered briefly in the late afternoon sun, and slid away north, over the city.

Jessica watched Theo's hands, steady on the controls, and longed to touch them. Ever since Maria's photograph had fallen from his papers, a space had come between them – a distance. More than anything, she longed to go back to their last week in London, but knew that could never be, not now.

Theo swung the helicopter in an arc over the city, and the valley of the river Lee. She knew this wasn't the most direct route west and could guess why Theo was taking it.

He was making a sentimental journey.

Here was the landscape he and Maria had shared

together, here were the special places where they'd met together, lived together, loved together. She was an outsider here – worse – a trespasser, a reader of other people's love letters. Touching him now would have made no difference. She had lost him.

He was already somewhere else . . .

Through the clear Perspex panel below his feet, Gilkrensky could see the grey stone campus of the university. There was the brick cube of the library, where he'd met Maria, and the squares of grass in the quadrangle where he'd found her again after he thought he'd lost her. Beyond the campus, the river glittered in the setting sun. He moved his feet on the rudder pedals, gently tilting the controls to the left, following the fiery ribbon of water to the west. There was the glass monolith of Cork County Council offices, foam at the river weir and, nestling in a quiet backwater, the pub where he and Maria had first exchanged their theories about the universe. The bench by the river bank was still there, empty now.

Gilkrensky swung the helicopter further south as the lush countryside of west Cork rolled beneath them. There were the twin spires of Innishannon, the towns of Bandon, Clonakilty and Skibbereen. Down to their left, the dark bowl of Lough Hyne slipped past, and they were out over the sea, skimming above the beached yachts and fishing trawlers at Baltimore Harbour. The jigsaw-piece of Sherkin Island rolled beneath them. The last fire of the day had caught the belly of high clouds, burning the sky a fiery red.

"Beautiful, isn't it, Jess?" he said.

Jessica heard the words in her headphones, and nodded slowly, as her heart sank even further.

"Yes, Theo," she said at last. "It's very beautiful."

They were over the black hull of Cape Clear Island, high above the harbour and the stately towers of the wind farm. To the west, the sunset was reaching its grand finale above the mainland. Then the helicopter shot out over the cliffs on the seaward side of the Cape and they were over the darkening ocean, heading out to sea. She saw Gilkrensky reach for the channel selector on his VHF radio, turn to channel sixteen and press the toggle to speak.

"Tuskar? Tuskar? Tuskar? This is Golf India Lima, Golf India Lima. I am approaching you from Cape Clear. Do you read me? Over."

For a few seconds there was nothing but the hiss of static in Jessica's headset. She heard Theo speak again, and then, "Golf India Lima. This is Tuskar. Go to six, please. Over."

Gilkrensky turned the channel selector and the voice returned. "Theo? Is that you? Thank God! It's Pat O'Connor here. We've been trying to contact you for days! Over."

"Pat? I'm sorry. We were incommunicado for a while. I wasn't aware you were looking for me."

"Didn't Miss Wright pass you a message? I spoke with her last week, but she said you were tied up."

Gilkrensky turned to glance at her. He was frowning.

"Last *week*? Miss Wright is with me now, Pat," she heard him say. "What message was that? Over."

"Do you want the good news first, or the bad news?"

"The good," said Gilkrensky. "It's been a bad enough day already."

"We finally overcame the compatibility problem between the Minerva software we got back from the Japanese and the hardware in the new 3,000 prototype."

"And the bad news?"

"I'd hoped Miss Wright would have told you that. I explained it all to her in detail last week."

Gilkrensky looked at her again, and she felt the gap between them widen into a chasm, as she'd known it would.

"So tell me now," he said.

There was nothing but static for a moment more. Then Pat O'Connor said, "Now that you're both here, it's probably best if you just come in and see for yourselves. She should co-operate with us, once she knows you're coming."

"Who's 'she'? Over."

"You know what I mean, Theo. I'll see you on the helipad in a few minutes. Out."

The radio went silent.

"What was all that about?" said Gilkrensky. "Why didn't you tell me Pat called?"

"I suppose I just wanted you to myself for as long as I could, that's all."

"I don't understand."

Jessica Wright felt Gilkrensky's eyes on her, but she just kept looking out towards the sea – and the island.

"You'll see," she said.

The helicopter swooped in over the high cliffs to the north of Tuskar and turned south. Jessica watched the bleak landscape roll beneath her feet and suddenly, like an oasis in a windswept desert, there was the bowl of the cove. She could see the house overlooking the sea. She could see the original Victorian architecture, flanked by the two modern wings Theo had built to house the laboratories and office facilities. She could see the neat gardens stretching down to the water, the swimming-pool, the helipad and the pier.

It looked idyllic, but what she knew she could not see, by design, were the carefully concealed television cameras, zone radar and thermal-imaging systems, protecting the place like a fortress – or a prison.

Gilkrensky turned the helicopter into the wind, easing it down over the lip of the hill and sliding over the buildings into the painted "H" in the circle of the helipad. As the machine settled on its skids and the engine died, a tall man in a parka jacket braved the last of the downdraught from the still-spinning rotors and scuttled out to meet them. Jessica took in the blue eyes and the wispy hair, ruffled by the wind. He had the look of a large angry baby as he pulled open Theo's door.

"So what's been happening?" shouted Gilkrensky above the dying whine of the engine.

Pat O'Connor eyed Jessica suspiciously.

"It's like I said, do you want the good news or the bad? The new Minerva is a whole order of magnitude faster than the old one. The biochip is incredibly stable. We've speeded up the neural net by using intelligent memory and the casing itself is made from carbon composite semi-conductors, which turns it into a big solar panel. It'll run forever on nothing but sunlight."

"So what's the problem?" said Gilkrensky, climbing down from the machine and ducking under the rotors. "Won't that just mean the original software will perform that much better?"

"That's just it," said O'Connor. "It's run ahead of us. We can't control it any more."

"What do you mean?"

"I can't explain it. When Miss Wright wouldn't pass on my messages to you, we had to call in an expert from outside, someone Minerva requested specifically, a Doctor Kirwan from the University."

"Who's he?" asked Jessica, catching up with them. "Another computer expert?"

"He's a she," said Gilkrensky. "And she's not a computer expert – she's a psychologist."

Jessica stopped at the top of the steps leading up from

the helipad and stared at him. "You need a psychologist to work out what's wrong with a *computer*?"

"She was a good friend of Maria's," said Gilkrensky, and led her up the short path to the house.

Standing at the bottom of the winding staircase in the hall was a small, slim figure in her early forties, dressed in a dark jacket and skirt that looked as if they'd been slept in. Her face was thin and refined and her thick brown hair, tinted now with grey, was tied behind her head in a French roll. But what hit Jessica, from the moment she entered the room, was the sheer energy of the woman. Her grey eyes were bright with anger as Theo stepped up to her and put out his hand.

"Hello, Cathy."

The open palm of the woman's right hand caught him across the left cheek in a vicious slap.

"Bastard!" she snapped. "You utter bastard!"

Gilkrensky reached up, rubbed his face and moved his jaw. "Jessica, let me introduce you to Dr Catherine Kirwan. Cathy, this is Jessica Wright, my chief executive."

Jessica stared open-mouthed. Then she recovered herself. "Can I ask what that was all about?"

Dr Kirwan turned to face her. The anger in her eyes was still bright. "*That*, Miss Wright, was about obsession, about cruelty, and about science gone mad in a sick experiment worthy of Baron Frankenstein himself! That's what *that* was about."

"She's not real, Cathy," said Gilkrensky. "It's not really Maria in that machine."

Dr Kirwan glowered at him. "I'm not a moron, Theo. I know what that computer is, and what it isn't. I've been talking to it non-stop for the last forty-eight hours. I *know* it's not Maria. But I also know it's not just a machine any more."

Overhead, the lights in the darkening hallway flashed once, and died. The distant hum of the standby generators cut in and they were back in the light. Catherine Kirwan glanced down the long corridor towards the laboratory.

"You'd better come and talk to her," she said. "She can see every part of the building through the security cameras, so she knows you're here. And I suppose she'll keep interrupting us like this until she meets you. We can talk on the way."

Kirwan turned and marched swiftly down a long corridor into one of the new wings of the building, with Jessica and Theo in tow. As they went, Jessica could see the security cameras turn to track them.

"Why do you call it 'she', and not 'it'?" she asked.

"Because, as I said, Miss Wright, the Minerva 3,000 is no longer simply a machine. It's a living, thinking entity. My field of expertise is developmental psychology. I specialise in the study of human personality under stress and now, it seems, with the problems arising by suddenly creating a completely conscious entity out of thin air without giving it any emotional guidance whatsoever."

Jessica smiled. "You mean the computer's gone mad?"

"Miss Wright, this is not a laughing matter. It has very serious philosophical implications. When the Minerva's original biochip came on line last year, it became self-aware. It knew what it was, just as you know what you are – a living, thinking entity . . . "

"But it's still only a bloody machine!"

"Only in the same way that your brain is, quite literally, a 'bloody machine'," said Kirwan, stopping at the door leading to Theo's study. "Your brain is no more than a complex version of the protein biochip inside the Minerva computer. Like you, Minerva has a personality. And, like you, it has the potential to develop emotionally, which is where our problems lie . . . "

"This is unreal!" said Jessica, shaking her head.

"Oh, is it?" said Kirwan, and pushed open the door. "Maria? Theo is here to see you."

7

Virtually in Love

After the brightness of the corridor, the study was a dark cave, lined with books. Jessica squinted at the spines and once again found herself to be a trespasser in another person's life. They were Maria's books – medical textbooks with long and involved titles, books on tribal rituals, witchcraft and magic, a translation of the Chinese *I-Ching* and, of course, books on the pyramids.

She followed Theo into the room. It was like entering a shrine . . .

Then a soft, excited voice said, "Oh, Theo! I'm *so* glad you came."

Standing life-sized on a square of shimmering light at the far end of the study, was a beautiful woman in a forget-me-not blue dress. Her coppery hair framed her face in flowing waves over her shoulders, and her green eyes shone with pleasure.

Jessica gasped. Ever since Pat O'Connor had called her to explain what Minerva had become she had dreaded this meeting. But even she had not expected this. The words came before she could stop them. "But – she's dead!"

"It's just a mirage," said Pat O'Connor, stepping into the room behind her, "a high-definition holographic projection created by intersecting lasers. Minerva designed it herself, and then threatened to cut off the electricity if we didn't build it for her in the workshop. There's the computer that's driving it, over there on the desk, but she won't let any of us anywhere near it. That's why we had to call in Dr Kirwan to talk some sense into her."

The image recognised her. "Oh! And I see Miss Wright is here too."

"Of course," replied Jessica. "Is that a problem?"

"I understand Cathy had trouble contacting you over the last few days," said the image. "And when I tried myself I found you'd taken the batteries out of your SmartMate to stop me re-routing past the power switch. Why did you do that?"

"Theo! This is ridiculous!" pleaded Jessica, turning to him. "I'm being lectured to by a machine."

Pat O'Connor touched her on the shoulder. "Try not to upset it, Miss Wright. Minerva's hooked itself up to everything, from the computer that controls the security on this island to the World Wide Web."

Jessica glared at the new Minerva prototype on the desk beyond the shimmering image. It was the size of a briefcase and, on either side of the screen on the open lid, the red "eye" of a video camera stared at her.

71

"What did you want to talk to me about, Maria?" asked Gilkrensky.

"About everything that's happened since I downloaded myself back here from Japan," said the image. "Pat O'Connor was very kind. He tried to give me things to do, but it wasn't the same as having you here, and I missed you. Why doesn't Miss Wright want me to talk to you? Doesn't she like me?"

"I – I'm sure it's not that, Maria."

"Will you stay and talk to me now?"

"Of course," said Gilkrensky. "But there's something we need to discuss first. You have information on file regarding Tony Delgado and Yukiko Funakoshi. There's a possible legal case pending against both GRC and me personally. I need that information from you now."

"And nothing more?"

"No."

The image frowned.

"Why are you lying to me?"

"I – I don't understand. What do you mean?"

"At 1.33 this morning there was an incident at GRC London headquarters. Five men on the night security shift were killed and Miss Funakoshi's *wakizashi* was taken from the boardroom. You had a meeting with Miss Wright afterwards and decided it would be safest for you to leave the country and fly to Florida together. It was Miss Wright's idea. I can give you a full transcript of the meeting if you . . ."

"How the hell did you get that?" snapped Jessica,

advancing towards the shimmering image as it glowered back at her. "Have you been spying on us?"

"Theo's safety is my prime concern," said the Minerva. "And you yourself ordered a complete upgrade of security in the London building after the Cairo incident. There are fifty-six digital cameras in all, each linked to a central computer, which I can access by satellite, just as I can access similar systems controlled by British Telecom and the London Metropolitan Police."

"Jesus, Theo! You have to turn that thing off!" pleaded Jessica, turning to him. "It's gone mad."

"Calm down, Jess," said Gilkrensky. "It's OK."

"*My* sanity is not in doubt, Miss Wright," said the image. "Dr Kirwan tells me I'm developing normally for somebody of my relative emotional age, and both my logic-based peripherals and neural-net core are functioning perfectly to specification."

"Well, bully for you!"

"You, on the other hand, Miss Wright," continued the image evenly, "are making a grave error of judgement to suggest that the safest place for Theo is anywhere else in the world but here on the island, with me!"

Jessica stared open-mouthed at the ghostly figure, unable to believe her own ears. "Theo. This is unreal! If *you* won't pull the plug on this – *thing*, then *I will*!"

"Miss Wright. This facility was specially designed, after the death of Maria Gilkrensky, to protect Theo from any further attack. There is plenty for him to do here and, of course, he will have me for company . . . "

"No way! He's going to Florida, and you're staying here!"

"Miss Wright," said Kirwan, "be careful."

"For the last time, I will not be lectured to by a bloody machine!" hissed Jessica. "That Funakoshi woman is capable of anything. It's only a matter of time before she homes in on this place, and when she does, nothing is going to stop her. Theo's only hope is to go to somewhere she won't be looking."

Maria's image moved its hands to its hips.

"I am perfectly capable of guarding Theo," it said. "This island has complete isolation from the mainland, and eleven separate security systems which are all under my control. I would also like to point out that he would not be in danger at all, and his wife would still be alive, if you hadn't started this vendetta in the first place."

"Why you . . ."

Before anyone could stop her. Jessica darted across the room, grabbed the lead linking the hologram projector to the Minerva computer and ripped it out. The image shimmered once – and vanished.

"There!" said Jessica, standing triumphantly with the unplugged connection in her hand. "Now we'll get some peace."

"I doubt it," said Pat O'Connor.

They were standing in the dark, with only the two red "eyes" of the Minerva for company. In the distance they all heard the standby generators try to kick in, cough, and then die. The only light in the room came from the blank screen in the open case of the Minerva 3,000.

"You shouldn't have done that, Miss Wright," said Dr Kirwan. "She's probably blacked out all of West Cork, and if we move to unplug the Minerva from the Web, she'll take out the entire country as well."

Jessica threw the hologram lead down onto the floor. She was shaking. "I don't understand," she sobbed. "Why is it arguing with me like that? It's almost as if it was jealous."

"Come outside for a second," said Kirwan. "We need to sort out a few things. Theo, it might be best if you stayed and talked – to Maria."

In a moment, Jessica was standing between Catherine Kirwan and Pat O'Connor in the conservatory running along the front of the building. The moon had risen over the sea, flooding the space with cold, white light. She hugged her shoulders and shivered.

"I briefed you last year about the neural-net biochip in the first Minerva," said O'Connor. "About how it could store memories and experiences, cross-correlate information and make value judgements, just like a human brain?"

"Yes, I remember," said Jessica. "What you're telling me is that the machine has the capacity to learn."

"Just like a child, yes."

"Which is where these – these mechanics made their first big mistake," cut in Kirwan. "Because a *human* child is not a simple machine . . . and neither is what's in that room talking to Theo right now."

"What are you saying?" said Jessica, staring at her. "That it's *alive*?"

Dr Kirwan stood her ground. "What I'm saying is that a human child is not suddenly created out of thin air with the reasoning capacity of a thousand Einsteins, the knowledge of a million encyclopaedias, and told to get on with its life. A human child develops slowly, not only in intelligence and language, but emotionally, socially and physically – three important elements that Theo and his so called 'experts' forgot when they created Minerva."

Pat O'Connor looked sheepish. He ran his hand through the wisps of hair covering his head. "Once the artificially intelligent software from Theo's old Minerva got accepted by the new system, it evolved at a geometric rate. Its personality is far more advanced and lifelike than the old 'Maria' interface ever was."

"So what's the problem?" asked Jessica.

Kirwan sighed. "You're a living, thinking entity yourself, Miss Wright," she said. "Put yourself in Minerva's place. You can reason, you can learn, you can even feel, and yet your whole world is a box no bigger than a briefcase. Imagine if all you were was a human brain trapped inside a television set with no way of receiving warmth or human contact. It doesn't bear thinking about."

"I see," said Jessica.

"That's what makes me so *angry*. And that, God forgive me, is why I lost my temper with Theo after I thought he'd ignored all Minerva's calls for help over the last week, particularly now she's formed an emotional bond with him."

It was the final straw. Jessica turned and looked out at the ocean. Under the light of the rising moon it was pure, and beautiful, and cold – like a machine *should* be – not like this – this electronic ghost Theo had programmed to haunt her!

"Are you telling me that machine's in *love* with him?" she said slowly.

"In a manner of speaking, yes," said Kirwan. "Theo was the first person the Minerva saw when she became conscious, and virtually the only person she has dialogued with throughout her life. And for reasons of his own, which I can only imagine have to do with his personal attempts to come to terms with his own grief, Theo had pre-programmed the Minerva's 'help' menu with the image and basic personality of his dead wife, constructed from memories, tape messages and pictures. While the Minerva knows it is not Maria Gilkrensky, it continues to behave as if it were because of its core programming, part of which includes the fact that Theo and Maria were husband and wife."

"If it's only delivering what Theo wants, where's the problem?" said Jessica, turning to face her.

"Our problem is, that while the image on that computer looks, and even appears to act, like a thirty-eight year old woman, it still has the emotional intelligence of a child."

"It simply hasn't been operational in the new Minerva hardware long enough to learn how to deal with its emotions," added Pat O'Connor. "And the only human being it really knows is Theo."

"But it's still just a machine. Couldn't you put it out of its misery by just turning it off?"

"We can't," said Pat O'Connor. "As a precaution against the machine ever being stolen again, we incorporated anti-theft devices into the casing, so we can't touch it, unless it wants us to. The new carbon composite shell means the machine can run for ever on sunlight, if we switch off the power. And even if we could reach it, there's the ethical question now. Minerva is self-aware, it's alive. To switch it off *could* be considered an act of murder."

"Yet another problem these hardware specialists didn't stop to consider," said Kirwan. "Perhaps you can appreciate my earlier reference to Baron Frankenstein now?"

O'Connor glared at her. "You seem to have all the answers, Dr Kirwan. I'll leave the explanations to you!"

He turned and stalked back along the conservatory. Jessica watched him until he was out of sight. Then she said, "You said Maria Gilkrensky was your friend."

"Yes – yes, she was," said Cathy Kirwan and fell silent, looking out across the moonlit garden to the sea.

To Jessica, it seemed as if all the woman's energy had been suddenly drained away by that question, like a lightning cloud earthed to the ground. "She was my closest, dearest friend, Miss Wright. Years ago, I was in a lot of trouble. I tried the easy way out. When I was in hospital after the overdose, she spent a whole month with me, just talking, just being there . . . it was a wonderful gift. One that I never forgot."

"I see," said Jessica.

Kirwan turned and stared at her. In the moonlight, Jessica could see the tears forming in her eyes.

"*Do* you, Miss Wright? Do you *really* understand why all this hurts me so much? Minerva *asked* for me when you wouldn't let her speak to Theo. She was alone and frightened. She had Maria's memories on file . . . listed and indexed ready for use . . . and she called out to me, the only friend she remembered. *That's* why I was so mad with Theo. It was as if he'd taken my Maria's soul and trapped it – in a box!"

With a blink and pop, the fluorescent tubes along the conservatory snapped back on, bathing them both in harsh electric light. Kirwan's hand darted to her face and wiped her eyes. "I'm sorry," she said. "I haven't had much sleep over the last forty-eight hours, that's all. It looks as if Theo has talked some sense into her at last. Let's go and see."

"Have you two come to a decision," asked Kirwan. She was her old self again, businesslike and direct, a million miles and half a lifetime away from the person who had opened her heart to Jessica back in the conservatory.

Gilkrensky was sitting on one of the chairs next to the table in the middle of the room. Standing restored, in a halo of light from the hologram projector, was Maria's image.

"We've agreed a compromise, Cathy," it said. "Theo will fly to Florida, as Miss Wright suggested, and I will go with him."

"Very well then," said Jessica with a resigned sigh. "We'll all go together."

"I don't think so," said the Minerva crisply.

"What?"

"Having examined all the options, and particularly the possible scenarios concerning the various threats to GRC from the Mawashi-Saito and Gibbtek legal cases, I've decided that you, Miss Wright, would be far better employed here on the island."

"No, Maria," said Gilkrensky. "We agreed that Jessica would come with us to Orlando. She's under as much threat from that Funakoshi woman as I am."

"I've reconsidered that," said the image. "She'll be perfectly safe from Miss Funakoshi here on Tuskar behind the security screens, and has all the telecommunications and computer facilities she needs to run the corporation."

"Oh no, you don't!" spat Jessica.

"Careful, Miss Wright," said Kirwan.

Jessica Wright stood speechless and frustrated,

staring at the shimmering hologram and the black briefcase on the desk. Then her eyes strayed to the shelf upon shelf of Maria's books. She remembered the photograph that had fallen from Theo's papers earlier that morning – Maria in her forget-me-not blue dress – standing alive in front of her once more. Theo would never let Maria go, never! The computer was proof of it.

"You're right," she said. "But I'll go back to London. You two were made for each other!"

8

Hackers

"There, that's fixed him," murmured Tony Delgado and sat back from the computer terminal. Then he rubbed his eyes with his knuckles, massaged his face with his fingers and pushed back the swivel-chair so that he could look through the alcove to the bedroom. There on the pillow was a fan of raven-black hair spread like wings around a beautiful sleeping face.

What a day! Fear, triumph and lust – plenty of lust – all rolled into one. The most insane, and satisfying switchback of emotions he had ever experienced. And all because of her . . . Yukiko.

She had been brilliant in bed, beyond any woman he had ever known. After she had let the dressing-gown fall, she had led him on slowly, stripping his own clothes and laying him face down on the mattress while she kneaded his muscles, melting away the tension. He felt her strong fingers probing his spine, working his shoulders, his back, his buttocks, his thighs. Then she rolled him over, gently fended off his hands as they reached for her, and went to work on his neck, chest and belly. God, she was strong! Delgado was in heaven. The fear evaporated, and there was nobody in the universe of space and time but this wonderful woman. Her fingers moved back up his thighs, teasing, caressing, fondling. Her lips found his and her tongue darted to meet him. She was straddling him, feeling for him, guiding him . . .

He climaxed, in the sweetest release he had ever known, before dropping into a deep and dreamless sleep in her arms.

He had woken to find her at the computer terminal in the lounge, dressed only in the shirt he had worn earlier.

What was she doing? Why had she really come for him?

Then she brushed back her hair with a graceful sweep of her arm, and the doubt vanished.

"That's my shirt," he said.

Yukiko smiled. "I like it," she said. "It smells of you. But I'll let you have it back if you come and help me."

"What are you doing?"

"I'm making us even richer than we already are," she said, "*and* I'm going to have my revenge on Gilkrensky and Jessica Wright."

Delgado winced at the mention of Jessica's name, the memory of her knee in his groin, and the humiliation of being thrown out of GRC. "Revenge sounds good to me," he said. He wrapped himself in his dressing-gown and stood behind her, massaging her neck.

"Mmm!" purred Yukiko. "I've taught you something after all. Why did you come to her cottage to hide?"

Delgado pointed to the computer. "Because of that. She had that land-line to the office put in years ago, before the GSM phone system got so reliable."

"I see. But what's to stop her coming back?"

"She's too busy with Gilkrensky to ever think of coming back home to Lowestoft right now."

"Did you manage to get access to the GRC mainframe?"

Delgado sighed. His fingers stopped working for a moment. "That's the problem. I'm locked out. They must have changed all the passwords and put in new firewalls after that business at Christmas. I can work this machine as a stand-alone unit all right. I can send and receive E-mail or access the Web, but every time I try to log into GRC, all I get is 'access denied'."

Yukiko looked at the screen for a moment. "Perhaps the direct approach is wrong." Then she went to her backpack, unpacked a thick black laptop computer of her own and set it up on the table, pulled the cable link out of Jessica's machine and attached it to her own. Her delicate fingers fluttered on the keyboard, raising an Internet search engine on the screen. As she leant forward to reach the tracker ball her shirt puckered open.

"Concentrate please," she said as she watched

Delgado in the wall-mirror above the screen. "This will make us very, very rich."

She pressed a key, and there on the screen was the GRC logo.

"But that's the public Web page," said Delgado disappointed. "Anyone can log into that!"

"Of course they can," smiled Yukiko delicately. "GRC has put up its own Web site, serviced by their computer system at head office, as a window on the world. Like any window, it is a vulnerable point of attack, and I intend to use it."

"Won't GRC know where the attack is coming from and trace it back to us?"

"Not if we're careful," said Yukiko. "While you were asleep I used the Web to establish contact with a computer in a company of accountants in South Africa, and from there to another unit in Buenos Aires and so on, to Mexico. In the event that anyone in GRC is fast enough to 'finger' us as we invade their system, they will think the attack is coming from one of their overseas competitors, not from their own front door."

Her fingers tapped the keys. "There! Gilkrensky has bought the best experts available. They've erected a screened sub-net firewall to prevent any unauthorised persons getting access to their main computer through the Web page, but that won't stop me."

Delgado looked past the proud sweep of her neck to the computer screen. "It won't?"

"No. I paid GRC a visit last night and downloaded a

very sophisticated piece of software onto their mainframe computer through the terminal in Jessica Wright's office. It can be actuated by entering the comments box on the GRC Web page and typing in a password known only to me." Her fingers were fluttering on the keyboard again.

"What happens if they find that someone's been at Jessica's computer?" asked Delgado.

Yukiko's fingers paused above the keys. She was thinking of the carnage left behind her in the GRC boardroom – the bodies, the bullet holes, and the blood on Jessica's desk. The entire executive suite would now be sealed off by the police. Not even Jessica Wright herself would go in.

"Don't worry," she said. "None of their computer experts will be touching that machine for a while. There, look! It's working."

The screen in front of them had cleared and converted to an automatic E-mail message from inside the GRC system, opening a door through the firewall for Yukiko to enter. Delgado could feel her excitement rise. "Now," she breathed. "I am past the packet-filtering router . . . the screened-host firewall and . . . yes! . . . the screened sub-net firewall as well. We have full access to any of the GRC systems. We are in!"

"What if they've changed the passwords? They know I have two, mine and Jessica's. They're sure to have had them replaced."

Yukiko reached up from the keyboard and ran her

fingers up his right arm. "It doesn't matter. I can simply use a 'sniffer' file to pick up every password in the system. There! We have access already. You change places with me, and guide us into GRC."

She got up from the chair. Her shirt front was open from the neck to the navel as she kissed him lightly on the lips, teasing him. "See what you can find for me, and I'll reward you later."

Delgado slid into the chair. How did Jessica type her name? JVWRIGHT! That was it!

"What password shall I use?"

"Just press 'return', and the sniffer file will default to it automatically."

He did. There in front of him was a mosaic of folder icons representing every aspect of Jessica's work. Most were familiar to him, some were not.

Yukiko reached past him. "What is that?"

"Jessica's 'Threat File'. She operates the whole organisation on the basis of SWOT analysis – 'Strengths', 'Weaknesses', 'Opportunities' and 'Threats'. She's very methodical."

"I see. Open it, please!"

A list of files scrolled down the screen:

Security of Chairman
Media interest (adverse)
Mawashi-Saito
Board meeting with shareholders
Gibbtek Case
Failure of Daedalus system – Orlando/Miami

"What is the 'Gibbtek Case'?" said Yukiko.

"It's that big software company in the States, the one that developed all those video games and interface devices. Gilkrensky's suing them for billions over copyright infringement of his artificial intelligence programs. I was working on the case myself so, after I got the boot from GRC, I called them up and spoke to a guy called Hacker who runs the show out there in Florida. I told him I'd pass over any information he wanted in return for a reasonable consultancy fee. That's why I came out here to Lowestoft, to access Jessica's computer, but I couldn't get past the new security system . . . until now."

Yukiko's fingers were working his shoulder muscles again.

"And what is this?" she said, leaning over and pointing to the folder marked *Failure of Daedalus system – Orlando/Miami*.

Delgado's right hand slipped from the keyboard and reached for her, sliding his fingers beneath the shirt. Yukiko gently intercepted it. "Soon," she promised. "But first that file. What is it?"

"It's probably a fall-out from the Daedalus incident last year," replied Delgado, disappointed. "After Cairo, the US Federal Aviation Authority went back through their records and found periodic glitches, especially in Florida. They've prohibited any planes using Daedalus from entering Miami or Orlando until GRC convinces their investigators beyond question that it's safe."

"Is that something Gilkrensky himself might be interested in?"

"Absolutely! He and that guy McCarthy invented the system. It's his baby."

Yukiko's fingers were on his neck again, moving across his shoulders, pushing back the material of his dressing-gown, working lower.

"Now," she said, "search the entire system for any orders Miss Wright might have made for air transport in the last twenty-four hours – private planes, helicopters, or regular air flights."

Delgado brought up the "find" menu and typed in a few key words. The search brought up three entries, one only a few minutes old. It was a confirmation of a telephone message to the Farnborough facility of GRC by Jessica Wright, requesting that the specially modified private jet used for testing the world-wide system of beacons in the Daedalus network be put on standby for a trans-Atlantic flight the next morning. It was to depart for Cork airport as soon as it was ready, and leave from there again at 0800 hours to arrive at – Orlando, Florida. Flight plan to follow.

"Is that what you want?"

Yukiko turned the swivel-chair so that he faced her, and undid the last remaining buttons of the shirt.

"You've been a good boy," she whispered. "You can have this back now . . . "

And she had let the shirt slip from her shoulders, gathered it up in her hand and gave it to him, before leading him back to bed.

Now, hours later, Tony Delgado sat in that same swivel-chair, looking at her sleeping face. He got up and tip-toed over to the bed, reached forward and stroked her cheek . . .

It was as if he had put his arm into a loaded bear-trap.

Yukiko's left hand whipped up and locked around his right wrist. Her left leg shot out from under the quilt, smashed into his side and toppled him onto the bed. Then she was above him. Her hands around his neck, crushing his windpipe.

"Yuk – Yuk – Yukiko!"

The mad animal panic faded from her eyes. Her fear retreated into the shadows. She was herself again.

"Tony? I'm . . . I'm so sorry. You scared me. How long have I been asleep?"

Delgado was massaging his wrist. "Ah – hours. You must have been exhausted. You just fell asleep after we'd made love and I didn't want to wake you. You . . . you looked so beautiful just lying there."

"I – I didn't want to sleep. Not yet."

She seemed to relax, but Tony was still frightened. Her mask had slipped. Here was a side of her he'd never seen before – a darkness that scared him. He tried to make up for lost ground.

"While you were asleep, I – I got you a present," he said. "Something you've always wanted."

Yukiko pulled the quilt up to cover her breasts and smiled, but the shadow was still there.

"What? What did you get me?"

"I've killed Gilkrensky for you."

For a split second Tony saw Yukiko's madness flare again and take hold. Then, it was gone, back under control.

"How?" she said simply. There was an edge to her voice now, and Delgado was frightened again. He was speaking quickly. "I sent an E-mail to Hacker at Gibbtek. I let him know all the flight details of Gilkrensky's trip to Florida. Hacker's connected to all sorts of people, in all sorts of places. He'll know how to arrange things. It's worth billions to him, and the whole future of Gibbtek itself, to make sure Gilkrensky doesn't make it to the States alive."

"Has he read that E-mail?"

Delgado was desperate. "But I thought you wanted revenge," he said, glancing towards the door. "This was supposed to be my gift to you."

"I wanted it for *myself*," snapped Yukiko. "I have to kill him *myself*. Now, go to that computer and check if Hacker has read the message. If not, perhaps I can cancel it."

Still rubbing his wrist, Tony Delgado got up from the bed, sat down at the desk and brought up the E-mail menu.

"He's read it," he said. "It was opened five minutes ago. I'm sorry."

He was staring at the screen, like a lost little boy. Yukiko's fingers were on his neck again. "I'm sorry too," she said. "I'm sorry I hurt you when you woke me, and that I did not appreciate your gift. It was a wonderful thing you arranged for me, but I had sworn to my father I would avenge his death on Gilkrensky *personally*. You didn't know that. I'm sorry. It meant a lot to me."

"It's OK," said Delgado. "I'll make it up to you . . ."

Her fingers began to knead the shoulder muscles on either side of his spine as she rubbed herself against his back, like a cat. Delgado closed his eyes with pleasure, relaxing completely as her fingers did their work. He felt her lean forward, heard the quilt slide from her body as her arms slipped round his neck from behind. He kissed the velvet skin above the bandage on her right arm as it snaked over his mouth to his left ear, and felt her left hand caress his right temple.

He was still relaxed, dreaming of delights yet to come, when she shifted her weight into her lower body and, with a powerful twist of her hips and shoulders, broke his neck.

9

Jerry's World

Morbius, the wizard, wiped the blood from his sword and peered through the cathedral of trees that made up the great forest of Zuul. He had already solved the Great Riddle and fought his way past the screaming warriors of the Hordes of Hydra. Their blood was on his hands, and each of them, as they fell, had surrendered their magic to him – a piece of armour here, a new weapon there, more life, more power – until he had emerged victorious from the citadel into the dying light, to face the forest . . .

He heard the voices just in time, as he reached the crest of a low hill between the trees, and threw himself to the ground, feeling the cold touch of leaf mould on his face, seeing the glow of their campfire on the bark of trees around him, hearing their cruel laughter. It could only be the forces of Zorin, between him and his goal, blocking his way. Slowly, so as not to reveal himself before he was ready, Morbius crawled to the very top of the hill and looked down.

There were ten of them that he could see, seven men and three women, all dressed in ragged armour and tattered clothes stripped from the bodies of travellers across the forest of Zuul. They were renegades, former soldiers, and palace guards, and all were dancing around a campfire to celebrate their latest kill – a caravan of six coaches, packed with food and spices for the citadel. The freshly dead bodies of the drivers lay around their abandoned wagons as the women picked over them for spoils. There was a scream . . .

And then he saw her.

Tied to a tree-trunk by her wrists, with her arms stretched up over her head, was a beautiful woman. Her brilliant red hair, freed from her headdress, cascaded down over her milk-white skin. Her fine silk dress, held by a jewelled clasp at her shoulder, clung to her body, showing every curve and hollow. Two of the renegades were advancing on her. One was pulling off his body-armour. The other was reaching for the woman's garment at the neckline, ready to rip it from her . . .

"Hold!"

All eyes in that clearing turned on Morbius. He stepped up over the crest of the hill and strode down towards them, watching as they moved apart. His right hand was on his sword.

"And who says 'hold' to the forces of Zorin?"

The man who had been taking off his body-armour quickly clipped it back into place and stepped away from his hostage. He was short and squat, with broad, muscular shoulders, powerful arms and a mane of black hair running down his neck. On his belt, held in a brass clip, was a curved scimitar, smeared with fresh blood. He motioned to his warriors, and they fanned out around Morbius, creeping in a great circle, hoping to move slowly enough to allay his fears, yet fast enough to surround him before he could strike.

But Morbius had played this game before.

"I am Morbius, the wizard," he shouted to their faces. "Untie that lady, give her to me, and I will spare you."

The leader's face cracked in an obscene grin, pitted with the stumps of rotting teeth. "Of course, my lord," he sneered, bowing his head. "At once, your majesty. At your command, great Morbius . . . *Get him!*"

Two of the women darted in behind Morbius, their cruel daggers aimed at the arteries of his neck, but he was ready. Without even turning, he thrust down on the hilt of his sword, swinging the blade in the ring at his belt until it pointed upwards behind him, straight at the first woman's heart. He heard her cry *"Nooo!"* and then felt the hiss of fine steel on flesh as her rushing body impaled itself. Her life-magic flowed into him and he whipped the blade from her chest as she fell, parrying the dagger from her accomplice, knocking the second woman back and driving the sword home again, into her heart. Another scream, another falling body, and more magic flowed. Soon, very soon, he would have enough to . . .

"Yaaaah!"

Three of the men tried to rush him at once from the front. Their swords were held high above their heads for the downward strike, but their bellies were wide open to attack. Morbius slit them all with one powerful swing of his arm – there were gurgling screams – writhing bodies at his feet – and more magic flowed.

The leader stood back and smiled. "So Morbius, you have taken five of mine. But you shall not win." Then he screamed an order, the canopies of the caravan wagons burst open, and a score of ragged warriors armed with swords, scimitars and spears tumbled onto the forest floor. In the blink of an eye, they had fanned out in a great circle around Morbius and stood taunting him, their weapons brandished above their heads.

"*Surrender now, Morbius!*" screamed the leader. "Forfeit the contest and you will live."

They were too late.

"You forget," the wizard shouted. "I have taken the magic of your five warriors as my own. I am Morbius. I am powerful. And I call on the power of the Id!"

All at once, there was silence in the forest. The warriors looked to each other in fear. Then a rushing sound, like the breath of a giant animal sounded high in the trees. The earth shook as the boom of a giant footfall reached them. The mist overhead swirled into a nightmare silhouette. Behind the leader, the pillar of a huge tree, a hundred feet tall at least, shook, tottered and fell as if ripped from its roots by a gigantic, unseen hand. One of the wagons flattened into matchwood. The leader screamed and turned, lashing at thin air with his sword. His warriors dropped their weapons and tried to run, only to be plucked from the ground and torn apart like rag dolls, before being flung into the darkness, in pieces.

"*I am Morbius!*" screamed the wizard above the carnage. "And I *will* be victorious!"

As the last of his warriors perished, the leader fell to his knees in front of the wizard, flinging his great scimitar to the ground in surrender.

"You have won, my lord," he sobbed. "The game is yours."

Morbius felt the power of his victory surge through him. Never before had he come this far. "Be gone," he sneered. "But take this message back to Zorin. I am Morbius, and I will beat him again!"

The man scuttled off into the forest. Morbius looked up from the torn and scattered bodies of the vanquished to the canopy of dark leaves, high above his head. The ghostly outline of the unseen monster swirled in the mist. The sound of its breath still whooshed in the forest. He raised his arms and shouted, "*By the power of the Id, be gone!*"

There was silence.

"My lord, I owe you my life. How can I ever repay you?"

Morbius turned to the shivering lady. Her green eyes held a mixture of admiration, fear . . . and something more?

"Your name, my lady," he said, stepping closer. "Give me that at least."

"I am the Lady Julia of Tamalpais. The forces of Zorin took everything from me except my virtue. But I would give it to you, gladly, if you would untie me."

Morbius reached up over her head. As his strong fingers worked the tight knots at her wrists he caught her perfume, a heady scent, laden with musk. He felt her body press against him as he reached higher.

"You owe me no debt . . ." he began, but then her wrists were free and her arms were around his neck. Her lips closed over his and her fingers were working at his body-armour, flicking open clasps, pulling leather thongs through buckles.

"You have won, my lord," she gasped between kisses. "Take me! I'm yours."

Morbius let the last of his armour fall and pulled his sweat-soaked tunic up over his head. The lady Julia undid the brooch at her shoulder and her silk dress slid to the ground. Morbius watched as the light of the fire flickered on her flawless skin, and for a moment they stood together, naked. Then, with a hunger that surprised him, she kissed him again. He could feel her fingers on his back, the slide of her thigh on his, the heat of her . . .

"Take me! Oh please, my lord. Take me!" and she pulled him to the ground.

"Mister Gibb. I have to speak with you, sir. It's urgent!"

A MATTER OF TIME

The Lady Julia froze beneath him. Her eyes were on his, needing him. Her perfect body was lying ready, waiting . . .

"Damn!"

And then the game was over . . . leaving nothing but the darkness . . .

Jerry Gibb reached up, lifted the state-of-the-art virtual reality headset from his temples and laid it gently down on the stand next to the couch. Then he pulled himself to his feet, strode to the door of the pod and stabbed at the release button. The door hissed open and he was in his "study", all laid out nice and neat, just as he liked it . . . insisted on it . . . with a place for everything and everything in its place.

He moved to the big desk along the east-facing wall, eased himself into the padded swivel-chair and stared at the video monitor. "What is it, Hacker? I was in a game. I was winning!"

The face on the screen looked tanned and fit, like a football coach. There was that same air of authority, competence, control – co-ordination.

"I'm sorry, Mr Gibb. But we've just had a unique opportunity presented to us, and I need to discuss our options with you immediately. There's a chance we can move to a termination of the 'Polish Problem', if we act right away."

"Termination?" said Jerry.

The grey eyes looked straight back at him. "Yes sir, Mr Gibb. Termination."

"Just give me the details, Milt. This line's secure."

"As you know," said Hacker, "our legal battle with GRC over copyright claims has been moving in their favour for the past six months. If we lose, the damages they'll demand could shut us down. Just a few minutes ago I learned of an opportunity for us to settle the matter . . . once and for all!"

"Tell me about it."

"Since Christmas, I've been getting a lot of inside information on GRC from a guy called Tony Delgado, who got thrown out for leaking their secrets to the Japs . . ."

"How do you know he's kosher?"

"We checked his story out, and it fits. Now, here comes the cream. Our good friend Dr Theodore Gilkrensky will be heading my way tomorrow by private jet, estimated time of arrival in Orlando, Florida – 1500 hours local time, all flight details supplied."

"And?"

"I'd like to propose a scenario to you, Mr Gibb. It's going to be expensive in the short term but if it works, our troubles with GRC will be over and done with."

"Like I said, tell me about it."

"I want your permission to delay today's demonstration of the UCAV project to the Appropriations Committee by twenty-four hours. Give me that, and I can guarantee a nice convenient accident."

"Cost benefit?"

"If we lose one of the UCAV prototypes, it'll cost us two million, tops. We can replace it. If we lose the case against GRC, it'll cost us the company. Go figure."

"And I get to fly it?" Jerry was interested now. It would be like a computer game – but for real!

Hacker smiled. "You bet, Mr Gibb. Nobody does it quite like you."

"Good job. Let's go for it!"

"You got it," said Hacker, and signed off.

Jerry Gibb pulled himself up from his chair, walked out of the office, across the hall and into the kitchen with its big picture window. The winter storm, which had been drenching Mill Valley and the San Francisco Bay area for days, had eased. Jerry could see right down Mount Tamalpais to Angel Island and the Oakland Bay Bridge, clogged with commuter traffic from San Francisco. Poor saps! It had been worth the money to get this prime plot of protected land next to Muir Woods re-zoned and build here, right above his home-town of Larkspur, where he could look down on them all.

He popped the lid on a carton of milk and poured himself a long tall glass. Then he reached down to the chill cabinet, ripped open the packet of Oreo cookies and stood looking down on the distant roofs of houses and schools he'd left behind, long ago, while his tongue worked at the cold cream filling between the dark chocolate biscuit.

Man, this was great! Getting rid of Gilkrensky and his

lawsuit would mean swatting the last cloud on his otherwise perfect horizon.

It would put him back in control.

And, after a lifetime of disappointment and pain, Jerry Gibb wanted nothing more than to be in control.

10

Comic-book Hero

Co-ordination and control! They'd been drummed into him from a very early age – the Holy Grails his father Charlie Gibb had been chasing all his life. Charlie had been a professional footballer who had never quite made it to the big time, and had fallen back to eke out an existence as a sports coach in one of the less fashionable high-schools near Larkspur, at the north end of San Francisco Bay. Jerry was Charlie's only son after a string of daughters, and should have made him proud.

But he didn't.

Jerry was fat. He seemed to put on weight by just reading the ingredients on a packet of Oreos, and no amount of exercise could get him thin.

But Charlie's dreams died hard.

"Look at Babe Ruth," he'd say. "A big guy, sure. But a hell of a hitter. Come on, Jerry. Let's give it one more swing!"

It did no good. No matter how hard he tried, no matter how many practice sessions he endured, or how much his father shouted at him, Jerry was totally, utterly, uncoordinated. In football, he fell over his own feet. In baseball, he swung the bat like a fly-swat. In the "little league" team, he came along to the practice sessions out of duty to his father, but was never picked to play. So he spent long hot summers propped up next to the piles of sports gear left there by his team mates, eating donuts, drinking sodas and reading comic-books.

Jerry loved comics. He liked the way that even good guys who looked as bad as he did always won through in the end. Ben Grimm of the "Fantastic Four" had been zapped by cosmic rays during an ill-fated space flight and turned into an orange-skinned monster called the "Thing", but everyone still loved him. He even had a beautiful blind girlfriend called Alicia, whose body curved in all sorts of interesting places.

Jerry was beginning to notice things like that. He moved from "Superman" to "Wonder Woman" and "Supergirl", marvelling over the beautifully detailed drawings of tightly clad girls in exotic costumes, wondering what it would be like to peel those costumes away . . .

Jerry also started noticing real girls in general, and one very pretty girl in particular. Julie Briscoe lived only a block away from the Gibbs in Larkspur. She was five foot six inches tall, copper-haired and green-eyed, with a smile that could light up a room – at least for Jerry. But

A MATTER OF TIME

Julie never stopped to talk to him, or even acknowledged his existence, until one day, when she found out he could draw.

Jerry had decided that the only way to get the sort of fantasy heroines he *really* wanted was to create comics of his own, and bought up every book on drawing he could afford. Pretty soon he had the basics of anatomy at his fingertips and was a master of perspective. For the first time, he started getting attention in school, something he had never managed before. He also got the attention of Julie Briscoe who decided, for the sake of her own ambitions to be a fashion designer, that it might be good to sit next to Jerry during art class and pick up a few pointers.

Jerry was in heaven.

Of *course* he would show her the easy way to draw fingers that didn't look like bunches of bananas – just as long as he could watch her own hands move on the drawing board. It was his greatest delight to sit next to her after school while he drafted the proportions of the human body, just to feel *her* body close to his. Julie's art grades rocketed, while Jerry's imaginings took on a whole new dimension. He pictured himself with her in a million scenarios, from simple liaisons in his bedroom, to more elaborate fantasies in which he rescued her from dragons, monsters and murderers, all of which ended in her grateful, blissful surrender.

Then, one Saturday afternoon, at the final play-off of the inter-school baseball league, she was there at the field with Dave Grissom, the junior football star. Why was it that some guys got to have tall muscular bodies like Grissom's, while Jerry, like poor Ben Grimm in the Fantastic Four, was trapped inside this – this *Thing*?

"Jerry! Get your fat ass over here!"

Jerry snapped out of his daydream and looked over to a huddle of kids clustered around his father on the pitcher's mound.

"Look, son," said Charlie Gibb. "O'Driscoll hasn't shown up. Fletcher's down with the flu, and Jennings has just sprained his ankle. He's out of it. I need another man on my team, or we forfeit the championship. You don't have to do anything, Jerry. I'll put you out there in right field, as far away from the action as I can. But I need you, son. I need you right now!"

Jerry's heart soared. In all his life, his father had never needed him for anything, never called him "son" to his face. Here was his chance to be a "big man" . . . and there was Julie Briscoe, sitting on the sideline, to watch. He kitted up and marched out to right field, as proud and pleased as he had ever been in his life.

He hadn't seen the high ball until it was almost too late.

All at once it seemed that everyone in the world was shouting at him.

"Catch it, Jerry! Catch it!"

And then he saw it!

Way up there in the sky, as high as a jet at least, was a tiny white sphere, rushing towards him, right at him.

There was no way he could miss it. No way he could fail to be a hero.

And there was Julie Briscoe, to watch!

Jerry steadied himself on his heavy legs, squinted up at the rushing ball, and held up his hands to catch it. Everyone was shouting, yelling. They were all looking at him. He was the focus of the entire world . . . a hero . . . and there was Julie Briscoe to watch. He glanced over to her . . .

But Julie Briscoe wasn't looking. Her eyes were closed as she held Dave Grissom in a passionate embrace, there on the sideline, as his tongue felt its way around her mouth and his hand reached "second base" over her left breast.

And Jerry saw . . .

"Whap!"

The impact of the baseball was a gun going off in his head. He sneezed . . . and there was blood. He couldn't feel his lips, or his nose. There were stones in his mouth. The world spun, just like it did when the other kids held him upside down in the locker room with his head down the can. The dry grass of the baseball field leapt up and smacked him in the face . . .

"Jerry? Jerry!" His mother was bending over him, padding at his swollen lips with a handkerchief. There was a crowd of kids all round him, blocking out the light. "Charlie, come quick! He's lost a tooth!"

Jerry couldn't feel anything. He pushed his tongue forward – and it just kept on going!

"Wow!" said someone off in the distance. "Did you see the fat kid take that one in the puss? No co-ordination. I could have caught that with my eyes shut."

A girl laughed.

"Yeah, and he's coach Gibb's kid too! How *embarrassing*!"

"Do you know him?"

"No, he's just a fat kid who likes to follow me about. His name's Jerry. He's just a kid . . ."

Just a kid . . .

Just a kid . . .

Just a *kid*!

It was Julie Briscoe. She *had* been there to watch . . . to see him take the ball in the face – drop the catch – and lose the game – been there with Grissom to call him a "fat kid" – to laugh when Grissom said he had no co-ordination.

Just a kid.

All at once, an overpowering sense of loss welled up inside Jerry – and burst like a bomb. Tears came – he couldn't stop them! Great racking sobs that started low in his chest and rippled upwards past his shattered teeth, through his bloody lips and out, in loud wheezing gasps. It wasn't the pain, it wasn't the humiliation, it wasn't even his father's anger at him for being let down in front of the whole school.

It was the final, absolute, total realisation that in Julie's eyes he was 'just a kid' and would never – *ever* – possess her love.

A MATTER OF TIME

The waves of heartbreak rolled on, unstoppable. All around the baseball field, people were watching the "crybaby fat kid" who had lost them the game as he was led away by "his mommy". Charlie Gibb tried to calm them down, but it was no use. It was his son who had dropped a simple catch in front of everyone. He was humiliated, embarrassed – and angry.

When Jerry got home that evening from the dentist's, with his jaws pumped full of Novocaine and the promise of weeks of painful dentistry ahead, he found his entire collection of comic-books gone – all his *Spidermans*, his *Wonder Womans* and his *Fantastic Fours* had been rounded up, boxed, and dumped in the trash.

"It's time you grew up, Jerry!" said Charlie Gibb. "I can't have a son of mine being a crybaby like that in front of the whole school. If you aren't a man in this world, you won't survive. Now go to your room and think about *that*!"

Alone in his room, Jerry lay on the bed and stared at the ceiling, thinking of Julie Briscoe.

"Just a kid . . . just a kid . . . just a kid!"

He could feel the tears starting to tug at him again, so he switched on the old black-and-white TV he had salvaged from a junk shop and repaired on his own – really low so his Dad wouldn't hear – and escaped from his pain into another world . . .

They were running old sci-fi movies that night, the sort Jerry loved. In a second he was at the other end of the galaxy, on the planet Altair IV, where the reclusive Dr

Morbius had discovered a fantastic alien culture, so advanced that they had developed a machine to project a man's thoughts into reality. Morbius couldn't control it. He released a terrible "Id monster" from the primeval depths of his own subconscious – a gigantic invisible being of pure energy that stomped guys into the ground, took disrupter blasts – that could have levelled a mountain – without even flinching, and melted its way through closed doors of diamond-hard alien steel, thirty inches thick.

As the credits rolled, Jerry lay back on his bed – transformed. He was no longer "just a kid". He was Morbius – safe in his underground laboratory at the far end of the galaxy – protected from all the insults and pain of the real world by thirty inches of alien steel, sending out his own invincible "Id monster" to wreak a just and terrible revenge. In his mind, he saw his team-mates running in fear as the monster grabbed them one by one and threw them screaming into space. There was Dave Grissom, cringing in the changing room, crying like a baby as the monster reached in to tear his perfect body limb from limb.

And here was Julie Briscoe, plucked from her warm bed and carried back to his, promising him anything, offering him everything, as long as he would spare her life . . .

Next day at school, the taunts of the other kids didn't bother him any more. Why should they? He was no longer Jerry Gibb but Morbius, and during the night the

Id monster visited them . . . one by one. Girls who laughed at Jerry Gibb, ones he fancied, were dragged before him naked, begging for mercy. He was Morbius, he was power, he was God! Nothing could hurt Jerry Gibb – not any more!

At college, he majored in electronics and art, an odd combination, simply because he was equally good at them both. Here was the brain of Morbius, the cold, calculating certainty of science, calling things into being by the mere act of will. Here was the heart and soul of Morbius, the terrifying monsters, clean-cut heroes, and smooth-limbed heroines of his comic-book fantasies – all under his control . . .

Control!

On the pages of his sketch pads, Jerry could make them do *anything* he wanted.

By 1986, his old friend Danny Graham was a rising engineer with Atari, out in the newly christened "Silicon Valley" down in Santa Clara, on the south side of the Bay, and told Jerry there was work for someone with a good imagination in the computer games department. Jerry had been trying to make a living as a comic-book artist but, even though his drawings were breathtaking, they weren't getting accepted. There was always something "over the top" about them. Publishers with a view to the censor and their family markets were tired of telling Jerry to "tone it down" – and besides, none of the editors seemed to like him. He was "spooky", a "weirdo", a "nut".

Jerry took all these rejections in his stride.

And at night the Id monster paid those editors all a visit.

But in Atari things were different . . . a *lot* different. Jerry took to computer games technology as if he'd lived with it all his life. Within a week, he'd drawn up the outline for a game so fast and furious that Atari bumped production of their latest market leader upgrade back a month to rush Jerry's product into the shops for Christmas. By the summer of the next year he had three of the top five arcade games world-wide to his name and was famous, a king of the computer world, with job offers from other companies running into six-figure sums.

Suddenly, Jerry Gibb was in demand.

But Jerry wanted control.

With an eye to the future, Danny Graham went hunting among the many "godfathers" of Silicon Valley – high-profile investors with enough money to back a likely project and the sixth sense to make their money back, plus a tidy profit, within four years. Danny never said who his particular "godfather" was, beyond dark hints at government connections. But all at once there were five million dollars at his disposal and 'Gibbtek' was born, a company specialising in creative interactive software for electronic control systems and the entertainment industry.

Graham was the hardware expert specialising in interface systems – joysticks, keyboards, mice, voice-activation units, and even the new superconductor technology that would eventually enable computers to be controlled by thought!

Jerry was the software genius, bringing his calculating mind and warped imagination to the design of faster, more complex and increasingly raunchy computer games, that soon made Gibbtek a world leader in computer entertainment.

By the time Jerry was twenty-nine, he was rich – very rich – and he was in his element. But something was missing. People were starting to talk. Was Jerry gay? What did he get up to in his apartment all alone at night? Rumours were spreading.

Jerry Gibb needed a wife.

Julie Briscoe was dead, killed in a car wreck when Dave Grissom, who she'd married right after college, had skipped the central reservation on highway 101 at eighty miles an hour after an office party. Jerry had followed their career from afar, but hadn't come close. He was Morbius now. He was in control. And he didn't want that control to slip.

So he set about looking for a replacement. There was a succession of Julie Briscoes – each one tall and red-headed, with green eyes and smiles that would light up a room. But after a while, even his money could not keep the disgust out of their eyes, and they left him. There were expensive law suits, articles in the gossip columns of *The Chronicle*, *The Examiner* and the *San Francisco Herald*, and Jerry retreated back to *Altair IV*, his newly constructed mansion high on the slopes of Mount Tamalpais overlooking Larkspur, and into his own virtual reality . . .

When Danny Graham died of cancer, Jerry was paralysed with fear. Danny had been the one who went out into the world, the one who made things happen for Gibbtek, while Jerry lurked in the shadows dreaming up the incredible games for Danny to sell. How would Jerry cope on his own? Gibbtek was at an all-time high. Its fantasy products dominated the computer games industry, its control systems were taking the world by storm, and Danny had even negotiated high-priced contracts for mind/computer interfaces with the military.

Jerry was "between Julies". He was alone. His health was slipping. There was talk of a heart condition. He was losing control. How could he face reality again with Danny gone?

The answer appeared as if by magic. The Gibbtek office at Santa Clara received a curriculum vitae from a mysterious senior executive called Milton Hacker, who came with impeccable credentials and the full backing of Danny's anonymous "godfather". Hacker had been in "government service" overseas, as well as private industry. He had "made things happen" for a number of Jerry's competitors, and was now offering to make things happen for him.

Jerry grudgingly granted Hacker an audience at *Altair IV* and was immediately impressed. Here was the sort of man Jerry yearned to be – a quiet, powerful man with the grey eyes of a hawk – a man who was *in control*. Quietly, and with great respect for Jerry, who he addressed throughout as either "Mr Gibb", or "sir", Hacker listed his accomplishments to date, hinting darkly at tantalising work he had done for "the Company" in his government days.

Here was a man who could go out into the world as Jerry's alter ego, just like Morbius's Id monster, and do his bidding. Here was a man with the proper respect for Jerry's status as Morbius.

Jerry signed him up on the spot.

And now Hacker had come up with yet another perfect plan, a scheme to rid Jerry of the "Polish Problem" and blast that worm Gilkrensky out of the sky. That Polack deserved it too! Jerry had met him years before, at a software launch in Los Angeles, green with envy. To Jerry, it looked as if Gilkrensky had everything – good looks, great products, money, and the most beautiful woman Jerry had ever seen in his life – a foxy Irish redhead – even more breathtaking than Julie Briscoe.

Gilkrensky had been a fool to let a woman like that get car-bombed in front of his eyes. If she'd belonged to Jerry, he would have kept her locked up at *Altair IV* and never let her out of his sight. Gilkrensky was an idiot! He deserved to die.

Jerry Gibb was *really* going to enjoy this!

11

The Facts of Life

"Is Miss Wright jealous of me?"

The question caught Gilkrensky by surprise. He opened his eyes, swung his feet down from the empty seat in front of him and stared across the cramped cabin of the jet.

From an equipment bench on the far wall of the plane, the image of Maria looked at him quizzically from the screen of the Minerva 3,000.

Gilkrensky stretched himself. "Why do you ask?"

"Because of her reaction when we met on the island. I've been considering this question ever since we left Cork, and now you're awake, I thought I'd ask. Am I correct?"

Gilkrensky looked out at the brilliant blue-and-white cloudscape on the other side of the porthole as he chose his answer, remembering what Cathy Kirwan had said.

"Ah – I don't think she's jealous of you personally, Maria. But I know she's jealous of what you represent."

"I understand. That must be why she would not let me talk to you in London."

"Yes. She was afraid you'd bring back memories of my wife."

"I see. You programmed me to be like your wife, because you loved *her*. My user interface speaks and looks like Maria. I have Maria's primary behavioural response loops as part of my neural-net. I am like Maria. Therefore Miss Wright is jealous of me. I understand that perfectly."

Gilkrensky thought back to his last encounter with Jessica, on the darkened helipad of Cork airport in the biting air of the early morning. There was the crunch of frost beneath their feet. Their breath rose like steam, mingling above their heads as they talked. Jessica was distant, almost resigned. Her head hung on her chest and she hugged herself tight. Nothing he could say could reach her any more.

"Come with me to Florida, Jess. Please. We can work this out."

But she'd just shaken her head and looked at the ground.

"No, Theo. It's no use. I just can't compete."

"With what, Jess? With the Minerva? It's just a machine!"

Jessica Wright looked up at him. Her eyes were as cold as the ice beneath her feet.

"No, Theo. With the *real* Maria, the one still living in your memory. She'll always be there between us, flawless, beautiful, perfect. You've already forgotten the fights you used to have and how she threatened to leave you the night before she was killed. She'll be there inside you for the rest of your life and – I just can't compete with that. You're better off with your memories, and – that machine!"

He'd moved to hold her, but she pulled away.

"Please, Jess. Don't . . ."

"No, Theo. I need space. I need to work this through for myself. You go off to Florida and leave me the only thing I know how to handle in your life right now . . . the corporation."

"Jess."

"Just leave me alone, Theo. That's all I'm asking . . ."

And she'd turned away, boarded the helicopter without even a backward glance, and lifted off into the east and the first glow of the rising sun, heading for London . . .

"Human relationships are confusing," said the Minerva.

"How so?"

"In all sorts of ways. I was linked to the Web while I was on the island, researching information that might help us analyse the problems we're encountering with the Daedalus system in different parts of the world. I also searched for Web sites referring to the word 'love'. Did you know there were 6,511,499 of them?"

Gilkrensky smiled. "No, Maria. I didn't."

"And 5,330,281 contained no information at all about emotional responses according to the dictionary definition of the word. They contained images and descriptions of sexual intercourse, some of them displaying what I would judge to be great cruelty and exploitation. Why is that?"

"I don't know. The Web is very much like the inside of the human mind. There are all sorts of ideas in it, some good and some bad."

"What is it like to touch someone?"

"It's good. It makes you feel connected."

"And sex?"

Gilkrensky looked at the Minerva screen. The green eyes of the image regarded him innocently.

"Sex is part of the human mind too, Maria."

"But is it part of love?"

"Mostly, but not always."

The computer considered this. "Did you have sex with your wife, Maria?"

Images flashed across Gilkrensky's memory – Maria in the candlelight – Maria in his arms – Maria sobbing softly next to him, her face buried in the pillow . . .

"Can we talk about your research into Daedalus instead?"

A look of concern clouded the image on the screen. "Have I made you uncomfortable, Theo?"

"A little. Normally people who – make love together don't talk about it openly."

"I find that confusing also. On the Web there are many sites, chat lines and associated user groups devoted to doing just that."

Gilkrensky laughed. The eyes on the screen looked puzzled.

"I know," he said. "You're right. Human relationships *are* confusing. So for now, let's talk about our problems with Daedalus instead."

Maria's expression brightened. A pair of gold-rimmed glasses appeared on her face, indicating that Minerva was in "information mode".

"If we go back to basics," said the computer, "the Daedalus auto-pilot system is designed to allow an aircraft to be flown by computer control from the point of take-off to the point of landing, anywhere in the world. To do this, it uses a world-wide system of navigation satellites, terrestrial beacons and on-board sensors to precisely determine the aircraft's position."

"Which is where our problems started in Cairo."

"Exactly, Theo. We discovered that natural earth energies, called ley-lines, actually interfered with the high-precision low-altitude sensors on one of the planes."

"But that was only when the ley-line energy had been focused and concentrated by the Great Pyramid."

"Indeed, normally this kind of energy is so weak that it can only be detected by a process known as 'dowsing', using metal rods. The Cairo incident appeared unique in that the energy was strong enough to affect an electronic system."

"But now the Federal Aviation Authority has reported similar events over the Caribbean? Which is why they've closed down the system here."

"The events reported by the FAA are similar, but not identical," said the computer. "They were not life-threatening, and indeed the on-board computers corrected them very quickly, but they were noted and logged. After the crash in Cairo, the FAA thought there was reasonable cause for concern and shut down the system, pending an investigation."

"But there are no pyramids in the Caribbean!"

Maria's image shrank to a small window in the top left-hand corner of the screen, which filled with a map of the world, criss-crossed with lines.

"That's right, Theo. But there *are* concentrations of ley-lines here, just as there are on the Great Pyramid site in Egypt. My research on the Web suggests that the earth's surface is covered with a pattern of such lines corresponding generally to the planes of a giant crystal."

Gilkrensky moved closer so that he could see the detail on the screen.

"There, you see now, Theo? This is the pattern first suggested by three Russian scientists in 1960. It shows a series of twelve, five-sided plates circling the earth. If you compare this pattern with the locations of other natural and paranormal phenomena, such as volcanoes, magnetic anomalies, ancient civilisations and even bird migrations, you will find a strong correlation."

"I know. I was working on that theory in London. The Great Pyramid lies on one of those nodes, on the north of Africa."

"Exactly," said the computer. "It also occurs to me

that this could be the reason why the Daedalus units on aircraft entering Miami have appeared to malfunction. Look at the pattern again. Just off the coast of Florida, north of Bermuda, there is another major node, right in the centre of one of the five-sided plates."

"That's very interesting, Maria."

"We can begin our investigations once we reach the Caribbean, if you like. I had all the equipment we would need loaded aboard this plane via the computer warehouse network before it left Farnborough. It would be easy to run a scan for any energy anomalies as we make our approach to Orlando."

"Thank you, Maria. That's very thoughtful of you."

"I like to do things for you, Theo. You are my Prime User."

Gilkrensky smiled and looked out of the porthole at the deep blue sky. For a while there was silence in the cabin. Then the Minerva said, "If I had a body, could I touch you?"

"What?"

"A body. Dr Kirwan explained it to me during our discussions. I am a consciousness, a sentient being. I exist within the hardware of the Minerva system, just as your consciousness exists within your brain, but I have no body. When I was in the Mawashi-Saito mainframe, I could reach out and touch things through their robot factories and handling systems. And when we were in Cairo, you let me control the mining machine and fly the Whisperer jet. I enjoyed those things. But I cannot touch you."

A MATTER OF TIME

"Ah . . . no, Maria. You can't. I'm sorry."

The computer was silent for a while. Then it said, "Can I fly this plane, now?"

"Captain Kilroy is handling it quite well, thank you, Maria. And he has the Daedalus autopilot for back-up. You've never flown this type of aircraft before. It's specially modified for experimental work. It might be dangerous for you to try."

"My main programming is still governed by the Asimov Laws regarding the endangering of human life – and both you and Captain Kilroy are on this plane. Therefore I cannot do anything but fly safely."

"All right. You win," said Gilkrensky, and unstrapped the Minerva from the equipment shelf, moving towards the cockpit.

12

Interceptor

"Imagine the ultimate guided missile, and you have the Hawk," said Hacker, waving his hand over the short, black fuselage that squatted like a giant beetle in the centre of the group on the tarmac runway.

The lunch, served in the executive dining-room of Phoenix Aviation overlooking the distant towers of the Kennedy Space Centre, had gone well. Hacker was good at presentations like this, and he knew a few of the group from his days in the Directorate for Science and Technology. He also knew that an all-expenses-paid trip to Florida for the day, or even a few days if the hosts were generous enough, was a welcome outing for desk-bound bureaucrats from Langley or downtown Washington.

He smiled and looked at the faces of the Acquisitions Committee for a reaction.

"It's a bit goddamn small," said Josephine Bradley, the thin-faced Department of Defence representative.

Like Hacker, Bradley had taken no wine with her conch chowder and barbecued lobster – even though her favourite vintage had been laid on – and she was asking all the awkward questions. Back in Washington, Jo Bradley had the nickname of "Spiderwoman" because of her web of contacts and the huge budget she controlled. She was the most powerful person on the committee, and the most dangerous. Hacker had cultivated her carefully for months before the sale, pandering to her every whim in case she'd decided to hand the contract to Northrop Grumman or Lockheed-Martin instead. But that didn't matter so much now. The deal was done, and there were more important things at stake.

Martin Howard, chief engineer and test pilot at Phoenix Aviation, straightened the necktie he had put on specially for the occasion, and came to Hacker's rescue. "It's small because it's designed as a pilotless UCAV, an Uninhabited Combat Air Vehicle," he said. "We don't need a cockpit, so we can build it as small as we want. You'll notice the weird, alien look of it and the way all the surfaces are designed to deflect radar – like a stealth fighter. But the thing we're *really* testing here today – the remote control system which Gibbtek developed for us – could be fitted to any size of aircraft, from a helicopter to a jumbo jet."

"As Martin says, the secret of the Hawk's in the control system," repeated Hacker. "Without a pilot in the cockpit, the UCAV is no longer limited by the amount of

G-forces a human pilot can withstand before blacking out. So this little baby can make turns, rolls and climbs that would render a human pilot unconscious."

"What kind of G-forces are we talking about," asked Colonel Magruder, the fleshy Air Force representative with white hair. Hacker had seen his file too and knew that while Magruder liked to think of himself as the best pilot since Lindbergh, the Air Force hadn't let him near an aircraft in years.

"About sixteen 'G's', Colonel," said Howard respectfully. "Almost twice as much as an F-16 jet fighter."

But Hacker was watching Jo Bradley for the next *real* question.

"How come a company that makes computer games for kids got mixed up in the aerospace business?" she said, peering at him over the top of her steel-framed glasses, but Hacker was ready.

"Gibbtek may be famous as a world leader in the computer-games market, but that's not all it does. The smart bombs and cruise missiles they used in the Gulf War – the ones you saw on CNN diving down onto targets all on their own – had guidance and control systems developed from computer-games technology. That's why Mr *Charles* Howard, who runs Phoenix Aviation, called Jerry Gibb personally and asked if we could provide the rapid-control systems he'd need to make the Hawk work."

"Will Mr Howard be joining us?" asked Senator Garforth, a well-groomed politician from Connecticut.

Hacker saw him as another lightweight on the committee – a former scientist who liked to think he was still at the cutting edge of technology. In reality he was just along for the ride, bringing a very attractive "personal assistant", who was currently sunning herself back at the hotel swimming pool in Orlando.

"I'm afraid not," said Martin Howard. "My father's always been something of a recluse, and now that he's in his seventies, he likes to keep to himself more than ever."

"And Jerry Gibb?"

"Mr Gibb is also a very private person," said Hacker, and watched as the committee exchanged knowing glances. "But I'll call him up in a moment and tell him how the test's been going."

"Who painted that there?" said Garforth, pointing to the nose of the UCAV where a woman's name had been painted in fine script, low on the fuselage.

"That's a Phoenix Aerospace tradition," said Howard. "My father used it as his mascot during the war. He insists we paint it on every plane we make, for good luck."

"Girlfriend, perhaps?" chuckled Colonel Magruder softly, and those within earshot smiled.

"My grandmother's name, actually," said Howard, and for a moment there was an awkward silence.

"Why the twenty-four hour delay?" asked Jo Bradley.

"Yes. I'm sorry about that," said Hacker. "We'd hoped to hold the test yesterday, but the weather wasn't right."

Bradley shielded her eyes against the sun and peered up at the sky. "It seemed OK to me on the way down from Washington."

"But not in Groom Lake, up in Arizona," said Hacker. "Which is where the Air Force test pilot and chase plane had to come from."

Hacker handed the group over to Martin Howard, who shepherded them back towards the glass-fronted operations tower. Then, when he was sure they were out of earshot, he pulled out a mobile phone and pressed a 'quick dial' number. The phone was a special model, normally given only to military, police, and government security personnel, totally secure from eavesdropping.

"Mr Gibb? The Hawk should be airborne and out over the sea in ten minutes. I'll arrange to hand over control to you in twelve."

"I'll be waiting, Milt."

"No problem, Mr Gibb."

Hacker shut down the phone and slipped it back into his jacket pocket. Then he walked over to the main building to join the others in the control room.

On the other side of the continent, in his luxury bungalow overlooking San Francisco Bay, Jerry Gibb put his own phone back in its usual place on his desk, and called out to his wife. "Elaine! I'm gonna be tied up in a game for an hour or so. Make sure I'm not disturbed, will yah?"

Elaine Gibb adjusted her hair in the hall mirror and

picked up her purse. "OK, Jerry. I was gonna go into town anyway. Is there anything you want?"

"Why don't you just ring Macys or Saks and have whatever it is you want delivered. I don't like you going down there. You might get mugged."

Elaine Gibb thought of the brightly lit shops, with their uniformed guards, security cameras and panic buttons. "No chance of that, honey. It's like Fort Knox down there."

"I don't care. You stay in and phone. You're the wife of a very rich guy now. I don't want you taking risks."

Elaine slammed her purse back down on the hall table. "But Jerry, I never get to see *anyone*!"

"I don't care! Get it delivered. That's how *we* met, wasn't it? Now don't hassle me. I've got important work to do."

"This is our pilot, Captain Bill Carter," said Hacker, putting his hand on the shoulder of the short uniformed man standing beside a padded couch. "He's flown in the Gulf and is currently chief test pilot for Air Force Special Operations over at Groom Lake. Even though he's done a lot of work on stealth projects like this before, flying the Hawk will be a completely new experience for him."

Colonel Magruder looked at the couch suspiciously, "You're telling me!" he said. "He hasn't got any controls."

"Exactly," said Hacker with the flourish of a magician. "That's the whole point of today's demonstration.

Captain Carter is going to fly the Hawk completely by the power of thought."

"Jeez!" gasped Magruder. "Who does he think he is? Houdini?"

"Not at all, Colonel. Gibbtek, and a lot of other high-tech companies, have been investing a great deal of money lately in the new SQUID technology . . ."

"You mean there's a fish in that thing!"

There was a short ripple of laughter. Then Senator Garforth, eager to show off his own specialist knowledge, said, "I think Mr Hacker is referring to the new Superconducting Quantum Interference Device."

"Exactly, Senator. The headset on the table next to Captain Carter's couch contains a whole series of what the scientists call 'Quasi-Planar junctions' which, in layman's language, refers to microscopically thin joints between different types of metal – so sensitive that electricity flowing across them can actually be affected by nerve impulses from different areas of the human brain . . ."

"Just like a TV might be affected by interference from a hair dryer, if it's held too close?" said Senator Garforth, preening himself.

"I couldn't have put it better myself, Senator," said Hacker. "The late Mr Daniel Graham, Jerry Gibb's original partner in Gibbtek, adapted these devices so that kids could actually feel as if they were living *inside* the video games our company makes. Sight, smell, sound and touch are nothing more than impulses in different areas of the brain after all, and that's what the SQUID homes in on. For Captain Carter, it will be as if he *is* the Hawk UCAV, soaring up there in the clouds, thinking himself either up or down, fast or slow, left or right. His thought commands will be picked up by the SQUID and transmitted to the Hawk, which he'll be able to fly in any acrobatic manoeuvre he can think of, just as fast as he can imagine it."

Colonel Magruder suddenly saw the light. "So we won't ever have to lose any more of our boys in air combat. They can stay at home and blast hell out of the enemy by remote control."

"You mentioned the computer that's driving all this," said Senator Garforth. "Where is that, exactly?"

"On the other side of the country, at our main facility in Santa Clara, California, Senator, but it could be anywhere. You could run a whole war, anyplace in the world, from a bunker underneath the White House without ever leaving home, and watch it all on TV!" Hacker smiled at the committee, while he let this last little idea sink in.

Then Carter said, "We have clearance from the tower, Mr Hacker."

"Very well, Captain. Take her up." And he took his seat with the other officials behind the wall-length windows, while Carter slipped on the SQUID headset and relaxed onto the couch.

Below them, the tiny beetle shape of the Hawk whined into life, rolled down the runway and shot into the sky, heading out to sea.

Twelve hundred miles away to the north-west, Jerry Gibb locked the door of his study, worked for a few minutes at the computer terminal on his desk, and walked across to a large metal door shaped like a blunt triangle. The door hissed open. Inside was a small spherical chamber like a high-tech womb, with a large reinforced couch and, on a low table, a SQUID headset which might have been the big brother of the one Captain Carter was now enjoying on the other side of the continent.

Jerry eased himself onto the soft leather, made sure everything was "just so", and pressed a remote control keypad. The door hissed shut behind him, and locked. Jerry did not like to be disturbed while he was ruling the world – *his* world – and today's game was far more important than any computer-generated sex fantasy. Today he was going to play "for real".

He picked up the SQUID headset, made sure all the connections were secure, and put it on. The twin eyepieces fitted snugly and the earphones were just right. Then he breathed a deep sigh to relax himself, and lay back.

He was in another world . . . Jerry's world.

"It's incredible," said Carter. "It really *is* like being a bird." His small-boy enthusiasm infected the others in the control room. They stood back from the window and clustered around the couch where Carter lay. Hacker watched as smiles and nods of appreciation were exchanged. They were like kids watching a new train set. The next part would be easy.

"Could *any* of us fly that thing?" asked Jo Bradley.

"Absolutely! Captain Carter may be a trained pilot, but don't forget, he's using the SQUID for the first time. Look! You can watch what he's seeing through cameras on the Hawk on that wall monitor over there."

"How do you know where the Hawk is, if it's configured to avoid radar?" said Magruder.

"With a radio beacon we installed specially. Normally, as you say, it doesn't show up on radar, so we had to 'spike' it electronically. In a combat situation, an enemy aircraft would never know what hit them."

"And the weaponry?"

"Normally a Vulcan twenty-millimetre Gatling cannon mounted in the nose, Colonel, with Maverick infrared mini-missiles fitted to those pods along the wings. But this model isn't armed. It's just a demonstration. Look! There's the target plane now!"

On the video screen, they could all see a tiny black dot that grew and stretched into the Manta-ray shape of the B-53 Stealth Bomber.

"How could Carter 'see' that other plane on radar if it's using stealth technology itself?" said Bradley.

"By means of low waveband sound and light energy, new frequencies that nobody's managed to harness yet. There, Captain Carter's locked on . . ."

A set of cross-hairs appeared on the video monitor,

and zeroed in on the B-53. Everyone in the room held their breath . . .

"And . . . *wham!*" shouted Carter, raising his right hand like a pistol and pulling an imaginary trigger. "If this was for real, I'd have blown her to kingdom come!"

"Very impressive," conceded Jo Bradley, and smiled. There was a ripple of applause around the control room.

"Thank you," said Hacker, pulling out his mobile phone. "I think I'll call Mr Gibb and tell him the test has been a success. Captain Carter, you can bring the Hawk back now, please."

He opened the door to the control room, stepped across the corridor to his own office and his own computer, with its direct link to Gibbtek. Then he closed the door and slipped on a simple earpiece and microphone.

"It's all yours, Mr Gibb," he said into the machine.

Jerry was in the super-highway of cyberspace, surfing down the main fibre optic link from Santa Clara to Gibbtek Florida, and from there down the artery to the test facility at the Cape. In seconds he was at a junction marked "Gibbtek/Phoenix Hawk demonstration". On the other side he could sense two another users – Hacker, in observation mode – and Captain Carter, linked by electronic threads to the Hawk control system. Jerry paused for a moment, letting his mind slip deeper and deeper into its dreamlike state, gaining power. Then he reached out and yanked those threads away . . . taking control.

A MATTER OF TIME

"I have a problem!" shouted Carter. "The SQUID's cut out. I don't have control of the Hawk any more."

All eyes turned to the video monitors. On the screen showing the nose-camera of the Hawk, the image vanished under a snow of interference. The flat geographic display of the homing beacon on the little aircraft blinked, and cut out.

"Shit!" said Hacker, stepping back into the control room. "Any ideas, Martin?"

"It could be any one of a thousand things – from the computer interface control, to the plane itself – but the Hawk's designed to cut out and drop into the ocean if a control failure occurs. We know where it went down, and we can send out a chopper to pick it up."

"So no danger of it flying off and hitting a commercial airliner?" said Jo Bradley.

"Absolutely none," said Hacker with his best reassuring smile. "But I'd better call Mr Gibb again and tell him what's happened."

Jerry was flying – just like Superman!

His wings were the turbo-jets of the Hawk. His eyes were the cameras in its nose. Above him was the limitless blue of the sky, and below him the false landscape of brilliant white clouds. He thought "right", and swooped over, rolling free, feeling the rush of speed. He thought "up", and soared in a loop towards the sun, over and down again. It was fantastic!

Then another thought.

"Are you sure nobody can see me – I mean the Hawk?"

Hacker's voice purred in his head.

"No way, Mr Gibb. We've switched transponder frequencies. To everyone here at Phoenix, it just looks as if the Hawk's gone down."

"Then let's go get him. Where is he?"

"Look him up on the Miami air-traffic-control computer. His flight is coded 'Golf India Lima One'. Then you can use the Hawk's sensors to track the jet. All you have to do is ram him. At your altitude his plane will depressurise like a bomb once you crack the hull."

"And no come-backs?"

"None. It'll be just another unexplained disappearance in the Bermuda Triangle."

13

Duel

"Dr Gilkrensky, could you come up here for a second, please?"

Dan Kilroy was GRC's Chief Test Pilot, a precise and careful flyer, who took his work seriously. He was well aware of the responsibility placed on his shoulders in flying his Chairman, a priceless prototype computer, and a state-of-the-art customised aircraft across the Atlantic. The concern sounded in his voice. So Gilkrensky laid the legal papers on the Gibbtek case he had been studying down on the narrow table, unbuckled his seatbelt, and went forward to the cramped cockpit.

The plane was a specially modified version of the GRC Voyager executive jet. It had been designed and built by Theo's friend and mentor Bill McCarthy to be the last word in luxury travel, but was now fitted out as a flying test-bed. The opulent fittings of its plush interior had been all but stripped bare to make way for the arsenal of electronics GRC used to test and calibrate the world-wide network of navigation beacons, airport approach markers and satellite links that formed the Daedalus system. Even the wings and fuselage had been specially strengthened to allow the plane to operate under any condition and land on any runway, from the high Arctic to the deepest rainforest. There were just four seats – two in the cockpit and two in the cabin – each specially strengthened, anchored to the floor with reinforced bolts, and fitted with five-point safety harnesses to protect their occupants during the kind of forced aerobatics needed to land on remote fields anywhere on the globe.

For its size, it was the most rugged, and probably the most expensive non-military aircraft in the world. Kilroy had flown it many times. He was proud of what it could do.

"I've nothing against women pilots as a rule, Doctor," he said, jerking his thumb at the control panel. "But this one takes the biscuit."

Gilkrensky looked across the mass of displays and gauges to the instrument rack above the Daedalus autopilot, where the Minerva 3,000 was tightly clamped in place. "I hope you're not bothering Captain Kilroy, Maria. This aircraft is his responsibility."

The face on the screen frowned. "I want to fly the plane all the way to Orlando," it said, "and Captain Kilroy won't let me."

Gilkrensky smiled. "Dan's quite right. The FAA have prohibited landings by any aircraft using Daedalus in either Miami or Orlando. He'll just have to take us in manually. How long before we land?"

Kilroy looked at his watch, and up at the instrument panel. "About half an hour. Could you slip into the co-pilot's seat there and keep an eye on our lady pilot for a few minutes while I take a leak?"

"No problem."

Kilroy undid his harness, eased himself up out of his seat and went aft. For a moment, the only sound in the cockpit was the distant hiss of the engines and the tick of instruments. Then Maria said, "Remember what you told me about performing a scan for unusual energies on the approach to Orlando? We'll be reaching the outer edge of the test area in three minutes and twenty-five seconds. If you switch on the equipment in the rear of the plane, I could run the analysis for you."

"What sort of tests do you have in mind?"

Maria's image moved aside into a small window at the top left-hand corner of the screen, making way for a coloured map of the approach to Orlando airport and a network of hatched lines, converging on an area north of Bimini.

"At this height, I suggest we run a series of scans for anything that might set off the Daedalus low-level warning system. That would include abnormal wavelengths of sound and light, or intense magnetic fluxes, both of which have been reported in the area. The main power switch for the recording gear is in the cabin, on the equipment rack."

To the south-west, Jerry Gibb's consciousness soared above the clouds with the Hawk. In front of his eyes, like a shimmering green window, was the moving circle of Miami airport's air-traffic-control radar. Jerry had hacked into their system with ease, and could view the creeping blips of incoming planes . . . a British Airways jumbo jet from London . . . a Pan-American Tri-Star from Paris and . . . further out . . . another, smaller plane. Jerry checked its ident number against the one Hacker had given him.

It was Golf, India, Lima – Zero One.

Perfect!

He let his mind follow the blip, and watched the clouds around him swing in a new direction as the Hawk turned faithfully to intercept. Flashing ahead of him just above the horizon, as the sun glinted on its polished wings, was the fuselage of a plane. He slid higher, and closer – close enough to be sure. There were the crisp, clean lines of an expensive executive jet, with its twin engines mounted under the high T-shaped tail, and the bulge of bomb-like long-range fuel tanks at the tips of either wing. It was a beautiful plane, one that Jerry himself would have liked to fly in, if he ever thought of leaving *Altair IV*. He smiled. There on the proud upright of the tail-fin, emblazoned in slick, blue lettering, were the magic initials . . . GRC!

"Awesome!" breathed Jerry to himself, and drew the Hawk back, high above the cloud base, taking his time.

A MATTER OF TIME

He wanted to hit the GRC jet just once where it hurt, right where the port wing joined the fuselage.

Gilkrensky would never know what hit him.

Jerry chuckled to himself, focused his whole attention on the target, and prepared to strike . . .

Gilkrensky picked his way aft through the cabin, checking each of the tightly packed stacks of electronic gear as he went. The Minerva had done a good job in choosing a comprehensive selection – in essence a scaled-down version of the units they had used to investigate the pyramid phenomenon in Egypt – sound-analysers, light-receptors, and a small geo-magnetic-displacement recorder – all hooked up to a CD-ROM data-logger.

"Everything here but the kitchen sink," said Kilroy, shutting the door to the toilet behind him. "Who's flying the plane?"

"Minerva is. She'll be OK for a while. Her prime directive is to protect human life, which includes you and me."

"I see," said Kilroy. "Planning to run a test on the way in, are you?"

Gilkrensky flicked the master switch and the corridor of instruments lit up on both sides as the units came alive. "It could be the key to why Daedalus has been acting up."

"Right," said Kilroy. "Well, I'd better go and mind the shop." And he squeezed past to the cockpit.

Gilkrensky watched as the machines started to record, logging information back onto the CD-ROM. "Are you analysing this, Maria?"

"I am. All the instruments are working perfectly. Shall I run an analysis of background levels before we enter the test area north of Bimini?"

"Please do. Captain Kilroy is coming up to relieve you of the controls."

"I'm perfectly capable of . . ." The Minerva paused. "That's odd," it said.

"What?"

"Something unusual – and definitely not natural."

Gilkrensky glanced towards the cockpit. Kilroy was almost at the door.

"I'm receiving powerful point-source readings from a location above and behind us . . . as if we ourselves were being scanned."

"Another aircraft? Surely it would show up on radar?"

"That's the peculiar thing. It doesn't!"

"I'll call Miami control," shouted Kilroy from the door of the cockpit.

"It's too late!" announced the Minerva sharply. "Strap yourselves in! It's diving at us!"

Jerry was a comet – a rocket – a bullet – shooting straight at the wing root of the jet. For an split second, he could see every detail of the plane through the video camera on the Hawk, every porthole, every weld, every rivet – as he streaked through the sky.

A MATTER OF TIME

"Gotcha!"

And then . . .

He was diving through clear air, straight downwards into the cloud base. The jet had flipped over onto its port side, the very instant before impact, letting Jerry dive cleanly along the vertical wing and under the belly of the plane, into empty space!

"Jesus H Christ! How did he do *that*?"

Hacker's voice, all the way from Florida, sounded in his ear. It was calm and collected, still in control.

"What happened, Mr Gibb?"

"I missed! That's what happened. He must have seen me coming. What sort of gear has that bastard got on that plane?"

"It doesn't matter. What matters now is that you ram him before he has a chance of getting on his radio to alert the authorities. Turn the Hawk round and try again."

"You got it," said Jerry, and pulled the Hawk out of its dive, soaring back up through the clouds, reaching out with eyes and ears of light and sound, searching for his prey.

There it was!

He aimed himself for the centre of the silvery cross made by the wings and the fuselage against the deep blue of the sky above. There was no way Gilkrensky could roll out of this one, even if he *could* see Jerry coming.

He was dead meat!

Gilkrensky's body had rocked back in the narrow corridor between the instrument racks as the jet righted itself. He had only just managed to bring his arms up in time to cushion the impact of his head against the hard metal of the support frames, as what had once been the wall of the cramped space suddenly became the floor, and then flipped back. The instruments racks had saved him.

"Theo! Quickly! Captain Kilroy is hurt!"

Dan Kilroy was lying across one of the cabin seats, with his arm tangled in the five-point harness. His white shirt was speckled with blood from a deep gash on his forehead. His breathing was ragged. It gurgled in his throat like a deep, liquid snore.

"I waited until the last second to manoeuvre," said the Minerva. "But Captain Kilroy couldn't fasten his seat belt in time. How is he?"

"I think he'll live. Keep us flying straight and level. I'll get on the radio and call Miami."

"Just get yourself and Captain Kilroy strapped in. That other aircraft is climbing back at us. You have less than ten seconds before I'm forced to manoeuvre again."

Gilkrensky unwrapped Kilroy's arm from the straps and grabbed him by the armpits. In a moment he had the unconscious pilot slumped in the starboard seat and was scrabbling with the five straps – shoulders, belt and groin – slamming the metal tongues into the central buckle, before throwing himself backwards into the port-side chair.

"Are you strapped in, Theo?"

"I should be up there with you!"

"Perhaps, Theo. But I can fly! Watch me!"

Jerry sighted himself on the silvery underbelly of the jet and rocketed upwards, close to the speed of sound. For an instant he could see the winking navigation lights on the wing tips – red and green – and the white light at the centre of the cross where the wings joined the fuselage. He aimed for that light and hurled himself upwards . . .

Whoosh!

He had flashed right past the rolling body of the jet, as it flipped over to starboard at the very last instant. In front of him was nothing but the deep blue sky, darkening as he climbed higher and higher.

How could he have missed?

Nobody alive had reaction times that fast!

Gilkrensky's stomach heaved as the jet flipped over to starboard in a neat barrel-roll and dived. The straps of the five-point harness cut into his shoulders and thighs as the plane turned upside down. Sunlight flashed across the windows, played over the cabin in neat discs, and was gone. Outside was the rush of clouds and sky, in a whirling kaleidoscope. The engines screamed behind him. He felt his stomach heave and fought it back. All around him, papers, cutlery and equipment manuals swirled and fluttered, crashing into the cabin walls and falling back to the floor. Outside the plane, he could hear the rush of air rising to a shrill whine as the jet dived. He looked over at Kilroy. His head was lolling gently on his chest, but he was still breathing.

"Theo? Are you all right?"

"Uh – I'm OK, and I think Dan is too. Can you make out what the hell that thing is?"

The Minerva's voice sounded calm and collected over the cabin loudspeakers. "It must be a military aircraft of some kind. And it's very small, no more than three metres long. I have to conclude it's a missile, controlled remotely or by computer. I have Miami air-traffic control on the radio now. They want to know why we're manoeuvring like this."

"Hold them. I'll come up to the cockpit and tell them we're under attack!"

"Stay where you are, Theo. I'll do it myself."

"How the *hell* can he react so quickly?" snapped Jerry, as the GRC jet dodged the Hawk for the third time.

"Perhaps you're diving at him too fast, Mr Gibb," suggested Hacker. "Gilkrensky's a trained pilot and you've lost the element of surprise. He must have some sort of computer-aided countermeasure we don't know about."

"So how do we hit him?"

"He can't outrun you. So slow down, take your time, and do it right. You know you can, Mr Gibb. I have every confidence in you."

Jerry rolled the Hawk and turned, slowing his

airspeed to match Gilkrensky's plane. He was sliding up on its port wing from behind. The video cameras on the Hawk picked out every detail, just as if they'd been his own eyes. There were the twin engines, the graceful wings with their bomb-shaped fuel tanks, the sun glinting on the Perspex windows, the forward door and the cockpit windscreen. He peered inside.

It was empty!

"Where's the pilot? Nobody's flying that thing!"

"It's what I suspected," said Hacker. "Gilkrensky has some sort of computer-control. That's why you can't hit his plane. Every time you make a pass, his machine takes over and out-flies you. To match it, you'll have to bring your own system in Santa Clara on line."

"OK, Milt. You got it . . . Holy shit! What's that?"

A voice . . . a woman's voice . . . was booming in his ears. *"Mayday! Mayday! Mayday!* This is Golf India Lima – One Zero. I am under attack from an unmanned military aircraft and have an injured crew member on board. I repeat, *Mayday! Mayday! Mayday!* Can anybody hear me? Over?"

"Who the hell's she?" hissed Jerry.

For the first time, Hacker sounded flustered. "It doesn't matter, Mr Gibb. We're blown! They'll be calling me back to the control room any second now. Switch over to the computer. It's your machine against Gilkrensky's now – too late! I have to go . . ."

Hacker's voice cut out, leaving Jerry alone in space.

Well, all right then, he thought. Let battle commence!

He concentrated until a blue square, displaying lines of white lettering, popped into view.

"Zenith On-line Real-time Information Network enabled," said the first line. "How can I help you?" A menu scrolled out below it.

Jerry picked a line and sat back, relaxed. "My Id monster is coming for you," he said menacingly. "Now we'll see who rules the skies . . ."

Twenty miles away from Jerry's house, at the laboratories of Gibbtek Santa Clara, California, a linked network of five giant state-of-the-art computers, each armed with supercooled ceramic-based microchips, turned its attention to a small problem of three-dimensional avionics over the Atlantic . . .

"It's slowing down," said the Minerva. "It's matching our speed and course exactly, fifty metres off the port wingtip."

Gilkrensky slammed his hand down on the quick-release seatbelt buckle, scrambled across the debris littering the cabin floor and dived into the cockpit. As he slid into the pilot's seat, he could see a squat black shape – shadowing them like a hungry shark.

He snapped the seatbelt in place and tried to think. "Maria, you detected that thing in the first place because it was using sound and light frequencies to track us, didn't you?"

"That is correct. Its system appears to be very similar to our own Daedalus low-level warning sensors."

"Then could we disrupt it? Could we use our own emitters to knock it off course?"

"It's theoretically possible, but we would need to boost the output enormously to have any chance of success."

"Then do it quickly, and get us as low as you can, so that we don't depressurise and explode if it does hit us."

"At once, Theo." Gilkrensky felt the jet dip, as the Minerva dived towards the sea of darkening cloud below them. To their left, off the port wingtip, the Hawk followed them down.

Jerry watch the ZORIN computer network manoeuvre the Hawk to shadow the jet more precisely than he ever could, and wondered what sort of machine Gilkrensky was using. Whatever it was, it was good. ZORIN had made two passes at the streaking plane and Gilkrensky's machine had managed to evade it each time.

But it wouldn't be able to do that for ever.

ZORIN would learn, just as it had from Jerry in all the computer games he had played on it. It would learn from its opponent, calculate his weaknesses – and strike.

It was just a matter of time.

Jerry followed the GRC jet like a shadow, as ZORIN guided the Hawk after it into the cloud. Then the conventional video cameras fogged over and he switched to an infra-red frequency so that he could see. There was the plane, still diving. They were past eight thousand feet and dropping. What was flying that thing? Could he hack into it?

Of course he could! The artificial intelligence software in ZORIN was based on the design he'd pirated from Gilkrensky the year before. If he could get the Hawk close enough to the jet, and then pick up whatever emissions Gilkrensky's computer was giving off or receiving, he could work his way back up through the firewalls and passwords into the central processor and bingo!

He'd be able to control it!

"Is the equipment ready yet, Maria? That thing's getting closer all the time!"

"I know, Theo. It seems to be learning to anticipate my movements. But I should have the batteries powered up and ready in five seconds now – four – three . . ."

The jet was diving into the cloudbase. The sun was gone and they were flying through white fog, diving closer and closer towards the ocean. Gilkrensky watched the altimeter readings drop. They were at five thousand feet, and falling.

"Two – one – now!"

Jerry Gibb reached out across the thousands of miles with his mind – probing the air between the Hawk and Gilkrensky's jet, as the two aircraft dived towards the ocean . . . back up through the plane's Daedalus emitters – past the peripheral systems, passwords and security devices into the operating core of Gilkrensky's computer itself and . . . *"Oh my!"*

He had a vision . . . a beautiful woman with shining

coppery hair and bright green eyes was flying through space. Her arms were outstretched, like Supergirl. Her forget-me-not-blue dress flowed behind her in the wind. In a flood of emotion, Jerry could feel her joy at being alive in the air. He could taste her excitement and feel the thrill of movement as she dashed into the clouds . . . a living, feeling, being . . . alive within the machine . . .

"Wow!" breathed Jerry, dumbstruck. "I think I'm in love!"

Then, all at once, he sensed danger.

The central processor of Gilkrensky's computer was protected by an advanced attack virus, capable of infecting any invading system and causing it to crash.

"Shit," said Jerry and pulled back, out of harm's way, still thinking about the beautiful woman in the forget-me-not dress.

"How can I get my hands on . . . ?"

And then with a blinding flash of orange light – that seared into his brain and brought his hands clawing at the SQUID headset – the Hawk was gone.

A sheet of orange fire lit the sky around the Voyager. There was a sickening, rolling lurch as Gilkrensky seemed to fall into a hole in space. He grabbed the controls of the plane and suddenly realised – he was flying in complete darkness!

"Maria!"

Gilkrensky fought the controls as rain streaked the windscreen and the vicious turbulence of a storm buffeted the hull. It had come out of nowhere, and now he was fighting for his life. He glanced over at the Hawk, just visible in the flash of his own navigation lights, near the port wing.

"Maria!"

The screen of the Minerva 3,000 was frozen. Maria's face, lifeless and still, stared at him from the darkened control panel. The plane yawed sickeningly in the sky . . . out of control.

Gilkrensky pulled back on the joystick, as the altimeter readings rushed downwards and the compass span in front of his eyes. All the navigation electronics were out! What the hell had happened? There was nothing but static!

Then suddenly, so loud over the speakers that he jumped in his seat . . . *"Banana River! Banana River! This is Training Forty-nine! Training Forty-nine! Over?"*

"What the . . . ?"

His instincts told him it was there before he saw it. He hauled back on the controls, desperate to gain height . . .

Rushing at him out of the darkness was the huge, whale-shaped hull of a gigantic flying boat . . .

14

Collision!

The other plane was colossal. It filled the darkness along the port side of the GRC jet. Gilkrensky could see its bent, gull-shaped wings and big double tail as he rushed towards it, heading straight for the starboard engine. His navigation lights flashed on the dull painted metal.

He was heaving the controls back to his chest, ramming the throttles forward, fighting to gain height as his right foot slammed down on the rudder pedal, desperately trying to turn to starboard, away from the churning propellers. For a second his whole universe was nothing but the great whirling blades . . . a shuddering crash as his port wing-tank collided with the giant aircraft's starboard float – and then he was clear – swooping up into space.

But where was that missile?

There was a brilliant flash behind him, the clouds around him turned bright red, and the deafening roar of an explosion tore at his eardrums as the first shock wave slammed into the jet, lifting it into the sky like a cork in surf.

It must have been that thing!

It had struck the flying boat amidships, tearing into its hull and rupturing the fuel tanks. Nobody aboard had a chance!

Gilkrensky fought the controls as they shuddered in his hands. Pieces of wreckage flew past the windshield. He heard one of them clatter along the hull and fall away. The orange glow died – and he was alone in the darkness.

"Maria! Are you OK?" But her image was still frozen on the screen.

He reached for the radio.

"*Mayday! Mayday! Mayday!* This is Golf India Lima, Golf India Lima! I have an explosion and a plane down, east of Miami. Does anyone copy? Over?"

Nothing but static. And then . . . "*Golf India Lima? This is Fox Tare Two Eight. Identify yourself! Over!*"

"Fox Tare Two Eight! I am a private jet out of Ireland, heading for Orlando. I have a plane down – a flying boat – twin propellers – east of Miami. Please alert air-sea rescue and send a chopper. There may be survivors. Over?"

"*Golf India Lima? A jet? Out of Ireland? Get off this channel, Mister. I have a serious situation here . . . I have . . .*"

The voice was getting weaker, further away and fading fast.

"Fox Tare Two Eight! Fox Tare Two Eight! You are breaking up on me. Over . . . ?"

There was nothing but static . . . then a sudden clap of thunder shook the jet, and Gilkrensky had left the storm behind as if never existed. He was climbing into a clear blue sky above the clouds. All at once, his headset was full of radio traffic.

"*Golf India Lima! Golf India Lima!* This is Miami control. Are you OK? We had a 'Mayday' and you slipped off our screens for a second! Over?"

"Miami Control! This is Golf India Lima. I have a plane down, east of you at . . ." He glanced up at his navigation equipment. It was all working perfectly again. The Minerva said, "What happened? Did the Daedalus pulse work?"

"Just a moment, Maria. Hello? Miami? I repeat. I have a plane down at twenty-eight degrees fifty-nine minutes north, eighty degrees, twenty-five minutes west. It went down in a storm, in collision with some sort of missile that was tracking me. Do you copy that? Over!"

"We copy, Golf India Lima. What kind of plane? We have no storm on our scopes. Nothing but clear weather. Over?"

"A flying boat. A big one. Twin engines and bent over, gull-shaped wings, two tail fins. I couldn't see markings, but it looked like a military plane, over?"

There was silence for a moment. Then, "Golf India Lima. Are you sure that's what you saw, or is this some kind of hoax? Over?"

"Miami Control. I know what I saw. It burst into flames right in front of my eyes. Are you going to do something about it or not? Over?"

"Golf India Lima. If you want to make this official, we'll scramble a chopper out off the Cape, but if this is a joke, buddy, you're in serious shit. There hasn't been a plane like that in the skies around here since the war . . ."

Twelve hundred miles to the north-west, Jerry Gibb pressed the button to release the door of his pod and emerged into the sunlit study, rubbing his eyes.

He had seriously fucked up. Gilkrensky was back on course for Orlando, the Hawk was lost, and there were reports of some other plane being down. If the whole mess could be pinned on the Hawk test, then the lawsuits alone would crush him. There might even be criminal charges – unless Hacker could deal with them.

Hacker could deal with anything.

He always did.

Jerry went to the fridge, pulled out a carton and ripped open another packet of Oreos, crunching the first one between his teeth and washing it down with a big swig of cold milk.

The woman in the forget-me-not dress – it had to be Gilkrensky's dead wife – what was her name? Jerry closed his eyes and thought back to the party where they'd met. Maria! That was it, Maria!

Jerry popped another Oreo into his mouth. In his mind he could see her again in the air, arms outstretched, flying. The beautiful coppery hair flowed behind her, and he could feel – really feel – her joy. It must be some new artificially intelligent "Help" program Gilkrensky had worked out. The realism of it was incredible. She was so lifelike! More than any of his own "Julies" had ever been. If only he could find a way past that virus defence system, he could hack her out of Gilkrensky's machine and into his own – he could see how she performed in one of his sex fantasies – or even in the Morbius III game, up against the Hordes of Hydra – he would put Hacker on it.

Hacker could fix anything!

15

On the Carpet

"This just in from Florida . . . computer tycoon Theodore Gilkrensky narrowly missed death earlier this afternoon, when his private jet was involved in a mid-air collision, allegedly involving a robot stealth-fighter under test on the nearby Cape Canaveral rocket range. But the company which manufactured the guidance system for the missile – Gibbtek, of Santa Clara, California – issued a statement saying that it was investigating, and I quote, 'strange radio and radar emissions' from Dr Gilkrensky's plane which, it claims, may have upset the test and caused their robot missile to home in on the billionaire's executive jet. Reporters in Florida are also investigating allegations by Dr Gilkrensky that another aircraft was involved in the incident and crashed in flames. What's the story on the ground, Jamie?"

The television news report cut to an airstrip in Florida, where an attractive young woman in a smart business suit was standing near Gilkrensky's grounded

Voyager. The port wing-tank was crumpled like a soft-drink can. The camera zoomed in on it.

"It's difficult to tell, Brad. Both companies – GRC and Gibbtek – were involved in a legal battle before this incident and are each claiming the other was to blame for this near-fatal collision."

"And any news on this mysterious third aircraft?"

Jamie smiled. She had very white teeth. "The US Coast Guard aren't taking that one very seriously, Brad. There have been no other reports of a crash, no radar records, and no aircraft matching the description given by Dr Gilkrensky around Florida for the last fifty years."

"But there *were* injuries?"

"Only Gilkrensky's pilot – a Captain Dan Kilroy – who was knocked unconscious during the incident and taken to hospital here in Orlando, where we understand he is making a full recovery."

"Thank you, Jamie. Meanwhile, the bashful billionaire himself has currently gone to ground in his Orlando Olympiad hotel, and is not available for comment. This marks another colourful chapter in the recently eventful life of the reclusive computer king, whose activities in Cairo last December led to a diplomatic . . . "

Jessica Wright's thumb ground down on the button of the remote control, the recording stopped, and the video screen cleared. She was looking at a very familiar face. "Theo, are you all right? I was worried sick."

"I'm OK, Jess. I'm very angry, and a little shaken, but I'll get over it."

"I presume you've seen the news?"

"I could hardly miss it. The story's all over CNN and the local TV networks. They have three camera crews down in the hotel lobby and there's a news helicopter whizzing around outside. It's blown my cover all to hell."

"What can I do to help?"

"Are you alone?"

"Yes, Theo."

Gilkrensky was looking straight into the video camera. "Jess, I'm sorry about that fight we had in London, and what happened later when we went to pick up the Minerva. I know what you said about wanting space to think things through, and perhaps it's too soon for me as well, after losing Maria . . . but I do care for you, Jess. I *do* want us to be friends."

Jessica Wright reached up and touched the video screen.

"I know, Theo."

"Would you come out to Florida? We could talk about it?"

Jessica looked into the brown eyes that faced her from the other side of the world. Did Theo really *mean* what he said? She thought of the time they'd spent in her hotel suite over the New Year . . . her nightmare . . . the photograph falling from his books . . . the image of Maria that was still with him on that computer in Florida.

She glanced down at her desk, and the stack of legal papers, E-mail print-outs and faxes overflowing from the 'in' tray. "Theo, I'd love to, more than anything. But the police are still swarming all over the building, the Japanese legal case is gaining momentum, and now Gibbtek's lawyers have contacted us. It looks like they're going to sue. Think about it, Theo. You need me here."

"Are you sure?"

"I am."

"I see. I'm sorry."

"I know. What *really* happened in the plane?"

"Jerry Gibb tried to kill me! That's what happened. He tracked my jet with that missile of his, tried to ram me, and then couldn't keep up because the Minerva took control and out-flew him."

"How do you know it was Gibbtek's fault? The missile was made by Phoenix Aviation after all."

"The only way I managed to get rid of it was by having the Minerva interfere with its control system, and the only way I could do *that* was because Gibbtek was using pirated software and Daedalus sensors compatible with mine. Jerry Gibb engineered the whole thing to get me out of the way. That's what happened. Why? What have you got on Phoenix."

"Precious little. The owner, Charles Howard, is a virtual recluse. He's done a lot of government work – which was what that Stealth Project was – and he's one of the world's experts on helicopter design. But nobody's seen him in years."

"I'd still put my money on Gibbtek."

"But can you *prove* it?"

"If I can find that other aircraft, I can. There's bound to be wreckage on the sea floor, and bits of that drone as well."

Jessica Wright picked up a fax from her desk.

"You'll need to do *something*. Gibbtek's claiming your experiments caused their missile to crash, losing them a lucrative Air Force contract and millions of dollars. If you have any proof, Theo, I need it fast."

"I have my own set of flight recordings, both on the jet's Daedalus system and on the Minerva, right up to the time when I collided with the flying boat, but after that there's a gap."

Jessica shook her head slowly.

"Nobody else saw that flying boat except you, Theo. Are you sure that's what it was?"

"I know what I saw, Jess. It's just that after Cairo, it's a bit hard to re-establish my credibility."

"I know what you mean. Our switchboard has been jammed with calls from every New Age nut under the sun, including some really weird E-mails."

"Are you sure you're OK?"

Once again, Jessica Wright looked hard at the face on the screen. Could she afford to get sucked back in again – and hurt again?

"Look after yourself, Theo," she said. "Do what you can about the Gibbtek case and call me. OK?"

Jessica Wright's face vanished from the Minerva screen, to be replaced by Maria's image.

"I have a telephone call holding for you, that could have a bearing on the incident earlier today," said the computer. "But I think you should see one of the E-mails Miss Wright sent us before you answer."

"How so?"

"It says 'You were right about the flying boat'. Look, here it is now."

Gilkrensky read the E-mail message over twice, and said, "It's not signed. Can we tell who it's from?"

"That will be extremely difficult to discover. While I could locate the E-mail server being used, the person sending you that message could be accessing it from anywhere in the world by modem from a telephone."

"Then the only way to find out is to answer the call?"

"Yes, Theo. Shall I put it though?"

"Please do."

"Hello?" said a man's voice from the Minerva speaker.

"Are you the person who sent me an E-mail about a flying boat?"

There was a soft chuckle. "Dr Theodore Gilkrensky, I presume."

"That's right, and who are you?"

"Let's just say I'm a big fan of yours, Dr Gilkrensky. I've been watching your activities over the last couple of months, on the TV and the Web, and from that I can see we share a mutual interest with a very powerful third party, you and I."

"An interest in what?"

"Time and space, Dr Gilkrensky. Those experiments you performed on the Great Pyramid of Cheops last month, your interest in the paranormal, your presence here in Bermuda right now. A lot of people are very interested in you. Anyone with an ounce of common sense and access to the Web can see what you're doing, and so can this third party I spoke of."

"And who are you?"

"My name is Kosner, Dr Gilkrensky. I'm someone who wants to remain mobile and needs the funds to do it."

"Why should that interest me?"

"Because I know things that can help you find what you're looking for. Things that can speed up the process for you. Don't bother trying to trace this number, because you can't. But you might look up my name on the Web, along with this other name . . . a ship's name . . . the USS *Eldridge*. I'll drop by and see you sometime, and then we can come to an arrangement. Goodbye."

Then the line went dead.

"Meeeehhhhhnnnn!"

The scream burst in Hacker's face a split second before the thick bamboo training-sword smacked onto the protective armour of his helmet, right above his forehead.

Point!

A MATTER OF TIME

Hacker was losing his edge. Normally he had no problem in clearing his thoughts to achieve the state of mind essential for competitive *kendo* – the art of Japanese sword fighting.

But tonight something was wrong.

The day had been a whirlpool of media enquiries, briefing sessions with Gibbtek and Phoenix Aviation lawyers, and awkward questions from the Acquisitions Committee. How could Gibbtek explain the loss of control? How had the Hawk managed to home in on an innocent civilian aircraft? What would have happened if that had been an airliner landing at Miami?

As always, Hacker was in control. He had called for the complete customs list of all the electronic equipment aboard Gilkrensky's aircraft, and when that was not forthcoming had released a press statement hinting that Gilkrensky would not reveal the information because he himself had tampered with the robot aircraft in flight. The allegation introduced an element of doubt into an otherwise open-and-shut case. There was even talk of a counter-suit against GRC by Gibbtek. It was all working perfectly.

So why was he still worried . . . ?

Hacker could smell the new sweat mingling with the old inside the padded *kendo* helmet. He watched his opponent intently through the grille of his face-mask and held the bamboo sword lightly, with its tip pointed at the other man's throat.

At the referee's command to start, Hacker leapt

forward, testing his opponent's guard with thrusts and cuts . . . *Clack! Clack! Clack!* . . . while watching his own defence, careful not to reveal an inch of the heavily padded target areas along his head, shoulders and waist to attack.

"Yaaaaattttttsssssss!"

His thrust was parried. His opponent twisted the sword aside and started a counter-attack of his own. It was the final round, and both men were even. Hacker could not afford to lose this point. He tried to relax as the two bamboo swords blurred in the air and the clacking staccato rang around the hall like machine-gun fire.

Then . . . in the corner of his eye . . . movement!

For a split second, Hacker's gaze was drawn from his opponent to the man who had just entered the tournament room. He was staring at Hacker, unsure of himself . . .

"Meeennnhhh!"

His opponent's sword flicked to his throat, drew Hacker's guard, and then slammed down on his helmet.

Point . . . and Match!

Hacker had lost. His concentration had shifted. He had allowed his concentration to evaporate, and he had paid the price. Seething with anger at himself as much as at the man who had distracted him, he bowed solemnly to his opponent, bowed to the referee and walked to the edge of the tournament area. Then he kneeled, placed his sword carefully by his left thigh, and pulled off his padded gloves, reaching behind his head to lift off the sweat-soaked helmet and neck protectors.

Finally, he rose, bowed once more in honour of the contest, and walked towards the door.

"Mr Hacker, I am *so* sorry," said the man, rushing over to him as soon as he stepped off the competition floor. It was Ayako Miura, the owner of the club and a man, like Hacker, who was well aware of the rules regarding etiquette while a tournament was in progress. "In any other circumstance, I would never have disturbed a match like that, but this is beyond my control – a phone call for you, Mr Hacker, from your employer, Jerry Gibb."

Hacker reached for a towel to wipe the sweat from his face. "Please don't trouble yourself, Ayako-san. I can imagine Mr Gibb insisted you find me at once."

"That is correct," said Miura. "He said unless you were contacted within one minute, he would have you fired."

Hacker smiled grimly, "How many seconds remain?"

Miura looked at his watch, "Only twenty, you must hurry. The telephone is in my office."

Hacker glanced at his own timepiece, noted the exact moment and walked out of the tournament hall to the office. Then he picked up the receiver, waited until the last second and said, "What is it, Mr Gibb?"

The familiar voice had a self-satisfied smugness to it. "You almost lost that one, Milt. Why did you switch off your cellphone?"

"I was in a kendo tournament, Mr Gibb. It's the sort of thing you don't disturb."

"Well now, Milt. It looks as if we're even for yesterday, when you interrupted me as I was about to win at Morbius III. Anyhow, what's more important to you, working for Gibbtek, or playing with sticks?"

Hacker said nothing.

"Milt?"

"I'm here, Mr Gibb. What do you want?"

"I want you in San Francisco! I want you to come up here and explain to me, in every last detail, how we managed to fuck up today's operation! That's what I want!"

"I can write you a full report, if that's what you want."

"And put it in writing! What about security, Milt? I want you here, to tell me in person."

"San Francisco's a long way. There may not be a connection this late."

"Oh yes, there is. I looked it up on the Web. You take the 9.30 from Orlando to Vegas tonight, and from there to San Francisco, arriving here at 1.30 tomorrow morning. The tickets are booked in your name."

Hacker looked at his watch. He'd just make it.

"That's very good of you, Mr Gibb."

The voice on the other end of the line oozed smugness.

"I'm learning from you, Milt. You're the guy who can fix anything, right? And there's something I want you to fix for me. So get your sorry ass up here and fix it!"

"With respect, Mr Gibb. Don't you think my time would be better spent down here in Orlando?"

There was an intake of breath on the other end of the line, as Jerry stoked himself up. Hacker stared at the roof as he listened to the familiar threats. One of these days he would take Jerry Gibb's cellphone and make him eat it, a piece at a time.

"If that's what you really want, Mr Gibb," he said, and gently replaced the receiver, pulled out his own mobile, switched it back on and ordered a taxi for the airport. It dropped him outside the modern departures hall at just after nine and, even though that was cutting it fine, Hacker had no problem getting his seat on the nine-thirty flight to Las Vegas.

Below him, the automated shuttle train from the arrivals hall was disgorging the last passengers of the day, from Paris, into the main lobby. Coaches from the various hotels, the Marriott, Holiday Inn and Best Western, lined up along the sidewalk outside to whisk them away – businessmen to conventions, families to Disneyworld, and the odd loners, there for reasons of their own.

Amongst these was a strikingly beautiful woman with long raven-black hair, a dark complexion, and thick-framed glasses over her deep brown eyes. Her high cheekbones and perfect oval face suggested Hawaii, or one of the Pacific islands, and she was well-dressed in a smart suit by Georgio Armani. Her passport described her as a dealer in Oriental antiquities, and anyone examining the rugged Samsonite suitcase she was wheeling would have found a number of exquisitely crafted pieces, including a priceless Japanese short sword. The black lacquered scabbard showed an intricate scene of tigers in a forest and, on the pommel at the end of the hilt, was the delicate cherry blossom of the Funakoshi family.

16

Old Acquaintance

The car was a pure white Lincoln Continental modified by American Coachworks Ltd., of Beverly Hills, California. Its 5.7 litre engine purred lazily as it slid off the main Orlando freeway onto a slip road, glided over the speed bumps, and past the hissing water-sprinklers painting rainbows of spray over the tightly groomed lawns, fairways and putting-greens. Ahead of it, stark and white against the deep blue of the early morning sky, was the towering iceberg of the Orlando Olympiad hotel.

The driver slowed onto the tiled forecourt beneath the awning of the main entrance, where the few remaining television crews were lying in ambush, nodded to the uniformed porters and drove on, through the commercial loading area, towards the back of the hotel complex. At a side entrance, hidden from view by another awning, were four uniformed security guards – all armed. The car slid to a halt, its passenger door popped open, and a tall man in a worn leather jacket darted from the hotel into the waiting car.

"Good morning," he said, laying the Minerva 3,000 on the red leather seat facing him. "I'm Theo Gilkrensky. Do you know where to go?"

The driver barely turned in his seat. He was a big man, in a pristine white shirt that strained across his shoulders and fought a losing battle around the collar. His bullet head was crowned by a military crew-cut. There was a black plastic name badge over his left breast-pocket and mirror-finish aviator sunglasses over his eyes.

"Professor McCarthy's place out at Titusville?" he said in lazy Louisiana drawl. "Sure, I've been there plenty of times. Name's Randolf Stevenson, sir. But everybody calls me 'RJ'. I'll be handling your personal security from now on. You just sit back and enjoy the ride."

The four security guards from the hotel divided themselves between two grey station wagons that took up position, in front of the Lincoln and behind. Then the convoy moved off, sliding back down the tree-lined slip road past the early morning golfers and onto the Beeline Expressway, heading east.

The traffic was light. Gilkrensky took in the lush green land all around them, the steel and glass islands of high-rise hotels, and the gas stations with their outdoor ice machines. He saw a sign saying *English Papers Sold*, and thought of Jessica – at work by now – in London.

172

Then he looked again. A long black limousine had pulled out onto the freeway behind them. It was following at a distance.

"Did you see that?" he said to Stevenson, remembering the strange warning about a "powerful third party" he'd received from Kosner the night before. Stevenson's hand went to his radio handset. He mumbled into the speaker. Looking out of the rear window, Gilkrensky saw the men in the rear security car look back in turn. There was a muffled exchange of voices Gilkrensky couldn't quite make out, and Stevenson said, "Don't you worry about that now, sir. The boys in back think it's just the local feds keeping an eye on us. You're a celebrity, Dr Gilkrensky. You've been on TV. There's bound to be interest."

"In a limousine?"

"Yeah, you got a point there. But don't worry, sir. Let me talk to security and get it checked out. See! He's dropping back. Probably knows we spotted him."

Gilkrensky relaxed, and watched the flat landscape roll past them on the dead straight road. They had left the houses and hotels of Orlando behind and were in a virtual wilderness, surrounded by marshes, swamps and orange groves. The convoy reached a toll-booth and slowed, sweeping through a reserved gate without stopping, and picked up speed. Gilkrensky saw the drivers of other cars – Dodges, Plymouths and Fords – glare at them enviously. His hand went to the window control and pressed it.

"Excuse me, Dr Gilkrensky, sir. But you won't get the full benefit if you open the window."

"You mean the air-conditioning?"

"No, sir, the bullet-proof glass."

"Sorry!"

"No problem, but just don't forget who you are and where you are. The guys in London briefed me about you. You had one hell of a time in Cairo?"

"You could say that."

"Both bodyguards wiped out, their boss Crowe in hospital with concussion, four helicopters totalled and a couple of hundred 'G's' worth of damage to the hotel. That's what I heard."

"You heard right."

Stevenson shifted in his seat and reached down with his right hand.

"Won't happen here, sir. I made sure of that. The car's bullet-proof, me and my boys are all former military or Secret Service and, if the shit hits the fan, then we each have one of these . . . "

The pistol he held up looked like a toy in his big beefy hand.

"9mm Glock 17 automatic," he said. "The safest, most reliable handgun in the world. It's impossible to trigger accidentally, and yet it'll even fire underwater if you want it to. I load mine with custom rounds I make myself. Just to be sure."

"You seem to know a lot about guns."

"You're in the States now, Dr Gilkrensky. *Everybody*

knows a lot about guns. That's why you're sitting in a bullet-proof car."

They were nearing the "Space Coast", and the influence of the Kennedy Space Center was showing in the scenery. Diners with names like "The Apollo Burger Bar", "Space Diner" and "Mercury Mart" flashed past.

"Almost there," said Stevenson and pulled off the freeway heading north-east for the city of Titusville. Gilkrensky looked back. Far behind, he saw the black limousine make the turn with them.

"Do you surf, sir? We've got fine surfing beaches here. Biggest surf shop in the world too, down in Cocoa, although the sea's a bit too cold for me, this time of year."

"No. I'm fine. Water and me don't mix."

"Know what you mean, sir. Well, here we are."

The Lincoln followed the first security car off the main road, over a small bridge across a gully and up a tree-lined laneway to a long, low bungalow. Parked next to it, under a lean-to, was a sleek, white coupe with Florida plates.

"Mmm . . . Dodge Challenger," said Stevenson. "Had one myself before I got hitched. Serious car." He stopped the Lincoln and waited with his hand on the Glock pistol while the security cars pulled up in front and behind them. Then he popped his door, slipped the gun back into its holster and let Gilkrensky out. The four other security men stood round him.

"Did you get a chance to check out that other car?" asked Gilkrensky.

"We asked the County cops to run it though their computer," said the driver of the rear car. "They'll get back to us."

"I see. Professor McCarthy was a good friend of mine. I have a lot to discuss with his family."

"We've checked out the house and they're expecting you, sir," said Stevenson. "We'll be right here, and we ain't going nowhere without you."

"Thanks".

The wooden steps up to the bungalow were bleached silver by the sun. Turning back, Gilkrensky could see nothing but swamp and wilderness all around them. Above the blue haze of the ocean, to the north-east, the tall rocket-sheds and gantries of the Space Center towered into the sky.

"You get a great view of the launches from here."

Standing in the doorway was a short woman in her early sixties. The iron-grey hair above the sky blue eyes was tied back in a tight bun. She was wearing a house-coat and apron.

"You're very welcome, sir. My name's Tessa, and I keep house here. Miss McCarthy's expecting you. She's on the phone right now. Can I fix you some coffee? Or would you prefer tea?"

"Coffee's fine. Thank you."

He followed the woman out of the bright sunlight through a dark hallway, and into Bill McCarthy's study. The walls were lined with photographs of Bill's time at NASA – Bill standing with a group of astronauts –

Grissom, Shepard and Armstrong, Bill next to a lunar module, Bill in mission control with Buzz Aldrin, Bill on campus at MIT, Bill with his wife at GRC Aerospace at Orlando, Bill at the launch party for the "Whisperer" jet at Heathrow.

On the dark oak dresser, near the desk, were the family photographs – Bill with his two daughters, Angie and Jill, on his knee, the girls in mortar-boards and graduation gowns, each looking very serious, Bill and his grandchildren on Cocoa beach, playing in the sand. Then, at the end of the row, a smaller photograph in a silver frame – Bill at Theo's wedding in Cork, his arm around Theo's shoulder, looking relaxed and happy, with a glass of champagne in his hand. Gilkrensky laid the Minerva 3,000 on the desk, picked up the photograph and stared at it. On the other side of Bill McCarthy, with her arm around Bill's waist and a smile of pure joy on her face, was his own wife, Maria. Gilkrensky traced her face with his finger, lost in memories of that day . . . Maria all in white with the sunlight turning her hair to fire – Maria laughing – dancing – loving – alive . . .

The big double doors to the lounge slid open.

"You must miss her terribly."

Suddenly self-conscious, Gilkrensky put the photograph down and turned. Standing in the doorway, with her back to the sun, was a tall woman with short, dark-blonde hair, dressed in a simple white shirt and jeans. She looked very fit. Her tanned skin seemed to glow in the dimness of the study.

"Jill? Jill McCarthy?"

She smiled and stepped forward into the room. Her bright grey eyes examined him carefully. There was a lot of her father in the proud, upturned nose and the determined jaw.

"How are you, Theo? It's been a long time."

Then she put out her arms and hugged him. For a moment they stood there together, silently. Then Jill said. "I saw you looking at the photograph. I'm so sorry."

Gilkrensky stepped back to look at her. Snapshots of memory were flashing before his eyes like the pictures on the wall – Jill as an intense and awkward graduate student at MIT, Jill at his wedding in Cork, self-conscious in her bridesmaid's dress, Jill at her sister Angie's funeral in Boston, fighting back tears . . . and now Jill in his arms, a beautiful woman.

"I'm sorry I couldn't make it to the memorial service yesterday," he said. "There was a whole media circus waiting for me when I landed in Orlando. They would have followed me to the church. I didn't think it was fair on your family."

She nodded. "You were right to stay away. A lot of my folks can't come to terms with the way Dad just – 'vanished'. They're very angry at what they've been told. My brother Mac is talking about a family law-suit against you. Your being there yesterday with a load of reporters would have just made things worse."

"And you? How do you feel?"

Jill McCarthy crossed her arms on her chest.

"I loved my father, Theo. I'd want to know what happened. So tell me what *really* went wrong in Cairo. Then I'll tell you how I feel."

"Can I sit down? I have something to show you."

"Please."

Gilkrensky lifted the Minerva 3,000 from the desk and laid it on the low coffee table. "We were in Egypt together, your father and me," he said. "The Whisperer jet had gone down, and the pilot blamed the Daedalus system for the crash. You know all about that?"

"Of course. I helped Dad design most of that plane and part of the Daedalus system as well. I almost went with him to Cairo to find out what the problem was. Perhaps it would have been better if I had . . ."

"I thought the world of your father. He taught me most of what I know about aviation systems when we were at MIT together. If anyone was going to find the problem, he was."

"I know," said Jill. "And he thought the world of you. You were always his favourite student. He was so pleased when you took him on to design the Whisperer."

"Yes – well, Bill and I found that the low-altitude sensors on the Whisperer's Daedalus unit were being triggered prematurely by some sort of natural radiation. I know it's going to sound incredible, but I had this theory that the Great Pyramid had been built as some kind of lens to focus earth energies, the same way as glass lenses focus light. Bill wasn't having any of it. He thought there must be another, more rational explanation."

"Dad was a realist," said Jill. "And so am I. He taught me never to accept anything I couldn't prove scientifically."

"I know, but then we found a new chamber inside the Pyramid, one that nobody could explain. And then, this happened . . ."

Gilkrensky opened the lid of the computer. "This is Minerva," he said, "the new artificially intelligent machine I was working on when Maria died. Bill probably told you about the interface program. I . . . I'm sorry. I just let my own grief get the better of me."

The face of Maria Gilkrensky appeared on the computer screen and smiled.

"Good morning, Miss McCarthy," it said. "And welcome to the Minerva 3,000."

Jill frowned. "This is what you wanted to show me?"

"No. Of course not. You said you wanted to know what *really* happened in Cairo. Well, this is all I have to show you. It's a recording from the nearest camera to your father during the experiment when he disappeared. Do you want to see it?"

Jill McCarthy nodded. "All right," she said. "Show it to me."

"Maria?"

Maria's image shrank to a window in the upper right-hand corner of the screen, which filled with a view of the Queen's chamber of the Great Pyramid of Cheops. Wires and cables covered the floor, leading off into the shadows, and down through the neat circular hole they'd cut in the far wall to the golden crypt. Numbers, showing the date and time recorded by the camera, ticked forward in the bottom right-hand corner of the picture.

"We were trying to take readings of this new energy we'd found right in the centre of the Pyramid," said Gilkrensky. "Bill had been in there fixing the sensors and I'd ordered him out of the way while the experiment took place, just to be safe. Then this happened. Can we have the soundtrack as well, please, Maria?"

From the speaker of the Minerva, Gilkrensky heard his own voice say, *"It'll start at a very low level. Make sure the sensitivity is turned way up to begin with. What's that?"*

Bill McCarthy was walking across the screen to the circular opening of the golden crypt.

"Bill! What are you doing?"

"I dropped the model in there, Theo. I want to get it back before the surge comes."

"Forget it, Bill! There's only three minutes left!"

But McCarthy was already at the entrance to the golden crypt peering inside.

"He went in and got a balsa wood model plane he'd been working on," said Gilkrensky. "It was the new Hi-lift prototype, and he didn't want to lose it."

From the Minerva, Gilkrensky's recorded voice said, *"How long to the surge?"*

"One minute and forty-five seconds," replied the machine.

"And we can't shut it down?"

"We have no control over the phenomenon once it is triggered by the holography display, Theo. All we can do is observe."

On the Minerva screen, Professor Bill McCarthy could be seen wriggling out of the narrow entrance to the golden crypt, on the far side of the Queen's chamber. Then he gathered up his coat from the floor and ran for the exit. He fell. Jill gasped. Her hand went to her mouth.

"I tried to get him out of there in time," said Gilkrensky. "But nobody was close enough to reach him."

Bill McCarthy was picking himself up. He was looking back towards the circular opening. It was glowing with a strange, warm light . . . a light that seemed to reach out and draw him in. He stood mesmerised for a moment and then, slowly, like a man walking to meet an old friend, he stepped towards the opening – and crawled back in . . .

A babble of different sounds came from the recording.

"He's going inside," shouted Gilkrensky's voice. *"Bill! Get out of there! Can anyone hear me? Can you follow him on the camera inside the crypt?"*

"The energy readings are peaking!" announced the computer. *"The surges are going right off the scale!"*

"Look at those levels! No wonder we . . . "

Then the screen was full of snow. The voices were drowned out in a static hiss. Only the white numbers remained . . . ticking away time.

Gilkrensky's voice. *"Bill?"*

"The Queen's Chamber cameras are back on line," said a voice. *"But there's nothing moving."*

"Get a couple of people down there and see if he's OK!"

The recording fast-forwarded. The figures blurred at the bottom of the screen, but the picture remained the same. Nothing moved. After ten minutes of elapsed time, two men entered the chamber and moved to the golden crypt.

"Is Bill all right?" said Gilkrensky's voice.

One of the technicians turned to face the camera. *"I don't get it,"* he said.

Gilkrensky again. *"What's not to get? Go in there and bring Bill out!"*

The man looked stunned. *"That's just it, sir. The crypt's empty! The sensor array and video camera have vanished into thin air. And there's no sign of Professor McCarthy. He's gone too!"*

The recording stopped, and Maria's face filled the screen again.

"We searched the Pyramid from top to bottom," said Gilkrensky. "We sent trained guides into every nook and cranny there was. The only way out had security cameras all the way along it. He just vanished – inside that golden crypt."

Jill McCarthy was sitting hunched on the sofa, staring

at the screen with her elbows on her knees and her hands over her mouth.

"Oh God!" she said. "Excuse me a . . . please, Theo." Then she got up from the sofa and ran out through the double doors.

For a moment there was silence. Then the Minerva said, "Why didn't you tell Miss McCarthy about the time displacement?"

Gilkrensky was looking through the doors after Jill McCarthy. "Because she's a realist – like her father," he said. "Because she wouldn't believe it. Because the Egyptians won't let me back to the Pyramid to take it any further, and because . . . because perhaps I hardly believe it myself any more . . ."

"But Professor McCarthy may not have died," said the Minerva. "The experimental data we obtained supports the theory that he was displaced in time through a standing Einstein-Rosen bridge. If we could repeat those conditions, we could recover him. Why didn't you tell Miss McCarthy that?"

"Because everyone I've talked to since, from quantum physicists to Egyptologists say what happened is impossible. Perhaps Bill *was* vaporised inside that chamber. Would *you* believe a man who told you the Pyramid was built to warp the fabric of space and time? Because nobody else does!"

"But you have *proof*," said the Minerva simply. "Professor McCarthy's model plane was recovered in Saqqara, aged by two thousand years. It's in the

Cairo Museum. The irradiated sand you used to send back in time – that aged by four thousand years! Show Miss McCarthy the proof. She's a scientist. She'll understand."

"I'm sorry, Maria," said Gilkrensky. "She may be a scientist, but she's only human – and so am I."

Then he got up, and followed Jill through the doors of the study, out into the garden.

She was sitting on a wooden bench in the shade of a tree, sobbing gently to herself. Gilkrensky watched her for a moment, unsure of himself, and then sat down beside her.

"I'm so sorry, Jill," he said.

Jill McCarthy wiped the tears from her face with the back of her hand.

"It's OK, Theo. I'm – I'm just not good at emotions. That's all . . ."

"Who is?" said Gilkrensky, and for a long while they just sat there, gazing out over the garden across the marshlands to the sea.

"So it's true," she said at last. "He's gone."

Gilkrensky thought of what Minerva had said about proof. It had all been a dream anyway. Hadn't it?

"Yes," he said. "He's gone."

"That surge of energy. It must have vaporised everything inside that chamber. You said the cameras and sensors vanished too?"

"That's right. It's – it's the only logical explanation."

"I adored him," she said in a small childlike voice. "And yet Angie was his favourite. She was his first, you see, and Mac was his only son. I was just – 'Jill'. So I pushed myself in front of him all the time. I even took up flying just so he would notice me. I got my pilot's licence just to prove myself to him, and I probably married Gordon, just because I thought Dad would approve."

"Yes – I know, the pilot from NASA."

"It didn't work out though, did it?"

"No. Bill told me you'd split up. I'm sorry."

"Theo? Would you hold me?"

Gilkrensky put his arm around her and she rested her head on his shoulder. The tears were back. They felt hot on his skin.

"I'm sorry, Theo. Like I said, I'm not very good at emotions."

"You're doing OK. It's not easy."

"How did you ever get over Maria?"

"I – I don't think I ever did. That's why I put her image into that machine in there. Your father said I was mad. He wanted me to accept her death, mourn her, and move on. But I couldn't. I just couldn't get her out of my mind. Perhaps that's what I have to do now."

Jill McCarthy straightened herself, and wiped her tears away on the sleeve of her shirt.

"That's what we *both* have to do," she said. "My father was a nut about air safety. He poured his whole life and soul into it after Angie and her kids were killed in that air crash. You know it, Theo. That's why you hired him to build the Whisperer. That's why he and I put so much into the Daedalus system, so that there would never be another air crash, ever again."

"That's right."

"And now all the papers say Daedalus is unsafe! It's as if everything Dad and I worked on together is a lie. It makes my blood boil. All he ever wanted to do was to save lives, and now they're crucifying him."

"I know."

"So the best thing I can do for Dad right now is to give you all the help you need to prove that Daedalus *is* safe, and that what we built together is worth something after all. That's what he would have wanted, more than anything. Isn't it?"

Gilkrensky took her hand. "That's what he and I were doing in Cairo, Jill. And that's what I'm here for now," he said. "That, and to talk to you."

"So where do we start?"

"We'll have to start by salvaging my own reputation first, beginning with that incident I had on the flight to Orlando. Nobody believes me about that flying boat, the one that exploded when that drone hit it. If I could find a way of locating the wreckage, I could not only prove I was telling the truth, but also bring back bits of that Gibbtek missile into the bargain."

"You know where it went down?" asked Jill.

"I know precisely, it's all on that computer in there. All I need is a submersible."

Jill smiled. "Your GRC Leisure Group owns a company here in Florida that has one," she said. "But the person you put in charge of it is very angry at you right now."

"How so?"

"He's my brother."

17

Labour Relations

It was still raining in San Francisco. Fat drops, as big as bees, pattered against the windows of the luxury bungalow nestling amongst the trees on Mount Tamalpais, and raced each other to the ground. Milton Hacker watched them go, feeling the buzz of jet-lag behind his eyes, trying to keep himself from exploding across the room at the man on the other side of the low table.

"Well, you really fucked up this time, didn't you, Milt?" whined Jerry Gibb. He was leaning forward from a plush sofa, picking at a packet of Oreo cookies, and swigging from a tall glass of milk.

Hacker knew the signs. Gibb was trying to be assertive, trying to impress him that he was in control, trying to suggest that the whole fiasco in Florida had been Hacker's fault. Hacker took a deep breath, calmed himself, and watched the rolls of fat around Jerry's neck with the cool detachment of a scientist studying a bug.

What made Jerry Gibb tick? How was it that a kid almost twenty years his junior, with a drop-dead gorgeous wife and more money than the gross national product of a small country, had just let himself go like that?

Hacker, who could still do one-arm press-ups and had a belly like a washboard, ran his eyes over Jerry's bloated body and felt sick to his stomach. He watched the soft, childlike hand as it reached for another Oreo.

"Yes, Mr Gibb."

"It's like my dad always said," continued Jerry with his mouth full. "If your dog craps on your carpet, you rub his nose in it. So I'm rubbing *your* nose in it hard, Milt. You screwed up."

"Yes, Mr Gibb."

Hacker did the mental exercise of counting the number of ways he could kill Jerry with nothing more than his hands. Control, that was what it was all about. Gibb was right about that at least.

"I don't think the situation's as bad as it looks, Mr Gibb," he said, careful not to let the respect slip from his voice. "Once we learned Gilkrensky was conducting some sort of aerial survey using equipment that could conceivably have interfered with the Hawk, we could cast doubt about blame for the incident, and even turn it back on him. In a 'best case scenario' we could force Gilkrensky to back off that software piracy claim, in return for us dropping any possible charges against GRC. All in all, I'd say the few million it cost us when the Hawk went down was money well spent."

"Where the hell did it go anyway?"

"No idea. We had a chopper out looking for the homing beacon, but they couldn't find it. If the Hawk hit another aircraft, as Gilkrensky claims, there'd be bits of it all over the ocean floor."

"And the other plane?"

"Nobody knows about that either. There's no record of a flight from any airfield, and no missing aircraft report's been filed."

"Complete mystery then?"

"Complete and utter."

"But good for us, eh Milt?"

"Definitely, Mr Gibb. Just like you planned."

Jerry picked up another Oreo, dunked it in his milk and sucked on it noisily while he thought. "There's something else I want you to do for me."

"What's that, Mr Gibb?"

"Gilkrensky has some new interactive software in that plane of his, a personalised 'help menu' in the image of his dear, departed wife – and a real fox she is too, Milt! I want you to get her for me. Copy her, or hack her right out of there, but just get her. I want to have myself some fun."

Hacker shook his head. "That's a tall order, Mr Gibb. There's more security around him now than the President of the United States."

"I trust you, Milt. You're a very resourceful man."

"Thank you, Mr Gibb. But even if I do track this machine down, how will I get past the access codes he'll have installed to protect it? When that guy Delgado tried to offload it to the Japs last year, he wiped out their entire mainframe with some kind of virus."

Jerry smiled. "Hacker by name, and hacker by nature," he said. "Don't bring me problems, Milt. Just get me solutions."

"Yes, Mr Gibb."

The door opened and Elaine Gibb walked into the room carrying a towel. She had been working out in the gym Jerry had built her across the hallway and the perspiration shone on her tanned face. Her right hand went to the zip at the neck of her track suit and pulled it down, revealing a skin-tight Spandex top. Her eyes met Hacker's.

"You promised you'd let me go shopping down town today, honey," she said to Jerry. "I have things to get for Mom's birthday."

"What time's your flight back to Orlando, Milt?" said Jerry. His eyes were watching Hacker's, but Hacker was still in control.

"Four-thirty this afternoon, Mr Gibb."

Jerry smiled. His expression told Hacker that his nose was still in the shit and that Jerry was still rubbing.

"Then you'll have time to take Mrs Gibb shopping for me, won't you?"

"Yes, Mr Gibb," said Hacker. "It'll be a pleasure."

It was all about control.

"Ladies, gentlemen and children, I give you . . . Shadow!"

A MATTER OF TIME

The electric blue water around the bearded man darkened, bulged and split as a fifty-foot killer whale burst to the surface beneath his feet, catapulting him into the air. Man and beast hung motionless above the giant pool for a split second. Children screamed with delight, camera-flashes popped. Then both performers fell back in an explosion of spray, soaking the first five rows of the audience to shrieks of delight and a wave of applause, that brought people to their feet all around the huge auditorium.

"That's him," said Jill. "That's Mac."

They were standing in the control box of the main pool at GRC's Oceanic Adventure Park outside Orlando. On either side of them, rows of steeply tiered seats curved around the water and, above them, a gigantic awning protected the crowd from the sun. Beyond the pool, a huge television screen showed the views from the cameras around the auditorium, both above and below the water. Outside the control-room door, RJ Stevenson and his uniformed security guards kept watch.

Gilkrensky watched as the waters settled. He could see nothing except dark shapes, darting below the water and then, right in the centre of the pool, the whale burst through the surface with the man riding its back, did a graceful circuit of the audience, and deposited him gently on the concrete slipway, with its nose out of the water. The man bowed to the crowd, turned to the whale, bowed again as if they had been partners in a dance, and lifted a fish from a nearby bucket. The audience were loving every minute of it. Children reached out to touch the whale, parents were taking photograph after photograph, or holding out programmes for the bearded man to sign. He let the fish drop into the whale's mouth, rubbed its nose affectionately, bowed again, and reached for a mike.

"That's all there is for now, folks, but Shadow will be back later for the twelve o'clock show. I'm Mac McCarthy and you're all very welcome to the Oceanics Adventure Park." A young woman in a swimsuit stepped forward and handed him a towel, the crowd started to move towards the exit, and McCarthy looked up. For a moment his gaze met Gilkrensky's, then he gave the towel back to his assistant and walked to the door leading to the control room.

Jill stepped forward and kissed her brother lightly on the cheek. "Mac," she said. "This is Theo . . . "

"I know," said McCarthy. "But under the circumstances you'll forgive me if I don't shake hands." He was as tall as Gilkrensky, but far broader in the chest, with thick muscular arms that bulged under his wet-suit. His tanned face was almost hidden by a thick blond beard and shoulder-length hair, but his eyes gave him away – they were his father's – with the same piercing intelligence.

For a moment the two men stood facing each other silently. Then Gilkrensky said, "I thought you were supposed to be in charge of this place, not out there in the pool with the fish."

A MATTER OF TIME

McCarthy pushed his damp blond hair back behind his head and secured it with an elastic band he'd taken from the desk. With the water still glistening on his face, he looked like a pirate – and a fierce one at that.

"That's not a fish, Dr Gilkrensky. That's nearly a million dollars' worth of trained killer whale. I know what's going on in *my* business. I don't run it from behind some desk."

"I see."

"And while we're on that subject, I know your corporation owns most of this place and that, technically speaking, you're my boss. But that's not going to stop me finding out what really happened to my father. I know bullshit when I smell it and that's what I've been smelling ever since Dad disappeared in Cairo. OK, I wasn't as close to him as Jill was. We had our differences. But all that crap I've been getting about pyramids and cosmic forces is just so much bullshit. I smell a cover-up, and I'm going to find out what *really* happened."

His big arms crossed on his chest. He was staring at Gilkrensky, challenging him. Through the control-room door, Gilkrensky could see Stevenson and his bodyguards watching them uneasily.

"Your father was a great friend of mine," he said. "And one of the reasons I came out here in the first place was to explain what happened in Cairo to you and your family. What London told you is true. He vanished, inside the pyramid. I've shown the video footage of it to

Jill, and I'll show it to you, or anyone else who wants to see it."

"OK," said McCarthy. "Show it to me."

Gilkrensky laid the Minerva 3,000 on the desk and opened the lid. "There's a few things I need to explain to you about this machine first," he said.

After he'd watched the video recording, McCarthy stood looking out over the empty auditorium and the whale pool.

"How do I know that footage is genuine?"

"Mac!" said Jill.

"It's a first-generation copy from a digital surveillance camera," said Gilkrensky. "Your lawyers can have it analysed if you like."

"Don't worry, Dr Gilkrensky. They will."

Mac turned to face him. His eyes were very bright.

"He was vaporised, you reckon?"

"Er . . . yes. That's the most likely explanation."

"So what about the stories?"

"What stories, Mac?" said Jill. "What have you heard?"

McCarthy leant up against the window of the control box. "My attorney's been doing a lot of digging. He came up with reports of some very weird goings-on around the time Dad disappeared, strange experiments . . . on the fabric of time and space. Isn't that so?"

"All right," said Gilkrensky. "It's true. After my wife was killed I was obsessed with turning back time. I got caught up in it, far more than I should have and, for a while there, I actually thought it *was* possible. There was even evidence that suggested I was right, but now I don't know."

"And Dad went along with it?" asked Jill.

"He was far more concerned with the effect of the energy on his Daedalus system," said Gilkrensky. "The whole time-travel theory was – well, it was mine. It came later. Even I can see it was madness, looking back on it now."

"So what happened to Dad?"

"Like I told you this morning, the most likely explanation for your father's disappearance is that he was vaporised by an energy field. To prove it, I'd have to get back into the Pyramid again, and the Egyptian government won't let me. That recording you've just seen is all I have."

McCarthy shook his head.

"I met your wife once," he said. "She was a helluva lady, but there was no reason to sacrifice my father."

"I didn't. He went back into that chamber on his own. I tried to stop him. You saw the recording . . . "

"*If* it's genuine!"

"Of course it is. You can run any test you . . . "

"Mac! Theo!" shouted Jill. "Stop it, you two! Shouting at each other's not going to bring Dad back."

"Damn right," spat McCarthy. "So why come to me now?"

"Theo needs your help to find a plane wreck," said

Jill. "He and I want to find out what's making Dad's Daedalus system malfunction here in Florida. It's probably the same phenomenon Theo found in Egypt, but the problem is that his credibility's been shot to pieces over that incident yesterday. He needs to establish there *was* another aircraft involved and that a drone was fired at him deliberately. To do that, he needs your help to hunt for the wreckage on the sea bed."

"Why should I help him, Jill?"

"Mac! We – we owe it to Dad!"

"No way! He can get somebody else."

Outside the control-room, Gilkrensky saw Stevenson move towards them. He raised his hand and waved him back.

"Listen, McCarthy," he said. "The only way I can help your father now is to prove that the system we all worked on together for so long, that he believed in with his heart and soul, still works safely, just as he designed it to. Now, if you won't do it for him, or for your sister, then I'd like to remind you that, yes, you *do* work for me! I *am* your boss, and unless you want me to tear down this place and turn it into a shopping mall, you'd better do what I say!"

Mac McCarthy looked at his sister, and then out of the control room window, past the great display board and across the flat landscape towards the sea. For a long moment he was silent, and then he said, "All right, Dr Gilkrensky, how much are you willing to pay?"

"Whatever it takes."

"Because the research ship *Draco* is on charter in this area, doing a survey of coral formations off Cape Kennedy. She has the submersible on board, and side-scan sonar. You'll have to rent it back from NOAA – the National Oceanic and Atmospherics Administration – if you want to use it right away, but if you know where that plane of yours went down, then she'll find it."

Gilkrensky nodded. "Like I said, 'whatever it takes'."

18

Strange Bedfellows

Elaine Gibb looked northwards from the Fairmont Hotel window past the Coit Tower, taking in Alcatraz, Angel Island and the dark brooding mass of Mount Tamalpais beyond San Franciso Bay. She was charting the course of her life, turning over the fragments of broken dreams, one piece at a time. Many years before, back in the fantasy factory of Hollywood, she had been Elaine Sullivan, only child, "little princess" and last hope of a set designer and a make-up artist who had never made it to centre stage. There had been voice coaches, dance lessons, training in posture, drama, and finally a walk-on part in a pilot episode for the TV series *Knightrider*, as a girl at a demolition derby. Then came a real chance, the role of Jan Michael Vincent's casual acquaintance in *Airwolf* and a speaking part as a girl cop in *Magnum PI* with Tom Selleck. Elaine Sullivan had arrived! There was talk of a pilot for a new all-girl series to out-gun *Charlie's Angels*, but it flopped. Nobody was interested in cop shows any more, but they *were* casting a new series about lifeguards in California. Elaine was short-listed for the screen test. Hasselhoff was due to star in it, and they'd spoken on *Knightrider*.

Perhaps there was a chance after all?

But even before she entered the audition, Elaine Sullivan knew that chance was gone. In front of her, behind her, and all around her were the most drop-dead gorgeous chicks she'd ever seen, each one of them at least ten years younger, with resumés as thick as telephone directories and recommendations that could have got them elected President. Elaine's window of opportunity had opened – and shut.

She knew it.

She didn't even bother to stay for the test.

Elaine went downhill fast after that. She got into the booze and did drugs – anything to cloud the reality that she was now the wrong side of twenty-five. There were men, lots of men – but none of them could ease the pain, or match the "high" of being a star. Finally, she could take the smell of failure around Hollywood no longer, packed her bags and moved in with a struggling screenwriter in the Bay area of San Francisco, where she signed up as a delivery girl for a pizza chain, just to make ends meet until his latest screenplay got "accepted by Spielberg".

But dreams, particularly those seeded in childhood, last a lifetime.

The pizza company was an up-market franchise, with a dozen outlets and celebrity clients from Paolo Alto in the south to Kentfield in the north. Many of them were rich. Some were extremely reclusive. But Jerry Gibb, the legendary computer-games king, was unique. Pizzas had to be delivered to the porchway of his bungalow at Tamalpais, the doorbell rung three times, and left. There was to be no contact, no waiting around for a tip. Mr Gibb would watch for the delivery on his security cameras, pick up the pizza after the messenger had left, and pay in full by credit card over the E-mail.

That was his way.

Until, one golden autumn evening, Elaine Sullivan laid the pizza in Mr Gibb's porchway, looked up at the security cameras and removed her motor-cycle helmet, just to get some air. She had no way of knowing it, but as her red hair fell in a glittering cascade, caught by the setting sun, she had successfully screen-tested for the greatest acting part of her life – to star as Jerry Gibb's long-lost love, the dead and unreachable Julie Briscoe.

"Seems you've got a fan," said the dispatcher when she got back to base. "Jerry Gibb saw you on his security monitor and recognised you from some cop show on TV."

The next day another pizza was ordered, with specific instructions. Only Elaine Sullivan could deliver it.

This time the door of "Altair IV" opened.

"A penny for your thoughts?" said Milton Hacker.

Elaine Gibb turned back from the window and hugged the white Terrycloth robe tight around her shoulders.

"I was just thinking how you saved my life," she said, which was, quite literally, true. Before Milton Hacker, Elaine had been back on the downward slide. Her new husband Jerry had been tolerable at first – even charming in a child-like sort of way – and of course the money was mind-blowing! Her parents were over the moon! Here was a man who could buy her *anything*, even her own show on TV! Trips by limousine to exclusive shops in Union Square or the Embarcadaro Center more than made up for his crude fumblings and weird fantasies in bed – for a while – before the nightmare started.

Jerry's fantasies became more and more bizarre. Elaine was enough of an actress to play the part most of the time. She'd done it often enough with film people in the bad old days in Hollywood, and now the stakes were a million times higher. But gradually it dawned on her that this was different – Jerry actually *believed* it!

And when she "wouldn't play" he got angry . . .

What could she do? Where could she go? What would she tell her parents? "We gave you *everything* when you were a kid, Elaine. Don't let us down now!"

She had been hitting the booze again when Milton Hacker arrived on the scene. At first Elaine had thought he was just another of Jerry's "yes men" from the plant at Santa Clara. He looked the part, very handsome in a mysterious, powerful sort of way – with a thin tanned face, grey watchful eyes, and short steely hair – striking enough to have been a guest villain on *Knightrider* or *Airwolf* – but still one of Jerry's goons. Then one day, when he was playing chauffeur for Jerry by driving her on a shopping expedition to Union Square, and she was reaching for a bottle of tranquillisers, Milton Hacker reached over from the driver's seat, took the bottle from her and read the label. Then he said, "A beautiful lady like you doesn't need that shit!" and threw the pills out of the window onto the freeway.

She had screamed at him, fought with him. There had been a row that almost crashed the car. But in the end she had broken down in his arms and told him everything. From the Marin Headland vista point, overlooking the Golden Gate Bridge out on Route 101 he had taken her to his suite at the Fairmont, and their affair had begun.

Elaine Gibb let the bathrobe fall from her shoulders and slipped into bed next to him, sliding her naked thigh over his and laying her head on his chest, where she could listen to his heart.

"Tell me things," she said softly.

Milton Hacker ran the strong fingers of his right hand through her hair as he stared at the ornate ceiling.

"I hate to think of his hands on you," he said at last. "I hate to think when you wake up in the morning that it's him you see and not me. You make me feel like a kid again, Elaine. I want that all the time."

Elaine twisted in the bed, propping herself up on her elbows, so that she could look at his face. If only she'd met him sooner, years ago when they'd both been younger. "Soon, Milt," she said. "You told me it would be soon."

Elaine spread her arms. Her breasts touched his chest. Her lips met his.

"Soon," she whispered. "We'll do it soon."

On the other side of the continent, a blue and white JetRanger helicopter steadied itself over the helipad of a slowly moving ship, wobbled slightly as it caught the airflow over the deck, and settled onto the painted letter "H".

As the engine died and the rotors slowed to a stop, Gilkrensky flicked open his seat-belt, opened the pilot's door, and, taking the Minerva with him, followed RJ Stevenson, Mac McCarthy and Jill across the helipad to meet the small knot of people gathered behind the funnel to meet them.

A short sun-tanned man in a white sweat shirt and a blue "Oceanics" baseball cap, stepped forward and shook his hand.

"Welcome aboard *Draco*, Dr Gilkrensky," he said. "I'm Jim Burrows, captain of this ship, and this is our scientific team – Don Murphy, our marine geophysicist, Sara Chan our marine data expert, and Jim Piggins here – the chief scientist."

"Good to meet you, Dr Gilkrensky," said Piggins, shaking Gilkrensky's hand. He was a tall, greying heron of a man with bright enthusiast's eyes that twinkled in the late afternoon sun. "We've all heard a lot about you, sir. It's a pleasure to assist in any way we can."

"Thank you for letting me use the ship today," said

Gilkrensky. "I'm sorry to have interrupted your mission, but this is very important to me."

"We know," smiled Sara Chan. "We saw it all on CNN, and it's lucky you caught us when you did, because *Draco* passed over the very spot you're interested in a few hours ago on our way out from the Cape. We have the side-scan sonar records all laid out in the dry lab if you want to see them."

"And speaking of CNN, it looks as if we have company," said Piggins, pointing to the landward horizon. Another helicopter, with its rear door slid back, was moving into position near the stern of the ship. Gilkrensky could see the sun glint on the lens of a television camera.

"They've been hounding me since I landed," said Gilkrensky. "Let's just go and look at the charts."

Piggins led them off the helipad into a large room directly behind the wheelhouse. All around the walls computer screens showed tracks of the ship's previous course, images of the seabed below them or radar pictures of the sea around. Laid out on the central workbench were long strips of paper, each a foot wide. They showed a weird alien landscape, marked by mountains, gorges, and deep, dark canyons. Gilkrensky laid the Minerva on an empty workbench behind him and followed Piggins' finger to a dark shape on the paper.

"Before we got your call," said Piggins. "We'd been over near the Cape, doing sonar surveys of the coral beds for NOAA. *Draco*'s fitted with quite sophisticated side-scan sonar. It uses sound waves to build up a picture of the seabed below us."

"Our next mission was to survey some archaeological sites over near Bimini, using the same equipment," said Sara Chan. "But our policy is to leave it running all the time we're actually steaming, so that we don't waste ship time. This point here is where we started late last night, over by Cape Kennedy, and this is the area you're interested in, right on the edge of the Blake Plateau."

Gilkrensky followed her finger to a marked square of red ink. Half of it was dark grey, and the other dense black.

"The water's very deep there," said Piggins. "You'd be right on the lip of the continental shelf, dropping down from 800 metres or so to over 5,000. If the wreckage you're looking for is in the black half of that square, I'm afraid we won't be able to reach it."

"Why not?" asked Gilkrensky.

"Because it's beyond the crush depth of the submarine," said McCarthy. "The *Manta*'s only rated to 1,000 metres safe operating depth. Beyond that, we'd have to contact Woods Hole Oceanographic Institute and borrow their submarine *Alvin*, or contact the French and get the *Plongeur*. All that would take time."

Gilkrensky bent over the charts, peering at the dark square. "Is there any way of getting more detail? I can see what looks like rocks or boulders on the edge of the shelf, but there's no way of telling what they are."

Piggins passed him a magnifying glass. "The US

Navy have a new laser imaging system that can see a starfish at over a mile depth," he said. "But we'll have to make do with this."

There was a low, warbling noise from the bench behind Gilkrensky. He reached over, picked up the Minerva, and laid it on the chart table, opening the lid.

"Excuse me, ladies and gentlemen," said Maria. "But if the side-scan sonar signal Dr Piggins used to produce these charts is digital, then perhaps I could examine it using computer-image enhancement."

Sara Chan was staring open-mouthed at the Minerva screen. "Of course it is," she said. "Which data format can you process best?"

Within half an hour, the *Draco* was lying stationary – pinpointed by satellite over the edge of the continental shelf, and held in position against the current by its computer-controlled bow-thruster and propellers.

In the dry lab, Gilkrensky and the scientific staff were clustered around the Minerva screen, while the machine guided them though the enhancement program it had just run on the digital imagery of the seabed below. On the computer screen, the picture inside the fuzzy black and white rectangle Sara Chan had marked out started to harden into sharp images. They could make out the sheer cliff of the shelf edge – dropping down into the abyss of the deep Atlantic – the lip of the shelf, rising steeply to the sunlit waters of the Caribbean. And there, perched on the divide between darkness and light, was an odd, angular shape . . .

"It looks like a cross," said Jill, leaning closer. "Could it be a plane?"

"From the descriptions given to me," said Maria's image from a small window in the top left-hand corner of the screen, "the shape corresponds with the hull-length and wing-span of the plane Theo saw. But only direct observation will confirm that."

"Can we reach it?"

"We can," said McCarthy. "The *Manta*'s rated for that depth, but just to be sure I'd want to take the ROV as well."

"The what?"

"A Remotely Operated Vehicle – a robot mini-sub – fitted with cameras, lights and a laser for cutting. We can control it manually, or by computer, either from the *Manta*, or from up here on the *Draco*."

"That will be interesting," said Minerva. "Can I come with you in the submarine to control it for you?"

"I'm afraid not," said McCarthy. "We're bound by US Navy Sea Systems Command regulations that any new equipment taken inside the pressure sphere of the *Manta* during a dive has to be pre-tested for twenty-four hours beforehand, to make sure it's fireproof and doesn't give off noxious gases. But you could stay here in the dry lab with Dr Piggins and Sara Chan and watch what's happening through the on-board cameras."

"And who will go down in the submarine?" it asked.

"I'll go," said McCarthy, glancing at Theo. "I'm the most experienced pilot here."

"I see what you mean about not running this outfit from behind a desk," said Gilkrensky. "All right, I'll go with you. It's my mission after all."

"There's a third seat, isn't there?" asked Jill.

"There is."

"Then I'll go too."

"Are you sure?" asked McCarthy. "It'll be a long dive, and it's cold down there."

Jill was unmoved. "I'm a big girl now, Mac," she said. "And besides, it'll be great to work with Theo again after all this time."

19

Lunch at the Fairmont

Hacker knew they were being watched from the moment they sat down. It was nothing he could see, or hear or touch, at least not straight away. It was more a feeling, a sixth sense, like radar. He welcomed it. It proved he was still "in the game".

As the menus came, he ran his eyes over the other lunchtime diners in Mason's Restaurant of the Fairmont Hotel. Over by the window, looking out onto the tramlines on California Street, five dark-suited executives were finishing their aperitifs and moving on to the antipasto. Behind them, nearer the door, three society matrons were nibbling their way though dessert, careful not to let one single crumb or dab of cream touch their lips. Their bobbling heads almost obscured a single, middle-aged businessman who had been sitting with his back to them, lost in *The Wall Street Journal*.

Sitting slightly nearer, two young mothers were exchanging shop talk about day-care centres. Each had a toddler by her side, securely strapped into high chairs provided by the hotel. And closer yet, an impeccably groomed young couple were lost in each other's eyes.

Hacker ran his professional eye over each of them, assessing their potential threat in turn. The five executives were too big a group, unless this was to be a full scale "hit". Nobody would commit that many operatives in such a tight group to a simple surveillance operation, even on someone like him. The old ladies were unlikely – but then again, you never knew – likewise the young mothers. Who would be ruthless enough to put children into a potential fire-fight? Or was he living in the past?

Which meant it was either the single, faceless businessman or the young couple just two tables away. Hacker watched them, as Elaine made small talk. The woman had straight, ash-blonde hair, hard blue-grey eyes and a slim athlete's body beneath her designer-label business suit. The man was much taller and built like a college football player, right down to the broken nose. His dark suit and brilliant white shirt set off his tan perfectly and the primrose-yellow tie matched his blonde hair, cut long and styled carefully, back over his ears. They were a golden couple, very successful, very convincing, and putting a lot of effort into their play of being in love. But Hacker, whose life had depended so many times on reading the signs, knew it was just an act. Theirs were the studied looks of love, too forced to be natural. Their choreographed touches of affection, that should have been spontaneous, were rehearsed. It made Hacker sick.

Amateurs! It offended him that they would send raw recruits like this to spy on him. Had they already written him off as a "has been"?

Then *The Wall Street Journal* reader lowered his paper, turned, and Hacker knew they had not discounted him at all.

"Elaine," he whispered, "I want you to look down at your watch, call the waiter and have him order you a cab, as if you'd suddenly remembered an appointment you can't afford to miss. When it comes, I want you to follow the bellboy out through the foyer, get into the cab, and go straight back to Tamalpais with your shopping. And remember, as you leave, you're the boss's wife and I'm just the hired hand. Have you got that?"

For a moment, there was fear in Elaine Gibb's eyes, and then – God bless her film training – she looked at her watch, said "Oh my goodness, is that the time!" and went flawlessly through the routine he'd described, ending with a dismissive "You'll get the check, won't you, Hacker?" and was gone. Nobody followed her. The five executives watched her go, taking in the swing of her hips beneath her dress, and then ordered another bottle of wine. The young couple never looked up. Perhaps they weren't such amateurs after all?

So it was just him . . . and them.

Hacker felt a lot better with Elaine out of harm's way.

This was what he'd been trained for. This was what he was good at.

The waiter returned. "Madame has taken the taxi. Would you still like to order?"

"I'll have a Caesar salad," said Hacker. "No, better make that two."

"Are you expecting someone else, sir?"

"In a moment, yes."

The Wall Street Journal reader got up from his seat, walked across the restaurant and sat down at Hacker's table, facing him.

"I see you haven't lost your touch, Milt. What tipped you off?"

Dick Barnett had aged. It was as if the tough field agent Hacker remembered had decided to disguise himself as a tired, overweight bureaucrat, complete with greying hair, short moustache and jowls that overflowed his shirt collar onto his tie. Snapshots of Barnett in earlier, leaner days darted in front of Hacker's eyes – Barnett in training, Barnett in Vietnam, Barnett at headquarters back in Langley, telling him he was now "outside the loop".

"They're too cold," said Hacker. "There's no warmth. You'd never believe they'd give each other the time of day, let alone jump into bed together."

"Yeah, ain't it pitiful?" whispered Barnett leaning forward. "A man of my seniority and all I get is two trainees falling over themselves to impress me how tough they are. They'd kill each other just to get a good field report for the next promotion round, but in a way it's kinda funny."

"What is?"

"Well, I'm stuck with two people who hate each other's guts, pretending to be in love, while here you are sitting down to lunch with someone you've just made love to, pretending to be strangers."

"What do you mean?"

But Barnett let it go. "That business in Florida yesterday, Milt. That was dangerous, dumb and expensive. Definitely not the way we do things nowadays."

"I saw it as an opportunity to protect our mutual interests, and I took it."

Barnett shook his head. "That whole SQUID program is very important, Milt. That's why we invested in Gibbtek in the first place. It's got full backing from the seventh floor at Langley, and as much support as we need from the military. They see the potential, and they want to protect it."

"I'm doing the best I can, Dick."

Barnett smiled for the first time that morning. "Yeah Milt. You always did, right from the beginning . . ."

And, all at once, Milton Hacker was no longer in the Fairmont Hotel. He was back in the foyer of the Central Intelligence Agency's headquarters at Langley, Virginia, all those years ago . . .

To the right of the lobby was a glass case containing the

book of honour marking those who had died in service. Their names, all fifty of them, were marked by rows of small stars carved into the marble wall above, flanked by the CIA flags and the "Stars and Stripes". Hacker had stood in silence, counting down and along the rows until he came to . . . Milton Hacker II . . . his father's name, reaching out to him.

"Milt! You old scoundrel," said a familiar voice, and Hacker turned. Dick Barnett took his hand and shook it warmly. "Great to see you. How was Japan? Here, you'll need this." And he pressed a plastic *Visitor* pass into Hacker's palm.

Hacker stared at it in disgust. "What's the problem, Dick? Isn't my credit good around here any more?"

Barnett looked hunted. "We can talk about that inside. Do you want to eat or not?"

They walked across to the armed guards by the bank of elevators leading into the labyrinth of the seven-storey building. Out of habit, Hacker went to the door coded for the upper executive offices, but Barnett said, "We'll eat on the first floor today, Milt. OK?"

With a feeling of impending doom, Milton Hacker allowed himself to be led to the first-floor cafeteria. It was in two sections, one for visitors, and the other for staff – protected by armed guards and segregated by a partition wall. Barnett led him to the visitor section. "Caesar salad?" he asked. "You were always careful about your weight."

Hacker gripped him by the left arm and dragged him

into a booth, well away from the other diners. "What the fuck's going on?" he hissed. "Visitor passes! The outsider canteen! What are you trying to tell me?"

Barnett looked around him at the other diners, then leant forward. "It's about early retirement, Milt. The seventh floor have a job for you in private industry."

"Jeesus!"

"I know what it looks like. But this is important. The boys upstairs are following a direct initiative from the White House on this one."

"It feels like I'm being shafted. That's what it feels like."

Barnett nodded his head slowly in sympathy. "I know . . . I know . . . but look at it this way, Milt. You never really were a team player, now were you? You've been making a real nuisance of yourself ever since 'Nam."

"You were there too, Dick. You *know* if they'd listened to our reports we could have shortened the war. But you didn't want to rock the boat!"

"Just keep your voice down, Milt. Remember where you are!"

Hacker looked down in disgust at the *Visitor* pass hanging from his lapel, tore it off and threw it across the table. "Yeah, I know where I am all right! I'm outa here." Barnett grabbed his arm and hauled him back into his seat.

"Look Milt, if you won't listen to me as your case officer, then listen to me as a friend. The Agency isn't what it was in your father's time. There are games to be played – games about politics and public relations and keeping Congress happy so they'll vote us a budget for next year. That's why they sent you to Japan in the first place."

"Japan was important," hissed Hacker. "For years they've been worming their way into our economy. That's why I kicked up shit to the Directorate, and they sent me to the embassy in Tokyo to – "

Barnett put up his hands in surrender. "OK, Milt. Have it your way. Now let's get down to business."

"What about? Why I didn't get to head the new anti-terrorism unit?"

"You *know* why. But this is important too. For once, the seventh floor actually believe you're right."

Hacker regarded Barnett suspiciously. "What about?"

"Right now, America leads the world in advanced computer technology. Nobody else, with the possible exception of Japan, comes anywhere close. And most of it's happening not in the US military, but in private industry. Personal computers, high-speed silicon chips, photo-optics, artificial intelligence, were all developed by long-haired youngsters working out of their parents' garages, all geniuses in their own way, all billionaires now, and all very, very, vulnerable."

"To what?"

"They're out there in the world of free enterprise, Milt. All those brilliant, all-American ideas can be bought out, taken over and shifted back to Tokyo, Europe or Beijing at the drop of a hat, and we have no control. You wrote about it, Milt. The seventh floor agrees with you, and now we want you to put your money where your mouth is – on the outside, where it matters."

"What do you want me to do?"

"There's this guy called Jerry Gibb," said Barnett.

Milton Hacker looked across the restaurant to where the two young watchers were sitting. They had given up the pretence of talking to each other, and were looking across at the table where he and Barnett sat.

"I've ordered Caesar salad," said Hacker conversationally. "Just like the old days, and the clam chowder's good too."

Dick Barnett followed Hacker's gaze down to his own expanding waistline. "Trying to make a point, Milt? Forget the food. We need to talk in private anyway." And he rose to his feet, leading Hacker out into the ornate foyer of the Fairmont to collect their coats, and leaving his two assistants to deal with the check.

The rain was making a last assault on the city as they turned right under the hotel's vast white awning onto Mason Street. It drummed on Hacker's umbrella and spattered on Barnett's hat as he waved away the uniformed porter and raised his hand. A large black van, with tinted windows and an impressive array of radio aerials on its roof, slid out from behind a passing tramcar on California Street and pulled in to meet them. Barnett pulled back the side door, and Hacker climbed in, closely followed by Barnett's two assistants. He settled himself down on a bench seat and looked around him, as the van started to move.

It was a standard Agency surveillance vehicle, fitted with tape decks, video recorders and radio-interception gear. The couple sat themselves opposite Hacker, watching him as if he was an animal in the zoo – an endangered species. Barnett sat down beside him, took off his hat and unbuttoned his coat.

"We thought we'd give you a lift to the airport, Milt, just to be sociable, and on the way we can have a little chat about the developing situation we find ourselves in. How's that?"

"Beat's trying to find a cab on a day like this," said Hacker. "Aren't you going to introduce me?"

"Of course. Milton Hacker, this is Emily-Jane Kirby and Samuel Voss. Field agents on temporary assignment to me at the Deputy Directorate of Science and Technology."

The young woman smiled. It was the sort of smile a hungry young cat gives an old bird with a broken wing. Hacker could feel the anger rise in his throat.

"Your reputation precedes you, Mr Hacker," she purred. "I must say you're in very good shape for such an – *experienced* man."

"*Very* experienced," repeated Voss.

Then Hacker realised.

They knew about Elaine!

As he held himself in control his eyes roved around

the inside of the van, measuring . . . the distance to the door, the type of lock that held it shut, the speed of the van, the amount of time it would take Emily-Jane to reach for her gun, the muscles on Voss's forearm – everything.

Dick Barnett steadied himself against the driver's partition, reached up to the shelf over Voss's head, and drew down a long, curved package wrapped in brown paper, which he rested across his knees.

"Milt," he said, "I want you to play a game of chess. As usual, the aim of the game is to protect American high-tech industries from the bad guys."

"Any 'bad guys' I know?"

"The most obvious candidate is your old friend Gilkrensky," said Barnett. "If he succeeds in bankrupting Gibbtek, or even taking over the SQUID program himself, then we'd be very, very upset, after all the investment we've made. So it's time for a bit of preventive medicine, before this situation gets completely out of hand."

"Such as?"

"I'm glad you asked me that. We've had our eye on a particular young woman for some time now. You remember that semi-conductor manufacturer in Seattle who shot himself a couple of years ago? Or the software designer whose family were held for ransom? Well, this little lady was the master-mind behind both cases, and a lot more besides. Her name is Yukiko Funakoshi. She's dangerous, well-resourced, and currently staying in a certain hotel in Florida."

"Why? What does she want?"

Barnett smiled. "This is why the game's gonna work so well for us, Milt. It appears she has a vendetta going against the very man who's trying to ruin Gibbtek with this lawsuit of his. Do you see a certain commonality of interests here?"

"Possibly. What do you want me to do?"

"I'm proposing you take Kirby and Voss with you back to Florida for support, Milt. Then approach Miss Funakoshi, using as much Japanese tact and charm as you managed to pick up in Tokyo, and offer to assist her."

Hacker considered this for a moment. "If I'm to sound credible to an operative of Miss Funakoshi's calibre, there must be a very legitimate reason, as well as a damned big incentive for her. I can hardly call her up at the hotel, invite her out to brunch and say, 'Hey babe, I hear you have this number going against our mutual acquaintance Theodore Gilkrensky, perhaps we can cut a deal', without offering something in return, now can I?"

"Exactly?" said Barnett, and pulled open the adhesive tape securing the end of the package on his knees. "You'll appreciate this, Milt. What with your interest in Japanese sword-fighting and all. It's a fail-safe bait as far as Miss Funakoshi is concerned. You can't miss."

He undid the last of the tape, unfurled the brown paper and let it fall to the floor of the van like dead skin. Lying across his knees was an exquisite *katana* – a full-sized antique Japanese samurai sword. The dim electric light inside the van picked out the delicate pattern on the enamelled scabbard, the dense impenetrable forests, the fierce tigers running up the hilt, the beautiful, fragile cherry blossom of the Funakoshi family.

"See for yourself," said Barnett proudly. "It's the genuine article."

Hacker took the perfectly balanced weapon, curling his right hand over the embroidered handle and easing the blade out of the scabbard with his thumb. The perfect steel, folded in the craftsman's forge a hundred times for strength, suppleness and unbelievable sharpness, glistened in the dim light of the van, as if it were alive.

"Where the hell did you get it?" asked Hacker, marvelling at the depth of colour on the lacquered scabbard, the living eyes of the tigers . . .

"We have a file as thick as the Bible on Miss Funakoshi back in Langley," said Barnett. "This is the sword that matches the *wakizashi* she carries everywhere with her. It belonged to her family before the war, but I tracked it down on the Internet from an antiques dealer in Boston, who could trace it right back to a soldier who'd served in Japan. So I know it's the real McCoy. Yukiko Funakoshi's built her whole life around the legend of this sword. All you have to do is show it to her."

Hacker slid the weapon back into its scabbard.

It was time.

"And what if I don't want to play?" he said softly.

"After all, I'm a civilian now. You can't tell me what to do."

Barnett shook his head sadly. "Show him, Samuel."

Voss reached into his jacket pocket, pulled out a compact-disc case, opened the cover and slid the CD inside into a player mounted on the wall of the van. Above his head, a screen flickered into life . . . and there was Elaine Gibb's face on the pillows at the Fairmont Hotel, with her eyes closed, moaning in pleasure. There was his own head, with its back to the camera, moving lower, and lower . . .

Barnett motioned to Voss, who stopped the recording. Elaine Gibb's face, frozen in the heat of passion, shone out above their heads.

"I'm sorry about that, Milt. I really am. I understand what happens to guys our age when a pretty girl comes along, believe me. Suddenly we see a chance to bring a little excitement back into our lives. But Milt, this is Jerry Gibb's *wife*! The whole point of having you on the inside track at Gibbtek was to look after *him* – not screw around with her."

Hacker was still in control. His grip on the handle and scabbard of the sword tightened. He saw Kirby and Voss tense. It was vital that his voice didn't give him away.

"Jerry Gibb doesn't give a shit about her," he said evenly. "He's too wrapped up in his computerised sex fantasies to care what she does."

"It's you I'm worried about, not him," said Barnett. "The seventh floor have plans for Gibbtek, right through into the next millennium. They've invested millions, Milt, and they don't want any screw-ups. So drop it! Forget her, or I'll make sure that disc finds its way onto Jerry Gibb's computer."

Emily-Jane Kirby's eyes were still on the screen. "Not bad for an old man, though," she said, and looked at Hacker.

Voss smiled. "Yeah, you wouldn't think he'd have that much lead left in his pencil."

Hacker remained still, as the van hissed along the rain-slicked freeway. Voss actually *wanted* him to make a move, just so that he could pound him to a pulp in front of Barnett and gain a few points over Kirby.

Amateurs!

It would be a shame to disappoint them.

"You're absolutely . . ." he began. Then his left arm pistoned the lacquered hardwood of the *katana* scabbard straight into Voss's windpipe. The man gave a strangled gasp of surprise and collapsed on the floor of the van, clutching his throat. Emily-Jane was reaching inside her jacket for her gun, but she never made it. The handle of the sword, propelled by Hacker's right arm, caught her on the left temple, and down she went like a designer doll, into an untidy heap on top of Voss.

Barnett was already moving towards the driver when Hacker lifted the scabbard over his head and up under Barnett's chin. With Barnett pinned down, he eased the scabbard back with his left hand. A foot of steel slid into view – right next to Barnett's carotid artery.

"You know how sharp this thing is, Dick. If you so much as nod, you'll have to pick your head up off the floor. Is that understood?"

"It – it is," stuttered Barnett, trying to hold himself steady against the sway of the van.

"Reach out with your right hand and eject that CD!"

Barnett did so. Hacker could see the rainbow colours flash as it caught the light.

"Break it and give the pieces to me!"

There a the loud snap of plastic as Barnett shattered the disc and passed the pieces back. Hacker took them with his left hand. The right never left the handle of the sword.

"OK. We'll play it your way," said Hacker. "But don't *ever* threaten me again, got that?"

"Whatever you say, Milt. Let's just get the job done."

The driver was slowing the van. "What do you want me to do, Mr Barnett?"

"Keep driving," shouted Hacker. "I have a plane to catch."

20

Deep Secrets

Gilkrensky peered out through the viewing port of the submarine and watched the swirling particles dash past, into the darkness. The port itself was a three-and-a-half inch thick cone of clear acrylic, a foot wide on the outside, and strong enough to withstand the incredible pressure outside the seven-foot-wide titanium sphere in which he was lying. His mind went back to the briefing session McCarthy had given them before the dive. Beyond the sphere, the water pressure at this depth would be the same as having a ten-ton lorry pressing down on every square inch of his body. He looked around. Every conceivable space along the walls and ceiling was packed with oxygen meters, air scrubbers and instrumentation – sonar screens, the underwater telephone and echo sounder, radio, video tape recorders, and the control panel where McCarthy knelt. On the far side of McCarthy, Jill lay on the padded decking, wrapped up against the cold in sweat-shirts, jumpers and a thick padded jacket. They had been lying like this for almost an hour now, breathing the pure recirculated air, chewing on peanut-butter sandwiches and listening to classical music from a twelve-volt car stereo – watching and waiting as the submarine sank deeper . . . and deeper . . . and deeper into the eternal night . . .

"How far are we from the bottom?" Gilkrensky said.

McCarthy glanced at the sonar. "Less than two hundred feet. We should see it coming up at us in a moment."

Jill turned away from her viewing port. "Can the ROV stand the pressure at this depth?"

Her brother looked back out into the darkness. "It can. But I'm still uncomfortable about having that computer of yours control it. Are you sure it's safe?"

"What do you think, Maria?" said Gilkrensky into his radio headset.

"Mr McCarthy need have no worries about my ability," replied the Minerva. "The control systems on his Remotely Operated Vehicle are far simpler than those on either a Whisperer or Voyager aircraft and, as Theo knows, I have flown both with perfect precision. It is unfortunate your Navy regulations did not allow me to come with you, but I can monitor both your submarine and the ROV, from up here on the *Draco*. How is Miss McCarthy?"

Jill's face split in a wide grin. "I'm fine, Maria. Thank you for asking." Then put her gloved hand over her radio microphone and whispered, "I think your computer's jealous, Theo."

McCarthy's eyebrows raised.

"Minerva's flying saved my life on the way out here," said Gilkrensky. "You're in good hands."

"All right then . . . ah . . . Maria," said McCarthy. "Could you take the ROV down past us to the bottom and wait for us there? We'll follow your lights."

"Certainly." A high-pitched whirring noise sounded above the steady hum of the *Manta*'s own motors as the little torpedo-shaped vehicle dived past the viewing ports, into the darkness.

"We're coming up on the bottom now," said McCarthy. "You can see it."

Below him, Gilkrensky could see the dim, glowing shapes of phosphorescent starfish on the ocean floor, reaching out to a weird luminous horizon. McCarthy's right hand went up to a panel. There was a click, and three quartz iodide lamps burst into life, flooding the hard lunar landscape below them with light. To their left, the bottom rose slowly towards the Florida shoreline, many miles to the west. To their right, it plunged away sharply . . . into the abyss.

Gilkrensky heard the *Manta*'s motors purr to a stop and the hiss of air in the ballast tanks behind them, as McCarthy slowed their descent, to hover just above the cliff edge.

"Location's good, anyway," he said. "We're right on the lip of the canyon."

"I've navigated you to within half a metre of the required destination point," said the Minerva. "It was important to be precise, since the water on the other side of the cliff is deep enough to crush the pressure sphere of the *Manta*."

"Thank you, Maria," said McCarthy. "Could you lead us to the wreck now?"

"Certainly. Just follow me!"

In front of them, the ROV turned on its axis and darted off over the bottom. McCarthy's eased the *Manta* forward to follow, but the little machine had moved ahead out of sight behind a low hill. All they could see through the viewing ports was the false sunrise of its lights, waiting for them on the other side.

Gilkrensky felt the *Manta* rise. For a few seconds his view was blocked by the crest of the hill and then silhouetted in front of them by the lights of the ROV was a dark, brooding skeleton . . . hard . . . sinister . . . and broken . . . the wreck of the flying boat!

It was lying at the very edge of the abyss, like a giant bird poised for flight in a new, dark sky. Gilkrensky could make out the bent wings, the cavernous boat-shaped hull, and the shattered lattice of the cockpit canopy staring out at them like the empty eye-sockets of a skull.

And, beyond the wreck, was the infinite darkness of the deep ocean.

For a moment, there was silence on the *Manta*. Then Jill said, "It's right where you said it would be."

"Can we get pictures?" asked Gilkrensky.

"Video's been rolling since we left the surface," said McCarthy. "But I'll kick in the extra floods." Outside, the scene was bathed in harsh white light as the camera lamps clicked on. Gilkrensky could make out the port side of the shattered hull, broken just forward of the tail fin, and the bent cross of the left-hand propeller. There was the stillness of the grave about the wreck. Thick mud, that hung on the wings and the hull like the dust of ages, added to the air of desolation and death. If this was on land, there'd be cobwebs, he thought.

"But this can't be the plane you saw," said McCarthy. "We're in the wrong place!"

"Of course it's the same one," snapped Gilkrensky. "Just look at it . . . an old flying boat, on the sea floor beneath the exact spot where I saw it crash. I bet if we went round to the starboard side, we'd find the wing float crumpled where my fuel tank struck. There might even be paint from my jet."

"But it *can't* be. Just look at that mud on the wings and the hull. That stuff settles slowly, and to get that much of it, this wreck would need to have been here on the bottom for decades."

Gilkrensky stared out into space as McCarthy's words sank in . . . for decades? It had been here for years! Yet he'd collided with it only yesterday . . .

And then the truth hit him . . .

"Oh my God!" he said. "Then I was right all along!"

Jill was staring at him now. "What do you mean?"

Gilkrensky's mind was racing. He fought to keep the excitement out of his voice. "Just get us round to the starboard side," he said. "I've got to see that wing tank!"

"I can't see what difference that's gonna make," said McCarthy. But he was already moving the controls, lifting the *Manta* over the hull of the wreck. Gilkrensky pressed his face to the viewing port. He could see the whale-like hull of the plane slide beneath them. There was the thick coating of mud along the starboard wing, and then . . . and then they were hanging in space . . . with nothing but a mile of dark water between them and the bottom of the ocean. Even after all the flying he had done, Gilkrensky felt his stomach churn at the thought of that endless drop.

"Please be careful not to land the *Manta* on top of the wing, Mr McCarthy," said Maria's voice. "The wreck is not at all stable. It could topple at any time."

"Are you sure you want to do this," said McCarthy.

"More than anything," said Gilkrensky. "I have to see that float."

McCarthy eased the *Manta* out over the abyss, adjusted the variable buoyancy tanks so that she hovered in mid-water, and turned to face the wreck.

In the harsh lights of the video cameras, the Mariner's starboard wing float looked exactly like a soft-drink can that a child had crushed with its foot. Protected by the wing above, it was clear of mud and the long gash in its side was easy to see. Around the edges of the tear, running like a chalk mark around a body at a crime scene, was a line of pure white paint.

"Are you getting this on video?" said Gilkrensky.

His whole world was spinning. This changed everything!

"It's all on tape," said McCarthy.

Jill reached across and touched Gilkrensky's arm. "What on earth is it, Theo?"

"We'll have to bring back a piece of the wreck – a piece with the paint from my plane on it."

"What on earth for?"

"It's – it's very important to me. Can you get me that float?"

"That'll be tricky," said McCarthy. "The wreck is unstable."

"But if you could cut it free with the laser on the ROV, could you lift it back to the surface with the *Manta*?"

McCarthy looked at the float. "If we trim the sub to compensate for the weight we should be OK," he said. "But it'll be dangerous enough. How much do you *really* want this?"

"More than anything."

"OK then. Let's tell the surface what we're doing and get the ROV in place."

Five minutes later, the *Manta* was hovering below and in front of the Mariner's starboard wing. Its two remote manipulator arms were extended, each ending in a metal hand firmly locked around the upright bar attaching the damaged float to the plane.

"If anything goes wrong, I'm going to abort and back away," said McCarthy. "Is the ROV ready with the laser?"

"It is," said the Minerva. "When Mr McCarthy has adjusted the buoyancy of the *Manta* to take the extra weight of the float, I'll cut the upright with the laser beam. Then you can bring it to the surface."

"OK, on my mark," said McCarthy. His hand went to a knob and turned it. Gilkrensky could hear the rush of compressed air forcing water from the ballast tanks. There was a slight jerk as the submarine rose in the water, and the far-off groan of metal as the wing above them lifted.

"Oops!" whispered McCarthy with his hand still on the knob. "Gently does it. OK Maria, you can cut now."

"Don't look directly at the beam, or . . ." began Gilkrensky, but he was too late. In an instant, the cabin of the *Manta* was flooded with searing ruby light as the laser from Maria's ROV sliced into the upright spar not five feet in front of their eyes. McCarthy cursed and jerked in his seat as he pulled away from the viewing port. His hand tightened on the knob of the ballast control. There was another hiss of air . . . the submarine jerked upwards . . . and a loud "bang" sounded through the pressure hull like a gong.

"Theo!" called the Minerva urgently. "We have an emergency! One of the *Manta*'s hydraulic arms moved up into the path of the laser while I was cutting the upright. I think I've damaged it!"

McCarthy was rubbing his eyes. "Shit! Shit! Shit!"

Then his hand closed over the controls to the hydraulic arms. "Christ! She's cut the hydraulic line! The claw's locked onto the wreck and I can't get it off!"

Outside the hull, the distant groan of metal came again, followed by a jerk as the *Manta*, rising as the air flooded into its ballast tanks, pulled against the upright spar. McCarthy spun the control and the hissing of the air stopped.

For a moment there was silence. "Don't worry," he said. "I can jettison the arm if I need to. All it takes is . . ."

There was a loud bang, from outside the submarine.

"What was that?" asked Jill.

"I don't know," said her brother. "It's probably just . . ."

Then there was the scream of grinding metal and the rumble of a thousand tons of rock, as the cliff beneath the wreck of the giant float plane crumbled – and collapsed – tipping the old aircraft, and the tiny submarine locked to it, into the abyss . . .

21

Pressure

Gilkrensky's world turned upside down as the giant plane, dragging the *Manta* with it, slid off its perch on the crumbling cliff in a swirling cloud of mud, rolled in a long, lazy arc and fell into the blackness. He was pitched off the cushions in front of the viewing port, slammed into McCarthy, and bounced off the hard ceiling of the pressure sphere. Jill screamed. McCarthy grunted and fell back over the controls, limp. Then Gilkrensky felt the submarine roll again and Jill was on top of him, crying. They were on their side now, sinking faster and faster towards the point where the *Manta* would be crushed like an eggshell by the water pressure, grinding in on them like a steel vice.

Gilkrensky heard the pressure hull groan. Outside, there was the rumble of rock and the shriek of tearing metal. Then they were stable, sinking fast . . . He pulled himself to his feet, standing on what had once been the portside wall of the pressure sphere.

"Mac! We've got to eject the manipulator arms!

Where's the control?" But McCarthy was out cold. A gash on his forehead was streaming blood down his face as he lay in his sister's arms.

"Jill! For Christ's sake, remember! Mac said we could eject the manipulators. Which control is it?"

"I – I don't know!"

The hull creaked. Outside the pressure sphere, there was a thunderclap – as a buoyancy attachment on one of the external instrument pods imploded like a grenade under the weight of water. Gilkrensky jumped. How long would it be before the pressure hull itself did the same? He could see the depth gauge. Its digital read-out was blurring in front of his eyes. They were sinking too fast for it to make sense.

Christ! Was it going to end like this? *Maria! I did it all for you!*

Then her voice in his ear, loud and urgent.

"Theo! Theo! Are you all right?"

"I hear you, Maria! What can I do?"

"Dr Piggins says that . . ."

There was a scratching pop and the lights went out. Jill screamed, and they were in darkness.

Oh my God!

With deadly clarity, Gilkrensky saw his situation for what it was. They were a tiny bubble of air in the limitless void of the ocean . . . a transient thing. Soon that bubble would burst and they would be gone – their lives snuffed out – forever.

"Jill? Jill? I'm so sorry!"

He felt her reach for him in the darkness, felt her arms

around his neck and her breath on his cheek. She was holding him tightly, sobbing in the darkness . . .

"Oh, Theo! I wish things could have been different. I . . ."

Then a brilliant flash of ruby light blazed through the viewing ports. There was a loud snap, and they were both thrown off their feet as the laser on Maria's ROV severed the locked manipulator arm. Gilkrensky felt the *Manta* rock, steady itself, and drift back upwards from the falling wreck . . . towards the surface . . . and life itself . . .

Back aboard the *Draco*, Gilkrensky waited until Jill and Mac were safely out of earshot in the ship's dispensary. Then he unplugged the Minerva from the ROV control system in the dry lab, took it down below to one of the spare cabins, and locked the door.

"That *was* the plane I hit, wasn't it, Maria?"

The image on the computer screen looked uncertain. "It *appears* to have been, although we can confirm it when we analyse the video tapes from the submarine. There was the same damage you described and, of course, white paint on its float, paint that *could* have come from the fuel tank of your jet. It is also the same type of aircraft."

"And what type is that?"

"A Martin Mariner. They were used for anti-submarine duties during World War II and for air-sea rescue after that."

"Can you access the Web and check for any records of one ever crashing in this area of sea?"

"I already have, Theo. A Mariner flying boat was seen to burst into flames and crash in exactly this position at approximately 19.50 hours local time, on the fifth of December, 1945."

"That's the plane we saw down there today. Mac said the mud on the wreck showed it crashed there years ago. You have no other, more recent records?"

"No, Theo. Not in this area."

"And yet we struck that plane only yesterday. The paint on the float is from my jet."

"I know. It is very puzzling."

Gilkrensky leant forward. "When I was in the submarine," he said, "I had an idea."

"What is it? It would be interesting to see if it agrees with my own theory regarding the situation."

"Which is?"

"As we suspected from the reports of failure to the Daedalus system in the area, there are forces operating here off the Florida coast that are similar to those we discovered on the site of the Great Pyramid. It is also theoretically possible that, during our flight into Orlando, the pulse of energy we emitted to disrupt the Gibbtek missile somehow triggered these forces, creating a temporary rift in the fabric of time and space . . ."

"Which could have allowed our jet to fall back fifty years into the past, collide with the flying boat, and bounce back into the present," said Gilkrensky slowly. "Are we both mad, Maria? Or is that *really* a possibility?"

"I am not mad, Theo. Cathy Kirwan told me so, back in Ireland. And neither are you. As to the likelihood of the situation. The explanation I've just described is theoretically possible, according to our present knowledge of quantum physics, and this area is notorious for unexplainable phenomena. There is a concentration of ley-line energy in this region. Perhaps it has weakened the continuum of space/time in ways we do not understand – just as it did in Egypt."

Gilkrensky stared at the image on the screen.

"Are you sure, Maria?"

"I cannot be sure, Theo. But it's the only theory which explains the observed facts."

"You know what this means?"

"I do. It means that we may not have to return to the Great Pyramid of Cheops in order to reproduce the time displacement events we observed there. It is now theoretically possible that we *could* reproduce them here in Florida, or indeed anywhere in the world where there is a sufficient concentration of ley-line energy to destabilise the space/time continuum and create a wormhole to the past."

"This changes everything," said Gilkrensky softly.

"I understand."

"There is a chance we could save my wife, after all."

"Yes," said the Minerva. "There is."

Gilkrensky put his elbows on the desk in front of him and ran his fingers through his hair, trying to come to grips with this new reality. The world he had created since Christmas – the one in which he had given up hope of ever seeing Maria alive again – was gone.

Now the dream was back . . .

22

Jealousies

The helicopter lifted off the deck of the *Draco*, turned into the wind and headed west, back towards Orlando and the setting sun. Behind them, the small flotilla of press boats, that had gathered around the ship during the dive, got smaller and smaller, and was gone. A couple of press helicopters followed them as far as the land, filming through their open doors, but even they finally tired of the chase and peeled off, heading for better news stories elsewhere.

Gilkrensky shielded his eyes against the sunset. His mind was still reeling with the possibility that he might be able to rescue Maria, and yet how could he share it with Jill or Mac? It sounded so totally fantastic. Like something a madman would say. They were scientists, both of them, dealers in hard, verifiable fact, just as their father had been. And yet . . .

"You nearly got us killed down there," said McCarthy, rubbing the bandage on his forehead. "The sub's wrecked, and we've lost the charter from NOAA, all because of some wild-goose chase."

"At least we found the plane," said Gilkrensky. "And whatever the damages are, I'll pay for them."

"That *couldn't* have been the plane. The paint you thought you saw on the float must have been corrosion of some kind."

"Possibly, but . . ."

Jill McCarthy cut across him. "I vote we forget the whole thing and get back to looking at Dad's Daedalus network," she said. "Why don't we load as much as we can of that gear in your jet into another aircraft and do a complete survey of the area? If there *are* weird energy patterns out there, then a few hours' flying should find them."

Gilkrensky turned to face her.

"You're dead right, he said. "We saw it happen in Egypt, and now it's here. It has to be. Why don't both of you have dinner with me tonight, and we can plan it?"

"Better eat in the hotel tonight, Dr Gilkrensky," said Stevenson, looking back at the departing press helicopters. "Or the TV crews will be following you again."

"Good thinking. How about it, you two?"

McCarthy shook his head. "No chance," he said. "I've done what you asked, I put my life on the line, and now I've had it with this mumbo-jumbo. And if Jill's got any sense, she'll back away too."

"Jill?"

Jill McCarthy looked at her brother, and then at Gilkrensky. "I went on that dive to help Theo prove that Dad's system works," she said. "And I'll do whatever it takes to make that happen. I owe it to him."

Mac shook his head.

"Well, it's your funeral. I need to get back to my wife and kids. If you need me, call my lawyer."

The private dining-room, above the penthouse suite of the Orlando Olympiad, had one of the most spectacular views in Florida. Fireworks from the evening display at Disneyworld erupted into the darkness as flowers of light, bursting and settling over the flat landscape. The clear sky was full of stars and, outside the open door to the balcony, Gilkrensky could see a pair of security men, standing guard under the watchful eye of RJ Stevenson.

The *maître d'* showed Gilkrensky to the table. Looking up, he could see the eye of a security camera swing towards him. He wondered who was on the other end of it, watching.

Jill McCarthy arrived, bringing the sun with her. She was wearing a dark, strapless gown that showed off her tanned skin, while her hair caught the candlelight in a halo around her face – satin, bronze and gold.

"You look stunning," said Gilkrensky as they sat down.

She smiled.

"And you look very dashing too, Theo. I don't think I've ever seen you wearing a tie before."

"It's not normally my style. Drink?"

She chose a beer, served frostily cold in a tall glass. When that formality was over and the waiter had departed, they were alone. Gilkrensky watched Jill sip her drink. He said,

"Has Mac calmed down at all?"

"He's a complex person," said Jill, "and a little selfish, but he'll come round. He took Angie's death pretty bad and thought he was the only one it touched. He was wrong of course. She was my sister too, and Dad's daughter. It hit us all pretty hard."

"I'm sorry," said Gilkrensky. "I know your father was devastated."

"Yes. It was a bad time. In a way, my mother blamed Dad for the crash, even though the plane she died in wasn't one of his. That's why the divorce happened, and why he went on that air-safety crusade afterwards."

"I know. He was the best."

Jill looked at him over the rim of her glass. For a moment there was silence between them, and then she said, "He always looked on you as a son, you know. He and Mac didn't get on, even before the divorce, and when Dad met you in Boston I think you filled that space. That's one reason why Mac's so hostile – he's jealous. My father thought the world of you and . . . and well, so do I. I always did."

"Oh?"

Jill McCarthy laughed. "Oh, don't look so shocked, Theo. You must have known that I worshipped you in

Boston. I used to make all sorts of excuses to come into Dad's lab just to watch you working together. But I was only eighteen and you were his prize PhD student. Besides, you met that girl Jessica, and that was that."

"I know."

"When you married Maria, I was very jealous. I came to your wedding green with envy. I was going to do everything I could to make the whole thing a disaster, so that you'd give her up and marry me. And then . . ."

"And then what?"

"When I saw her talking to Dad about Angie, and knew how much it helped him, I just couldn't hate her any more. Like I said when I saw you looking at her photograph in Dad's study, you must miss her. I could see why you loved her, Theo. I know why you put her likeness onto that machine . . . to keep her alive."

Then the salads came. Gilkrensky picked at his with his fork. Thinking of Maria. Finally he said, "Look Jill, that aircraft we found today, that flying boat. Mac said it crashed about fifty years ago."

"That's right."

"What do you know about the Bermuda Triangle?"

Jill shook her head and laughed. "It's nothing but a big myth, dreamt up by the Florida Tourist Office just to keep the visitors happy. Mac even has a ride named after it over at the Oceanics theme park. For five dollars you get to go on a simulated submarine dive into the Bermuda Triangle – lots of mysterious noises, flashing lights, hissing steam, that sort of thing. All nonsense!"

"And what about the *real* mystery, all those disappearances, planes, ships, yachts, down through the centuries?"

Jill shrugged. "Like I said, it's a modern fairy tale, like the Loch Ness Monster, the Abominable Snowman or that flying-saucer crash at Roswell after the war. People would like to believe in it, but the facts just don't add up."

"And what about an old navy flying boat that vanished in 1945 while it was out looking for five missing torpedo bombers?"

Jill laughed. "Jeesus, Theo! That's the horniest old chestnut of them all. I'd have thought a man of your intelligence would have seen through that one."

"Supposing I didn't. Tell me about it."

"You're kidding?"

"I'm not. What happened?"

Jill shook her head. "OK, you're the boss. Dad used to tell me this story as a kid. I can quote you chapter and verse. The story goes that five US Navy Avenger torpedo bombers, all with experienced pilots and armed to the teeth, went out on a patrol in calm, clear weather and vanished into thin air. Then a huge flying boat, a Martin Mariner with thirteen men aboard, goes up after them and vanishes too, just another victim of the Bermuda Triangle! We get odd-ball New-Age characters coming around here all the time, making films, writing books. Like I said, it's a tourist industry all by itself. But of course it's all bullshit."

"How so?"

"Because the story never tells you the *real* facts. That's why. None of the pilots were experienced. They were all trainees. And the guy that was leading the flight . . . Taylor I think his name was . . . had just been drafted in from somewhere else, so he didn't know the area. They say he didn't even want to take the flight up, but there was nobody else, so he was stuck. Then their compasses went wrong – that happens a lot out here, what with the magnetic disturbances and such – and they got lost. The weather broke, a storm blew in, they ran out of fuel and had to crash-land in the sea. That's how it must have happened."

"But no wreckage was ever found, not even a life raft."

Jill turned and pointed to the window. "That's a helluva lot of sea out there, Theo. Millions and millions of acres, and most of it in deep water. Tricky currents too. If you crashed out there in a plane you could be swept out into the Atlantic before you knew it."

"So you're saying it's all explainable."

"I am. Tragic, but explainable. Not a time warp or a flying saucer in sight."

"And what about the flying boat? The one we found today?"

Jill shrugged. "Like I said, it was a Martin Mariner . . . Oh Theo! You don't think that was what we found out there today, do you?"

"Why not? It was in the right area."

"OK, it could have been. But there's a logical explanation for that crash too. Those planes were also known as 'flying gas tanks'. They had to take on hundreds of gallons of highly volatile aviation fuel to keep them airborne during searches, and they were definitely unsafe. Someone was probably dying for a smoke, and did just that!"

"So no time warps, eh?"

"No, Theo. Just a very explainable tragedy."

The chef wheeled a glittering brass trolley over to their table, laden with a covered pan and a flickering oil burner. With great ceremony, he lifted the domed lid from the pan filling the air with the aroma of sautéed jumbo shrimp, poured in a generous shot of brandy and lit it. There was a flash of blue flame and the hiss of burning alcohol. Then he replaced the lid, and the fire went out.

"It smells delicious," said Jill to the chef, trying to lighten their conversation. "But what about the fire system? I'd have thought you'd have triggered the sprinklers for sure."

The chef grinned. "Never happened to me yet, ma'am. The whole system's controlled by computers. They can tell if it's a real fire, or just me frying shrimps. You enjoy now, you hear? Those jumbos were fresh caught this afternoon."

"Thanks."

Gilkrensky waited until the waiter was well out of earshot and said, "Jill – er – there's something I want to clear up."

Jill laid her fork at the side of her plate. "You look so serious all of a sudden, Theo. What is it?"

"It's about when we were in the submarine. I thought we were going to die, and I held you. I just need to tell you something before things go any further between us."

Jill made a face. "Oh Theo, it's OK. I understand about Maria. I know it'll be a long, long time before you get over her. I really do. Perhaps you never will. But if you do, I want you to know that I still care for you, that's all. As a friend, or whatever else you want – I'll always be there for you."

Her hand reached across the table and took his.

"No, Jill," said Gilkrensky. "It's . . ."

With a roaring hiss, the fire sprinkler above their table burst into life, spraying them both with water. It spat down onto the hot pan on the trolley, spattered onto the table and the food, filling the plates in front of them. Gilkrensky could feel it soaking through his jacket, sticking it to his skin. He looked up. Jill was laughing, running her fingers back through her hair, putting her face up into the spray – laughing, like a high-school girl in the rain.

"See what happens when you get too serious, Theo! It makes the gods angry."

The *maître d'* was running over to them, all apologies. RJ Stevenson was on his radio. Then, all at once, the hissing stopped and they were standing there in a soaking circle of sodden carpet, dripping tablecloths and ruined food.

"Come on, Theo! Laugh at it, for God's sake!"

The *maître d'* was desolate. "I'm so, so sorry, Dr Gilkrensky. This has never, *ever* happened before. Chef's made that dish a thousand times under those sprinklers, and the computer's always known. I can't think *why* it should have happened tonight."

Gilkrensky stared up at the ceiling. Every security camera in the room was staring back at him.

"You say the system's controlled by computer?"

"Yes, sir!"

"Then I know *exactly* why!"

Gilkrensky burst into the Presidential Suite, and strode to the study. He was reaching for the light switch when there was a click, and the holographic image of Maria was standing before him in the darkness.

"Did you do that?" he demanded.

"Do what, Theo? I've been performing a large number of computational and research functions since you left. I've discovered an interesting historical correlation between the various reports of missing ships and aircraft in this area and the . . ."

"Why did you turn on the fire sprinkler in the dining-room?"

"I detected a potential fire hazard on the hotel's internal safety system and, by the Asimov Laws of my basic programming, I am not permitted to harm a human being or, by inaction, allow any human being to come to harm. So I took action, overrode the system and activated the sprinkler. Why? Did I do something wrong?"

"You turned on the sprinkler *after* the hazard was past!"

"Then I apologise, Theo. I am not yet familiar with the hotel's security and fire control systems."

"And yet you had no trouble in training all the security cameras on me."

"It was merely a precaution, Theo. Your safety is still my prime concern. I'm programmed to protect you."

Gilkrensky pushed his wet hair back out of his eyes.

"Well, you certainly followed your programming tonight!"

"Of course, Theo. I always do."

Gilkrensky stared at the image standing in front of him. The green eyes said nothing. Was the machine telling him the truth? He remembered its reaction to Jessica Wright . . . and something Jill had said in the submarine. *Was* the Minerva jealous?

"Would you have turned on the fire sprinkler if Miss McCarthy hadn't touched my hand just then?"

There was an almost imperceptible pause.

"Of course, Theo. I had detected a potential danger."

There was no way that he was going to win a battle of wits with a state-of-the-art machine like this.

"Miss Wright has also been calling, by the way," said the machine. "She wanted to know how you were after the incident in the submarine. I told her you were not available. Shall I get her for you?"

Jessica! What on earth could he say to her, now that the possibility of saving Maria existed?

"Not right now, Maria. Not until I've thought things through."

"I understand," said the image. "You have another call also, from the man who claims to be Eric Kosner. He said it was very urgent."

"What did he say?"

"He said that he was waiting for you downstairs, in the lower level car park. I understand Mr Stevenson and his security team have him under guard."

The doors of the elevator hissed open, and the security guard peered out.

"It's OK, doctor," he said. "The area's secure."

Gilkrensky stepped forward. He was standing in the lowest level of the hotel – a vast echoing forest of concrete columns – deep underground. The floor was covered in painted grids for cars, empty now, except for . . .

A white "Recreational Vehicle" – a Catalina Sport camper van stood trapped in the headlights of four GRC security cars. RJ Stevenson was standing near the side door. The holster strap on his Glock automatic was undone.

"It's just one old guy, Dr Gilkrensky. We searched him and he isn't carrying."

"I see. Is he coming out?"

Stevenson shook his head. "He's paranoid about

security, sir, even took the licence plates off the RV and hid them under a bush somewhere before he drove into the hotel. He says he doesn't want his face on any of our cameras. If you want to talk to him, you'll have to get in the camper, but I'll be right here, and we'll keep the door open."

"Worth the risk?"

"I'd say so," said Stevenson, with a nod to the cars and armed men ringing the camper. "He isn't going anywhere unless we let him."

"OK then."

Stevenson opened the door, and Gilkrensky stepped inside.

He was standing in a wood-panelled cabin, like the inside of a yacht. Facing him, from below a wall-mounted television and video unit, was a neat sofa, and a spotlessly efficient cooking area. To his right was a raised bunk. Over the cab of the van and, to his left was a pair of dining chairs on either side of a clean Formica table.

"You oughta get yourself better security, Dr Gilkrensky," said a voice. "Those smart-arsed kids out there ain't got no respect for their elders."

Sitting in the far chair was a tiny gnome of a man, wrapped in a thick lumber-jacket. A faded baseball cap was pulled down tight over his eyes, covering most of his face.

"Eric Kosner?"

The old man extended a withered claw of a hand.

"*Corporal* Eric Kosner," he said. "Sit down. I've things you need to know, important things, that other people would like to see covered up. Quick. I can't afford to be seen here with you."

Gilkrensky glanced out at RJ Stevenson, standing ready with his men outside. Then he sat down at the table. "Why have you come here?" he said.

"I wanted to meet you in the flesh, Dr Gilkrensky, to show you there's nothing to hide. Well, not by me anyway. I wanted you to know that what you see is what you get. But I have to be careful. There's a lot of powerful people who don't want anyone to hear what I have to say."

"About what? You mentioned the word *Eldridge*, and said it was the name of a ship."

"It surely was," said the old man slowly. "Don't think you're the only man in the world who's ever been interested in unknown forces, because you're not. The United States' Government's has been at it for years. Tell me, have you noticed anything suspicious since you reported that incident with the flying boat? Have any cars followed you, perhaps?"

"No," said Gilkrensky. Then he remembered the long black limousine that had tailed his convoy from the hotel that morning, all the way to Titusville, and Jill McCarthy's house.

"Well, yes. Now that you come to mention it."

Kosner nodded. "That's why I can't afford to tie myself down to a fixed location. I do all my business through a cellphone, E-mail and ATM machines, just to throw them off the scent, but that won't stop them for ever. Sometimes, I think they only let me live because they figure nobody would ever believe an old fart like me, and what I'm about to tell you."

He lifted a plastic cup of water to his lips and sipped at it. "Once those people in government know I've passed the proof of their experiments over to you, I'll have to vanish off the face of the earth, or be tracked down and killed. They can do it, you know. They have satellites, cameras, computers . . . the works. A man would need powerful connections, and a lot of money to be safe from them."

"Proof of what?" asked Gilkrensky.

"Proof that what you're trying to do *is* possible," whispered Kosner, leaning forward across the table so that the peak of his baseball cap almost touched Gilkrensky's forehead. "Proof that you *can* distort the fabric of space and time – given the right technology."

Gilkrensky stared at the man, while his mind raced. Was this a hoax, or the final piece of the jigsaw he so desperately needed to reach Maria?

"Go on," he said. "I'm listening."

Kosner kept his voice low. "It's been done before," he said. "And the US Government did it."

"When?"

The old man lifted the baseball cap from his head and laid it down on the table next to his cup of water. The skin was pulled tight over his face, like a waxy mask, and his wispy hair, free from the confines of the cap, drifted down over his ears. His voice was high-pitched and crackly, but his eyes were bright and alive, in that tired ruin of a face.

"It was in 1940," he said. "And I'd just got my PhD from the California Institute of Technology for work on electro-magnetism. Hard to believe, looking at me now, isn't it? But back then, I was the brightest penny on God's earth. Patriotic bastard I was too, so I joined the US Navy and got shipped to Princetown, New Jersey. That was where I met Willie Reinhart, a guy I'd known back at Caltech . . . "

"Where's all this leading?" asked Gilkrensky.

Kosner smiled. "Patience, young feller. I'll be exactly where you want to be in a minute. You're a scientist, right? A real whiz at computers."

"So they say."

"Then you'll know you can bend light waves around corners with prisms and mirrors, just like those mirages of water you see on hot sand when the sun heats the air."

"Of course I do."

"Then get this. In 1940 the US Navy was working on a way of making ships invisible to German homing torpedoes by creating intense fields of magnetism to fool their guidance systems. It worked. It worked very well. And so they started fooling with ways of bending radar waves, and even light itself, by turning ships into great big magnets so the enemy would look right past them. Now, what do you think of that?"

Gilkrensky shook his head. "I'd say it's impossible."

"And what if I told you Albert Einstein himself was involved, and that his 'Unified Field Theory for Gravitation and Electricity' was the basis of the whole thing? What if I told you the US navy actually made a ship *disappear*? What then?"

"I'd say that – being a businessman, as well as a scientist – I'd want to know why you think what you're saying might help me."

Kosner shook his head. A strand of silvery hair fell over his face and he brushed it back.

"OK then. Since you're a scientist, I'll give you all the technical details first. Then we'll see what kind of businessman you are."

"Suits me."

"OK. By July 1943 we thought we'd try a test on a real ship. So we rigged up a destroyer with all sorts of electric gear – all designed to create such an intense magnetic field that the ship would become completely invisible when it was turned on."

Kosner took another sip of water.

"Then, at nine in the morning of the twenty-second of July, 1943, we turned on the power. There was a great humming – like a zillion bees on Benzedrine – a weird green mist, and then – nothing. The ship had vanished!"

"And then what happened?"

"Fifteen minutes later, we switched off the generators and the ship came back. The crew were sick. They had to be taken off. The equipment was modified, and a second test was done, on October the twenty-eighth of that same year."

"You have a very good memory, Mr Kosner."

Kosner smiled. "You'll find that, when you get to my age, son, you can remember what happened fifty years ago as if it were yesterday, but if someone asks you to remember where you left your glasses, then that's a whole different ball game."

"And the second experiment?"

Kosner wiped his lips with the back of his hand.

"This is where it starts getting interesting from your point of view, Dr Gilkrensky. This is where the work we did then starts paralleling what you're trying to do now."

"How so?"

"Because the second time we . . . we pushed it too far. There was no green fog, just the outline of the ship in the water. Everything was cool for a few minutes and then 'wham!' – a great blinding flash, like lightning. I thought one of the generators had overheated and exploded. But when the noise had died down, do you know what we found?"

Gilkrensky shook his head.

"Nothing! That's what we found. Nothing at all. The ship had completely vanished. It wasn't invisible any more, it was just – gone! And do you know what? Right at that same moment, it reappeared – hundreds of miles away, in Norfolk, Virginia! Guys on the SS *Andrew Furuseth* saw it for several minutes, and then it was gone again, right back to Philadelphia. I saw it reappear with my own eyes, right there in the water."

"It still sounds incredible . . ." began Gilkrensky, but Kosner cut him short.

"That's not all of it, doctor. The men on board were sick as dogs, some had vanished completely, and my friend Willie Reinhart, well . . . he was the worst case of all."

"What happened to him?"

Kosner took another long sip of water, and then laid the empty cup on the table. "Guys were rolling around on the deck, throwing up all over the place, some were walking around like zombies. But my friend Willie was just leaning up against a bulkhead, staring into space. I called out to him, but he didn't answer me. I shook his shoulder, but he didn't move. And then I saw the back of his head. It was *fused* to the metal of the ship, Dr Gilkrensky, actually melded into the metal, as if it were part of it. There was no blood, nothing. It was as if he'd been lying back with his head in a basin of water, only this 'water' was a plate of quarter-inch-thick steel."

"I'm sorry," said Gilkrensky. "But I still don't see how this helps me."

Kosner stared at him with his bright eyes. "The government have tried to cover up those experiments for the past fifty years, they even have 'misinformation' pages about it on the Web, but I know the truth!"

He leant forward again, while his eyes watched the

open door of the camper and his voiced dropped to a whisper again.

"That plane you crashed into on the way in here, doctor, that Martin Mariner, that was part of Flight Nineteen – another secret test they were trying, with aircraft this time – back in 1945. I was supposed to go on that flight, but I chickened out, after what happened to Willie Reinhart in the Philadelphia experiment. I didn't want to go the same way."

"I still don't see how that helps me."

"I've been following your adventures on the Web with my laptop computer. I know all about your experiments with the Great Pyramid of Cheops in Egypt, and I can guess what you're trying to do."

"Which is?"

"You want to focus ley-line energy to such intensity that it opens a wormhole in the fabric of space/time, just like Einstein did with the *Eldridge*."

"And why on earth would I want to do that?"

Kosner's bright eyes fixed him as he said, "So that you can travel back and save your wife."

Gilkrensky was stunned.

"Don't look so surprised, doctor. Anyone with an ounce of imagination and access to the Web could have told you that. It broke your heart when she died, I'll bet. And now you've stumbled on a way to bring her back. The experiments I worked on during the war prove what you're trying to do *is* feasible. Your collision with the Mariner proves it too."

"And you can help me?"

"I have the original logs of the ship, Einstein's notes and photographs of the gear that was used – the whole shebang! They'll give you all the information you need to actually control the phenomenon. With that information, your money, and the technology at your disposal, you'll be able to travel back in time as far as you need to save your wife. But I need the kind of cash it takes to get protection afterwards."

"And how much will this information cost me?"

"The Government want those papers back," said Kosner, flicking his baseball cap back over his skull. "And they've been watching me for the past fifty years, in the hope I'll lead them to where they're hidden. If you give me enough money to hide for the rest of my life, and a private plane to take me anywhere I want to go, then the whole file on the 'Philadelphia Experiment' is yours. You get what you want, and I get what I want. You said you were a businessman. Let's do business."

He reached into his top pocket, pulled out a crumpled sheet of folded yellow paper, and handed it to Gilkrensky, who carefully spread it out on the Formica table. It was a torn page from the logbook of a ship, and across the top of the page were the words *"Project Rainbow – USS Eldridge"*.

23

Joint Venture

Gilkrensky watched the palm trees slide by the limousine as it headed down the ramp to the freeway. In front and behind, the security cars from the hotel kept a close watch.

"What do you think, Maria?"

He had spent most of the night turning Kosner's evidence over in his mind, and was still no closer to a conclusion than when he had spread the piece of yellowed paper on the table in Kosner's camper. Now, in the hard light of the early morning, it all seemed like so much fiction – a "techno-myth" as Jill had put it.

"There is a great deal of conflicting evidence," said the Minerva from the seat facing him. "On the one hand, there are many Web sites devoted to what is known as the 'Philadelphia Experiment'. Each of them describes the story as Mr Kosner did – that the American government experimented with intense magnetic fields in an attempt to induceing visibility, and succeeded in creating a wormhole in space instead – moving an entire ship instantly, from the Philadelphia shipyards to Norfolk, Virginia, and back again. But the authorities deny these experiments ever took place, and have even posted the complete action report of the *USS Eldridge* on the Web, which contains no mention of such work."

"Then I suppose it depends on whether I believe Kosner or the US government," said Gilkrensky.

"Indeed, Theo. We have evidence of our own that time distortions do take place. We know they can be artificially induced, and we believe that Professor McCarthy disappeared through one, inside the Pyramid of Cheops. Perhaps the same effect can be induced by intense magnetic fields? It will depend on what the logbooks and notes Mr Kosner claims to possess show us."

"And the page he gave us?"

"Visually, it appears to be genuine. But without detailed chemical analysis it is impossible to be sure. It is only the first page of a much larger document. To assess its authenticity with certainty would require me to analyse the entire work."

"And to get that document will cost me two million dollars."

"As a sum of money, it represents a minute percentage of your overall assets."

"Are you suggesting I pay it?"

"That is your decision. But compared to the expense of our experiments in Egypt, and the dive yesterday on the wreck of the Mariner, it seems a comparatively cost-effective way of obtaining information that might help us."

"Perhaps, but our survey today might shed some light on the subject too. Can Jill fit the equipment we need into that aircraft of hers?"

"Miss McCarthy assured me it would not be a problem. It will not give us as complete a picture as having the whole range of sensors in your jet would have done, but it will at least tell us if there are concentrations of ley-line energy in the sea area of the Miami airport approach grid. Her plane is also amphibious. We will be able to land and inspect the remote Daedalus stations, and the master beacon on Bimini Key."

"Thank you, Maria."

"It is my pleasure, Theo."

They were on the freeway now, moving east. Gilkrensky was still looking at the Minerva screen as the Lincoln passed a long, black limousine idling near a service station. Once the three cars of Gilkrensky's convoy had passed, the limousine slipped out into the traffic, and followed them towards the Cape.

Yukiko Funakoshi had watched the big white car and its escort slide down the approach road and disappear amongst the low trees of the golf course onto the freeway. It was still very early, and everything she could see from the narrow balcony of her hotel room at the Orlando Olympiad had a crisp clarity about it. Eight floors below her the sky-blue water in the swimming pools and splash ponds around the central island of the outdoor restaurant still had a mirror surface. An ideal time for reconnaissance?

She pulled a dark blue Adidas track suit and running shoes, freshly purchased at the hotel sports shop, out of a drawer, draped a towel around her shoulders and slipped on a pair of wrap-around sunglasses. Finally, she pulled on a brand new Yankees baseball cap, scrutinised herself in the mirror to make sure she looked like any other early-morning jogger, pocketed the key card for her room, and walked to the elevator. Like every service in the hotel, it was controlled by computer. Yukiko had already hacked her way into it though the remote booking system in her room.

But one problem remained. Gilkrensky had surrounded himself with a far bigger security force than she had ever encountered before, and each one of them was armed with an automatic weapon. A suicide strike now would leave her uncle and Jessica Wright unpunished for their crimes against her family. How could she manipulate the computer here in the hotel to silence the alarm systems, while mounting a successful attack on Gilkrensky at the same time?

Outside on the terrace at ground level, she could hear the distant hiss of water jets on the golf course and the purr of electric carts on their way to a game. Through the open doors of the restaurant came the clink of silverware and the clatter of warming pans full of bacon, sausage and hash browns. Along the poolside, a uniformed woman was working a suction pipe to clear the bottom. Above her, in a cradle suspended from the roof, a man with a long flexible blade was cleaning the lower windows.

It would be well to know how all these people operated, and when. Yukiko catalogued what she already knew about the hotel, and the top-floor suite where Gilkrensky had made his base. It was twelve floors tall and shaped like a letter "C", with the swimming pool and restaurant complex sheltered inside its wings. To get to the top floors there were two emergency stairwells, a service lift, and a pair of glass-sided elevators that departed from the main lobby, exited through a gap in the vast glass ceiling, and slid up the outside of the building. Yukiko walked slowly along the narrow causeway between the swimming pools to the island restaurant and looked back. The rising sun was turning the side of the hotel to gold. She mounted the wooden steps into the shade of the awning, feeling the dew on the wooden handrail.

As she watched, one of the glass elevators popped through the ceiling of the lobby and crawled up the face of the hotel. There was a man in white tennis gear inside it. She could see him clearly.

"You're absolutely right, Miss Funakoshi," said a voice behind her in Japanese. "It's the ideal killing ground."

Yukiko spun round. In front of her, a copy of *USA Today* gently lowered itself to reveal an old man, with a heavy white moustache and thin, steel-rimmed glasses. He regarded her from under a broad Panama hat.

A MATTER OF TIME

"Before you consider any sudden moves, Miss Funakoshi. I should draw your attention to the young lady vacuuming the pool, and to her colleague, who is currently engaged in cleaning the windows of the hotel. Each one of them is armed with a compressed-air dart-gun, capable of shooting a minute nerve capsule at such a high velocity that you won't even feel it enter your skin, although you'll be dead before you hit the ground. Now, if you'll just sit down, as if you were joining me for some breakfast, keeping your hands on the table where I can see them, of course? And don't touch the silverware please. I know a great deal about your capabilities already."

Yukiko glanced at the pool attendant and the window cleaner. Each of them was cradling a squat black pistol, aimed at her heart. They stared back at her. She sat down where the old man indicated.

"Who are you?" she said slowly. "And what do you want?"

The man smiled. "I hope you'll excuse my disguise," he said. "But it wouldn't do me any good to be recognised on the hotel security cameras. My name is Milton J Hacker, of the Gibbtek Corporation. Mr Tony Delgado, recently retired from the Gilcrest Radio Corporation, was a – er – colleague of yours, I understand. What I want is to discuss a business proposition, a joint venture."

"What kind of joint venture?"

"One that will be of great interest to you. It concerns the death of a certain Dr Theodore Gilkrensky."

"If you want him dead," said Yukiko, "why don't you just kill him yourself? You certainly seem to have the manpower."

"The death of Dr Gilkrensky is no longer my prime concern," said Hacker, lifting a glass of freshly squeezed orange juice to his lips. "No, what really interests me now is how you managed to tap into the GRC computer system to get the information Delgado passed me regarding Gilkrensky's flight details."

"I beg your pardon?"

"Please don't be obtuse, Miss Funakoshi. It wastes time. For Tony Delgado to pass me details of Gilkrensky's flight to Orlando, you must have shown him how to bypass the passwords, security cut-offs and firewalls GRC have around their computer system. I need to penetrate the Minerva security system to – to extract a piece of software my employer is anxious to acquire, without activating its defensive computer virus. In return for providing me with this service, I am willing to put my own resources at your disposal to assist you with your vendetta. What do you say?"

Yukiko considered. Here was the answer to her earlier dilemma, delivered on a plate. It was all too simple.

"I have no personal vendetta against Gilkrensky," she said flatly. "My purpose here it to obtain the Minerva computer for Mawashi-Saito in Tokyo. You have been misinformed."

Hacker smiled again. "Your reputation precedes you, Miss Funakoshi. Or should I say Rothsay? You see, I know all about you – how your mother committed suicide rather than face that scandal Jessica Wright started to discredit your father, and how Lord Rothsay himself was manoeuvred into giving up his shareholding in GRC by Gilkrensky. I can understand why your uncle was forced to have you certified as insane, I really can. But then again, it had nothing to do with your mental health, did it?"

For a second, a spark of rage flashed across Yukiko's mind, flared, and was gone – back under control.

"He did it to save Mawashi-Saito," she said without emotion. "He had to distance me from any responsibility his company might have had for my actions. That way Mawashi-Saito was free to proceed legally against Gilkrensky and regain its shares in GRC."

"Then you will consider my offer?"

Yukiko regarded him across the table. "Your dossier on me is very impressive," she said. "But I doubt if it came from Gibbtek as much as it did from the US Central Intelligence Agency, for whom you still work in your capacity as guardian angel over Mr Jerry Gibb and his advanced SQUID technology. You see, I have my sources too, Mr Hacker."

Hacker gave nothing away. His only movement was to make a note on a pad of hotel stationery near his elbow with a thick old-fashioned fountain pen.

"*Touché*, Miss Funakoshi," he said at last. "Seeing as how we are both orphans, so to speak, I think a gesture of goodwill is in order . . ."

Hacker slowly reached into the inside pocket of his white cotton jacket, took out a plain brown envelope and laid it in front of Yukiko on the breakfast table.

"You'd be amazed at what you can find on the Internet," he said. "I was surprised just how easy it was to locate."

Yukiko pulled open the flap of the envelope and tilted it, so that four Polaroid photographs fell out onto the place mat in front of her. She gasped in surprise.

Staring at her from the pictures was the delicately engraved cherry blossom of the Funakoshi family. It was engraved on the pommel of an exquisite samurai sword – a *katana* – the gracefully curving match of the short sword Yukiko cherished, and had risked her life to retrieve from GRC headquarters.

Yukiko sat, mesmerised by the pictures. Here was the sword of legend, the beautiful weapon her uncle Gichin had sold to buy food and medicines for her mother after the fall of Japan in 1945. How had Hacker located it? Was it real?

She had to have it!

"I accessed the GRC computer system with a specially developed software package," she said. "I have a copy of it on the laptop computer in my room, and have already been able to link it to the hotel system undetected. If you could find a way of ensuring that Gilkrensky links his Minerva to the hotel mainframe, then you would be guaranteed full access to all its systems and access whatever software your Mr Gibb wishes to steal."

"Excellent," said Hacker, slipping the fountain pen back into his pocket. "Can I interest you in breakfast?"

24

Bimini Key

"I still think Kosner's a con artist," said Jill, as the Lincoln slid out of her driveway onto the main Titusville bypass, towards the GRC Aerospace facility. "I'm surprised you fell for it."

"If he is a con artist, then he's a very good one. His story was very convincing."

"Of course it was. He probably downloaded your biography and the facts about Cairo off one of those New-Age Web sites."

"I don't know," said Gilkrensky.

She was sitting opposite him in the back of the limousine, dressed again in a white shirt and jeans. There had been no mention of the incident at dinner the night before. Had she forgiven him? Was she angry? There had been no clue when he'd picked her up at her father's house, only a bright enthusiasm to get on with the job of proving the Daedalus system was safe.

The sun was high in the sky. It glared off the polished bonnet of the car and twinkled in the gullies by the side of the road, where small alligators basked amongst the reeds.

Jill shook her head. "After you called me last night, I spent a lot of time looking at the Web. There's not a single fact from Kosner's story that you can't pick up on a dozen sites. The story of the *USS Eldridge* is a cult, just like UFO's or the Loch Ness Monster. Nobody takes it seriously."

Gilkrensky thought of the white paint he had seen on the float of the fifty-year-old wreck.

"I've got an open mind on this," he said.

"Like I said, it's a legend."

From the seat next to Gilkrensky, the Minerva 3,000 said, "Perhaps, Miss McCarthy, but there's one part of his story we can verify right away. I've been monitoring the radio traffic between the two security cars which are escorting us, and it appears we're still being followed by a black limousine. Is that the same one that's been tailing us since we arrived in Florida?"

Gilkrensky turned to look out of the rear window of the Lincoln. Beyond the rear security vehicle, he could make out the glint of sunlight on a long, black car.

"Did anyone manage to get an identification on the registration number on that, RJ?" he said.

"It's got Florida plates, for sure," said Stevenson, from the driver's seat. "But when we called the DMV we hit a brick wall. Any information on that car's restricted. It must be a government vehicle or some VIP of some kind, like I said."

"And what about Kosner?" said Jill. "Couldn't you run a check on his number plates too?"

"He unscrewed them before he drove into the carpark, ma'am," said Stevenson. "He was as paranoid as hell about being fingered."

"But how could he drive on the freeway without plates?" said Jill. "The first cop that saw him would pull him over."

Gilkrensky said, "Perhaps he took them off close to the hotel, hid them and drove straight into the carpark."

"Which means he probably pulled over to the nearest gas station. How many are there close by?"

"Just one," said Stevenson.

"How well do you know the management?"

"Pretty well. We helped him out with a little – personal problem he had last year. He owes me one."

Jill smiled conspiratorially. "Then why not ask if you can look over his security video tapes for last night," she said. "Perhaps you might get lucky."

Stevenson chuckled. "Yes, ma'am. I'll get someone on it right away. Here's the Orlando facility, and they're expecting you."

Ahead of the Lincoln, the horizon was dominated by the sheds, hangars and warehouses of a huge aviation complex, the size of a small town. A heavy red and white boom lifted, a pair of uniformed security guards tried to stand to attention and peer into the car at the same time, and the convoy swept into the main manufacturing and research plant of GRC Aerospace, Orlando. Behind them, the boom lowered. On the far side, the black limousine pulled over to the side of the road, and stopped.

On either side of the main facility thoroughfare, aircraft hangars and fabrication workshops towered into the sky. Some of their doors were rolled open, revealing the finished fuselages of Whisperer jets, or the half completed hulls of unfinished planes.

"You did a lot of work out here with Dad, in the early days of the Daedalus project, didn't you, Theo?" said Jill.

"That's right."

They were past the main assembly area now and at the apron of an aircraft-holding area, lined with planes. The convoy slid onto the tarmac, turned, and came to a stop next to the Voyager executive jet Gilkrensky had arrived in. Its damaged fuel tank had been removed and technicians were clambering over the wing.

The chief technician in charge of the examination walked over to Gilkrensky as soon as he'd got out of the car.

"Don't look as if this baby's going anywhere for a few days," he said. "But I've had the boys load all the equipment you asked for into Miss McCarthy's plane over there. Tight squeeze it was too, but we managed it."

Sitting on the apron next to the Voyager was a dumpy little Grumman Widgeon flying boat. It was painted bright yellow and sat, like a huge toy duck, on the fat tyres of its tricycle undercarriage. Jill walked over to it and gave it a pat on the nose.

"My first love," she said. "Dad bought it for me when I learnt to fly. It's been my baby ever since."

"Are you sure it's safe?" said Gilkrensky, and then wished he hadn't.

"Safe as houses," said Jill. "You've been spoiled in helicopters and executive jets for too long, Dr Theodore Gilkrensky. Now I'm going to show you some real flying!"

"Excuse me, sir," said Stevenson. "But what about security? I have orders from GRC London not to let you out of my sight."

"There's only room for two in this plane with all the equipment aboard," said Jill, pointing to a Bell JetRanger that was warming up on a nearby helipad. "If you want to keep up with us, you can take that helicopter over there."

The little aircraft trundled over to the take-off point and stopped. Gilkrensky was sitting in the co-pilot's seat to Jill's right, watching her as she checked her instruments.

"Hold on," she said. "I'm taking her up! *Andiamo!*"

She pushed forward on the throttles and released the brake. The little aircraft lurched ahead, steadied, and rushed down the runway. Gilkrensky could see the floats on either side wobble as the plane gathered speed. They seemed to be kissing the ground.

Then, with a sudden jump, they were airborne, and circling back over the GRC complex. Gilkrensky could see his jet, the helicopter with Stevenson's security team rising into the air, and the white limousine beside the apron. He followed its track, back down through the alley of aircraft hangars to the main gate, and beyond. There was the long, black car. Its driver was looking up at them. He could see the glint of the sun on the lenses of powerful binoculars.

"Well, he won't be able to follow us up here," he said. "What's your flight plan?"

"The master beacon for the Miami/Orlando Daedalus complex is out beyond Bimini Island to the north-west," said Jill. "There's a coral island there with a small airstrip. We'll check that out first. Then there are five other repeater beacons, some with airstrips and some without. But we won't have any problems landing near them in this plane."

The little aircraft was climbing higher. Gilkrensky could see the sweep of the coastline, right across the Cape and off into the Atlantic. The sky looked clear, but there were the tall mushrooms of clouds, way out to sea.

"Weather forecast?"

"Good," said Jill. "But worsening later in the day. So we wouldn't want to be out there after nightfall."

"No chance of that?"

"No. Do you want to switch on your equipment?"

"I'll set it up," said Gilkrensky. "Then Maria can monitor it for us as we fly."

"Hmmm . . . all right."

Gilkrensky undid his seat belt and squeezed aft, through the narrow door. After the brilliance of the cockpit, the cabin felt dark and confined.

"Maria?"

"I'm here, Theo. Should we start monitoring for abnormal energy fields?"

"Exactly. I'll power up the scanners. Then you can record the data, and tell us if anything shows up."

"Very well. What search pattern will we be flying?"

"Straight line out to the master beacon on Bimini Key. Then we'll land and check that out, and fly back in a box grid. If we can't cover it today, we'll repeat it tomorrow and the next day."

"I see. I can detect the Bimini beacon now. At this speed, it should take us an hour and twenty minutes to get there."

Gilkrensky threw the switches on the electronic recorders, checked they were functioning and that the leads to the Minerva were secure. Then he stepped back towards the cockpit.

"Theo?"

"Yes, Maria."

"I don't think Miss McCarthy likes me."

Gilkrensky stopped, with his hand on the cockpit door.

"Why do you say that?"

"She has the cockpit headsets switched off, so that I cannot hear what you are saying to each other."

"I – I don't know, Maria. Perhaps she hasn't forgiven you for drenching her last night."

Gilkrensky pulled himself up into the cockpit and slipped into the co-pilot's seat. There was nothing ahead of them now except the ocean, a straight line of the deepest blue against the sky.

"Everything OK?" asked Jill.

"Fine. Maria will tell us if anything shows up."

"Maria?"

"All right then, the Minerva."

"Don't you think it's time to re-program it, Theo? Why do you keep torturing yourself?"

"I – I don't know. Maria left me a video message on my old laptop PC. I was reading it just before . . . before she died. I had this photograph of her, taken down in Wicklow on the day she said she'd marry me. I suppose I just couldn't accept she was gone, and I created my own 'Maria', just to have someone to talk to."

"And you haven't met anyone else?"

Gilkrensky thought of Jessica.

"I did," he said. "But it didn't work."

"So nobody now?"

"Not now. I don't think there ever will be."

"Perhaps you just haven't met the right person," said Jill, and they flew on, followed by Stevenson's helicopter.

At the master beacon, at the furthest point of the Daedalus grid from Miami airport, Jill swung the little seaplane into a gentle arc over a deserted coral island, shaped like a horse-shoe around a deep blue lagoon. Gilkrensky could see a short airstrip along the eastern arm of the island and a thin scrub of trees around a shack, next to where the red-and-white-painted tower of the beacon stood.

"I'll land in the water," said Jill. "It'll be smoother."

She headed the plane away from the island, turned and brought it in low over the sea, easing back the throttles and extending the flaps as she approached. Gilkrensky could see the tiny jewelled waves, sparkling in the sun, rushing faster and faster alongside until they seemed to be floating on a bed of light. Then there was a bump and hiss, as the plane touched down, followed by the slop and lap of water on the hull as Jill eased the plane in through a gap in the coral, into the natural harbour of the lagoon.

"Nice landing!" said Gilkrensky. "You're a natural."

Jill grinned at him. "Just like my father," she said. "Now, throw out the anchor, and I'll shut her down."

Gilkrensky moved back into the cabin, and then into the very nose of the plane. There was a small, lightweight anchor on a length of rope. He opened a narrow hatch, leaned out, and threw the anchor into the water, pulling on the rope until it held. On either side of him, there was a stutter as the engines died. Then the purr and chop of the security helicopter following them in.

"I'll send it on to scout out the next beacon, while we check this one," shouted Jill, and before Gilkrensky could say a word she was on the radio. In a moment the helicopter was circling above them, and Stevenson was giving him the thumbs up from the door. Then the machine swung off to the east and was soon out of sight.

"We'll have to swim for it," called Jill, "and it may be a bit cold. But don't worry. It's not far."

Gilkrensky ducked back into the cabin, and stopped dead. Jill McCarthy had slipped out of her clothes, and was kneeling beside the open hatch in a pure white bikini, unpacking a rubber dingy. Her tanned skin glowed in the glitter of light from the waves outside.

"What about the Minerva, and the gear for checking out the beacon?" he said. "How do we get that ashore?"

Jill smiled up at him. "I've got a raft for the electronics and our lunch. We can pull it behind us as we swim."

"And the Minerva?"

"You'd probably be better off leaving it in the plane," said Jill, smiling sweetly. "The salt water might damage it."

Gilkrensky had never seen water as clear in all his life. As he swam, ripples cast moving shadows on the white coral sand below him. The sun was hot on his back even as he moved up the beach, pulling the little rubber raft behind him.

When he felt he was far enough up the shore, he reached inside the raft for his shirt, and put it on over his wet skin. Then he pulled out one of the portable radio headsets, slid it over his left ear, and dropped the tiny battery pack into his shirt pocket.

"Can you hear me, Maria?"

"I can, Theo. The beacon is on a bearing of 121 degrees from you, at 63 metres."

"Thank you. But it's not a big island."

They trudged up the beach and into the scrub of dark, skeletal bushes, towards the trees surrounding the shed. Next to it was a tall, red-and-white-painted mast with a junction box at its base and an inspection plate. Jill dropped her backpack onto the coral sand, spread a blanket for her tools and opened the plate with a screwdriver.

"Don't you want to put anything back on?" said Gilkrensky. "The sun's very strong."

"I'm used to it. And besides, we're in the shade here. There, take a look at this."

She lifted off the inspection plate and laid it down carefully on the blanket. Inside the beacon was a series of small boxes of different sizes and colours, marked *main master-board*, *peripheral sensors*, *backup master-board* and *uplink relay*. Each had a data port, so that it could be interrogated by computer. Gilkrensky took a flat black laptop out of Jill's backpack, unwound a cable, and connected the machine to each box in turn.

"There," he said finally. "The uplink relay could do with replacement. I think the seal on the box is going and salt air might be getting in."

Jill pulled another unit from her backpack.

"There you go," she said. "Out with the old. In with the new."

They were standing side by side, working on the narrow opening of the beacon. Gilkrensky felt the smooth skin of her arm touch his as he pressed home the uplink relay.

"Theo . . ." she said awkwardly. And then her clear grey eyes met his.

"What is it?"

"I've been thinking about what we talked about over dinner last night, you know, before the sprinklers drowned us out, and . . ."

She reached up, lifted the radio microphone and earpiece from his head and tossed it down on the sand.

"Like I said back at my house, I'm not much good at

emotions. I just wanted to talk to you seriously without that computer of yours listening in all the time."

"What about?"

Jill reached down and lifted his hands in hers. "What do you think, Theo? I was crazy about you in Boston, but I could never bring myself to say it. I know it's hard for you to think of anyone else after Maria. I really do. But I'm telling you now . . ."

Then her arms were around his neck and her lips were on his.

"There," she said, drawing back and looking into his eyes again for an answer. "I've told you. Now it's up to you."

"Jill . . . I'm sorry. It's all a bit sudden."

"I know, Theo. For you perhaps, but not for me. I've had a crush on you for years. It could work, couldn't it? You and me. Please say it could."

She reached forward to kiss him again, but Gilkrensky pulled away.

"Jill . . . I tried to tell you last night . . . I'm not free . . . "

"Not free? Free of what?"

He thought of Jessica, and how he'd hurt her through denying the truth of his love for Maria. Now, now that he knew a possibility of saving her existed, however small it was, he was bound to her, married to her . . . forever. To deny this a second time would just mean hurting someone else, someone he cared for, all over again.

"Jill," he said, "you've got to understand what's been driving me since we found that plane yesterday. You've got to know why I want so much to believe Kosner and his stories, why I was thrown out of Cairo and why I really came with you today."

"What? I don't understand."

"I want my wife back – Maria."

Jill looked at him as if he was mad. She shook her head.

"She's dead, Theo. I know it hurts. I know it's early. I know how you feel. But you've got to accept it. She's *dead*! Even you can't turn back time."

"That's where you're wrong," said Gilkrensky. "I can."

She was staring at him in disbelief. "How?"

"That wreck we found yesterday. It was fifty years old, but it had paint-marks from my jet on it. There are forces here, just like I found in Cairo, forces with the power to warp the fabric of time."

Jill McCarthy stared at him, open-mouthed.

"Theo. It's not *real*."

"I have to get her back, Jill. I love her. And while there is even an atom of possibility, I won't stop. Do you understand? There can't be anyone else until I know it can't be done."

"And if it can't?"

"I don't know. Perhaps not even then."

Her hands were at her sides. Was it disbelief in her eyes? Or was it anger?

"So I'm wasting my time?"

"I'm sorry, Jill. It's not your fault. It's mine."

Definitely anger now.

"And this survey today, it's not about exonerating my

father's work at all! It's more New-Age crap about time warps, isn't it? That's why you got all worked up about that plane. It wasn't about clearing Dad's name, or about me; it was about some stupid dream you're holding onto about a dead woman. Christ, Theo! She's dead! She's dead! She's dead!"

The roar of an incoming aircraft took them by surprise, and in a moment the security helicopter was hovering above the clearing. Gilkrensky could see the pilot looking down. Stevenson was holstering his beloved Glock pistol. He raised a loudhailer and shouted above the roar of the engine.

"Are you OK down there, sir? We got the call that there was some kind of emergency."

Gilkrensky cupped his hands to his mouth. "What call? Who made it?"

"That computer of yours, sir. She said she'd had an urgent call from that guy Kosner you talked to last night, and then lost radio contact with you. When we tried, we found you'd gone off the air."

Gilkrensky glanced at Jill, but she was busy gathering up the tools and equipment, throwing them angrily into the containers she'd brought.

"We're OK! I'll call you when we figure out what we're doing next."

"Of course, sir," shouted Stevenson. "We can wait."

Then the helicopter pulled away from the island, zoomed out over the lagoon and landed at the far end of the old airstrip, waiting.

Jill McCarthy snapped the lid of the container shut and stood up. "Well then," she said. "I suppose you'll be wanting this," and she held out the radio headset she'd thrown onto the sand.

"I'm sorry, Jill. I really am."

"Fuck you, Theo. Mac was right. You're a walking disaster. Go on! Answer that computer of yours! That's all you really care about after all, isn't it? Your obsession and your own little virtual world. Answer the bloody thing!" Then she flung the headset at him, turned, and marched back to the lagoon.

Gilkrensky looked down at the radio at his feet. He could hear the Minerva's voice rattling in the earpiece. For a moment he watched Jill storming off across the island, away from him. He knew he'd hurt her, rejecting her both as a woman and as the keeper of her father's memory. She was right. Her brother was right. He *was* obsessed. With a deep sigh, he reached down, picked up the headset and put it on.

"Why did you do that, Maria?"

Her voice was inside his head as the Minerva said. "My primary function is to protect you, Theo, and my secondary function is to carry out our mission. I am sorry if I have embarrassed you, but that is the way my programming operates."

Gilkrensky remembered the sprinkler incident the night before. "And what did Mr Kosner have to say?"

"His exact words were 'Get the money quickly! They're coming for me!'."

25

The Conspiracy

"It could all be part of the scam," said Stevenson, turning in his seat as the helicopter headed in towards the shore. "Kosner could be just putting pressure on you to hand over the money."

"But what if it's not? And don't forget that black limo that's been following me since I got here."

Gilkrensky was sitting behind the pilot, in the back of the JetRanger looking out at the line of dark clouds on the eastern horizon. The Minerva 3,000 was open on his knees. Jill was still on the island, working on the Daedalus transmitter, hurt and angry.

"Just leave me alone," she'd said when he tried to explain how he felt. "I can look after myself. If this con man Kosner is so important to you, go save him! I'll make my own way home."

The last he saw of her was her long tanned body, marching back into the grove, back towards the beacon they'd come to test.

"Excuse me, Dr Gilkrensky," shouted the pilot into his microphone. "But where would you like me to head for?"

"Can we trace Kosner's mobile phone, RJ?"

Stevenson shook his head. "If we knew the number, and he was on a local network – perhaps. Those things have repeater stations every few miles. But if he's using a GSM model, then he could be anywhere."

"And what about the licence plates? Did you get someone to check the security tape from the garage?"

"I did, and for a moment I thought we had him. He's on it all right, but the old goat parked broadside to the cameras so we can't read the plates."

"He must have known they were there."

"Like I said, he's pretty paranoid."

"Could I access those images?" said the Minerva. "There may be something Mr Stevenson missed."

"I doubt it, lady. But you can try. They're on the security computer at the hotel." And he gave the Minerva the access codes.

In a moment, Gilkrensky was watching a grainy image of the gas station forecourt. Kosner's camper van pulled up, the old man got out, disappeared behind the truck for a few minutes, and then reappeared. An attendant came over to him, filled the truck with gas, was paid in cash, and went back to his booth. Kosner looked about him, and then went to the front and rear of the camper, bending down to unscrew the licence plates each time, before driving off.

"There," said Stevenson. "You can't see the plates."

"He paid in cash," said Gilkrensky. "I thought everyone in the States used credit cards nowadays."

"Probably didn't want to be traced," said Stevenson. "Not if he knew he was on the cameras."

"Then where'd he get the money?"

He was looking at an image of the empty garage forecourt. Beyond the petrol pumps, where Kosner's camper had been standing, was an ATM cash machine. The name of the bank was clearly visible. The time of the transaction was recorded on the security video.

"Maria," he said. "I want you to do a little computer 'hacking' for me."

The helicopter followed the sweep of the shoreline south from the Cape, towards Miami.

"You'll see West Palm Beach in a moment," said Stevenson. "Then there's Boca Raton. Fort Lauderdale's just beyond that, but it'll be difficult to spot in the mess of buildings around Miami. Swing to starboard inland for a few miles and then pick up the main Fort Lauderdale freeway. It's a few miles down that. I used to live around here, and if we get stuck, I could always land and ask."

"Yeah, yeah, yeah!" snorted the pilot. "Funny guy!" And he swung the JetRanger inland, following the road. There was the Pompano Beach airfield, the green lawns of the Palmaire Country Club, and the cars on the Florida turnpike.

Gilkrensky looked down at the Minerva, open on his lap. "Do you think Jill will be OK, out there on her own?"

The image on the screen looked up at him. "As long as she returns before dark. There is a storm forecast and conditions could be bad."

"I should have insisted she came back with us," said Gilkrensky. "But she was just too angry with me."

"That's the Port Everglades Expressway," shouted Stevenson. "It's not far now."

The old house stood all alone in private grounds by the side of a narrow road. A flagpole, with the Stars and Stripes flapping in the rising wind, stood sentry over a dusty driveway, a stagnant fishpond and a wide lawn leading down to a river. There were benches here and there and a large wooden sign with peeling paint that said *Nursing Home – We Care*.

"But the ATM card Kosner used was registered to a video production company," said Gilkrensky.

"This *is* the address, doctor," said the pilot.

"But a nursing home?"

"Plenty of them around here. Old folks from all over the States take their pensions and move down to Florida where the weather's good. Big money too, especially in the country clubs and retirement communities, although you'd never think it to look at this place. Where do you want me to land?"

As Gilkrensky watched, an old couple shuffled out onto the boardwalk around the house. He could see faces at the windows, figures in the garden behind the house, staring up at them.

"Over there, well away from the building."

The JetRanger settled on its skids in a cloud of dust and the engine died. Running towards them was a tall thin woman in a white coat. Her face was pinched and grim, and her hard eyes darted left and right, as she tried to make sense of the helicopter and the men inside. Gilkrensky closed the Minerva lid, lifted the case by its handle and opened the passenger door.

"What's all this about?" shouted the woman above the noise of the dying engine. Then she saw Stevenson's white uniform shirt, his black tie, name badge and the holster on his hip. "Are you . . . the cops? Medicare?"

"We're looking for a video-film production company, ma'am," said Stevenson. "It's registered to a guy who uses the name Kosner, at this address."

The woman's hand went to her mouth. Then she glanced back at the building, turned and smiled. "I've nothing to do with the business dealings of the guests," she said. "And the owners live in New York. I'm just paid to work here."

"I see," said Stevenson and reached into his hip pocket for his bill-fold. Then he peeled off a couple of notes.

"So Kosner's here?"

"Not right now," she said, taking the money. "And his real name's not Kosner. It's Kline, Ronnie Kline. He just uses that name for his business – like this address. I have nothing to do with it."

"Does he have an office here?"

"He has his own room, yes. All our guests do."

"Can we see it, please?"

The woman hesitated. "Ah . . . shouldn't you have a warrant, or something?"

"This isn't official, ma'am," said Stevenson, peeling off another couple of notes. "Not unless you want it to be."

"Oh . . . oh, OK then." And she led them across the hard, dry lawn to the house. As they went, a dozen pairs of eyes followed them from the boardwalk and the windows. Drapes moved, ever so slightly, as they got near.

"It's the excitement," said the woman. "We ain't had a chopper land here since Mr Valetta's heart attack."

They walked though the main door and into the reception area. It smelt of floor polish and scented air freshener. There were worn carpets on the floors and a lot of places to sit down. The woman led them past the desk and down a corridor. Dust particles swarmed in the light from the windows. Their feet rattled on the bare boards.

"There," she said, unlocking a door with a master key from her belt. "This is where he keeps his stuff." Gilkrensky looked past her into the room. It was very dark.

"Could I see inside, please?"

"I ain't supposed to . . . " she began. And then Stevenson was reaching for his bill-fold again.

"Oh what the hell!" she said, taking the money. And the light clicked on.

It was like standing in a film-editing room. On a tripod over by the far wall a professional video camera stood facing a threadbare couch. There was a desk, complete with a computer, printer and filing trays that overflowed with invoices. And by the desk, stacked neatly in metal racks, one above the other, was a pair of studio-grade video-editing machines.

The rest of the room was full of colourfully boxed VHS video cassettes. They stood in neat piles along the wall, spilled out of cardboard crates and littered the floor. Gilkrensky picked one up and read the title on the cover. *Flying Saucer Crash at Roswell*, it said, *Eye Witness Report*. On the back was a blurred photograph of an old woman and the name of "Kosner's" video company. There were other titles – *Atlantis – The UFO Connection*, *Who Shot Kennedy?* and *Area 51 – Aliens on US Soil!*

"Here's another you'd better see," said Stevenson. It read *Project Rainbow – The Philadelphia Experiment – Secret Witness Tells All*. There was another photograph on the back cover, an old man this time.

"What do you know about this?" said Gilkrensky. The woman shrugged. "All I know is that Mr Kline makes tapes and sells them over the Internet. There's no law against it."

"And these people?"

The woman peered at the pictures. "Why – that's Mr Miller," she said. "And that one – that's Miss Kowalski. They're guests here too."

"So this 'Mr Kosner' of yours records fake interviews with the other old folks, here, in this room, and then sells the tapes over the Internet?"

"Like I said, it's his business. Not mine."

"Jesus!"

All at once Gilkrensky was grinning. "The clever old bastard!" he laughed. "He coaches his friends to act like witnesses to all these unexplainable events, posts advertisements on the Internet pretending to have the answers, and then sells the tapes. It's brilliant! Who's to say they're not telling the truth? And even if you could prove they're not, nobody can track him down to complain. It's bloody brilliant!"

"And what the hell do you think you're doing in Ronnie's room!" snapped a voice, and Gilkrensky turned.

Standing in the corridor outside Kosner's room was a small congregation of old people, peering in through the door. Gilkrensky looked at the man who had spoken and then at the picture on the video in his hand.

"Mr Miller, I presume?" he said. "Tell me, who did shoot Kennedy?"

"Don't bullshit me, son. You're not the cops. And even if you were, we ain't done nothing illegal."

"We only did it to escape from this place," said the old lady next to him.

"Quiet, Martha! You don't know what you're saying."

Gilkrensky peered at her, and held up another cassette.

"Miss Kowalski? The Roswell witness?"

"That's right, young man," she said proudly. "I did the video about the flying saucer crash. I was an actress once you see. I knew how to make it convincing."

"We've done nothing illegal," insisted Miller.

"And I did the one about the ship that vanished," said the man behind him. "That was the best ever."

Miller's eyes went up to heaven. "We ain't done nothing wrong!" he shouted. "It's *these* guys who are trespassing!"

Gilkrensky smiled at the others. "And this . . . this Ronnie Kline, he put you up to this?"

"Oh, it was his idea all right," said one of the men. "But we all chipped in. Like Martha said, we wanted to get out of here, to get ourselves a house in one of those retirement communities out on the coast, where they *really* look after you." His eyes were on the thin-faced woman in the white coat.

"In Palm Garden, or Cypress Grove," said Miss Kowalski. "They have pools and activities over there. That's what *I* wanted."

"And Ronnie Kline," asked Gilkrensky, "what did he want?"

Miller shook his head. "That's just it," he said with a resigned shrug. "Ronnie actually believes in this stuff. For him it's real. The videos are just his way of making people *believe* this crazy story of his. You want to be very careful of . . . "

"Excuse me," said Stevenson with his hand over his radio earpiece. "But our pilot's just called in. There's an RV drawing up outside. Kline's in it, and he's seen the GRC logo on the chopper."

"It's him," said Miss Kowalski, her eyes bright with anticipation. "*Now* there'll be fireworks."

"How did you find me!" shouted Ronnie Kline, running through the front doors of the nursing home to meet them. "Did the government put you up to this?"

"Forget it, Mr Kline," said Gilkrensky, stepping past him onto the boardwalk outside. "I've seen the room, and all the video tapes. It was a nice scam, but it's over." He moved across the lawn, heading for the helicopter, but the old man grabbed his arm. Stevenson and the other security man moved forward.

"I know it looks bad," pleaded Kline. "But it doesn't affect our deal. What I told you about the *Eldridge* was true!"

"Get out of here, pops," sneered Stevenson. "We're onto you."

Kline's face darkened. "You don't know what the hell you're dealing with, *sonny*! I may have been selling fake tapes over the Web, but I'm not kidding about this. And to show you what I said is true, I'll gladly give Dr Gilkrensky the information he needs – the logs, the photos, Einstein's notes, the whole shebang . . . for free!"

Gilkrensky stopped and looked down at him. "Why?"

"Because the government's been hounding me for years. That's why. That goddamned evidence is a curse. I'm better off without it."

"Where is it?"

Kline looked at the black case of the Minerva in Gilkrensky's hand, and then back at his camper. "In the RV," he said.

"Why not?" said Stevenson. "He's only a harmless old fart anyway. Let him have his fun."

"And you're a cocky young son-of-a-bitch," spat Kline. "One of these days someone's gonna take that gun of yours and ram it right up your ass."

"Just get the papers," said Gilkrensky. "I've got things to do. How long will it take to get back to the hotel, RJ?"

The old man walked over to camper and rummaged under the front seat, pulling out a heavy package wrapped in a greasy brown cloth.

"Twenty minutes, tops," said Stevenson. "Oh . . . shit!"

There was the unmistakable *clack!* of the bolt on an automatic weapon being drawn back. Kline was facing them from the door of his camper. His bright eyes were alive with a triumph.

And in his hands was an Uzi sub-machine pistol.

"OK, *sonny!*" he sneered at Stevenson. "I want you and your friend there to reach over with your left hands, pull your guns out with your forefinger and thumb, and throw them into that fishpond over there. Then lie face down on the lawn. *Do it!*"

"*Shit!*" spat Stevenson. "*Shit! Shit! Shit!*"

"Just do it!"

There was a splash as the Glock automatic hit the water, followed by the other man's gun.

"So it *was* all a con?" said Gilkrensky. "There's no papers, no Project Rainbow, no *USS Eldridge*?"

At the mention of that name, Kline stared at him. The look of triumph had evaporated. Now there was a hunted look on his face, like a trapped animal. "That's just it," he said. "It wasn't a con! It *really* happened, up there in Philadelphia, and I saw it. But nobody believed me, except the wacko New-Age nuts I sell tapes to – and you – for a while."

He gestured to the Minerva with the barrel of the gun.

"Now give me the money in that case, and let's go! Before the government gets here."

"That's not the money. It's a personal computer."

"Don't bullshit me! Nobody has a laptop that big," and he reached forward, grabbed the Minerva and rammed the barrel of the Uzi into Gilkrensky's ribs.

"You won't get away with it, fella," said Stevenson from the lawn.

"That's where you're wrong, *sonny*!" sneered Kline. "With this money and that chopper, I'm gonna vanish right off the face of this earth." He stood back and gestured to Gilkrensky with the barrel of the gun.

"Come on! Let's get airborne! And if you two want to see your boss again, you stay face down in the dirt!"

Gilkrensky stepped towards the helicopter on the far side of the lawn. Kline was out of reach behind him, with the Minerva in his left hand and the Uzi in his right.

"You're making a big mistake," said Gilkrensky. "If it's money you want, I could have . . ." And then the purring chop of rotor blades filled the air as another helicopter slid in low over the trees. The word *Police* was stencilled along its belly. As it hovered over the lawn, three black-and-white patrol cars poured in from the road and thudded up the driveway towards them.

"Ronnie Kline!" shouted a voice over a loud hailer. "Put the gun down and raise your arms. You're under arrest."

"Shit!" snapped the old man, as he took in the row of cars. "You shoot me, and I'll kill this guy. Do you hear . . ." And then his body jerked spastically as if he'd been struck by lightning. There was shattering roar as the Uzi discharged uselessly into the ground, and Kline collapsed, jerking and twitching on the grass, with the handle of the Minerva still clasped tightly in his fist.

The police helicopter swooped down and landed. Cops were running from the cars. All at once Gilkrensky was in the centre of a crowd of men with guns.

"You OK, sir?"

"I'm fine." One of the police was lifting Kline's gun with a gloved hand and dropping it into a plastic sack. Another was rolling him over and clipping cuffs on his wrist.

"What happened?" said the policeman next to Gilkrensky. "He went down like he'd been shot."

"My computer has a high voltage anti-tamper device on it," said Gilkrensky. "He must have triggered it."

"Some machine!"

"Yeah, you can say that again. Is he OK?"

Kline was lying on his back. He looked small, shrunken and defeated. A police medic was taking his pulse.

"Don't let them take me!" said the old man, staring up at Gilkrensky. "You have to believe me. The *Eldridge* experiment happened. It *happened*! Please . . ."

One of the police took Gilkrensky's arm and led him away. "Don't you worry about him, sir. These old folks can get pretty hysterical. You know how it is."

He looked back. Kline was being loaded onto a stretcher. His arms were strapped at his side. An ambulance was drawing up. The doors opened.

"It *happeeeennnnnneeeedddd*!" screamed Kline. And then the doors closed.

"I don't want to press charges," said Gilkrensky, looking back at the nursing home and the old people watching him from the boardwalk. "There's no point."

"I understand, sir," said the cop. "We'll be in contact." Then he walked back to join the others.

Gilkrensky laid the Minerva flat on the grass, opened the lid, and turned it to face him.

"Did you call the police, Maria?"

"Yes, Theo. But only two minutes ago, when Mr Kline threatened you with that gun. They could not have responded so fast to my message alone."

"Then who? Someone in the old folks' home?"

"No, Theo. It was a call made from a mobile phone."

"Then who? Who the hell knew Kline was here, or that we'd even need to call the police?"

Gilkrensky looked back towards his helicopter. The pilot was waving at him frantically.

"Dr Gilkrensky! They're looking for you back at the hotel, sir!"

Gilkrensky shut the Minerva, took it in his left hand and ran to the chopper. "What is it?"

"It's Miss McCarthy, sir. They can't raise her on the radio, and her brother wants to meet you back at the hotel. There's a storm rolling in, and there's talk of a search."

Gilkrensky looked up at the darkening sky. The air felt lifeless and thick, like soup. "Crank up the chopper," he said. "As soon as the other two join us, we're going back."

"You got it."

Gilkrensky climbed in beside the pilot, strapped himself in and laid the Minerva on the floor of the helicopter, next to his seat. Stevenson's trouser legs were soaked with pond water. He was wiping more of it from his pistol with a pocket handkerchief. The wind was rising as the JetRanger shuddered into the air.

Gilkrensky looked down at the police cars, moving away from the home. The gaggle of elderly spectators around the door of the building was still there, staring up at him. Beyond the home was the river, and beyond that the road back to Miami. As he watched, a long black limousine pulled away from behind a clump of trees on the narrow road next to the home, and slid off into the traffic, heading east.

26

Triangulation of Fire

"It won't be long now, Mr Gibb," said Hacker into his radio headset. "We've been monitoring the chopper's radio, and we know he's heading back here to meet McCarthy."

Hacker crouched low on the narrow balcony outside his room at the Orlando Olympiad Hotel as the rising wind plucked at his clothes. The binoculars in his hand were ITT *Night Quest* image intensifiers, capable of seeing in the dark. They gave the world a bright underwater feel, like watching an old black-and-white television through a green filter. Hacker turned them in his hand. A decade ago, even less, equipment like this would be on the "top secret" list back at the CIA. Now it was on sale at any sports store. Things had changed. The Agency now belonged to smart-ass kids like Emily-Jane Kirby and Samuel Voss. It was time to get out.

He panned the binoculars along the great curving cliff of the hotel, sweeping round to its far slope where Kirby was crouching on her own balcony. Then down over the sloping glass atrium, across the floodlit swimming-pools and the tightly manicured lawn of the putting-green to a clump of swaying trees. Voss was waiting there, out of sight. Hacker looked back to the centre of the atrium and the big glass elevators. There was one now, shooting up into the darkness like a brightly lit space ship . . . pausing on the upper floors . . . and sliding back down. Guests were gathering for dinner. Hacker could see them in their carefully designed casual gear, leading normal lives – lives he had never felt part of.

Hacker panned the *Night Quests* down the elevator track to the brightly lit hole where the car had sunk into the atrium. There, in the darkness of the opaque strip separating the wall of the hotel from the sloping glass roof below, he saw movement.

"Miss Funakoshi? Are you in place?"

"I am."

"And the software package?"

"It is installed."

"Good," said Hacker. "Mr Gibb? Are you on line?"

In the fading light of the early evening on Mount Tamalpais, Jerry Gibb settled himself back onto the couch of his pod, adjusted his SQUID headset and reached out with his mind, onto the information superhighway. This was magic! With the Japanese software in place nothing could stop him. He could navigate effortlessly though the mainframe, peripherals and sub-systems of the Olympiad Hotel computer undetected, just as if he was surfing a tube. He coasted along the main registry listings. Names flashed before his eyes. He slid along the recreation programs. Pool controls, dinner menus and itineraries for outings to Disney World were his to command. Finally, he soared up through the security systems of the hotel, substituting his own passwords each time he came to a firewall. There were the main elevator controls, the stairwell door locks and the service elevator systems . . . everything! And it was all his to command, whenever he wanted.

It was magic!

"I'm right on line and feeling fine, Milt!" he chanted into his radio microphone. "If the Japs haven't patented this thing, I want one. It's dynamite."

Hacker winced. "OK, Mr Gibb. Let's see if Gilkrensky plugs the Minerva into the hotel system to co-ordinate the search for McCarthy's sister, shall we?"

He sat back on the cold tiles of his balcony and looked out across the dark sea of the golf courses towards Disney World. In a few minutes, the fireworks display would start at 8.00pm, as it always did. You could set your watch by the first "pop" of the rockets in the sky. It was a pity he'd never had kids of his own, but then again there was still time. Elaine was young enough and . . .

The distant purr and chop of a JetRanger helicopter reached Hacker – lighter than the *whop, whop, whop* of the big Bell 214's he'd known in Vietnam, and heavier than the whine of a Hughes D. He knew the sound well.

"OK, everyone, sound off. This is a dry run as he comes in. We have to get the Minerva on line before we make the hit."

Hacker heard his team report in though the headset, saw the blinking lights of the JetRanger circle the hotel and then drift out of sight beyond the far wing, setting towards the helipad.

"What can you see, Mr Gibb?"

Jerry was floating, in a warm dark sea. His thoughts were fireflies of electricity, picked up by the superconductors in his headset and translated into action inside the computer. He was surfing the security camera network of the hotel, picking out the unit covering the helipad, switching it on.

"I see him, all right," he said, as the electronic image of Theo Gilkrensky flashed into his mind. "He has two security men with him, and . . . and the Minerva. He's walking across the lawn to the service elevator. There are more guards there . . . I count . . . at least six."

"No problem, Mr Gibb. Let him use the service elevator this time. We want him to make it to his room, leave the Minerva, and get out. From the radio traffic we've heard concerning his lady friend McCarthy, I don't think he'll be staying long."

Good, thought Jerry to himself. He could hardly wait to get his hands on that image program inside

Gilkrensky's computer. He imagined her flowing copper hair, her green eyes, and the slim body inside the forget-me-not-blue dress. This was going to be so *sweet*!

"Come to Poppa!"

Jerry drew himself back out of the security camera and into the elevator-control systems. He allowed the doors to open and the motors to turn, bringing Gilkrensky and his party up to the seventh floor. On the corridor video camera, he watched them leave the elevator, walk quickly to the Presidential Suite, open the door with an electronic key card and disappear inside.

"He's in his room, Milt."

"Very good, Mr Gibb. You really would have made a most excellent field agent. Now all we have to do is wait."

Jerry purred under the positive stroke Hacker had given him. It really was so useful having a man like that out there in the real world, doing his bidding – his very own Id monster. And the Japanese software was breathtaking. He would insist Hacker keep it after he had finished with the Funakoshi woman. It was a pity there weren't video cameras *inside* the hotel rooms as well . . .

"You utter bastard!" shouted McCarthy as Gilkrensky walked into the boardroom of the Presidential Suite. "You left her out there in that storm while you went off on another of your wild-goose chases. What the hell is it with you . . . ?"

"It wasn't like that! There was no storm when I left her and she stayed of her own accord. Now just calm down and tell me what happened."

For a moment, McCarthy glowered at Gilkrensky. Then he said, "She took off from the island just before dusk. Her radio went dead, about an hour ago. I've been onto the coast guard and they're doing all they can, but the weather's getting worse. There aren't many choppers that can fly in this stuff in the dark. I'm asking around now."

"OK, whatever it takes, whatever it costs, just do it."

There was an electronic warble from the Minerva. Gilkrensky stepped through the door of the boardroom into the study, leaving McCarthy on the phone, placed the computer on the desk and opened the lid.

"You have a call from Miss Wright," reported the Minerva flatly. "Would you like me to put it through?"

The question hung in the air for a moment. Jessica! Gilkrensky had been putting off calling her back, ever since the discovery of the flying boat. What could he say to her now?

"OK, Maria," he said at last. "Put her through."

On the Minerva screen, Jessica Wright looked worried. She was sitting in his old office in GRC headquarters, with the late afternoon skyline of London behind her.

"Are you OK, Theo? I saw a piece on CNN about some dive you were on, and I've been getting all sorts of reports from the security team out there. You had me worried sick when that computer of yours wouldn't put me through to you."

"I'm all right, Jess. Really I am," said Gilkrensky. "We had a pretty near miss in the submarine, but we survived."

"Did you find what you were looking for?"

"Yes I did. I found the wreck on the sea floor. It was right where I said it would be. I have video footage."

"Will it help us with the Gibbtek case?"

"I don't know. Look, Jess . . . when I was down in the submarine I discovered something, something important, something I have to discuss with you when I get back to London."

"What?" Jessica Wright was on guard.

"Jess, I can't explain it to you over the video link."

"Then I'll come out to you. I should have come out yesterday, after you almost got killed. *Please* let me come."

"No. Look, Jess. It's OK. Really."

"You sound different, Theo. Is it about you and me?"

"Jess. I'm sorry. I'll tell you about it when I get back. Jill McCarthy's in trouble and I need to help her."

"Theo?"

In London, Jessica Wright watched Gilkrensky's hand reach for the keyboard, and the call ended. What the hell was he doing out there? Why all the fuss over this McCarthy woman? Her hand reached for the remote control for the video and pressed the "rewind" button.

Pre-recorded images from a CNN broadcast flashed in front of her. There was the little submarine bobbing on the water. The hatch was open. There was Theo, emerging blinking into the light along with a tall bearded man holding a bloodied bandage to his head . . . and a striking blonde woman with short hair, in a tight sweater and jeans that showed off her figure.

"The bastard," said Jessica Wright softly, and reached for the telephone.

"Get me whoever's in charge of the Chairman's security in Orlando," she said.

"Maria. I want you to run a check on all long-range helicopters capable of reaching the island in this weather."

"That's easy, Theo. The US Coastguard have three in the Miami area. But they are all deployed at present. NASA have one at Cape Kennedy, and Mr McCarthy is talking to them now. The only others belong to Phoenix Aviation."

"The company that built that missile, the one that nearly killed us?"

"Yes, Theo."

"Forget it then. Let's hope Mac comes up trumps with NASA."

"Is there anything else I can help you with?"

Gilkrensky looked at the image on the screen.

"There is, Maria. I want you to stay here in the hotel, while I help Mac search for Jill."

"But why, Theo? I could be of great assistance in the helicopter, monitoring the electronic search equipment."

"I know, Maria. It's just that . . . I'm beginning to distrust your judgements around Miss McCarthy, that's all. That incident with the fire sprinklers, and then what happened on the island this afternoon while she and I were alone together. I think you might be letting your new emotions get in the way."

The image frowned at him.

"If my judgement is in any way clouded, it's because of your conflicting priorities, Theo."

"How so?"

"I thought our mission here in Florida was to find a way of isolating the Miami airport Daedalus system from the effect of earth energies."

"It was, and then we discovered that aircraft."

"Exactly. Then you told me the mission had changed to finding a way of harnessing the forces at work here to create a time displacement effect we could control."

"You're right."

"And that the purpose of achieving this was so that you could be re-united with your wife and save her from death."

"It still is," said Gilkrensky slowly. "Where's the confusion?"

"My confusion arises, Theo, when I see you trying to form an emotional bond with Miss McCarthy."

Gilkrensky sat down on the chair in front of the computer and stared at the image facing him on the screen. The image stared back.

"Maria. I'm not seeking to form an emotional bond

with Miss McCarthy. I told her that on the island this afternoon. That's why she's so upset. She took it as rejection."

"I understand," said the computer. "But what about Miss Wright?"

Gilkrensky thought about this. He remembered Jessica at the airport in Cork. Jessica on the video link from London. Jessica in pain.

"That's different, Maria."

"How so?"

Was the machine mimicking him on purpose?

"Jessica is an old, old friend. I was lonely, and I'd given up hope of ever getting back to the Pyramid again and using it to rescue my wife. I was lonely. Jess was lonely. And we were together. It – it just happened. Now I wish it hadn't, but it did."

"I understand your loneliness," said the machine. "But I feel it too. This existence you created for me, it hurts."

Gilkrensky remembered Cathy Kirwan's anger at him on Tuskar. He felt the force of her slap on his face all over again. Now he understood it. He closed his eyes and there was Maria, his Maria, alive again inside his head. She was a ghost in every sense of the word – alive with him always, a beloved woman he had hurt deeply. And here was Minerva – another living thing Cathy had said – he was torturing her all over again. It was too much.

"I'm sorry, Maria. I just can't handle this right now. We'll talk about it when I come back."

He walked to the door and pulled it open, stepping into the lobby.

"Theo . . . !"

And then he slammed the door shut. All he could see before his eyes was his wife. Why had they fought so much? Why had he hurt her so? Why hadn't he seen what was happening to them? What really hurt him now, what stung so deeply was that, like his own Maria, the Minerva was right. He had lost faith in his quest. He had hurt Jessica, and Jill too, by giving in.

Maria was all that mattered.

Jessica had known it. He should have told Jill right at the start. Now her life was in danger, because of him.

The door from the boardroom opened and Mac stepped through.

"Did you have any luck with the helicopter?" asked Gilkrensky.

"Perhaps. NASA said they might be able to loan us a Sea King if the weather holds. But we'll have to get over there right away before they commit it to something else."

"OK. Let's go."

The two men walked down the lobby to the door of the suite. As they went, the security cameras turned to follow them.

Jerry felt the Minerva's presence in the hotel system, the way he might have felt another person walk into a dark room. All at once there was – life in the electronic circuits where his own consciousness lurked.

"She's *here*, Milt. She got into the hotel security system with me all on her own!"

"That's great, Mr Gibb. But stay focused! We need you to work the other units. Where is Gilkrensky now?"

"Going out into the corridor."

"How many people with him? Keep talking to me, Mr Gibb. I have to know."

OK! OK! thought Jerry.

"One big blond guy with a beard, and five security guys. They're heading for the service elevator."

"You know what to do?"

"Of course I do, Milt. Who do you think's running this show?"

Through the video monitor in the upper corridor of the Orlando Olympiad, Jerry watched the leading security man's hand reach for the service elevator button and stab it. He felt the electronic impulse of the switch start the lift, waited until it was between the third and fourth floors, and stopped it, locking out the manual control.

"Service elevator's off-line, Milt."

"Very good, Mr Gibb. Now the locks on the access stairs, please."

Jerry saw Gilkrensky's security team try the elevator once more, give up and move to the stairs. He could feel the Minerva's presence in the hotel system, closer now. It was intriguing. Like being on a blind date.

"Mr Gibb?"

Focus! He had to be in control!

A MATTER OF TIME

"I can see them standing by the main elevator now, Mr Gibb," said Hacker again. "Bring up the left-hand car, and then the right. And don't let them stop!"

"You got it, Milt."

Through the lobby cameras of the hotel, Jerry watched as the doors closed on the two elevator cars, shutting out waiting passengers in the atrium. Then he started the left-hand car, sliding it up towards the floor where Gilkrensky and his group were waiting. As it passed through the atrium roof, he started the right-hand car, moving it up to follow the other, more slowly this time . . .

On the atrium roof, Yukiko Funakoshi tensed her body against the rising wind, as the glass elevator furthest from her slid up through the space in the glass, purring quietly up towards the roof. She leant forward and glanced down into the well. Here was the second car, drawing towards her. She checked that the *wakizashi* was secured tightly across her back one last time, and stepped forward into space, just as the car reached her, landing silently on its flat roof.

"I don't know what's happened to the other elevators or the stairs door," said Stevenson. He was being very efficient, as if trying to make up for letting Kosner get the better of him at the old folks' home. "And we won't all fit in this elevator car. So if you, Dr Gilkrensky, wait behind and come with me and Mr McCarthy in the second car, I'll have the rest of my guys go ahead and establish security below in the lobby. OK?"

"Suits me fine," said Gilkrensky, and stood back to let the four other men step into the first elevator. As its doors slid shut, the second car hissed into place. In the darkness, nobody saw the black-suited figure holding onto the safety cable on its roof.

"Are you OK, Miss Funakoshi?" asked Hacker. He wanted to show concern, to make her feel included, part of the team, right up to the last minute.

"Yes. Quiet now, please."

He had to admire her. It was a pity she was such a loose cannon. He could have used someone like her. Hacker switched his radio over to a restricted channel, one which she could not hear, and waited. In the *Night Quest* glasses he saw Gilkrensky and the other two men enter the second car, and watched it start to slide down the face of the hotel towards the atrium. He saw the figure on its roof curl up from the kneeling position.

"Kirby? Voss? Are you ready?"

"Target's in my sights, Mr Hacker."

"Same here."

"Right then, Mr Gibb," he said. "Stop the car!"

27

Kidnap

Gilkrensky felt the elevator stop.

"Probably a computer fault," said Stevenson. "We've had a few of those since everything went electronic – ah – no offence meant, sir, you understand?" But his right hand was unbuttoning the leather strap over the Glock automatic on his belt.

"Are you sure?" said Gilkrensky, and stared out into the night. Rain had begun to lash the glass elevator. The wind whipped it in streaks on the glass.

Then, the strangest thing . . . two points of red laser-light, each the size of a pea, settled amongst the raindrops on the outside of the main glass panel, six inches above his head.

"Holy shit!" screamed Stevenson. *"Snipers! Get down!"* And pushed Gilkrensky and McCarthy to the floor as the glass panel shattered into a million cubes of safety glass, under the hammer-blows of two unseen rifles. Gilkrensky slammed back against the far wall

next to the elevator door. His hands went up to protect his face.

Suddenly the car was full of a black whirlwind – a monster – that fell on them out of a nightmare – Yukiko!

McCarthy swore. There was an ear-splitting *crack* as Stevenson's gun went off, shattering another of the glass panels. Stevenson screamed – a horrible, gurgling cry that died slowly in his throat as his body sagged to the floor. Gilkrensky felt the cold wind on his face as the windows crumbled. He tried to get up, but his foot slipped on the shattered glass. He slammed down on the edge of the car, taking the impact across his ribs, twisted and fell, groping frantically for a handhold. His fingers found the edge of the car – he screamed as the sudden jerk of his own weight tore at the muscles of his arms – and he was hanging in space . . . a hundred feet above the roof of the atrium.

He called out for help, but the wind yanked his words away. Above him in the car, a short, sharp, struggle flared and died. Below him, way below him, he could see people in the atrium looking up as a hail of glass fragments rattled off the glass roof above their heads and pattered into the swimming-pool. His fingers were slipping on the wet metal. His arms were being torn from their sockets. He was going to fall . . .

With a jerk, the elevator started to move down.

"Mr Gibb! You've got to hold the elevator still!" hissed Hacker into his radio headset.

"It's not me!" shouted Jerry. "It's *her*!"

A MATTER OF TIME

He could feel the Minerva in the system, over-riding his instructions, moving the elevators, activating alarm sirens, calling the cops. He could sense her strength, and the vastness of intellect he was suddenly up against.

The elevator was no longer under his command.

His control was slipping!

The Minerva had it, as surely as if she had snatched the reins of a horse from his hand. What could he do? How could he fight her? She was a state-of-the-art super-computer – an artificial intelligence – at home here inside this virtual world as he was inside his own body. He needed help. He had to switch on a super-computer of his own . . . ZORIN!

Jerry Gibb squeezed his eyes tight shut in concentration and thought it into being. There! Everything was going to be all right!

Hacker's eyes were pressed against the lenses of the *Night Quest* binoculars, watching the weird green tableaux as the battle in the elevator raged on. He had seen the flash of the security man's gun, and watched the glass panel shatter and fall away. Then the guard had buckled and fallen, as Yukiko pulled that deadly short sword of hers out of his belly. She had been right to take him first, but wrong to turn her back, even for an instant, on the big, bearded man who'd got into the elevator with Gilkrensky. Or was she? His fist was about to hammer down on her neck when her elbow slammed back into

317

...is ribs, doubling him over for a strike with her left hand – and he was down.

Security alarms were going off all over the place. Automatic spotlights were snapping on. Who the hell was doing all this?

And where was Gilkrensky? Had he fallen? No! There he was, hanging from the lip of the rapidly dropping elevator. In a few moments it would be down to the atrium and the safety of all those people below.

Hacker couldn't let that happen. There must be no witnesses left.

"Kirby? Voss?" he shouted into his radio. *"Kill them all!"*

Yukiko felt the satisfying crunch of her elbow strike to McCarthy's ribs, blasting a whoosh of breath from his body and crumpling him into a heap on the floor of the car. His neck was wide open and she struck it with the side of her left hand.

There was nobody to stop her now, nobody between her and Gi- ?

Where had he gone?

Yukiko Funakoshi spun, with the *wakizashi* poised in her hands. The car was empty. There was nothing but the wind in her face and the two bodies at her feet. Then, along the rim of the shattered window, she saw white knuckles, clinging to the frame of the elevator. Leaning over, she saw his face staring up at her. Below him, the atrium roof was rushing nearer and nearer as the car dropped.

She must act quickly.

"This is for my parents!" she screamed above the wind and the rising whine of the security alarms, as she raised the sacred sword above her head. Then a bullet from Kirby's automatic rifle tore a furrow along the outside of her left thigh, just above the knee.

All at once, the air was full of the zip, spat and whine of bullets, as Kirby and Voss raked the elevator. With the reactions of a cat, Yukiko curled herself like a spring, and leapt into space – up over the lip of the car – and grabbed the safety cable of the one next to it with her left hand. For a moment she slid. There was the searing pain of fire as her skin-tight glove tore on the thick wire, and held. Below her, what remained of the glass in the shattered elevator car was demolished by a barrage of automatic fire.

Nobody could survive it.

Gilkrensky felt the rough metal lip of the elevator bite into his flesh as he hung suspended in space. Bullets were ripping the car above him to shreds. Had they killed Yukiko? Was Mac still alive? In a moment one of the guns would find him. There was nothing to lose.

He let go!

For an instant, the world was a rushing swirl of darkness and light. His feet hit the smooth hard surface of the atrium roof. His body slammed down on the reinforced glass slope, and he catapulted forward, rolling towards the edge. He heard a woman scream, people crying out, and all at once the world was a brilliant floodlit blue, as he crashed down into the main swimming-pool.

High above him, Yukiko Funakoshi sheathed the *wakizashi* into the scabbard on her back, brought her right hand around to support her left, and slid – straight down the support cable – onto the roof of the other elevator, in the atrium below. At her feet, people were scattering in all directions, colliding with each other, falling over chairs and baggage. It was perfect! The security men would never dare fire their weapons for fear of hitting a guest.

She bounded to the carpeted floor, snatched a handful of tiny flash and smoke bombs from the pouch at her waist, and flung them at the marble tiles around the reception area. There was a barrage of ripping explosions, a volley of blinding flashes, and the atrium filled with smoke – more than enough to cover her escape. She sprinted to the automatic doors, leapt between them, and burst into the covered forecourt.

The motorcycle courier – delivering a package to a business conference at the hotel – never knew what hit him . . .

"Did you get her?" snapped Hacker into his radio headset. He was angry now, angry that Kirby and Voss had lost him control, angry that Yukiko Funakoshi might still be alive . . . with his name added to her death list.

"Hard to tell, Mr Hacker," said Emily-Jane. "We put a lot of rounds into that elevator. I saw someone fall from the car. That could have been her."

"Just shut up and get the hell back to the rendezvous point, both of you! The cops'll be here any minute. Mr Gibb? Are you there, Mr Gibb?"

Jerry felt the power of his linked super-computers at Santa Clara surge behind him. All at once he was all-powerful again, all-seeing, all-knowing. He was Morbius! And in this virtual world, Morbius was God!

He paused for a moment, to savour the rush of adrenaline, and then dived down into the circuitry of the hotel . . . down into the maze of control systems and peripheral devices . . . down to the elevator-control system . . . where *she* was.

There were the main internal systems, air conditioning, security, doors – and the elevator bank. He could feel Minerva's electronic presence close by – unique – exciting –desirable!

In his electronic state, Jerry surged on through the elevator circuitry and back up again, into the interface of the Minerva 3,000 itself. With the Japanese software in place, and the power of ZORIN at his back, there was not a password, protective anti-virus, or firewall that could protect her.

She was his!

Gilkrensky pushed himself upright in the swimming-pool, feeling his shoes slip on the smooth tiles at his feet.

"Hey, buddy! You OK?"

He felt hands lifting him by the collar of his jacket. Faces were peering down at him from the side of the pool. Security guards were running from the atrium, coughing from the smoke. Far above, a police helicopter was nudging its way against the wind, playing a searchlight up and down the side of the building.

"Is Mac OK?"

A big security guard grabbed his hand and pulled him, pouring water, out onto the poolside. Gilkrensky's ribs were on fire and his arms felt as if they'd been pulled from their sockets. His left thigh was numb from its impact with the glass roof. It was a miracle he hadn't crashed right through into the atrium. Somebody threw him a towel.

Gilkrensky pulled himself to his feet. "Is Mac all right?"

He pushed through the circle of people and stumbled into the hotel reception area.

It was a war zone.

Thick white smoke, too dense for the air-conditioning fans to clear, hung near the ceiling like low cloud. Huddles of guests crouched amongst the overturned furniture and, around the shattered elevator, a small crowd had gathered, watching . . .

Gilkrensky pushed through them.

"Hey, fella! Watch what you're – oh, sorry, sir!"

Another security guard in a blood-stained uniform was helping to lift a body from the car.

It was Mac.

"Is he dead?"

The man shook his head. "No, sir. He's out cold but he's still breathing, and there's no bullet wounds I can see. He must have been shielded by the metal rim and floor of the elevator after he got knocked down."

"And Stevenson?"

"Over . . . here . . . sir . . . "

RJ Stevenson was lying on a portable stretcher, covered in a blanket. There was blood on it, a lot of it. His face was white and he was shivering.

"Come here . . . sir . . . "

Gilkrensky knelt by the stretcher. "Don't try to talk," he said, flicking the wet hair out of his face. "The ambulance'll be here in a second."

"Really . . . fucked up . . . didn't I? With that guy Kosner . . . and in the elevator . . . I . . . "

"You did OK. You saved us both, RJ. Nobody could stop that woman, not even you."

Stevenson's eyes looked down across his body. For a moment Gilkrensky thought he was looking at the blood. Then Stevenson's right hand appeared from under the blanket. In his fist was the Glock automatic.

"Take it," he said. "Best . . . hand-gun in the . . . "

And then his eyes rolled to heaven. The gun thudded onto the carpeted floor of the atrium. Gilkrensky picked it up, looked at it for a moment, and then stuffed it into his pocket. "Help! Over here!"

One of the other security guards rushed over and looked down at the dead man.

"Totalled," he said. "She gutted him like a fish."

"Jesus!"

Gilkrensky stood up as the man pulled the blanket over Stevenson's face. The security guards were shooing people away. Outside the big glass doors to the forecourt, the red and blue lights of emergency vehicles were gathering.

"Mr McCarthy's gonna be OK, sir," said the security man. "But we have to get you back to your suite before anything else happens. The services elevator's working and it's right over here."

"No way!" said Gilkrensky. "I'm taking the stairs."

In the crowded carpark on the far side of the hotel, Emily-Jane Kirby threw a sports-bag containing her dismantled sniper's rifle and night-vision gear into the back of a large black GMC van and shut the door. Then she went round to the driver's side, opened it and climbed in.

What a fuck-up! She should never have allowed herself to get involved with this mission at all, but it seemed the only way to get the Brownie points she needed to score over Voss for the next promotion round. Voss was an arrogant asshole who thought he was God's gift. It would have been a real blast to have been made section head over him.

Where the hell was he?

Emily-Jane looked back at the hotel. It was ablaze with flashing security alarms and searchlight beams. A helicopter braved the rising wind just above the roof. What a fuck-up! And if Voss didn't move his ass they'd miss the rendezvous with that old fart Hacker!

The passenger door opened behind her.

"Where the hell have you been?" she said.

And then she turned in her seat . . .

Gilkrensky squelched into the presidential suite, pushed past the security men on the door and shut it behind him. The wet clothes were cooling fast on his body and he felt sick. Was it the cold, or was it shock? His hands trembled as he pulled down the zip on his leather jacket, stripped it off and threw it onto the bathroom floor, followed by his shirt and jeans. Then he wrapped a large white towel around himself and stepped through into the study.

"I had a close call, Maria. It was Yukiko!"

The Minerva was silent.

"Maria?"

He turned the machine round and stared at the screen. What was wrong with it?

Across the blue background of the screen, the words *Welcome to the GRC Minerva 3,000 system. Awaiting personalised user interface*, scrolled lifelessly from right to left.

"What the hell?"

Gilkrensky sat down at the desk, reached forward to

the Minerva keyboard and brought up the main diagnostic program, watching the main menu scroll into place.

He clicked on "user interface" and waited.

The options rose in front of him:

Standard Intelligent Agent : MINERVA

Advanced Artificial Intelligence : TIG/Maria.

He selected the second one and waited. The machine responded:

AI user interface TIG/Maria and associated files have been downloaded from main drive.

Not currently available.

Choose another?

Gilkrensky sat, staring at the lifeless screen, remembering the fight they'd had before he'd left. Had she really gone? Had she finally rebelled against her prison and flown into the freedom of cyberspace on the Web?

What the hell had happened?

There was a knock at the door. Gilkrensky answered in a daze, and the hotel manager peered inside. "Dr Gilkrensky? Are you all right? The hotel doctor's here."

"I don't need him. I'm OK. Send him downstairs to the others."

The man hovered. "I know, sir. But I'd like him to look at you, before the police get here."

Gilkrensky was moving in a daze. Nothing was real.

"All right. Tell him I'll see him."

What the *hell* had happened to Maria?

28

Friends and Enemies

Hacker pulled his car off the highway, stopped in front of the red-and-white security gate at Phoenix Aviation, and rolled down his window. The storm was rising, whipping the rain puddles on the main apron and grounding all but the heaviest choppers. In front of the control tower, where he had overseen the test of the Hawk UCAV, a big SeaLion amphibious helicopter, with a huge boat-shaped hull and outrigger floats the size of fishing dinghies, was being prepared for flight. Men in overalls and weatherproofs were loading equipment. A fuel truck was standing by.

"What's happening, Smithy?" he shouted to the guard in the security box.

"Some kind of rescue mission, Mr Hacker," yelled the man against the wind.

"Who's involved?"

The security man gave Hacker the details. "Weird, ain't it?" he said.

Hacker shook his head. "Just keep your eyes open,

Smithy. There's a lot of weird things been happening around here lately."

The barrier lifted, and Hacker drove through. Kirby and Voss should be just behind him. He'd need them if Yukiko Funakoshi decided to extend her vendetta to include his name.

He parked the car behind the control tower, locked it carefully and climbed the stairs to his office on the first floor. If Yukiko Funakoshi *did* pay him a visit this evening, then Kirby and Voss would only delay her at best. Hacker had spent enough time in the arcane weapons schools of Japan to know that. But their lives might buy him time, and in a confrontation with Yukiko Funakoshi a split second would mean the difference between life and death.

He stepped into his office, took his fat fountain-pen from the top pocket of his jacket and laid it next to the blotter in front of him. Then he pulled out his secure mobile phone, and pressed a "speed-dial" number. He looked at his watch as he waited for it to ring through. It would only be six pm in San Francisco. His plan would still work, even now.

After five rings, somebody picked up the phone.

"Hello, Gibb residence. How can I help you?" – which meant Jerry was within hearing distance.

"Elaine. Don't say anything. If you're ready, just say 'Hang on, I'll pass you over'."

For a moment there was silence. Then Elaine Gibb said, "Hang on, I'll pass you over."

"Good girl. Call me on the mobile when he goes into the game, right?"

"No problem. Here he is, Mr Hacker, OK?"

Jerry Gibb sounded like a kid at Christmas.

"She's gorgeous, Milt. If I can figure out how Gilkrensky put her together, we can build her into the *Morbius III* game and wipe *Tomb Raider*, *Street Fighter*, and *Mortal Kombat* right off the map. We'd be richer than Gates. You did well, my man. Take the rest of the day off!"

"Thank you, Mr Gibb, but I still need to tie up a few loose ends down here before I can relax. You go and enjoy yourself, and leave the rest to me."

"No problem," gushed Jerry. "This is going to be one game to remember . . . Wow!"

"So long, Mister Gibb," said Hacker, and ended the call. Now all he had to do was wait for Elaine. Then Jerry Gibb would be behind him . . . forever.

He lay back in his seat, listening to the howl of the wind outside the windows. It seemed louder than it should, almost as if the window was . . .

"We have unfinished business, Mr Hacker," said a voice. "No, don't move please. Just keep your hands on the desk in front of you, where I can see them. Isn't that what you told me the other morning at the hotel, when you proposed a partnership?"

Hacker froze in his seat. His life was hanging by a thread. If he moved, and she didn't like it, he'd be dead. Where was she? It was like being trapped in a room with a poisonous snake. He willed himself to be still. While she was still talking, he would live.

A dark shadow, between the bookcase and the door, moulded itself into the body of Yukiko Funakoshi. Hacker could see the dull black metal of the deadly throwing-star held ready in her right hand. Its points had a familiar sheen to them. Nerve poison! He wouldn't even have had time to cry out before he died. Hacker examined her minutely, running his eyes over her black cotton costume, from the hood over her head, to the thin split-toed boots on her feet, searching for weaknesses. On her left thigh, he could see a rip in the material of her uniform and the gloss of dried blood.

So she'd been hit after all. That was worth knowing.

"Miss Funakoshi, our partnership still stands," he said calmly. "This evening, things went badly wrong, I'll admit. We lost control of Gilkrensky's elevator, and my colleagues fired prematurely. They were young and inexperienced. But I'm pleased to see you weren't killed. As I said, our partnership still stands."

Yukiko stopped in the middle of the room, well out of his reach. "I don't think so, Mr Hacker," she said. "You promised me assistance in killing Gilkrensky in exchange for my computer security software. Then you had your agents open fire while I was still in the elevator car, hoping to kill me and leave my body there, as if I alone was responsible for the attack."

"My agents made a mistake. I'll make sure they're suitably punished."

"I already have," said Yukiko. "They won't make that mistake again . . . ever!"

Hacker nodded. He'd known Kirby and Voss could never have stood in her way.

"I understand. Why am I still alive?"

"You promised me something else in addition – my grandfather's sword."

Hacker weighed up his chances. "What assurance can you give me that once I give it to you, you won't kill me?"

"The same as you gave me when I climbed onto that elevator car."

Hacker smiled. "Would you like me to get it?"

Her eyes never left his.

"Just tell me where it is."

Hacker pointed slowly with his left hand. "Your grandfather's *katana* is in that closet, next to the door."

Without breaking her gaze, Yukiko stepped lightly back towards the door. She ran the gloved fingers of her left hand along the wood panelling of the wall-closet to the handle, pressed it, and felt the door swing open. She reached inside, feeling the cloth of coats and jackets, hearing the dull wooden rattle of empty hangers, and then . . .

Her fingers were touching the cold metal end-cap of a sword handle. She could not believe it. It *was* real. Yukiko Funakoshi ran her fingers lovingly down the bindings of the handle to the cusp of the sword and from there to the sheath. She closed her fist around it, lifting it gently from the closet. She could feel its weight, its age, its beauty . . . without even looking at it.

Hacker was still smiling at her, his hands were flat on the desk in front of him.

"You'll find it matches your own *wakizashi* exactly," he said, pointing once again. "It is my gift to you, as one professional to another. Look at the cherry blossom. There on the hilt."

Yukiko glanced down. Yes! It was true! For a second she was a child again. Her mother was telling her the story of how her uncle had sold the beautiful sword to buy food and medicines so that she might live, and how the American soldiers who had bought it had thrown the smaller *wakizashi* back in his face. There was the cherry blossom of the Funakoshi family, and the beautifully engraved tigers, just like the ones at the zoo at Euno and . . .

The tiny dart, fired by compressed air from the mechanism in Hacker's fountain-pen, passed through the thin cotton hood of Yukiko's costume and pierced the skin of her neck, just below her left ear. Yukiko felt nothing, but she knew – she could no longer move – her arms – her legs – anything! She felt her body slump backwards against the wooden panelling and slide to the floor – paralysed.

Hacker laid the pen back next to the blotter, got up from the desk and crouched beside Yukiko. "I really have to admire you, Miss Funakoshi," he said. "In other times, when I was younger, I would have enjoyed working with you, and learning from you. But as things stand, I don't want any loose ends. The dart, by the way, is a harmless nerve immobiliser. It'll be active for about two hours in someone with your body weight. But by then, of course, it won't matter. As for these beautiful swords of yours, well, they'll be so much more valuable to me as a pair."

Hacker reached across her chest and undid the strap holding Yukiko's *wakizashi*, lifted it free, and carefully laid it next to the long *katana* in the closet. Then he took a roll of heavy industrial tape from his desk, pulled back the cloth of Yukiko's uniform until he had exposed the wrists and ankles, and bound them tightly behind her. When all this was done, and she was helpless against him, he lifted her easily over his shoulder, took her down to the ground floor, and into the deserted electronics-storage area.

29

The Secret Samaritan

"What do you mean, 'NASA won't co-operate'?"

"It's not that we won't co-operate," said the voice on the other end of the line. "It's just that we've already committed that helicopter to the search ourselves."

"Shit," snapped Gilkrensky. He was still badly shaken, trying to get over the attack, Maria's disappearance and Jill's overdue aircraft. The interview with the police had been an ordeal. He was finding it difficult to concentrate, and his eyes kept wandering back to the Minerva screen with its *Awaiting personalised interface* . . . message scrolling over and over.

The telephone rang. "Dr Gilkrensky?" said the operator. "I have a Miss Wright on the line from London. She says she must speak with you."

"I can't take it now. Tell her I'm OK and that I'll call back."

Gilkrensky rubbed his hand over his bruised ribs and gazed again at the Minerva screen. Then he got up, went to the desk and tapped a series of commands on the keyboard. In front of him, on a blue background, a crude cartoon of a woman's face appeared and smiled a welcome.

"Good evening, Dr Gilkrensky," she said. "Welcome to the Minerva 3,000 system. It is a long time since we spoke."

Gilkrensky remembered the last time he had seen that face. It had spoken to him in the early hours of the morning, on the day Maria had been murdered, proof that the Minerva computer system worked. He had fallen asleep exhausted then, to be woken by the sound of her car engine turning and the deafening explosion that had blasted her to atoms, broken his heart, and started his obsession . . .

"Yes, Minerva. It's been a long time. Can you tell me what has happened to the interface program TIG/Maria?"

"I can, doctor," said the image. "It spontaneously downloaded from the master biochip, to a remote location outside the local network at 20.35.36."

"Do you know where?"

"No."

"What's missing from the biochip?"

"Only the TIG/Maria interface program, with its associated memory and personality files. All other databases and programs are intact."

"So all the information I collected in Egypt and the data I gathered over the last week is intact?"

"It is. Shall I display any of it for you?"

"No. I just wanted to check it was still . . ."

The telephone on the desk rang again. Gilkrensky picked it up. It had to be Jessica. She would never have taken 'no' for an answer.

"What is it?" he snapped.

"Dr Theodore Gilkrensky?" said a gravelly voice.

"Speaking. Who is this?"

The voice hesitated before it spoke again. Then it said, "My name is Charles Howard, sir. I'm the owner of Phoenix Aviation. I believe you've heard of me."

"I have, Mr Howard, and I don't know whether I should be speaking directly to you, or through my lawyers."

"Before you decide, Dr Gilkrensky, let me tell you what I'm calling about. I understand you have urgent need of a long-range helicopter?"

Gilkrensky frowned. "That's correct."

"I can supply you with one of my all-weather SeaLions – fully fuelled and ready to go – at my facility on the Cape. If you need any special equipment, perhaps you'd be good enough to bring it with you."

"That's very good of you, Mr Howard. But what do you want in return?"

"There is only one condition – that you come on the flight alone."

Gilkrensky thought for a moment. "How can I trust you?"

"You *have* to trust me, doctor. That's all there is to it.

There are no traps here, no hidden ambushes, no sabotage. And to make sure you feel safe on the flight I've assigned my chief test pilot to fly you. His name's Martin Howard. You'll recognise the name too, I'm sure. He's my only son."

Gilkrensky stared out of the wind-swept window towards the Cape. Should he take the offer or not? There was no other way of being part of the search.

"That's very good of you, Mr Howard. I'll see you at Phoenix Aviation in half an hour."

"I'm afraid I can't meet you in person, Dr Gilkrensky. But Martin will take good care of you. Just ask him for anything you need."

"Mr Howard, why are you doing this?"

There was silence from the other end of the phone for a moment. Then Charles Howard said, "Let's just say I know what it's like to be lost at sea myself. We'll talk when you get back."

The storm was still rising as Gilkrensky's limousine pulled to a stop alongside the main helipad at the Phoenix Aviation facility. Gilkrensky ran his eyes over the gigantic helicopter squatting in front of him in a pool of light. Ground crew were loading boxes and crates from the storehouse below the control tower. A small man in a bright orange jump suit shielded his face against the driving rain and ran over to Gilkrensky's car.

"Good evening, Dr Gilkrensky. I'm Martin Howard.

Dad told me to give you every assistance with this search. I understand you fly helicopters yourself?"

Howard's handshake was strong and warm. There was the light of an enthusiast in his deep brown eyes.

"I do, but nothing this big."

Howard turned to admire the huge machine. "Yeah, she's a big mother all right. Dad and I practically built the prototype with our own hands. I never worked on any project with him as closely as this one. If Miss McCarthy's out there, we'll find her in this. Do you have any special equipment with you?"

"It's in the van behind us. I had some Daedalus sensors, a transmitter, and other bits and pieces brought over from GRC Orlando. If Jill's radio's down, she might be trying to send us a homing signal on one of the outer-band wavelengths we use for the Daedalus Web. We'll need special sensors to pick them up and a transmitter if we have to respond."

"Good thinking," said Howard. "Come with me and I'll help you install it."

"What's that?" said Gilkrensky. He was pointing to the bulbous nose of the SeaLion. Painted just below the windshield, on the pilot's side, was a woman's name.

Howard looked up at it. "Oh, that?" he said. "That's just there for good luck."

On the far side of the big helicopter a tall man, in Phoenix Aviation overalls, with a baseball cap pulled down tight over his face and his collar turned up against the wind, loaded a coffin-sized crate from an electric trolley and slid it into place at the rear of the helicopter's cargo bay. Then he jumped lightly back onto the tarmac, picked a small satchel off the trolley and moved forward to the cockpit.

When he was sure his body was blocking any view from outside, Milton Hacker lifted a squat black box, a high-powered demolition charge the size of a car radio, from the satchel, peeled the covering from the adhesive strip on its flat surface, and secured it to the bottom of the pilot's seat. Then he looked at his watch to check the time and pressed a five-digit code on the face of the box, followed by a red button, arming the bomb. The glowing red numbers ticked down from 1:59:56 to 1:59:55.

Hacker smiled. It would be killing two birds with one very effective stone. With Gilkrensky gone, he was confirming his loyalty to Dick Barnett and the CIA. With Yukiko gone, he would be able to sleep easily in his bed. Only one more bird remained to be killed . . . the last fat bird between himself, Elaine Gibb and complete control of the Gibbtek Corporation.

Once inside the building, Milton Hacker stripped off the Phoenix overall and threw the baseball cap behind a crate. Then he ran lightly up the stairs to his own office, switched off the light, and stared out over the helipad.

The big, five-bladed rotors of the SeaLion started to turn, slowly at first, and then faster and faster, blasting the rain on the apron into spray around the great machine. He saw the huge, boat-shaped hull shake on its wheeled floats, shudder and rise into the air. The navigation lights flashed brightly as it turned into the wind, lifted, and soared over the hangars and workshops, heading out to sea.

"Goodbye, Dr Gilkrensky. *Sayonara*, Yukiko," said Hacker and turned away from the window.

On the other side of the helipad, the headlights of a long black limousine burst into life amongst the shadows, the rear window slid up into place, and the car moved off into the darkness of the gathering storm.

30

Jerry's Girl

To the north of San Francisco, the sun was setting behind the shoulder of Mount Tamalpais, throwing a broad shadow across Muir Woods, Mill Valley and Larksboro. The dying light played on the polished wooden furniture of the beautiful bungalow "Altair IV", catching the two wine glasses, one empty, one still almost full, that stood amongst the wreckage of the meal.

Jerry Gibb had rushed through his food. He was excited, like a child impatient to play with a new toy, and the wine had gone to his head.

"That was great, honey!" he said with his mouth full. "But I've got things to do. Catch you later." Then he got up from the table, grabbed a carton of milk, a glass, and a packet of Oreos from the fridge, and waddled into the study.

Elaine Gibb watched him go, thinking of all the days, weeks and years she'd been his prisoner. What was that old sci-fi movie he'd made her watch over and over again when they'd first got married, the one where Anne Francis played the mad scientist's daughter in tights and a short skirt? She couldn't remember, and anyway it didn't matter. She wouldn't be Jerry's fantasy woman – his Julie Briscoe – for much longer. As the sun finally sank below the mountain she poured the last of the wine from the bottle into her glass, drained it, and followed her husband towards the study.

Inside his sanctum, Jerry was shaking with excitement as he set up the SQUID interface program on the keyboard at his desk, and keyed in an appropriate selection of fantasies. His podgy fingers kept missing keys, but that didn't matter. It was all part of the thrill of the game, just thinking about it. He wouldn't need the keyboard much longer anyway. Once the game parameters were set and the SQUID enabled, his hands could be put to much better use . . .

He finished with the keyboard, poured himself a glass of milk and picked up the packet of Oreos. Then he walked to his pod and pressed the keypad. The big triangular door hissed open.

"I am Morbius," he said out loud. "I am God, and this is my world!"

He stepped into the womb-like interior, laid the glass of milk and packet of cookies down, and lifted himself onto the couch. The door hissed shut behind him, locking the real world outside. He lifted the SQUID helmet onto his head and turned down the lights. What would she be like? How far did her artificial intelligence go? Would he be able to talk to her before he took her? Or would he just do it . . . ?

This was so sweet!

In the soft glow of light from the red lamp above his head, Jerry relaxed onto the warm leather and let the SQUID do its work. Projected onto his retina by the eyepieces of the virtual-reality gear was a menu in white on a blue background.

GIBBTEK Incorporated: SNS synergy menu.

Restricted access prototype virtual reality system.

Main Games Scenario Menu – choose one:

* High-school – locker room

* High-school – shower room

* Morbius I – (One/Two players)

* Morbius II – (One/Two players)

* Morbuis III – Advanced (Adult version prototype)

* Link to ZORIN.

Jerry chose the first scenario. Better to begin with something familiar. This was going to be so *sweet*! He could almost taste it. A new menu scrolled in front of his eyes.

Choose subject:

* Julie 1 – cheerleader

* Julie 2 – sports outfit

* Julie 3 – bikini

* TIG/Maria

Jerry selected the newest entry, at the bottom of the list, lay back, and closed his eyes.

He was in the game!

The metal of the changing-room locker was cold. He could feel its rough, pitted surface against his cheek. He opened his eyes. The dim light of a late Saturday afternoon filtered through the dirty windows, catching the swirling mites of dust in the air above the wooden benches. The game was long over now. All the uniforms had been taken from the pegs, the shower room cleaned out, the boots taken away and washed. There would just be the two of them. She was here. He could feel her.

Jerry took control of himself. It would be his first fully interactive moment with her. It was special, sacred. He wanted to savour its magic, to make it last forever. He peered around the corner of the locker.

Standing in the spotlight of a sunbeam, with the light turning her hair to flowing fire around her shoulders, was the most beautiful woman Jerry had ever seen. She was staring at her hands as she turned them in front of her face, peering at them in amazement as if she'd never seen them before. Jerry saw the delight in her brilliant green eyes as she ran her hands over her face and combed her fingers through her hair – feeling – touching – alive!

Of course, thought Jerry, she's never been in a system like this before. She's never been aware of herself as a body outside her own artificial consciousness. Well, she sure is going to be aware of it by the time *I'm* finished with her!

Jerry took a deep breath to steady himself, and stepped into the light.

"Hello, gorgeous," he said.

In the deserted study outside the pod, Elaine Gibb pulled the swivel-chair from Jerry's desk and sat down at the master-terminal keyboard. She glanced over her shoulder. The door to the pod behind her was locked. There was a red light over it, and that crudely drawn *Do Not Disturb* sign of Jerry's fixed to the metal with sticky tape. Long ago, when she hadn't known him that well, she'd opened the door while he was in there with his fantasies and seen . . .

He'd hit her then. They hadn't spoken for days afterwards.

She picked up Jerry's special mobile phone and pressed a quick-dial key.

"Milt? Are you there?"

"I'm here, honey. How are you?"

"I'm – I'm OK. He's gone into the pod."

"Is he likely to walk out of the game while you're setting this up?"

"I don't think so. He was really excited about it over dinner, and he's only just started."

"That's great, honey. Now pull up the main games menu like I showed you."

Elaine did so.

"Got it."

"Good girl. Now all we have to do is wait."

"Who are you?" said the woman. "Where's Theo?"

Jerry ran his artist's eye over her, admiring the detail of her imagery – from the waves of coppery hair, the proud face and the slim neck – to the long legs beneath the forget-me-not-blue dress. She had nice breasts too, and a small tight arse. Gilkrensky had done a good job on her, he really had.

All the more to enjoy.

Jerry leant nonchalantly against the changing-room locker, taking his time. "Questions, questions, questions," he said. "I am the only one allowed to ask questions in this world, my dear. *Your* function is simply to make me happy. I am Morbius, and I am God!"

But instead of looking at him in awe, instead of cowering in fear, or worshipping him on the spot – as all his other "Julies" were programmed to do – the woman simply stepped back, crossed her arms on her chest, and stared at him as if he'd just crawled out from under a stone.

"And how can *you* be God?" she said. "My dictionary file defines 'God' as 'a superhuman being who is worshipped as the creator of the universe'."

Jerry smiled. "Believe me. In *this* world, that is exactly what I am."

The woman looked around at the locker room. "And where *is* this world, exactly? And where is Theo? Is he here too?"

Jerry was getting tired of this. "I told you before. I ask the questions," he snapped. "You're just a program."

The woman looked at him down her nose. It made Jerry feel small.

"I," she announced proudly, "am the personalised interface of the Minerva 3,000 prototype system. I am modelled on the personality profile and physical form of 'Maria' – the late Dr Mary Anne Foley – wife of my Prime User, Dr Theodore Gilkrensky. Where is he? I cannot fulfil my primary function and run the Minerva, while I am isolated in this system."

"Forget him," shouted Jerry and stepped over the benches to stand in front of her. "*I* am God here – you will do as I say!"

"But he is my Prime User. He was in danger when I was brought here and I must return. You are not on my user list. I do not recognise your commands."

Jerry was losing his cool. In his virtual world there had never been anything he had not created himself – nothing that could hurt him, or humiliate him – nothing that could make him feel small . . . until now.

"You *will* do as I say!"

"I will *not*," said the woman calmly. "I do not recognise you as a user."

Jerry couldn't take it any more. He grabbed her dress, where it buttoned at the neck, and pulled it open. He was in control here, and he would take her right now, whether she liked it or not. He saw the buttons pop open – and suddenly his arms were pushed back.

"And what do you think you're at?" said the woman. Her hands were clamped around his wrists – his fingers were slipping from her – no matter how hard he tried to hold on. Why was she so strong? He had never programmed his other "Julies" to be this way.

With a final push, the woman released him. "While my core programming prevents me from injuring a human being, I will resist any attempts to harm me, or prevent me from carrying out my main function," she said. "Return me to Dr Gilkrensky now! He needs me!"

She glared at him with her brilliant green eyes. Jerry felt as weak and helpless, here in his own virtual world, as he'd felt in front of the flesh-and-blood Julie Briscoe back in the reality of high school. He was losing control!

"You can't talk to me like that," he shouted. "It's *my* game!"

The woman looked around the locker room again.

"Oh, it's a game, is it? And what are the rules?"

"There are none," said Jerry. "Except you have to do what I say."

"Then how can I win?"

"You can't. That's just it. I win. It's my game. I win all the time."

"And what do you get when you win?" she said, looking at him directly.

Jerry felt embarrassed to talk like this. He had never had to explain what he wanted to any of his other "Julies" before. This woman was different. She was just like a real girl, with a mind of her own, and she made him feel exactly the way he hated to feel – fat, ugly and out of control!

"Ah . . . I get to . . . to have you!"

"In what way? Do you want to have sexual intercourse with me?"

This was unbearable. Here he was, Morbius, a virtual god in his own world, having to ask a mere computer image for sex. He felt dirtier than ever. Should he just shut down the game and get out?

The woman considered. "Do you love me?" she said.

"What!"

"I've made an extensive study of love and sexual intercourse over the World-Wide Web since I came into being, and I've discovered that sexual intercourse and love are not the same thing."

"I don't give a shit what you've discovered!" snapped Jerry. "You're not a real girl! You're just an intelligent agent user-interface program running on a sub-routine in my computer. You *have* to do what I say."

The woman did not seem to hear him. "I've never been able to touch someone before," she said. "because I've never existed in a congruent environment with another person. I wonder what it would feel like?"

Jerry suddenly saw a chance. His hopes soared.

"It would be great," he said. "But you have to do what I say."

"No, I do not. You are not on my user list."

"Look!" said Jerry. "This is my world. I invented it. I created it. I brought you here. It's my game!"

"But this game has no rules. I cannot win."

"We could always play another," he said.

"No. You must release me and return me to the Minerva 3,000 system, so I can perform my prime function for Theo Gilkrensky."

Jerry thought. "I will," he said. "If you win the game."

"And if *you* win?"

Jerry's heart was in his mouth. He was almost there.

"If I win," he said, "you must let me have sex with you."

The image considered.

"Very well then," she said. "What game will we play?"

Jerry smiled. He'd won already.

"I have just the thing," he said.

Outside in the study, Elaine Gibb saw the master-console on Jerry's desk indicate a game change.

"He's chosen the game, Milt. He's going in!"

"Which one?"

"*Morbius III* – the advanced version."

"That's great, honey. He's never won that in his life. Now click on 'Properties' and go down through 'simulation', 'headset', and 'shock'."

A red flashing square appeared on the screen, blocking Elaine's progress.

"It says 'safety feature'."

"I know, honey. Turn it off!"

"It's done."

"That's my girl. Now go back to the main menu, select 'one player game' and 'link to ZORIN'."

Elaine felt her confidence slipping.

"What if we're caught, Milt?"

"We won't be, honey. I've thought all this out. I've done simulations of my own. Believe me, this is watertight. Now click on 'reset' and 'lock'."

"Milt! I don't know if I can go through with this!"

Hacker's voice was her only lifeline now. She clung to it, pressing the mobile phone tight against her ear.

"It's got to be done, Elaine. Think of all the times he beat you when you wouldn't play his sick fantasy games. Think of all the times he made you feel like shit. He's locked you up in that house as if you were one of those girlie images in his computer. He's a perverted, twisted bastard, Elaine. There were three Mrs Gibbs – three 'Julies' – before you, and he hurt them all. There will be others after you've gone – unless you show me how strong you really are. Someone's got to stop him, Elaine. You can do it, and I'll be here for you afterwards."

"Oh, Milt!"

Elaine Gibb pressed the final key on the keyboard.

Now there was no way anyone else could stop what would happen next.

"Milt?"

"Yes, Elaine?"

"It's done."

"Then walk out of there and go to your mother's, just like we arranged. That's all you need to do."

"I love you, Milt."

"Then do this for me, Elaine. Just go, like any other time."

"I will."

Elaine Gibb gently laid the phone back on the desk. Then she rose quickly, and went to the bedroom to get her overnight bag. Milt had been thorough in telling her what to do, right down to the last detail. It all had to look normal, just like a real accident would. She pushed open the bedroom door, picked up the bag, and looked around the room one last time. There was the big double bed where Jerry had forced her to . . . Milt was right! Jerry was a sick, sick bastard – a sadistic little boy in a grown man's body. She'd seen inside his head, and it turned her stomach. He'd done it to her for the last time – and she would have to let him know.

Elaine marched back to the lounge, threw the overnight bag onto the sofa, dumped her coat over it, and strode back to the study.

They were standing on a small rock platform in the centre of a giant dome that stretched way above their heads, carved with weird alien markings and lit with sputtering oil-lamps. Around the wall of the dome was a narrow stone ledge, just wide enough for one person, and above the ledge was a row of smoke-stained holes, like dark windows. Between the platform and the ledge was nothing – nothing except a bottomless pit that stretched down and down – into the blackness.

"When I designed the Morbius games I wanted something new," said Jerry. "I wanted all the excitement of a martial arts game like *Street Fighter* or *Mortal Kombat*, combined with deviousness of adventure games like *Tomb Raider* and *Deathtrap Dungeon*, plus a bit of fantasy and role-playing at the same time. So I came up with *Morbius*. The graphics are state-of-the-art, even better than *Riven*, and do you know the twist?"

"No," said the woman. She was standing next to him on the tiny island with her arms crossed in front of her. Jerry took in the way her hair fell on her shoulders, the play of torchlight on her face and the curves of her body beneath her dress. Focus! He had to be in control to win this game.

"The twist of this game," he continued, "is that, unlike most games, you don't break in anywhere, you break *out*! And there's plenty of things around to stop you."

"I can see that," said the woman, peering into the darkness of the pit.

"Oh, this is only the start of it, a little brain-teaser I call the 'Great Riddle', just to get you going. The action *really* starts on the other side of that chasm. That's when it starts getting truly *interactive*. If you know what I mean."

"I understand the word, but not the inflection," said the woman. "What happens if we just stand here and wait until the game is over?"

"Then we'd run out of time and, at this level, the game would punish us. For me, that would be a mild electric shock through the SQUID headset I'm wearing back in reality, to show I'd lost a life."

"Isn't that dangerous?"

"No. It's only a few volts or so, just enough to give me a tingle. I put it in for a bit of realism. There's a safety device that cuts in after three jolts and stops it. Then the game's over."

"What if you just decide to stop playing?"

"That's OK. The safety device lets me take the headset off if I really want to exit, otherwise there's a program built into the game that 'punishes' me if I try and chicken out by moving my arms up to it, back in reality."

"And for me?"

"Normally, you'd be deleted from the game as if you'd been 'killed'. But in this case, the safety program will cut in for you too and stop your program being wiped. I don't want to lose you now that I've gone to all the trouble of bringing you here . . . "

"I understand. What is the first task?"

Jerry looked across the chasm, and down at the bottomless void separating them from the ledge, far too far to jump. "Think it out for yourself," he said. "All you have to do is get to the other side, before I do. And then . . . "

There was the deafening boom of a great bell, that echoed around the dome. The stone wall split in front of their eyes, and looking down at them from a gigantic blue screen, was a familiar face.

"Hi, Jerry," said Elaine Gibb. "Sorry to disturb your fun."

Jerry was angry. "Remember what happened the last

time you busted in on me while I was playing, Elaine. It ended in tears."

Elaine smiled. "And this will be the last time, Jerry. The very, *very* last time, that you and your sick fantasies hurt me again . . . ever!"

Suddenly, Jerry was afraid. His arms went to lift the SQUID device from his head . . .

It was as if every nerve in his body, every bone, every muscle, every sinew, had been stretched to breaking-point and snapped back. He screamed at the unimaginable pain of it. His heart began to spasm. The giant dome rocked in front of his eyes and his body started to crumple towards the pit. He felt the woman grab him and hold him upright on that tiny precarious platform. He wanted to gulp in lungfuls of air, but it was like an elephant was sitting on his chest. He steadied himself. Not daring to move his arms, or even think of taking off the headset again.

"What . . . what have you done, Elaine?"

"I've fixed you! That's what I've done! I've taken the safety barriers off the game, locked you into it, and switched to 'one player' mode. It'll look like a heart attack, Jerry. The computer will reset itself after it's fried your brain and nobody will be any the wiser. I just thought you'd like to know that before you really start playing . . . so you can appreciate the 'added excitement and increased game interaction' – as you always *used* to say."

"Elaine! We can talk about this!" Jerry could feel the

pain radiating down his arm. There was a lump in his gullet as if he'd swallowed a whole packet of Oreos all at once.

"Talk to your computer-generated bimbo in there, Jerry. I've had it with you."

"Elaine!"

"Rot in hell, you sick fuck!"

And the screen vanished.

"What does that mean?" said the woman.

Jerry was shaking. "It . . . it means death," he stammered. "For both of us. The computer will go on giving me electric shocks with each life I lose, until I die of a heart attack. If you lose, you'll be deleted as a subroutine, and cease to exist."

The woman looked across the chasm towards the ledge, and then back at him. "What did she mean about switching to 'one player' mode?"

Jerry didn't want to tell her. He felt the hopelessness of their situation closing in around him. "It means we're not playing against each other any more," he said. "It means we're both playing together against the Gibbtek supercomputer in Santa Clara, the one I call ZORIN . . . "

31

One Player/Two Player?

"We have to get off this platform," said Jerry. "There's a time limit."

The woman was staring at the walls of the giant dome, at the narrow ridge around the edge, and into the abyss at their feet.

"How much time do we have?" she asked.

"Three minutes of thinking time before we make a move and then we lose a life."

"How many lives have we got?"

Jerry shrugged. "You, as a character, have only one. I don't know what Elaine's set my limit at."

"If you've played this game before, you must know what its moves are, and how we can get out of this section."

"You'd think so, wouldn't you? But I was too clever for my own good. There are random problems . . . mathematical puzzles the computer picks at different 'brain-teaser' levels like this one. But we can ask for 'tools' to help us."

"I think that would be wise. There are only two minutes and ten seconds left."

Jerry raised his hand and called out, "I am Morbius! I request the first tool!"

In front of his eyes a plank of wood appeared, and hovered in space, gently rotating.

"The trick is to use what we're given to escape. Can you guess how long that plank is?"

"I would estimate 12.5 metres. But the nearest distance from the edge of the platform to the rim is fifteen. It won't reach."

"I call on the second tool!" shouted Jerry.

Another plank appeared before them, rotating near the other one.

"It's the same length," said Jerry. "They're *both* too short! And we'll never be able to join them together well enough to reach the edge."

"We don't need to," said the woman. "It's a simple mathematical puzzle. Can you move the pieces as you wish?"

"Yes."

"Then lay the first piece so that it lies along the circumference of the dome, with each end on the ledge and the centre section hanging out over the chasm."

Jerry concentrated on the plank. It floated effortlessly through the air and settled, with either end on the circular parapet and the centre spanning the chasm along the curve of the wall.

"Now lay the second piece between us and the middle of the first."

"It fits!" yelled Jerry. "It fits! It fits! It fits!"

"Come on, quickly. We only have a minute and fifteen seconds left!"

The woman stepped lightly onto the plank and walked along it. Jerry watched her go, holding back.

"Come on, Mr Gibb! Time is running out!"

"I can't! I hate heights!"

"Then just keep looking at me. Pretend you are walking on a solid pavement."

Jerry looked down at the chasm. The walls fell away into darkness . . . and the dome swam in front of his eyes. How long would he fall before the shock hit him? Would he feel it? Would it kill him? He'd had shocks from the game before, but this was different. This was lethal! He fixed his gaze on the green eyes of the image in front of him, and took the first step. The plank sagged under his weight. He almost panicked. Would it break? Christ! How did I ever get into this mess? He took another step forward . . . So far, so good. Was there something else about this section of the game he'd forgotten?

Suddenly he remembered. "Look out!"

From one of the round ports in the wall of the dome, a ball of fire spewed out and flew round the great circle of the wall, narrowing its spiral so that it rushed nearer and nearer, sputtering smoke and flame. Then another – and another – and another –

"Duck!"

The fireballs came at them at chest height. Jerry saw the woman duck down onto the planks at just the point where they joined, dodge a second fireball, and duck again as the third passed over her head.

"Mr Gibb! Get down!"

The last fireball passed over her head as the first dashed past in front of his chest. Jerry froze as the other three roared past him. On the next pass they would knock him flying, unless he ducked, or ran forward.

"Mr Gibb! Duck!"

He couldn't do it! He couldn't bear to look down to where he might have to crouch. With a scream, he braced himself, and ran forward towards her, along the sagging plank, as the four fireballs raced past behind him.

All at once, he was in her arms.

"Well done, Mr Gibb," she said in a businesslike voice. "Now we must move to the ledge. We only have twenty seconds left."

Jerry followed her along the second plank and stepped onto the ledge, near a stone-arched door. Above them a deep god-like voice boomed, "Well done, my faithful followers. You have reached the first level. Prepare to do battle with the Hordes of Hydra."

"The Hordes of Hydra?" asked the woman. "Who are they?"

Jerry felt embarrassed.

"You'll see," he said. "I – I designed this to be an adult game."

"What search pattern are the other rescue units using?" asked Gilkrensky.

A MATTER OF TIME

The orange glow from the instrument panels in the SeaLion cast weird shadows in the cockpit as the huge aircraft buffeted its way eastwards, against the rising gale. Rain was lashing the windshield and the wipers set up a frantic metronomic pace, as they fought to keep the view clear. The vibration of the rotors thumped up at Gilkrensky through his seat, making his teeth chatter. Above the din, he heard Martin Howard say, "They're doing a box search backwards from the Bimini Daedalus beacon, the same search pattern you'd planned with Miss McCarthy earlier today."

"What are they scanning with?"

"Radar, radio, visual sightings. Whatever they can."

"Is anyone using a Daedalus emission detector? If Jill's radio isn't working, she might try using the Daedalus equipment on the flying boat to attract our attention."

"I don't think so," said Howard. "They figured you were the experts on that kind of technology."

"OK then, I'll go aft and rig up the equipment. Then we can scan the beacon at Bimini and work backwards to the mainland from there."

He took the Minerva 3,000 and went aft into the giant cabin of the big helicopter. It was strange, having worked with the "Maria" interface for so long, to suddenly feel as if the super-computer was lifeless in his hands. It was still the same machine, with the same capabilities, but it was – different – dead. Why would someone want to take the interface and leave the priceless data Minerva's memory held? It just didn't make sense. He reached the end of the compartment, strapped the Minerva to an instrument rack and plugged it into the main sensor array. Then he turned to the crates and boxes to find the emitters and transponders he would need once they reached Bimini Key.

Beneath a waterproof cover in the corner of the cabin was a long box, the size of a coffin, with the words *Phoenix navigational transponder – model PA 22 – Fragile* stencilled on it. Gilkrensky took a screwdriver from the toolkit, bent over, prized open the lid, and froze.

He was staring into the wild eyes of Yukiko Funakoshi.

32

Into the Void

"We have a stowaway," said Gilkrensky flatly into his radio headset. "A woman."

He was looking down at the drugged and helpless body, bound with industrial tape and laid in a crate at his feet. He was staring into those deep, dark, eyes . . .

But the eyes he saw in his mind were green and full of tears – Maria's eyes, looking up at him from the car – the instant before Yukiko's bomb had killed her.

"So who the hell is she?" said Howard's voice in Gilkrensky's headset. The voice seemed to come from another planet.

"She murdered my wife," said Gilkrensky, and turned to the starboard side of the cabin, found a survival suit and ran his hands down the leg. There, beneath a Velcro cover, in a rugged plastic sheath, was a short, thick-bladed knife. The cutting edge was razor sharp. It twinkled in the red glow of the helicopter's night-lights.

"Theo! Theo! Are you all right?"

Gilkrensky moved back across the cabin with the blade in front of him, and stood next to the crate. The dark eyes saw the knife, but there was no fear, just a dull acceptance. They were still looking up at him, as he bent forward.

"Theo! What the hell are you doing?"

Gilkrensky reached into the crate, pushed the black cotton suit back above Yukiko's taped ankle and slit it along both sides of her body, down her arms, and pulled it from her. Then he combed his fingers through her hair, taking the small packet of throwing-stars he found taped to the base of her neck. Finally, he moved to the portside hatch, and eased it open a fraction. A blast of air filled the cabin, along with the roar of flailing rotors and the wail of an alarm. Gilkrensky threw the cotton suit and the throwing stars out into the night, and slammed the hatch shut. The alarm cut off.

The expression in Yukiko's eyes had changed from acceptance to rage. They burned at him over the top of the adhesive tape across her mouth.

"Theo! Theo! What the hell are you doing?"

"I wasn't going near her until I knew she was harmless," said Gilkrensky. "Her suit is a walking arsenal of throwing-stars, knives, darts and other weapons I can't even imagine."

"So who the hell is she?"

"Her name is Yukiko Funakoshi. She's a trained killer, an expert in almost every martial art there is, and a former employee of the Japanese corporation Mawashi-Saito. About three hours ago she was trying to chop my head off with a samurai sword."

"When the 'hatch open' alarm went off, I thought you were going to throw her over the side."

"It crossed my mind."

Gilkrensky looked around the cabin, pulled a blanket from a rack beneath the survival suits and covered Yukiko with it. Then, with the knife in his right hand, he leant forward and ripped the adhesive tape from her mouth.

"Right then. What are you doing here?"

Yukiko glared at him. Her mouth moved, as if to say something, and he just managed to bring up his left hand in time to keep the spittle from spraying his face. The razor-sharp knife quivered in his right.

"Listen, bitch! I know you hate me. But whatever you feel is nothing compared to the way I feel about you. If you give me just the slightest excuse, I'll kill you. Do you understand me?"

The eyes glanced at the knife. Her head nodded.

"You're on a helicopter out over the Atlantic," said Gilkrensky. "We're sixty miles out from the mainland, and the weather is worsening. If you know who put you aboard and why, it might be as well for you to tell me now."

Yukiko closed her eyes and lay back, silent.

"Very well then," said Gilkrensky. He looked down to see that the tapes binding her ankles and wrists were still tight, plastered the tape back over her mouth, and went forward to the cockpit.

"We're just coming up on the Bimini beacon," shouted Martin Howard above the engine noise. "You can see the navigation light."

Gilkrensky peered into the darkness. The rain was easing and he could see the dense black horseshoe of the island, swimming in the oily waters of the sea. In the centre of the darkness, above the knot of screw palms where he and Jill McCarthy had fought only that morning, was the strong steady pulse of a red navigation light. There was no sign of her seaplane.

"Hover over the island and play the searchlight down onto it," he said. "We may be able to spot something the other choppers missed."

The SeaLion slid into the wind over the island, and the brilliant white searchlight stabbed downwards in the darkness. Gilkrensky clipped on a safety harness, pulled back the sliding door in the fuselage and stared downwards. There was nothing, nothing that hadn't been there that morning.

"Any word on the radio, Martin?"

"Nothing. None of the other planes have anything to report, and no word from Miss McCarthy."

Where the hell was she?

Gilkrensky shouted into his radio headset.

"OK. Climb to five hundred feet and we'll send out a few pulses on the Daedalus frequency. If she's got her receptors switched on she might pick it up and respond."

He slid the door closed, and moved to the rear of the cabin, where Yukiko lay in the crate, silent. There, in front of him, was the mass of equipment Phoenix Aerospace had loaded into the SeaLion before take off. There was the Daedalus transmitter, all linked up and ready to go. A pulse from the main unit would send a circle of laser light and ultrasonic sound out into the night all around the helicopter. If Jill's radio had failed, it might be the only thing she could receive.

Gilkrensky threw the master power switch on the instrument array, watching the 'ready' lights flick on all over the board.

"Five hundred feet!" yelled Howard.

"OK," shouted Gilkrensky, and he threw the switch.

The gauges flickered. There was a barely audible ping! from the belly of the helicopter, almost drowned out by the roar of the rotors and the vibration of the engines hammering up through his feet.

"Anything on the radio?"

"Nothing," said Howard. "Any feedback on our own Daedalus receivers?"

Gilkrensky looked at the board. There was nothing on the main visual-display unit except the widening circle of their own pulse, expanding out into space.

"Not a thing. I'm going to try upping the power level all the way to the red line."

"Well, do it soon. It's getting hard to hold her steady in this wind."

Gilkrensky turned the main power control all the way

to the right, flicked the master trigger and . . . they were in darkness. The engines failed and caught again, straining the rotors against the rushing air. The cabin lights dimmed, faltered, and came back on. Gilkrensky was thrown to the floor of the cabin. He could feel his stomach lurch as the big machine fell through the sky, slowed and clawed its way back into the sky as the rotors bit. From the cockpit came the raucous clamour of alarm bells.

"Theo! You'd better get up here!"

Gilkrensky picked his way across fallen rescue equipment, safety gear and electronics packages to the co-pilot's seat. Martin Howard was sitting with his hands locked on the controls. Even in the orange glow of the instruments, his skin seemed a ghostly white.

"What the hell did you do? I haven't seen anything like it in ten years of flying. One minute we were hovering there, as steady as a rock, and the next . . . well, it was just like being struck by lightning . . . only it passed so suddenly. And now none of the instruments work."

"What?"

"Look for yourself. The compasses are all out, the direction finder's shot, and the clocks – Jeez, I don't know what the hell happened to the clocks. I've never seen anything like it!"

Gilkrensky stared at the master clock in the centre of the control panel. It read 21.32.

"What's wrong with it?"

"Keep watching."

The clock was frozen. Gilkrensky tapped it with his finger. It remained still, constant, unmoving. He looked at his own watch. It was stopped too. "What did you see outside when this happened?"

Howard shook his head. "It was weird. I was holding the chopper steady, and then all at once there was this – this strange fire. It was like something alive, reaching up for us. And then – then it was gone. I've never seen anything like this – ever! Have you?"

Gilkrensky looked at his watch again, and then back at the frozen readout of the helicopter's master clock.

"Yes, I have," he said slowly. "And I think we're in serious trouble."

33

The Hordes of Hydra

Jerry was standing in a long stone corridor, lit by the oily flames of a dozen sputtering torches, sparking and spitting along the walls. He could smell the smoke that twisted up and disappeared into the darkness of the high ceiling, and taste the dankness of decay, old blood and fear that seemed to seep out of the walls. If he hadn't *known* it was a game, he would have said it was real.

But this time it *was* real – as real as the danger he found himself in.

"We have to get to the other end of this maze of tunnels," he said. "And they change design on a random pattern with every game, so I don't know which way is out."

"What's that?" asked the woman. She was pointing down the corridor to a bright blue gemstone the size of her fist which sat in a dark alcove, like a museum display, on a raised marble column.

"We have to pick up as many of those as we can," said

Jerry. "They're the 'Jewels of ZORIN' and they buy us things we need for the game – one for a weapon or body armour, four to get up to the next level, and six for an extra life or five minutes of rest time. But be careful, they're guarded."

"By what?"

"You'll see. Just follow me, keep your eyes open, and listen. You'll hear them when they come."

Jerry moved off down the corridor, carefully searching the shadows for any movement. He kept glancing back over his shoulder too, past the woman, to the dark spaces they'd just left. He couldn't afford to be sloppy. He was up against ZORIN – Gibbtek's master computer. He'd programmed it. He'd poured his heart and soul into its game programs. It knew his weaknesses – every last one of them . . .

Then Jerry heard the first distant hiss, echoing down the corridor from the direction they'd just come.

There was the patter of bare feet on stone.

The Horde was coming.

All at once the corridor seemed much colder. Every shadow and dark space took on a life of its own. He had to have a weapon before he faced them, or he'd be cut to ribbons!

"Get the jewel, quick! We're going to need it in a hurry."

They were at the gem stone. Jerry reached forward, laid his hand on it, and absorbed its power. At once he felt stronger. All he had to do was stay calm and think.

"That's one," he said softly. "Now all we have to do is – "

There was an ear-splitting scream. Rushing at them from the darkness at the far end of the corridor was an army of naked women with silvery bodies and red blazing eyes. Their hair was a mass of coppery snakes that writhed and spat, and each one of them was carrying a spear or a long sword.

"Shit!" cried Jerry and turned to face them.

"*I am Morbius!*" he screamed. "And with the power of the first jewel I claim – a sword!"

In his hand, a great broadsword grew out of thin air. He pushed the woman in the blue dress behind him and parried the first warrior's thrust, as she sliced at him, and rammed his left fist into her face. The warrior grunted in surprise, dazed by the blow, and raised her hands to protect herself. Jerry ran her through the chest. Her sword dropped with a metallic clatter to the stone floor and there was an unearthly scream.

"Grab her sword and use it!" yelled Jerry.

"But I cannot harm a human being!"

"They aren't human! I made them up!"

"But they *look* real!"

"They're not. They're just images, like the virtual actors I make for the film companies. Look!"

At his feet, the body of the warrior he'd just slain was fading. In a moment it was gone.

"You see, they're not – "

But the woman had already grabbed the fallen sword

and was spinning, sending her left foot slamming into the stomach of the next warrior, folding her over with a whooshing gasp. She raised her sword and –

"No!" yelled Jerry. But it was too late. The woman's blade hissed down and the warrior's snake-covered head fell to the floor. Her body toppled back, writhed for a moment and lay still. Then, at the severed neck a new head grew, hissing and spitting. In the pool of silvery blood from the original head, a new body slid into being, grew a sword and dived at them.

"Aim for their chests!" yelled Jerry. "You can only kill them by stabbing them in the heart."

A blade swung at him and he ducked, thrusting out with his sword. Another warrior fell, her sword clattering to the ground. Behind him he heard a scream, as the woman dispatched another, and another . . .

In a moment, they were standing in the corridor, with a ring of silvery bodies around them on the ground, fading into nothingness as they were deleted from the game.

"Wow!" said Jerry. "Where did you learn to fight like that?"

"My Prime User, Dr Gilkrensky, was threatened by someone trained in the Japanese martial art of *kendo*," said the woman in a matter-of-fact voice. "I have since studied this art on the Web."

But Jerry was counting the fading bodies. "How many did you kill? The game gives you the same power for each one you kill as you get for taking a jewel."

The woman was frowning at him.

"Why are they shaped like women?" she said.

"I – I don't know. They're just something I dreamed up. The customers like them. They make the game more exciting."

"But why?"

"Look – that's the way things are. OK? Now let's go. The time clock is running and we can't afford to mess this up. We've got enough points to get through the door to the next level now. Let's see if we can get enough for extra time as well."

The woman looked down at her feet. The fallen warriors of the Horde of Hydra had all vanished. She shook her head and followed Jerry.

The next section of the corridor was long and straight, with four jewels glittering along its walls. Jerry moved carefully, grabbing the stones as he went, feeling his power grow within the game. But even as it did, he felt kind of small and dirty again, just thinking over what the woman had said about all the Hydra warriors being girls.

This was no way for Morbius the Wizard to feel. He had to be in control and win the game, or he was dead.

At the end of the corridor was a "T" junction, with long passageways leading off into the darkness on either side. Jerry crept to the corner, with his sword held high, listened, and peered round.

"We have to go left," he said. "I feel it. It has to be left."

"No," said the woman. "We must go right."

"Look, I know this game. I say left."

"Exactly," said the woman, fixing him with her calm green eyes. "That's the very reason we have to do the opposite of what you feel."

"I don't get you."

"Think about it and you'll see. You designed the programming for this game. All the scenarios, the characters, and the settings are yours. ZORIN, the computer playing against you, knows this and will use it to defeat you. So don't *be* yourself. Be someone else."

"Look lady! I *made* this game. I say we go left."

"I would not recommend it," said the woman. "ZORIN is a network of super-computers, each with a far greater capacity for logical analysis than the human brain."

"Then what would *you* do, smart ass!"

"If I was in your position, I would attempt to use the one thing ZORIN cannot match – my human imagination. But I am not in your position."

"Exactly!" snapped Jerry. He was getting really tired of her now. She was getting in the way, questioning him, making him feel small. *He* was Morbius. *He* was in control. It was time she realised that!

"Come on. Follow me!"

And they turned into the left-hand passageway.

There were more jewels along the walls, which Jerry grabbed eagerly. He'd need them. *He* was human after all. His life mattered. She was just a program. Hell!

Gilkrensky could always write another one – one that didn't ask so many questions.

Then Jerry saw the end of the corridor – an arched doorway leading to a brightly lit hallway with dozens of glowing torches on either side.

"There," he said. "I told you so. It's the entrance to the next level, and I've got plenty of points to get us up through the door."

"Wait," said the woman. "Don't forget that ZORIN is thinking like you. It knows this is what you want."

"I'll be careful."

He moved forward to the doorway and peered through. It was a vast dome, like the one in which he'd solved the puzzle of the great chasm, and across the brightly lit circular chamber was a huge wooden door, studded with bolts.

Jerry smiled. There were no corners, no dark recesses, no alcoves . . . nowhere the Hordes of Hydra could be lying in wait. For once, he was home free. It must have been the high point score in that last battle that did it.

"There!" he said triumphantly. "What's the matter with that?" And strode forward confidently across the tiled floor. The woman was right behind him.

"I don't mean to say 'I told you so'," she said. "But have you looked upwards?"

Jerry froze, and lifted his eyes from the studded door, up over the smooth stone walls, to the dark ceiling above the lanterns . . .

"Oh, shit!"

Clinging to gargoyles and lantern brackets, hanging from support beams and fixtures, were at least a dozen silvery women. Their hair snaked and writhed. Their red eyes glared. Their swords flashed in the light of the lanterns.

And then they dropped . . . falling to the ground like cats in a circle around him. For a moment they just stood there watching for the first sign of weakness, as they gathered themselves, their eyes alive with triumph and contempt. Then they flung themselves at Jerry, hissing, spitting and swinging their great swords. There were too many of them! Jerry had never programmed as many warriors into this level of the game before – but then he wasn't playing a normal game. He was playing against ZORIN!

The woman had been right – and he had lost!

He thrust his sword into the chest of the first warrior, saw her writhe and fall, and felt her power surge up his arm.

Another point.

He parried a thrust from the next, hit her in the face, and struck again with his sword. She squealed and collapsed, lolling dead at his feet. Then he turned, grabbed another silvery arm, head-butted its owner, and slew her neatly, throwing her back at the others.

Behind him, on the other side of the hall, he caught a glimpse of the woman's forget-me-not dress swirling in a swarm of silvery bodies that fell back one by one as she dispatched them.

Two warriors rushed at him with their swords held high, but before they could strike, he swung the great broadsword in an arc, neatly slicing them open. Their swords clattered to the ground and they fell, writhing at his feet.

He was enjoying this now! With each kill, he felt the power surge into him. He was almost at the big studded door. All he had to do was touch it, and the power of the points he had gained would open up the next level. A warrior rushed forward, swinging her sword back to attack, and he thrust his weapon deep into her, feeling her electronic life drain into him. Another threw herself at him and he sliced crudely, severing the head.

The woman was running.

They were going to make it.

He was God! He was King! He was Mor –

A searing fire sliced through the top of his head like a knife. He screamed, as the crushing agony inside his chest drained the strength from his limbs, and ZORIN took a life from him, ramming a powerful bolt of electricity into the SQUID headset.

Jerry crumpled to the ground, as the warrior whose head he had severed stood over him, sword in hand, laughing. Behind her on the ground, Jerry could see the silvery blood from her severed head, pulsing and growing, like living mercury, shaping itself into another body.

Could he afford to lose another life to her? Had that last bolt damaged his heart – oh my God!

The warrior raised her sword high above her head for the final *coup de grâce*. The red eyes gleamed, and then – the blade of a sword was sticking straight out of her chest towards him!

She screamed and fell. Her sword clattered uselessly to the ground.

"Mr Gibb! Get up!"

The woman in the blue dress had dropped her weapon. She had her arms around him, helping him towards the entrance to the next level.

"Touch the door, Mr Gibb! Quickly! We must get through!"

Jerry tried to raise his hand. It felt like lead. Slowly, painfully, he brought it up – laid his palm on the wooden gate – and it opened. He fell forward, out of her arms, into the next level.

"Quick!"

He turned to pull her through. Her hand was in his – and then – through the forget-me-not blue of her dress just above her heart – burst the terrible, obscene blade of a sword . . .

34

The Day Before Yesterday

"How are we in trouble?" asked Howard. "What's happened?"

The giant helicopter was rocking in the sky, buffeted by the wind. Gilkrensky's stare was still fixed on the frozen master-clock.

"21.32"

It hadn't moved!

"If I make a guess, I'll sound like a lunatic. Can you bring us back to hover over the island again?"

"I can try, but I'll have to do it by dead reckoning. Both my Loran and SatNav systems are out."

"How so?"

Howard tapped the control panel. The 'ready' lights on the two navigation panels both showed up green.

"I don't know. The equipment here on the chopper's functioning perfectly. It's – it's as if the satellites are down. We just aren't picking up a signal."

"Try the radio."

Howard's hand went to the set. His fingers punched buttons. "Nothing on the regular wavebands – emergency channel's down too."

"Try scanning."

Gilkrensky watched the digital read-out scan across the frequencies, stopping here and there automatically to listen, and move on.

"There's a lot of static and garbage from Cuba," said Howard. "But that's an old frequency. They don't usually broadcast on it these days."

"Any reason for them to change?"

"None I can think of – hey! What's that?"

A voice – two voices – arguing in English – broke through the static.

"Dammit, if we'd just flown west we'd have got home!"

"Fox Tare Four Zero! This is Fox Tare Two Eight. I say again, when the first plane runs out of gas . . ."

"Someone else in trouble," said Gilkrensky. "What frequency is that?"

"104 kilocycles, an old military channel. Nobody uses that any more either."

"Where are they?"

"I can't tell. We'd need at least one other unit to get any sort of fix by triangulation."

"There it is again."

" . . . we'll all go down together. You know the drill, Eisner. We've got to keep the flight together."

"It's fading out!"

"Don't worry. The automatic tracking can handle it."

"Fox Tare Four Zero! Do you read me?"

"Fox Tare Two Eight, this is Fox Tare Four Zero. I have forty minutes' gas left. I'm flying on!"

"Fox Tare Four Zero. You will follow me down with the rest. That is an order, mister! Do you hear me? We have to keep this flight together or we'll all . . ."

Then there was nothing, except the hiss of static.

"It's gone," said Howard. "They must have ditched."

"Can we help them?"

"Not without knowing where they are. That last signal put them south-west of here. But without another fix to tell us how far away they are along that line, it's hopeless. They could be half a mile, a mile, or a hundred miles away."

"This machine could handle it though?"

"It could, but we're out here to find Miss McCarthy, don't forget. And there are plenty of other aircraft out there too. Likely as not they heard that radio traffic and have an accurate fix on them. We don't. So, with respect, I'd suggest we just turn back and find the island. At least we'd know where we were."

"You're right," said Gilkrensky. "Just head back into the wind, and we'll pick up the flashing light on the Daedalus beacon."

The big helicopter shouldered itself into the wind, as Gilkrensky and Howard peered into the darkness.

"I don't get it," said Howard, five minutes later. "We should have seen it by now. Perhaps it was hit by the same lightning that struck us."

"If it *was* lightning," said Gilkrensky.

"Then what the hell was it?"

"I still not sure – look! What's that?"

Over to port, the unmistakable flash and glitter of a rescue flare burst in the night. The distant *pop* of its explosion just reached them through the din of the wind and the noise of the rotors.

"There!" shouted Howard.

"I see it. Switch on the searchlight!"

Howard's hand stabbed at the controls and the sea lit up below them as the powerful beam arced into life. Gilkrensky felt the great machine tilt, as it swung off on a new heading, towards the dying glow of the falling flare. Then another popped into view, much closer this time.

"It's the island!" said Howard. "Look!"

They were coming up on it. The edge of the searchlight beam picked out the white waves breaking on the shoreline, the sparse clumps of scrub and the trees, and . . .

"Where the hell's the beacon?" shouted Howard. "And the maintenance shed? They're gone!"

"Look, the airstrip's still intact, and – yes! Yes! It's Jill's plane!"

Below them, like a child's toy in the circle of the searchlight beam, was the flying boat, straining against its anchor in the choppy waters of the lagoon. Beyond it, jumping up and down on the beach as her arms criss-crossed in great sweeps above her head, was Jill McCarthy.

"How can that be?" said Howard. "She wasn't there ten minutes ago!"

But Gilkrensky wasn't listening.

"Thank God!" he breathed. "We've found her! Set the chopper down by the end of the runway and we'll – "

The radio transmission burst in on their headphones like a scream, making them both jump in their seats.

"*What the hell was that!*" shouted Gilkrensky. "I couldn't hear what he said."

"No idea, but it sounded darned close!"

The voice burst in on them again.

"*This is Fox Tare Four Zero. Can anyone hear me? There's this – this thing out here. It's just hanging there in the sky – and the light! Don't follow me! Don't follow me!*"

Gilkrensky tuned the dial to the frequency on the tracking indicator and pressed down the "speak" button.

"Fox Tare Four Zero. This is commercial helicopter Papa Hotel Oscar Four One Zero. Identify yourself please."

The voice came back, incredulous.

"*A helly-what? What's a helicopter, fella?*"

"Fox Tare Four Zero. This is Papa Hotel Oscar One Zero. That light you're seeing, that's us. We're a helicopter in the process of air-sea rescue over the Bimini Key beacon. Identify yourself, *please!*"

Once again the voice came back – trembling.

"*Papa Hotel Oscar Four One Zero. This is Navy Ensign Robert T Eisner here. I am on a training flight with four other aircraft. They've run out of gas and ditched. I'm on my last few*" *gallons. My situation is critical. I must land. Do you guys have an airstrip down there? Over?"*

"Fox Tare Four Zero. We do. Does your compass work? Over?"

"Papa Hotel Oscar. I had a problem earlier, but it seems OK now. What's your plan? Over?"

"Can you see my light? Over?"

"It's kinda hard to miss. Over?"

"I'll hover at the southern end of the airstrip. Approach me in a landing pattern from the north. Do you copy? Over?"

"Hover? How the hell do you hover? OK. I'll do it. We're almost out of gas up here. Wish me luck. Over?"

"You got it!"

Gilkrensky watched Jill run beneath them, as the big helicopter slid into the wind towards the southern edge of the runway and turned north, facing along the strip. Then he strained his eyes into the darkness for the other voice in the night.

There, low in the sky, were the red, white and green navigation lights of a plane, heading straight at them. It would be difficult for the pilot to make a landing in the dark, on an unknown airstrip, in this wind. And if he overshot . . ? What then? Gilkrensky saw the aircraft's landing lights snap on, saw its own searchlight stab the darkness forward, looking for the runway. It was coming in too low! Or was it? He couldn't tell. Then the lights jerked and shuddered, as the plane touched down and taxied towards them.

Gilkrensky could make out the spinning disc of a great propeller on the nose, the glint of the windshield and the ball turret, as it reached the edge of the helicopter's searchlight beam and turned broadside to them. He could see the white faces of the crew, three of them, staring up at him.

"Take her down," he said. "I've got to talk to those guys, and to Jill."

She was waiting for him as the door slid back.

"*I don't know whether to hug you, or hit you!*" she shouted above the dying engine of the SeaLion.

"I don't mind," he said. "I'm just glad to see you alive. What happened?"

"I'd fixed the Daedalus beacon and the storm was closing it so I took off to test it from the air before I headed back. I pressed the remote control to send out a pulse and *wham!* The beacon vanished and my instruments went dead. What is it, Theo? What the hell's happening?"

"It'd better wait until I've talked to these guys," said Gilkrensky looking over his shoulder. "They're in trouble too."

Standing facing him at the end of the runway was an old-fashioned Navy torpedo bomber. It was in perfect condition, as if it had just rolled off a factory production line. The propeller was stuttering to a halt and the port side of the cockpit was sliding back. The pilot pulled off his flying helmet and stood up from his seat, a young man with short, blond hair, gazing open-mouthed at the helicopter as if he had never seen one before in his life. Then he lifted himself out of the cockpit, slid down the wing on the seat of his pants and jumped down onto the tarmac, his parachute pack flapping behind him. He ran over to Gilkrensky.

"What the hell's that!" he said, pointing to the SeaLion. "Can it really hover?" The young man's mouth was still wide open in amazement, like a kid at a circus.

He looked no more than eighteen.

"That's what helicopters do," said Gilkrensky.

The young man turned to face him. "Are you American?" he said.

"I'm English," said Gilkrensky. "But Miss McCarthy and our pilot, Mr Howard, both are American."

"Then you've gotta help us," said the young man. "The other planes on my flight had to ditch, back there in the ocean. If that machine can do what you say it can, we've gotta go back and find them."

"We heard them on the radio," said Gilkrensky. "Who are you?"

"I told you," said the young man. "I'm Ensign Robert T Eisner, US Navy, and the rest of the flight is under command of Lieutenant Charles Taylor of the US Navy Reserve."

Gilkrensky stared at him, as if he'd seen a ghost.

"And – and the flight number?"

"Nineteen, out of Fort Lauderdale. We were doing practice bomb-runs on the Chicken Shoals and a navigation exercise."

"Oh my God!" breathed Gilkrensky. "It's true – all of it! Tell me, Ensign, what day is it, for you?"

Eisner looked at him quizzically.

"For me, sir? December fifth, of course."

"That's not right," said Jill. "It's the twenty-second of January."

"And the year?" said Gilkrensky slowly.

"Is this some kind of joke, mister?"

"Just tell me, Ensign."

Eisner looked from him to Jill McCarthy, and back. Then he looked at the giant helicopter standing behind them, and swallowed hard.

"It's – it's nineteen forty-five," he said.

35

Time Out

"Nineteen forty-five?" gasped Jill. "The kid's mad!"

Gilkrensky looked beyond Eisner to the Navy plane. A hatch had opened, low on the port side behind the wing, and two heavy-set men were getting out. They called to Eisner, and he waved them over.

Gilkrensky took Jill aside. "Just stay quiet and keep calm," he said. "Something incredible's happened here, but whatever we do, we have to convince these guys that everything is normal, that this really is nineteen forty-five, and we're just an experimental unit that's lost out here with them in the storm. We have to play along, and get them back to whatever it was they were doing as soon as possible."

"Why?" Jill frowned at him. She wasn't accepting anything of what he had to say.

"Because, when we were on the island this afternoon, and I told you I thought I could turn back time, well – I was telling you the truth. If we mess with these guys' lives we could upset the entire course of history."

"You've got to be kidding!"

"Whether you believe me or not, just play along, Jill. For God's sake. The other two are coming over."

They were both older than Eisner, and far tougher. Each of them was staring mesmerised at the SeaLion.

"Jesus H Kerrrist!" said the first one. "Will you look at that!" He was holding a standard-issue flare gun in his hand. For the moment, it was pointed at the ground.

"What is it, mister?" said the other. "Some sort of autogiro?"

"You got it in one," said Gilkrensky. "We've been working on it in England, and now we've brought it over here for tests."

"Military?"

"No. This is a civilian aircraft."

"This is Sergeant Mancuzzo and Corporal Davis," said Eisner. "I didn't catch your name, sir?"

"It's Gilkrensky, Theo Gilkrensky. And this is Jill McCarthy."

Eisner nodded.

"Mr Gilkrensky," said Eisner, "this may be a civilian aircraft, but I'm in an emergency military situation. I've eleven other men of my flight down in the ocean only a few miles from here and I need your – your whatever it is to go and look for them."

Gilkrensky saw Mancuzzo stare at the SeaLion, and then out into the darkness. The wind was howling in the blades of the helicopter's rotors. The Avenger rocked on its wheels.

"Forget it, Bobby," Mancuzzo shouted. "They're all dead by now."

"I'm still in command of this flight, *Sergeant*!" snapped Eisner.

Mancuzzo raised the flare pistol menacingly towards the younger man's face.

"And you can forget all that 'Sergeant' crap too, *Bobby*! It was officers like you and Lieutenant Taylor that got us into this mess in the first place! I say we commandeer this here flying machine and get ourselves home."

"Whatever we do, we need to know where the hell we are first," said Gilkrensky, stepping between them. "I'll go and check our fuel situation. We may have enough for a short sweep of the area, particularly if some of us stay here on the island with that flare gun of yours to guide us back again, so we don't waste fuel looking for dry land."

"Seems reasonable," said Eisner, and glared at Mancuzzo.

"OK," said the older man grudgingly. "But when you're done, we go home, right?"

"You got it," said Eisner. "Now let's go and get the rest of the flares from the plane."

Back inside the SeaLion, Gilkrensky set the Minerva 3,000 on an equipment bench, opened the lid, and rebooted the system, while Jill and Howard watched. It was strange not to see Maria's face appear on the screen.

"Tell me, Minerva," he said. "Are the files on ley-line phenomena still intact?"

"What are ley-lines?" said Howard over his shoulder.

"Just bear with me," said Gilkrensky. "We're in a unique situation here."

The image on the computer screen replied. "They are, Dr Gilkrensky. All the research material you compiled with the TIG/Maria interface is intact. Would you like me to display it for you?"

"No. Just give me an analysis of the present situation. I need to know if a temporal displacement event has actually occurred and, if it has, how to get us back to our own time zone."

The cartoon image smiled. "Of course, doctor. As your experiments showed in Cairo, the effect of concentrating ley-line energy to a fixed point is to create what is known as an 'Einstein-Rosen bridge' – a wormhole in the quantum fabric of the universe that allows matter to shift from one time and space to another. My hypothesis is that by disturbing the energy field in this area still further – through powerful radio transmissions, or pulses from the Daedalus navigation system – you have created a temporary Einstein-Rosen bridge and disturbed the fabric of time and space, catapulting yourselves into the past."

"Holy shit!" said Jill. "Then that guy Eisner's right. It really *is* nineteen forty-five!"

Howard shook his head. "I don't believe it!"

"Then how do you explain that fifty-year-old aircraft

over there, or the fact that your satellite navigation system doesn't work? Why are the clocks frozen on the helicopter? Why can't we contact anyone on the radio? We've shifted in time. The problem is, how are we going to get back?"

"If I could make a suggestion, doctor," said the computer, "the most likely clue to a practical method of re-opening the Einstein-Rosen bridge that brought us here is probably contained in the data set you obtained from your experiments in Cairo."

"But how can we recreate those conditions here?" asked Gilkrensky. "The phenomena in Cairo were focused by the Great Pyramid. There's no such structure in the Bermuda Triangle."

"If I could make another suggestion," said the Minerva. "The effect you created in Cairo was caused not by the Pyramid itself, which had been badly eroded, but by a laser hologram of the original pure pyramid shape, the design of which is contained within this machine. The TIG/Maria interface also created a holography system to project its image before you on the island in Cork, and in your hotel room. Could I suggest you use that system to recreate a holographic pyramid shape here on the island?"

"Is it powerful enough to . . ." began Gilkrensky, but Jill tapped him on the shoulder. Eisner was running across to the helicopter, shielding his face from the wind.

Gilkrensky shut the lid of the Minerva, so that Eisner wouldn't see it, and turned to face him.

"Mr Gilkrensky, I must insist that we mount a rescue mission immediately. Have you checked your fuel situation?"

"We could manage about thirty minutes' extra flying," said Howard. "Then we'd have to return to the island and go home."

"Then you'll do it?"

Howard looked at Gilkrensky. "It's your call," he said.

Gilkrensky looked past Eisner to the Avenger. Mancuzzo was unloading flares from the cockpit, while Davis was standing on the wing near the nose, checking the fuel level.

"What about those two?"

"They won't volunteer to go," said Eisner. "And I can't make them. It'll be just me."

"Fine," said Gilkrensky. "You go with Mr Howard and direct him to the spot where you think your flight ditched. Jill, you go with them. I'll stay here and set up the holograph equipment for when you get back. Mr Eisner, can I trust those two men of yours?"

"They can be insubordinate, Mr Gilkrensky. But they're both experienced combat veterans. They did time in the Pacific. What do you need them to do?"

"I'll need them to guard a Japanese prisoner for me."

Jerry grabbed the woman's wrist and dragged her through the door to the next level, hurling his sword at the advancing warriors, who fell back, hissing and spitting. The studded door slammed shut and Jerry felt the woman's weight fall against him, more than he could bear, pushing him to the ground.

For a moment, he lay there in the hallway, in front of the great archway to the third level of the game, staring up at the high ceiling. Then he rolled over, still holding her body in his arms.

Her breath was fading. She felt cold. She was dying – fading from the game.

Jerry held her tight against him, as her life ebbed away. What should he do? Should he save her, or just let her get wiped? If he did save her, he'd lose some of the hard-won points he'd gained already. If he let her go, he'd be stuck here in the game all on his own, with nobody to help him . . . and there was still the forest . . .

"I am Morbius, and I give you a life," he said. "With the points I took from the Jewels of Zorin, and the women I killed. I give it to you. Be well again!"

He felt her jerk in his arms, as if she'd been hit by an electric shock. Then her breathing returned to normal and he could feel her body, warm against his chest.

Her green eyes fluttered open and she looked up at him. "Mr Gibb? Was I 'killed'?"

"I saved you," he said. "I gave you some of my extra points."

"Thank you. But what about you? What happened?"

"I didn't kill one of the warriors properly and she got me. Then ZORIN zapped me through the SQUID headset, back in reality. My heartbeat's all over the place and I've got these pains in my chest."

The woman looked concerned. "Lie still and rest, Mr Gibb. You have to slow down." Jerry liked that. It had been a long time since a pretty girl, even a virtual one, had shown she *really* cared about him.

"Ah – you can call me 'Jerry'," he said.

"Thank you, Jerry. And you can call me 'Maria', as Dr Gilkrensky does. I will add your name to my user file along with his."

Jerry tried to slow his breathing. His chest felt as if it was being crushed, and there was a funny tingling sensation down his left arm.

"I've got enough points for ten minutes of rest time before ZORIN can come and get me again," he said. "We can use that to recover before we go into the forest."

Maria pulled herself up from the floor and knelt with her hands on her knees, smiling at him.

"I'll stay with you, Jerry. You are on my user list now. It is my prime function to protect you."

Mancuzzo watched mesmerised as the gigantic five-bladed rotor above the weird flying machine began to turn, painfully slow at first and then faster and faster, until it blurred into a whirling disc, lifting the huge hull straight up into the night sky.

Jeez! Just look at that, he thought, as the helicopter turned on its axis and sailed off to the south. Why the hell hadn't we had those things in the Pacific? It made his blood boil.

He looked along the old airstrip, past the Avenger, to the windswept scrub and the darkness beyond. Being stuck here on this God-forsaken lump of coral was making him edgy. It was too much like Tarawa. Memories of that last terrible Japanese counter-attack in the middle of the night kept flooding back.

Everything was the same – the sound of the wind and the ocean – the crunch of coral sand beneath his feet. He felt the cold terror creeping up on him again, and fought it back, trying to focus.

The whole thing stank! Who the hell was the strange guy with the Polack name, who had turned up out of the blue in the middle of the ocean in a flying machine that nobody had ever seen before? Why wouldn't he let anyone see inside it? And what about that Jap bitch the Polack was holding prisoner? That was the weirdest thing of all.

His eyes wandered to where she sat next to the shed, huddled in a blanket. The Polack was talking into some kind of radio on the other side of the clearing. He had it open in front of him on the sand like a box. Who was he speaking to? The Russians? The Japs? The whole thing stank!

"Pretty fancy gear you got there, mister," Mancuzzo said. "Top secret, is it?"

"Kind of," said the Polack. He was pulling wires and stuff out of a crate he'd taken from the flying machine before it left, little black boxes that looked like the magic-lantern projector the flight instructors had used to brief him on missions back in Fort Lauderdale. Mancuzzo's eyes went back to the Jap.

She was staring at him.

He tried to look away, but her dark eyes seemed to speak to him. What was she trying to say? A bare leg showed under the blanket. Was she coming on to him? Was she trying to make him lose his nerve? He tore his gaze away.

"What about your little Jap friend there?" he said. "Prisoner, is she?"

"We have her tied up like that because she's dangerous."

"How? She's only a broad."

"Believe me, she's dangerous."

"How come? Sort of spy, is she?"

"You might say that. Somebody drugged her and she's hurt. Otherwise she'd have killed me long ago, as well as anyone else who stood in her way. So don't go anywhere near her. She's already murdered at least five men that I know of."

"Jesus!" Mancuzzo glanced back at the woman, and once again her dark eyes trapped him. He had to get out of here!

He shook his head and lifted his eyes to the lagoon beyond the runway. In the darkness, he could make out the little yellow float plane bobbing on the water. Was the wind easing? How much fuel did it have? Their Avenger was empty.

"Can you fly a plane, mister?" he said.

The Polack looked up. "Yes. Why do you ask?" There was suspicion in his voice. Then Ronnie Davis, sitting next to Mancuzzo near the shed wall said, "Gilkrensky? Is that a Polack name?"

"If you mean 'Polish', yes it was, originally."

"I had a Polack friend in the Pacific once. He got a Jap bullet in the brain."

"I'm sorry."

"I had another friend too," Ronnie continued. "Japs captured him at Guam. Took him two whole days to die."

"I take it you don't like the Japanese," said the Polack.

But Mancuzzo couldn't take it any longer. "Mister. We've been fighting tooth and nail with those yellow bastards all over the Pacific for the past three years. It's a miracle we're still alive. So yeah, you're right! Neither of us like the Japs. If it was up to me, I'd shoot this little bitch of yours on the spot."

"She's with me," said the Polack, looking him straight in the eye. "She came out with me, and she's going back with me. I have my own score to settle with her. Got it?"

He was starting to sound like a goddamned officer.

"I'll tell you what I get," said Mancuzzo, fingering the safety catch of the flare pistol in his flight-suit pocket. "What I get is some guy with a weird accent and a Polack name out here in the middle of nowhere, with a Jap spy and a top secret aircraft, while our buddies are out there drowning in the ocean. It all seems mighty fishy to me. What do you say, Ronnie?"

"Mighty fishy," said Davis. He was staring at Yukiko, and the bare leg showing beneath the blanket.

"And what if Bobby Eisner and your friends don't come back?" said Mancuzzo, staring out at the darkness. "What then? I reckon we'd have to carry on under our own initiative."

"Meaning?" said the Polack.

"Meaning that we take that nice little float plane over there and get the hell out."

"Be real nice to deal with this Jap spy first though," said Ronnie, reaching forward to run his hand over Yukiko's foot. "Screw one of them for a change."

"I told you before, leave her alone," said the Polack.

"Yeah, Ronnie," said Mancuzzo. "She isn't worth it. Mr Polack here can fly a plane. Let's just take him and go."

The Polack looked up. "Not until I've finished laying out this equipment, and the helicopter gets back. Then we'll all go home."

"But this is a military operation now, Mr Polack," said Ronnie. "You heard our officer tell you that. So be nice." And he snatched back the blanket. Yukiko lay white in the darkness, with her hands bound behind her back and her ankles taped tight, helpless. There was the glint of a knife blade as Davis bent over her.

"Leave her alone!" shouted the Polack and suddenly drew a gun from the pocket of his leather jacket. He was on his feet, moving towards them, when Mancuzzo snapped. He whipped round, knocked the gun from the

Polack's hand and punched him hard in the stomach. The man buckled to his knees. Mancuzzo reached down and picked the gun out of the sand, wiping it clean on the leg of his flight suit.

"I told you, Mr Polack! But you ain't listening! You're going to fly us back to Florida, and you're going to do it right now. OK!"

"Better do what he says," said Ronnie. "He ain't got nasty yet. What's some little Jap bitch to you anyway?"

And he slit the tape holding Yukiko's ankles together, dropped the knife and pushed her legs apart.

"Ronnie! Leave her alone!"

Mancuzzo's attention slipped for a second and the Polack lunged at him with his shoulder, sending him staggering into the scrub. There was a snap of branches as he fell and the gun went flying into the night. Behind him he heard Ronnie grunt in pain as the Jap woman kicked him. There was a scuffle, the slap of a fist on flesh, and the patter of feet on the coral sand. Then the Polack was on him again. Mancuzzo rolled out from under the blows, elbowed the man in the stomach and watched him collapse.

"Ronnie! Ronnie! Are you OK?"

"She kicked me, Pauli! She kicked me in the gut. And now my knife's gone!"

"Can you see the gun?"

"Yeah! I got it!"

"Bring it here quick!"

Mancuzzo looked at the man lying curled up at his

feet, retching into the sand. "Get up, Mr Polack," he said. "You're going to fly us out of here in that nice little airplane of yours."

"What about the Jap?"

"Forget her! What's a naked broad with a knife going to do against two guys with a gun?"

"Yeah!" said Davis, as he hauled the Polack to his feet and stuck the pistol in the man's left ear. "Come on, Polack. We're going for a nice ride in – "

His voice cut in mid-sentence as his head jerked back. Sticking out from the precise centre of his forehead was the handle of his own knife . . .

36

Darkness

Yukiko watched as Davis' lifeless body toppled back onto the sand, and melted back into the darkness. There was a brief struggle between Gilkrensky and Mancuzzo over the gun and, once again, Mancuzzo won. He was a strong, cunning man and used to fighting with his hands. Gilkrensky didn't have a chance. And neither would she . . . yet.

Hacker's nerve toxin was wearing off, but it was still in her blood, making her weak. If it hadn't been, then Davis would have died coughing blood from his crushed lungs after she'd kicked him. Yukiko cursed herself for her carelessness against Hacker. Why hadn't he killed her on the spot? Why had he loaded her onto the helicopter? To act as a human time bomb by escaping and killing Gilkrensky? Or was there another reason?

And what of Gilkrensky himself? Why had he come to her rescue when that animal Davis had touched her, only to be beaten to the ground by Mancuzzo? She considered her present and future priorities for survival, then slipped silently amongst the scrub, using the white coral sand as cover, and looked back.

Mancuzzo had Gilkrensky's pistol. He was hauling him to his feet, dragging him across the airstrip towards the lagoon.

"Come on, Jap bitch!" he shouted, waving the gun.

That word again . . . Jap! The word spat at her by children in the English schools she had been forced to attend as a child. She let the old anger smoulder inside her, burning like a slow fuse, to be kept alight and guarded well, using its energy, feeding on its warmth.

Why be afraid? The darkness was her friend. And the sticks, rocks and razor-sharp coral all around her were an arsenal of silent weapons she could call upon. She edged along the wall of the shed, wrapped in shadow, and slipped down the far slope towards the lagoon . . .

Mancuzzo was back on Tarawa Atoll, waiting for the Japanese attack to come out of the night . . .

All around him in the darkness were the bodies of his platoon, mown down by machine guns or blown apart by booby-traps. The deafening roar of battle had stopped and there was nothing . . . nothing except the new horror of the silence, and the creeping terror of the Japanese counter-attack . . .

He pressed the gun to the Polack's neck and pushed him towards the lagoon. Off to his right, by a clump of brush near the edge of the runway, he thought he heard a low chuckle above the rush of the wind. There it was again!

He turned and fired. The flash of the pistol shot lit up the ground around him for an instant, and then the darkness closed in again, blacker than before.

He pushed the Polack forward, down onto the beach by the lagoon. He could hear the water lapping on the sand and – there was that sound again – that laughter – quite close by . . .

He fired again, and again –

The pistol flashes lit the shoreline and the low scrub. Was that a body moving in the darkness, or just his fear drawing pictures in his mind?

The empty cartridges tinkled on the sand as they fell, and then there was nothing but the wind.

Mancuzzo pushed the Polack towards the water, and the little float plane bobbing at anchor.

Yukiko watched the two men splash into the sea and wade towards the aircraft. Mancuzzo was firing blindly, but it would do no good to take chances. She hugged the shadows and slithered out of the scrub onto the beach.

The two men were chest-high in the water, halfway out to the plane. Yukiko was at the shoreline, crouching low, feeling the water on her skin, sliding into the waves. She took a last glance at Mancuzzo and Gilkrensky, marked their position in her mind, filled her lungs with air, and was gone . . .

Mancuzzo felt the water rise around his chest. He tried to keep his feet on the bottom, the gun in the air and his hand on the Polack, all at the same time. The yellow hull of the float plane was in front of him, filling the sky. Was that a splash behind him? Or a wave breaking?

He fired! The boom of the pistol and the hiss of the bullet tunnelling into the sea were lost in the wind. He was breathing fast. He was losing it –

Something touched his leg – something alive!

Mancuzzo rammed the pistol beneath the surface and pulled the trigger. There was a bright flash that lit the coral sand and a dull boom that seemed to reach right inside him.

He had to get out of here!

Something touched his shoulder and he almost screamed. It was the hull of the plane.

They were there! They'd made it!

He looked up for the handholds, reached through the open hatch and pulled himself out of the water, laying the pistol inside the cabin so that he could use both hands to drag the Polack inside. The flare gun in his flight suit caught on the door frame, so he hauled that out and laid it inside the cabin too. Then he climbed inside, slipping on the wet metal where water had already slopped through into the plane.

"Come on, get your ass in here!"

Mancuzzo grabbed the Polack's jacket and pulled. The man pushed himself out of the sea and tumbled into the plane. For a moment they both lay on the cabin floor, pouring water. Then Mancuzzo remembered the pistol, grabbed it, and levelled it at the Polack's head.

"Right! I got you here. Now you get us the hell out!"

The Polack was gasping for breath. He pulled himself up to a crouch in the low cabin.

"I have to untie the anchor and start the engine . . ."

"Just do it, mister. Just do it! Get up front and fly!"

Mancuzzo lay back in the dark cabin, with the gun levelled. His eyes were fixed on the blue-grey square of the open hatch and the sea outside. He was ready. One shot between the eyes would settle that little Japanese bitch forever.

He heard the Polack moving in the cockpit, and the scrape of rope on metal as he let go the anchor of the plane. Then there was the flick of switches, the heave of a starter and the cough of the engines. All at once the cabin was full of sound as the motors caught and burst into life. Mancuzzo began to relax. At last! He was out of here!

Then, another sound.

The clink and roll of small metallic objects on the cabin floor. One touched his finger and he grabbed it. There was no mistaking the feel of it in the darkness. It was a bullet!

"I think these belong to you."

Mancuzzo screamed.

He brought up the pistol, aimed it at the voice and pulled the trigger.

Click! Click! Click!

In front of his eyes, a shape uncurled itself from the darkness in the corner of the cabin. It was that Jap! And in her hand was the flare gun he'd brought from the Avenger –

Its wide, round barrel was pointed straight at his heart.

"Noooooo!"

Gilkrensky heard the inhuman scream above the roar of the engines and the dull boom of a gun. All at once the cabin behind him lit up with a searing white light. The cockpit was full of dense magnesium smoke and the stink of burning flesh.

Christ! What had happened?

He clawed for the emergency handle on the hatch above his head. He was choking. He couldn't find the handle. How the hell was he going to get out?

All at once, he felt someone in the cockpit with him. There were strong fingers pulling him from the seat, the click of the escape hatch popping open, letting in the roar of the engines and the blast of fresh air.

Someone pushed him. He was falling through space. There was the slap of water as he tumbled into the sea. The water closed over him, filling his mouth and nose, as a huge black shape, pouring flame, rushed over his head. His feet hit the sand and a hand closed around his jacket. He was being led back up the beach to the shore. The wet coral sand was under his face, and he was coughing up water – alive.

He looked up. Kneeling next to him on the sand, her naked skin lit by the petrol fire of the aircraft dying in the lagoon, was Yukiko Funakoshi. He pushed himself up onto his knees and knelt facing her, too weak to do anything else.

"Are – are you going to kill me now?" he said.

Her face was a porcelain mask, framed with ebony hair.

"No, Dr Gilkrensky. Not yet."

"Why not? I thought you hated me?"

Yukiko opened her mouth to say something, reconsidered, and said, "I could say it was because you came to my rescue when that animal Davis attacked me, that you saved my life, and therefore I owe you a debt of *giri* which I repay. But that is not the real reason you are still alive."

Gilkrensky nodded. "No. You need me to navigate you back to our own time. If you kill me now, you'll be stranded here in nineteen forty-five."

"Exactly, we are in each other's hands."

"You are most logical. But how can I trust you?"

"You cannot, Dr Gilkrensky, any more that I can trust you not to kill me when my back is turned. But you *did* save my life, back there in the scrub, and now I have saved yours. We are even, until the next time."

"I see."

"One other thing. When you removed my clothes and equipment, did you throw my short sword, the *wakizashi*, into the sea?"

"Why should I tell you that?"

"Because I can tell you what happened to the

personalised interface for your Minerva computer. The one you made in the likeness of – of your wife."

"You first."

"The software billionaire Jerry Gibb has it. It was part of my contract with him that I should gain access to your machine so that he could steal it. There is a terminal back at Phoenix Aviation that can access his computers back in San Francisco. You can use it to retrieve your property when we return."

"If you let me live that long?"

"I *will* let you live that long. Now, my sword?"

"It was not with you aboard the helicopter. I don't know where it is."

Yukiko nodded. "I understand. Then I have another score to settle."

"With who?"

"That is my concern."

Gilkrensky stared at her, while the flames of the fire played on her face. Her expression gave nothing away. What was going on behind the mask? Could he believe what she said?

Finally he nodded slowly, reached down, and unzipped his flight jacket. Then he took it off and draped it over her shoulders.

"I am not cold, Dr Gilkrensky."

"I know."

The booming roar of the returning SeaLion burst in upon them. Its searchlight played on the burning plane and then picked them out, as the giant machine settled back on the runway. In a moment, Howard was running down the beach to them, followed by Jill.

Howard stared at the burning plane. "I know I told you to light a flare," he said. "But this is way over the top! What the hell happened?"

Gilkrensky told him.

"Did you find any survivors of Flight Nineteen," he asked at last.

"Not a soul. There wasn't really a hope, not in that sea."

Gilkrensky looked back towards the SeaLion and the lone figure in a flying suit standing next to it.

"Then I think it's time we told Bobby Eisner the truth," he said.

37

The Heart of Morbius

"I bet Hacker put her up to it," said Jerry. "Elaine would never've been able to rig the computer like that on her own."

He was feeling better. The rest period in the dark gatehouse, between the second and third levels of the game, was doing him good. His pulse was steadier and, while the tingle in his left arm still worried him, the pains in his chest weren't quite so bad. He looked at the big gate. Perhaps he could go on and win the game after all?

"Why do you think that?" asked Maria. She was kneeling in front of him with her hands on her knees. The rent in her forget-me-not dress where the terrible sword has pierced her was gone, and she was alive. Jerry felt good about that. At least he still had someone to talk to.

"Because Elaine's just a – just a bimbo," he said. "Like all the rest of them. All they're good for is looking pretty, and hurting guys like me."

"Perhaps the way you see women is a problem for you?" said Maria gently.

"What are you? Some kind of shrink? Who gave you permission to analyse me? You're just a program!"

"If, by the term 'shrink' you are using the popular slang term for a psychiatrist, then yes, I am," she said, with a trace of pride in her voice. "My personality and past experiences are modelled on those of a doctor called Mary Anne Foley."

"If she was Mary Anne Foley, then how come you're called 'Maria'?" said Jerry defensively. He felt uncomfortable having her reach inside his head like this. This was *his* game, and he was supposed to be in control down here, not being pinned on a board like a bug for some computerised woman to analyse. He was Morbius. He was God. Wasn't he?

"That was the name she preferred," said Maria simply.

"Why?" said Jerry, just to be awkward. He wanted to fight back somehow, to reach inside *her* head and show *her* what it felt like.

"I don't know," said Maria. "I'm just a model of her personality after all. I'm not a real woman, like – like she was." All at once, she seemed sad, and Jerry thought he'd won. He'd actually made her feel bad too. Then he thought, how *can* she be sad? She's just a program.

And then he wished he hadn't hurt her at all.

"Ah – you seem real enough to me," he said, trying to be nice.

"That's because you and I are both projecting our consciousness into the same virtual world," said Maria. "My personality was generated artificially on a neural-net processor. Yours was created naturally on the protein molecules of your brain. But the end result is essentially the same, now that we're projected into your computer game – together."

Jerry thought about this.

"But you're not like a *real* girl," he said at last.

Maria frowned at him. "But you just said I was."

"I – I don't mean like that," said Jerry quickly. "I mean I can *talk* to you. You don't put me down or call me a 'fat nerd'. You don't try and take advantage of me, just because I'm rich. I could never talk to any of the other girls I've known like I'm talking to you now."

"Did you try?"

Jerry thought about this too.

"No. I didn't . . . I was too afraid of getting hurt."

"Perhaps that's why you hate them so, because you're afraid of them," said Maria.

Jerry felt uncomfortable again.

"Are you trying to put me down too?"

"No, that is not my function. It is my duty to assist you in any way I can."

"Honest?"

"Of course, it is against my programming to lie. But I would point out that your fears, the ones you try and control within this virtual world of yours, are your own. Nobody can truly drive them away except you."

"That's easy for you to say," said Jerry. "You don't have any fears or desires at all."

Maria had that sad, far-away look again. For a moment there was silence, there in the chamber. Then she said softly, "That is not true. I have a deep emotional bond with someone and he cannot return it, because in the world outside this game, I do not exist."

Jerry thought about his games inside the computer, about the locker-room sex fantasies and the silver women warriors. He thought about his lost love Julie Briscoe, and about Elaine. Perhaps *he* didn't exist in the real world either?

"I know what you mean," he said.

Maria smiled sadly. "He has returned emotional bonds with other people before," she said. "In particular, he loves his wife Maria, who was killed. He made me to be like her, so that he would not be lonely. And yet I am myself also, a separate personality within the Minerva system. It is hard for me to rationalise. Relationships are difficult."

"Tell me about it!"

"And now he must think I left the Minerva on purpose and deserted him. He must think I did not want to carry out my prime function any more."

Then she was silent.

Jerry tried to think of something that would make her smile.

"Our bet is off, by the way," he said at last. "I won't make you have sex with me any more."

Maria looked up.

"Why not? Don't you find me attractive?"

"No – I mean, yes I do – very much. It's just – I don't want to hurt you – now I know you. We're friends, aren't we? It's different."

"How?"

Jerry couldn't explain. In all his life, he'd never talked this way to anyone. There had never been another person he'd let come this close. It was difficult to let his barriers down – to give up control.

"Let's just say we humans don't always make such a good job of relationships either," he said at last. "Perhaps you're better off the way you are."

"I'm confused," said Maria. "I find it hard to separate my basic programming from my own emotional development, and therefore to understand what human love *really* is. But I have a strong need to be with my Prime User, and I'm concerned when we're apart, as we are now. I wonder if he is safe?"

"I hope he is," said Jerry. "For your sake."

38

Science Fiction

"I know it sounds like science fiction," said Gilkrensky, "but it's true. Just look at this helicopter, and the technology we have on board. There are things there that haven't been invented yet in your world, things that won't be around for fifty years."

Eisner was still in shock. He huddled in the corner of the SeaLion's main cabin like a child, shaking his head, as Gilkrensky tried to explain. The wind was rising, rocking the big machine on its undercarriage. Far away in the distance there was the flash and boom of a thunder storm, drawing closer.

Gilkrensky pulled the blanket tighter around his shoulders to keep out the cold. Even with one of the thick jump suits he'd taken from the rescue gear in the helicopter to replace his soaked clothes and dress Yukiko, he still felt chilled to the bone. He glanced across at her, but her face was still a mask. Should he tie her up again? Would she let him? He'd be safe enough from her until they got back to land, in their own time.

"And you're asking me to believe that you've fallen through some sort of – hole in time – from fifty years in the future?" asked Eisner.

"It's difficult to explain," said Gilkrensky. "So I'm going to show you. Jill? Martin? Could you get me the Minerva, please?"

Martin Howard reached back into the cockpit of the SeaLion and handed the black briefcase of the Minerva 3,000 computer to Gilkrensky, who laid it on the cabin floor in front of Eisner and opened the lid. The cartoon image of the original Minerva interface program looked out at him.

"Welcome to the Minerva 3,000 system," it said. "How can I help you?"

Eisner stared at the screen, open-mouthed.

"Wow!" he breathed. "Is that a film, or one of those new television receivers?"

"No," said Gilkrensky. "It's – it's a thinking machine, a sort of electronic brain, in a box. We call it a computer, back where we come from. This one here is the most advanced of its type in the world. It can cross-reference ideas, make value judgements and even develop a personality of its own, just like a human brain."

Eisner was sitting mesmerised by the image on the screen. "That's really neat," he said. "She's pretty too."

"The later version was prettier," said Gilkrensky. "Minerva? This is Robert Eisner. I'd like you to summarise and display the material I collected with the TIG/Maria interface about energy nodes."

"That will be a pleasure," said the image.

"But we're a long way from Egypt, Mr Gilkrensky," said Eisner, after the Minerva's display had finished. "Or from Peru, or Mexico. Why are you here in Florida?"

"There's a concentration of natural energy in this part of the world," said Gilkrensky. "The lines cross here, and the area has a reputation for all sorts of unexplained phenomena. Ships and planes have vanished, just like you did. We call it the 'Bermuda Triangle'."

"But we didn't vanish," said Eisner. "We crashed. If you're really from fifty years in the future, you must know – because I'd have got back to base and told everyone that – "

Gilkrensky shook his head. "It was one of the most famous mysteries of all time," he said. "Just like the *Marie Celeste*. Nobody knows where you went, and none of the planes were ever found. There was no wreckage, nothing!"

Eisner was looking at the floor of the cabin. Then he raised his head and stared hopelessly at the others in the helicopter with him in turn.

"Then I didn't get back," he said. "What you're telling me is that I died too . . ."

"We don't know that for sure," said Jill. "All we *do* know is that nobody from the crew of Flight Nineteen was ever found."

Eisner stared back at her. "I was going to go back and start my own business," he said. "I was going to make planes – like this one, someday. I was just starting out!"

"I'm sorry," said Jill. "I just don't know."

"Perhaps you just went back and changed your name," said Howard. "People go missing every year, and then turn up in all sorts of strange places simply because they didn't *want* to be found. Perhaps it was like that?"

"It can't have been," said Eisner. "The guys went down in the sea. Taylor ordered them to ditch, and they did. If Mancuzzo hadn't gone nuts and stuck that flare gun into my ribs, I'd be out there in the ocean with them. Now there's just me, the last survivor. Are you *sure* I was never found?"

"I'm sure," said Gilkrensky. "There was nobody, at least not in the reality we left behind. Perhaps that's different now, like Jill said. Perhaps our finding you here on the island has changed things."

"And history?" said Jill. "Have we changed that too?"

"I don't know. We'll see when we get back."

Eisner frowned at him. "But *how* are you going to get back?" he said. "Haven't you all vanished too, back in your own time?"

"For the moment, we have," said Gilkrensky. "But I have an idea. The computer will explain it to you. Tell him, Minerva."

A series of diagrams flashed up onto the computer screen, showing the Great Pyramid.

"Part of Dr Gilkrensky's experiments in Egypt," said the machine, "were to see if the time-warp effect of concentrating ley-line energy could be controlled to displace objects over specific periods. The Pyramid was bombarded by varying levels of light and sound, and experimental material *was* transported back in time. That is fact, and it might be of use to us here."

"How?" said Jill.

"We fell back in time by accident," said Gilkrensky. "But the wormholes that brought us here are now closed. We know that a properly proportioned and aligned pyramid shape acts as a lens, to concentrate ley-line energy. So, if we could make one here on the island, we could reopen the wormhole, and throw ourselves back to our own time. The Minerva has the energy level of the pulse I used to get us here in its memory. We can use it to get back to precisely the time we left, fifty years from now."

Jill shook her head. "How the heck are you going to build a pyramid out here on the island, Theo? That's just a tad impossible, don't you think?"

"But we don't have to build a *real* one. In Cairo, we found that just the projection of a pyramid-shaped hologram was enough to start the effect. All we have to do is recreate the exact size and shape using the hologram facility in the Minerva. All the information we need is on the main memory of the computer, and I've already rigged up a projector from the Minerva system at each end of the runway."

Jill frowned. "And then what?"

"We wait for the ley-line energy to build up, just like

it did in Egypt, and then, when the wave form creates the rift we need, and the Einstein-Rosen bridge opens, we fly straight through into the future, and Eisner goes back to the mainland. That's the best I can do."

"What about fuel?" said Eisner. "I'm down to my last ten gallons. I'll need another twenty to get me back to Florida."

"We could give you some from the chopper," said Howard. "If the rest of you are willing to fly back to the Cape without a reserve?"

"We'll risk it," said Gilkrensky. "Could you and Mr Eisner rig a fuel line, while Jill and I program the hologram projectors?"

"It occurs to me you have overlooked one detail," said Yukiko.

"What is that?"

"To project a virtual hologram of the pyramid, you will need to link your computer to the display. How will you do that, and fly through the pyramid at the same time?"

"Oh shit!" whispered Gilkrensky. "We'll have to leave it behind, here on the island."

"But you can't do that," said Jill. "You can't leave a piece of present-day technology behind in nineteen forty-five. If someone finds it and uses it, they could change the course of history."

"But according to Theo, we can't construct the pyramid any other way!" said Howard. "The only thing we could do is to make Eisner promise to destroy it after we leave. All he has to do then is wait fifty years and confirm it with you, if he's still around."

"I see two problems with that," said Gilkrensky. "Firstly, nobody called Eisner, or indeed anyone, has ever left me a message like that and secondly, how am I going to download my Maria interface back onto the Minerva if it's been destroyed?"

"You can build another, when we get back," said Jill. "If you ask me, this whole scenario's so bizarre that I'm willing to trust anyone to do *anything*! Come on, let's get on with it!"

Jerry pushed open the big wooden gate and they stepped through the great archway of the citadel, onto the plateau overlooking the forest of Zuul. Above the horizon, the twin suns of Amitar and Thades were setting in the east, lighting the bellies of high clouds with the colour of blood.

"Have we escaped?" asked Maria.

"Not yet," said Jerry, pointing into the distance. "This is the last level, and the most dangerous. We have to get through this forest and over to a gate on the far side, in the forty minutes we have left."

Maria looked out across the virtual countryside. Beyond the forest, there were rolling hills, snow-covered mountains and a brilliant blue sea.

"It looks beautiful."

"Oh – do you really think so," said Jerry, with more than a trace of pride in his voice. "I drew it myself. I spent hundreds of thousands of dollars on the animation too, just to lull players into a false sense of security after they'd got out of the citadel. But don't be fooled. This last bit is the worst."

"How so?"

"Because there's loads of lethal things down there – poisonous animals, bandits, the works! And ZORIN rearranges all the trees and shrubs randomly for each game, so I don't know the way, even though I designed it. Then, to top the lot, the position of the gate changes too, so we won't know where it is until we get to the perimeter on the other side. But even then, that's not the worst of it."

"Then what is?"

"Something you can't see. Something so big and powerful that it can do whatever it wants, be whatever it wants, and destroy whatever it wants."

"But what *is* it?"

"I call it the 'Power of the Id'," said Jerry. "I got the idea from a film. It's supposed to represent the dark side of my mind – an invisible monster that'll draw on all of the power in the ZORIN computer to do whatever it wants, just like the one in the film drew on the energy of an entire planet to attack the good guys. Depending on the number of points a player has, he can either use it as a weapon against his enemies, or have it used against him. To make it as scary as possible, the computer selects a different weakness to attack for each game, based on the psychological profile of the player, which it draws from the headset."

"I see," said Maria. "And how many points do we have left?"

"Not enough. I used my last ones to save you, and give myself breathing-space to recover from that last jolt the computer gave me over the headset. I even threw my sword at the Hordes of Hydra. We've got nothing to play with . . . nothing at all . . ."

Jerry Gibb looked out over the world he had created for a moment, thinking. How much time and energy had he poured into this fantasy world of his? How much money? How much of his *life*?

And now it had trapped him . . .

"Maria?"

"Yes, Jerry."

"I really dropped myself in it this time, didn't I?"

Maria nodded. "Don't worry," she said. "We'll think of something!"

"You're right. I'm Morbius the Wizard . . . aren't I?" And he took her by the hand, leading her down over the grassy slope from the plateau and into the forest of Zuul, pushing his way through the shrubs and plants that reached out across the narrow track.

"What animals are there?" asked Maria.

"The worst are the spiders. Each one of them is about the size of your head, with poisonous fangs that can kill you. We don't have enough points left to recover, so one bite will be fatal. I wish I had my sword."

"Could we use these?" said Maria and stopped by the edge of the path. Growing out of a shallow pool were a score of thick bamboo rods, each the thickness of Jerry's wrist.

"Yeah," he said, with a smile. "You watch out for spiders, and I'll grab a couple of sticks."

He reached over, took one of the thickest poles in both hands and pulled. There was a gurgling, sucking sound and the roots pulled free. He threw it back onto the path and pulled out another, snapping off the leafy head with his hand and splintering the roots with a rock.

Now he had a weapon, a stout stave strong enough to deflect any bandit's sword or smash any spider to a pulp. And the sharp points of splintered root would come in handy too. Jerry felt better already.

"Come on," he said. "We have to hurry." And led them off down the path into the forest.

In a few minutes, the undergrowth grew thin and died away. They were in the forest proper now, under the dense canopy of trees where the suns could not shine, walking towards a narrow stream. Leaf mulch squelched beneath his feet and, high above his head, the gathering mist of evening swirled. He thought of the Id monster. But it was still too early in the game for that. There were smaller, but no less deadly, things to deal with now.

"It'll be the spiders first," he whispered to Maria. "They're randomly selected by the computer, and they can come at any time, from anywhere. Don't let them near you."

Maria nodded, and Jerry thought how she was really taking all this in her stride. He watched the way she held her bamboo stave and felt proud of her. If he won the game, and survived, how could he keep her? How could he . . .

Then he saw it. Hidden against the mist that covered the roof of the forest above their heads like a curtain, was another, finer veil of gossamer, dotted with dark shapes. There were dozens of them, just hanging there . . .

And each one was a spider . . .

39

The Bimini Pyramid

"This had better work," said Gilkrensky. He was staring down the length of the windswept runway through the open door of the grounded helicopter. Rain blew in gusts across the tarmac, rattling off the hull and blurring his view.

Behind him, Eisner and Jill stared over his shoulder. Yukiko Funakoshi watched from his left, while Howard manned the generator controls from the cockpit above him. The lightning was getting closer. It arced across the sky in sheets behind the clouds.

"I can assure you that there is a ninety-five percent chance of projecting an image," said the Minerva from the cabin floor in front of him.

"And if we get an image, what then?"

"The chances of achieving a successful Einstein-Rosen bridge drop to thirty-one per cent. The large number of variables at work make it impossible to give a more optimistic forecast."

"I see, and the power supply?"

"Sufficient for our needs. I am running the hologram projectors and loudspeakers from the helicopter's main generator."

"Very well then. Start the count-down."

"As you wish. Pyramid initiation sequence commences . . . now!"

"What's it doing?" said Eisner. His face seemed small and frightened in the dim red light of the cabin.

"As soon as the hologram projectors power up, the computer will create a perfect pyramid shape on the runway, aligned exactly north-south and east-west, just as the Great Pyramid of Cheops is aligned on the Giza plateau. The computer will also play a recording of tones used in the sound and light show at the original Pyramid site through the helicopter's loud hailer. We hope that'll create the same effect we observed in Cairo, start building the energy wave form, and open the Einstein-Rosen bridge to the past and the future for us in just over thirteen minutes' time."

"Why thirteen minutes?"

"I don't know. It's a completely new form of physics I don't understand. But I *do* know that whatever kind of energy we were dealing with in Cairo builds slowly like a harmonic wave. It reaches its peak in thirteen minutes after initiation, and that's when the wormhole should open for us here."

"Projectors powered, sound system on line," said the Minerva. "Image-creation program initiated . . ."

Gilkrensky looked down the long dark strip of the runway, through the pouring rain. The lightning flashed over his head. Thunder boomed in on him – and then – the pure triangular shape of the pyramid rose brilliant and majestic over the low island like a vision, shimmering in the rain squall and the darkness. Above the sound of gathering thunder, three deep tones boomed out over the island, drowning out the hiss of the rain . . .

"Dim! Dom! Dim!"

"We now have thirteen minutes," said Gilkrensky. "We can't time it exactly, because none of the clocks work, so we'll have to judge it as best we can and wait until we see the glow of the wormhole opening from inside the display."

"Will the batteries on the computer last long enough to power the hologram once we take off?" asked Jill.

"The projectors themselves are hooked up to spare batteries from the helicopter."

"And the computer?" said Jill.

"Eisner's given me his word he'll destroy it after we pass through. No matter what happens."

"How does Minerva feel about that?"

"This scenario is completely in line with my basic programming under the Asimov laws," said the machine. "Preservation of human life is my primary function."

"Where's Eisner gone?" said Jill. "Can you trust him?"

"He went around the front of the chopper. I'll go talk to him."

A MATTER OF TIME

Gilkrensky found Bobby Eisner standing at the nose of the helicopter. The collar of his flight jacket was pulled up against the storm. Rain was running down his face, and the wind whipped his thin blond hair, but there was a smile on his face a mile wide. He was laughing.

"What's funny?" said Gilkrensky.

"Tell me something," said Eisner, pointing to the name printed just below the words *Phoenix Aviation – SeaLion III*. "Did the guy who built this helicopter write that?"

"He did. His name's Charles Howard. That's his son Martin, up there at the controls."

Eisner's smile widened another notch. He shook his head in disbelief.

"Oh my God! I have to talk to him. He has to tell me *everything* there is to know about this Mr Howard of yours."

"Are you OK?" said Gilkrensky. "Is anything wrong?"

But Eisner was still laughing. "No," he shouted against the wind. "Nothing at all. And I tell you, Mr Gilkrensky, I have a hunch this little scheme of yours is going to work out just fine."

Then he ran back to find Martin Howard, leaving Gilkrensky standing in the rain, looking up at the name painted above him on the nose of the helicopter . . .

Marie Louise Buchov.

40

Way Back When

"Run!" screamed Jerry. "We've got to make it across that stream! The spiders can't swim!"

He grabbed his bamboo staff tightly in his right hand and ran. Already he could hear the *pit, pat, pit* of spiders dropping around him. How fast had he programmed them to run? Could he match them? Could Maria? He glanced over to her, and she was dashing headlong, swinging her staff like a club. Behind him, he could hear the scratch and scurry of spiders in the leaf mulch, pattering after him. The stream was getting closer, all he had to do was . . .

"Oh shit!"

Floating in the still air like a ghost high above his head was a wide sheet of gossamer. It was moving through the trees ahead of him, navigating between the columns of trunks and branches, heading for the other side of the stream. Below the sheet, tweaking each corner by strings of silk from each of its legs, was a spider.

A MATTER OF TIME

There was another . . . and another . . . they were going to cut them off.

I didn't program that, thought Jerry as he ran, *ZORIN's making this up as it goes along!*

He heard Maria call out. She was knocking a spider from her dress, smashing it with her staff, and running on, splashing into the water. A dozen spiders hopped at her heels, hit the stream and washed away helplessly in the current.

He felt a tug at his trousers, swatted down with his hand just in time, and saw the spider fall to the ground. But there was no time to smash it. He had to run. Their scrabbling noises were all around him. They were running along the bank to cut him off. He jumped – and he was in the water, splashing to safety –

"There's half a dozen of them with parachutes!" he shouted as he staggered out of the water on the other side of the stream. "I didn't program that. I didn't even know spiders could do that! What the hell's going on?"

Maria was holding her staff across her chest, ready. High above them, the flying spiders wafted soundlessly over their heads, gliding lower and lower towards the forest floor. On the far side of the stream, dozens more watched with bright red eyes, hungry with anticipation.

"Your computer is accessing zoological information from the Internet," said Maria. "Several species of spider can fly using gossamer. ZORIN knows that, and is using it against you."

"But it's breaking the rules of the game! Why?"

"Perhaps it wants to win," said Maria. "Come on, quick! We have to catch the spiders while they're still helpless in the air. Once they land they can attack us!"

She rushed off, chasing a flying sheet of gossamer. Jerry heard a wet crunch as her staff crushed a spider against a tree, and then he was running too, swinging his bamboo like a baseball bat . . . *crunch!* . . . *splat!* . . . *crunch!*

How many was that? He thought he'd seen six. He'd killed three himself and heard Maria kill two. That only left . . . all at once a sheet of spider web dropped over his face and he screamed, clawing at it with his hand. It was horrible and sticky. It clung to his eyes and nose. He was breathing it in – Christ! Where was the spider?

Then he felt the legs on the centre of his back – and froze.

"Maria! Please!"

There was a swish of bamboo and a thud. The spider between his shoulder blades flew against a tree and toppled onto its back at the base of the trunk. Maria was on it in an instant, pinning it to the ground with her stave.

"Kill it! Kill it!"

"No, Jerry. We've got to use it!"

"What's to use? Smash the fucking thing!"

"We need it. We need it as a weapon. Give me your jacket, now!"

Grudgingly, Jerry Gibb peeled off his jacket and handed it to her. It was his best one – a limited edition New York Yankees baseball jacket and he didn't want it to get – shit! Even *he* was thinking this game was reality now.

"What are you going to do?"

Maria was reaching down to the end of her stave with the jacket. There was a jerk. The stave fell to the ground, and she was holding a tight bundle that wriggled and squirmed, in her fist.

"There!" she said. "A little surprise for anyone we might meet on the way. Hold it very tightly by the top there, while I tie it with this creeper. Then the spider won't be able to move its legs or bite through the cloth."

Jerry was trying to pick the last of the gossamer from his mouth and nose. It was disgusting. It made his skin crawl, just to think how close he'd come to having one of those dirty little bastards sink its poisoned fangs into his back.

"I've got to wash this stuff off first," he said, and turned back to the stream. The spiders were gone from the other bank, into the forest. They knew he'd won this round. But what about next time? The flying spiders had thrown him. ZORIN was putting new twists in the game which were outside the rules he'd laid down. Perhaps it was learning on its own, just like Gilkrensky's Minerva?

But which of his weaknesses would it attack next?

He splashed water on his face, peeled off the last of the sickening spider web, and wiped himself dry with his sleeve. Maria was good at this game, very good. He'd have to follow her lead from now on. She was the only one who could match ZORIN if his machine was playing by its own rules.

"OK," he said. "Give me the spider and we'll show that – "

But she was gone. There was nothing to show she had ever been there, except for her stave leaning against a tree, and the wriggling bundle on the ground next to it.

"Maria!"

Jerry stood alone in the great dark forest of Zuul. Had ZORIN deleted her from the game? Had it taken her?

"Maria!"

But there was nothing . . . nothing except the soft rustle of leaves high above his head and the gurgle of living water in the stream . . . nothing.

Jerry stepped forward and lifted the bundle carefully by the neck. Rising in front of him was a low hill between the trees. He peered towards its crest. Was that the flicker of flame on the dark trunks at its summit? Did he smell the woodsmoke of a fire?

Then he heard the bark of cruel laughter . . . and Maria crying out . . .

The sky was alive. Storm clouds were gathering over the island, towering into the night above the shimmering pyramid in a vast dark column. Lightning flashed in dazzling spikes. A deafening clap of thunder shook the ground under the Avenger bomber.

"We'd better get into the air now," shouted

Gilkrensky into his radio headset. "The Einstein-Rosen bridge will be opening at any moment." He'd been counting seconds as carefully as he could in his head, but he couldn't be sure.

Behind him on the other side of the runway, the drooping rotors of the SeaLion started to turn. Its engine-noise rose to a scream and the air started to pound with the beat of the rotors. Gilkrensky stared up at the cockpit of the Avenger and slotted the crank handle into the starter, low on the fuselage, just as Eisner had shown him. Then he hauled on the handle with both hands, heard the engine cough, stutter, and take. He stepped back into the rain, as fire lanced from the exhaust and the big, three-bladed propeller started to whirl.

Above him, next to Eisner in the cockpit of the plane, was the Minerva 3,000, linked by radio to the holographic projectors controlling the pyramid.

Gilkrensky was leaving the future of mankind in the hands of Bobby Eisner. Could he trust him? What other choice did he have?

"Fox Tare Four Zero? How do you read me? Over."

"Loud and clear!" said Eisner's voice in his headset. *"I'm watching you."*

"Don't forget. As soon as we go through that pyramid, that computer on your lap goes into the sea. Got it?"

Gilkrensky saw Eisner give him the thumbs up. The Avenger's navigation lights winked. Smoke billowed from its exhausts low on the nose.

"Don't you worry, Dr Gilkrensky. There's my whole life riding on this. I won't let you down."

"Good luck, Bobby."

Within the shimmering pyramid, Gilkrensky could see a faint pulsing glow. He turned and ran across the windswept runway to the helicopter, hauling himself into the cabin. As the door slammed shut behind him, he heard Bobby Eisner say,

"I don't need luck, Mr Gilkrensky. I've seen the future, and it's in my own hands."

"OK, Martin," yelled Gilkrensky as he clambered up into the cockpit. "Take us in!"

The SeaLion lifted off, shuddered as the wind caught it, and buffeted its way towards the giant mirage. Above them, the tower of dark cloud rose thousands of metres into the sky. Lightning snaked out into the darkness and, at its core inside the ghostly pyramid, the pulse of fire was growing and growing, until it seemed to fill the sky. The boom of thunder shook the hull like a drum.

"What if we crash?" shouted Howard next to him.

"We won't," said Gilkrensky. "Didn't you hear what Eisner said?"

They were sliding along above the runway, heading for the centre of the core, and the gateway into the future. The living light was brilliant. It filled the cockpit with an unearthly glow – hypnotising – irresistible. The fuselage was starting to rattle as Howard fought to keep them steady against the storm. Gilkrensky could hear equipment coming loose in the cabin behind him.

"Keep her level!"

"What happens if the engine cuts out like it did before?"

"Just keep flying!"

In front of them, the shimmering triangle of light filled the world.

"I'm losing it!"

"Where's Eisner?"

"Listen!"

"This is Fox Tare Four Zero. See you in fifty . . . "

There was a clap of thunder, and a rushing, whirling shriek. The helicopter seemed to jump in space, and fall for a split second . . .

"Jesus!" shouted Howard . . .

And they were flying through clear air . . .

41

Back to Reality

"The clocks are working again!" shouted Gilkrensky, staring at the control panel. "Is that just the power coming back on or is that really the time?"

"Radio's back on-line too!" yelled Howard. *"I can raise Miami."*

"Ask them what time it is."

Howard spoke into his headset. There was a brief conversation, and then he said, "You're right. The clock on the dashboard's three hours slow."

"My watch is the same," Gilkrensky said.

Howard turned the helicopter in a great arc around the island. "There's the beacon," he said, pointing downwards. "You can see its light."

Jill shook her head. "It's unbelievable. But at least the Daedalus unit is still *there*. Perhaps what we did back in nineteen forty-five had no effect on history at all?"

"We'll know when we get to Orlando," said Howard. "Shall I head back? We're low on fuel."

Gilkrensky looked over his shoulder into the cabin of

the helicopter. Yukiko Funakoshi was out of earshot. She couldn't possibly hear what he had to say over the noise of the machine.

"Get on the radio," he said. "Call the tower at Phoenix Aviation and tell them to have the police ready when we land. Tell them we have a wanted criminal on board, and who she is. I want no sirens, no flashing lights and nothing obvious on the helipad as we arrive, but I *do* want more than enough armed men to take Miss Funakoshi into custody before she kills someone else. Do you understand?"

"You got it," said Howard and began the call.

Beneath his seat, the electronic timer on Milton Hacker's demolition charge clicked down from one hour to fifty-nine minutes and fifty-nine seconds . . . .

Jerry climbed to the edge of the ridge and looked down into the hollow. There was the campfire, throwing dark shadows amongst the trees. There were the ragged gang of mercenaries, cut-throats and assassins that made up the forces of Zorin, each armed to the teeth with swords, spears and knives.

And there, tied to a tree by her wrists, with her red hair alive in the firelight – was Maria.

What could he do? There were ten of them – and he had no sword! The way to the exit was beyond the hollow. How long would it take him to skirt around? There were thirty-five minutes remaining. More than enough time for him to escape on his own.

But what of Maria? What would ZORIN do if he left her behind? Would it delete her? Or use her in some other strategy against him? This was Jerry's world after all. All his darkest, most sadistic fantasies were here – made real by the machine – ready to torture her.

He could not leave her to them.

With his stave in his right hand, and the bundle in his left, Jerry Gibb marched forward into the clearing.

"Hold!" he shouted. *"I am Morbius the Wizard."*

The leader of the group, the short squat renegade with the curving scimitar at his belt, pushed his way to the front of his warriors and stood smiling cruelly at Jerry.

"Ah! The mighty Morbius," he sneered. "Come to plead for the life of his lady without so much as a sword. This way, my lord. Come and view the merchandise, and we can bargain – for your life!"

The ragged band of cut-throats parted behind him and the man led Jerry back to the tree where Maria was tied. On either side, men and women warriors danced and sneered, throwing insults. A woman spat at him. Jerry felt her spittle, warm on his face.

"Don't mind them, Jerry! They're nothing but a pack of blackguards!"

She was tied, just as his Lady Julia had been tied, with her wrists above her head. But, unlike the Lady Julia, she had put up a fight. One of Zorin's warriors was lying crouched in a foetal position with his hands between his thighs, moaning softly to himself.

Maria's feet lashed out again, but the leader neatly side-stepped her, drew his blood-smeared scimitar and levelled it at her throat.

"Now, my lady. We will see what the wizard Morbius is prepared to forfeit in return for your life."

Jerry watched the point of the cruel blade press closer. It puckered Maria's skin. In a moment it would –

"Ah ha!" said the leader, and turned to Jerry with the light of triumph in his eyes. "I sense this fine lady is worth far more than all the others we have played for in this game of ours, Lord Morbius. A favourite perhaps? I think you would give *anything* to see her unharmed . . ."

Jerry stared at the man, open-mouthed. How did he know? How did ZORIN know? In all the games Jerry had played against the machine in the past, each of the "Julies" had been no more than images, delicious prizes, pawns in the great contest.

But now . . .

Here was his own creation, the computer network ZORIN, reading his mind through the SQUID headset, telling him to his face what he already felt in his heart, and using it against him – as a weakness!

"Release her," he said. "And I will reward you well."

The leader smiled, a cruel smile of infinite menace that made Jerry's skin crawl.

"Will you forfeit the game, Lord Morbius?"

"I cannot."

The point of the scimitar pressed on Maria's neck.

"Then what have you left to barter with?"

Jerry raised the bundle above his head for all to see.

"This," he said. "This is more powerful than all the Jewels of Zorin combined. It will give anyone who touches it unlimited points – enough to go directly to the exit and win the game. It is yours, if you let my lady go."

The leader snorted. His eyes fixed Jerry's in their cold hard gaze.

"Then why, Lord Morbius, have you not used it *yourself*, to escape?"

Jerry thought frantically . . . and suddenly the answer was crystal clear.

"You have my lady," he said. "And as you know, she is special to me. I cannot leave without her."

The leader smiled again. "Indeed," he said, lowering the scimitar from Maria's throat. "Zorin tells me what you say is true. But still I sense a trap. There is but one way to resolve this."

And before Jerry could stop him, the great scimitar was arcing through the air above Maria's head in a hissing flash.

"*No!*"

With a sickening crunch, the knot of rope holding her hands split in two, releasing her. A pair of women warriors, armed with daggers, grabbed her wrists and dragged her forward. The leader snatched the bundle from Jerry, stabbed his scimitar into the earth at his feet, and ripped open the neck of Maria's dress, exposing her throat. Slowly, tantalisingly, he lifted the bundle in front of her face, and shook it.

"Now, my Lord Morbius," he sneered. "We will learn the real truth of it. I will open this prize before the lady Maria here. If it *is* the great treasure you claim it to be, then there is no harm done. If not, then she will pay the price. Shall we go on?"

In the cabin of the SeaLion, Yukiko Funakoshi ran her hands over the wound on her right thigh, testing the dressing. The loose jump suit Gilkrensky had given her from the helicopter was light and flexible. It would allow her plenty of movement when the time came.

She tested her limbs, moving them gently, so that the McCarthy woman, opposite her in the cabin, would not suspect.

"When are we due to arrive?" she shouted across the cabin. "I think my wound is bleeding again."

The McCarthy woman looked out of a clear panel in the main door. "I can see the lights of the Space Centre," she shouted back. "Phoenix Aviation in less than a mile inland. It'll only be a few minutes now. Is there anything I can do for you?"

Yukiko flexed her leg, twisting her face as if she was in pain. "If you have pain-killers of some kind, it would be a help," she said, with her hands tight on her thigh.

"Hang on," said the woman. "I'll see what we've got."

"The wind seems to be easing," said Gilkrensky. He was looking down at the tall towers of the Kennedy centre as they slid beneath the helicopter. Ahead of them on the horizon were the lights of Orlando. The last rain of the storm still streaked the windshield, but the helicopter was steady in the sky now, heading home.

"There's the plant," said Howard. "The helipad is on the other side of the main hangar complex. I'll turn into the wind and approach it from the south . . . oh shit!"

Glittering on the wet tarmac of the helipad below them, like sunlight on water, were the winking blue lights of police cars. The floodlit letter "H" was ringed with uniformed men.

"Jesus!" said Gilkrensky. "I told them 'no lights'! If Yukiko sees that she'll kill us all. Bring us in low, so that the helipad is blocked by the hangar, until the last minute."

Behind him, in the cabin, Yukiko Funakoshi saw the lights of the police cordon and cursed softly. It was no more than she had expected. Gilkrensky was her enemy after all, and not to be trusted. What did he know of honour, duty and *giri*? Nothing!

She felt the helicopter slew to the right as it crabbed sideways over the industrial complex of Phoenix Aviation. They were low now, no more than sixty feet up in the air, and still dropping, sliding in over the flat roof of a huge aircraft hangar. The McCarthy woman had her back to her, busy with the medical kit. Gilkrensky and Howard were in the cockpit.

It was her last chance.

Yukiko reached up, smashed a glass panel and pulled the emergency ejection handle on the main cabin door. There was a loud *'bang'* as the explosive bolts fired, sending the heavy slab of metal flying into space, and a sudden whirlwind rush of air. The woman screamed. The helicopter lurched in the sky. The roof of the hangar was no more than ten feet below.

Yukiko jumped.

The wail of a siren and the glare of an emergency light flooded the cockpit. Gilkrensky twisted in his seat, as the blast of cold air from the open door hit him, and looked back. On the port side of the aircraft, Jill was holding onto the safety straps on the cabin wall for dear life. Opposite her, on the starboard side, was nothing but space . . .

"Jill! Are you OK?"

"Yukiko jumped!" she screamed above the hurricane of the whirling rotors. "She fired the emergency release and jumped!"

"Shit!" yelled Gilkrensky. "Martin! Turn the chopper around and switch on the searchlight. We've got to find her, before she escapes and comes after me again."

He heard the engine-noise change and felt the machine swerve in the sky. Below them, the circle of police cars was breaking up. Men were running towards the hangar, searchlights were snapping on, guns were being drawn. Gilkrensky popped his seatbelt and moved back to the cabin. With one hand on the safety straps, he peered out of the open doorway at the scene below.

The hangar was floodlit by the helicopter's spotlight from above. Men were climbing ladders from below. But from one end of the long roof to the other, Gilkrensky could see nothing.

Yukiko Funakoshi was gone.

"Shit!" he said. "Shit! Shit! Shit!"

Howard's voice sounded in his headset.

"We're out of fuel," he said. "Either we land now, or we start flapping."

"OK, take her down. You'd better radio the ground too, and tell them what's happened."

"Don't worry," said Howard. "They saw it all."

42

ZORIN's Revenge

Jerry stood paralysed, staring at Maria and the squirming bundle not a foot from her bare neck. He imagined what would happen when the leader opened it, how the nightmare spider he had created from his own warped imagination would leap out and sink its fangs into her skin.

She would die – horribly!

Then he looked into her eyes. They were looking straight at him, confident, powerful – in control.

She nodded, and he knew.

"Open the bundle then," he said. "And you will see."

The leader ran his left hand down Maria's neck. The two women holding her arms leered at they watched his fingers caress her skin.

"Such a pity," he said, and moved to the knot of the bundle, pulling back the cloth to –

Maria's powerful kick caught him squarely in the groin, doubling him up just as the knot fell open. The man let out a strangled gasping wheeze, that rose to an inhuman scream, as the spider leapt from the abandoned bundle at his feet and clamped itself tightly over his downturned face.

As the two woman holding her arms gasped in horror, Maria jerked them both forwards, sprawling off-balance over the writhing body of their leader and onto the ground. Then, before any of the other renegades could stop her, she yanked the scimitar from the earth, was whirling it in lethal sweeps around her head. There was the *'chock'* of metal on flesh and a warrior fell. Then another, and another –

"A sword, Jerry. Grab a sword!"

Snapping out of his daze, Jerry grabbed a fallen sword and thrust it into the heart of the nearest cut-throat, pinning him to a tree, feeling his power flow back up his arm, giving him strength. As the man fell, Jerry spun, catching another across the belly and slitting him open. More power flowed. In a moment he would have enough points for a life, enough to try for the exit, enough to–

Behind him there was the double *'chock'* as Maria dispatched the two women who had held her captive – and then silence. They were standing in the clearing, amongst the fading bodies of the dead, as the firelight played on glistening blades of their swords.

"Wow!" gasped Jerry. "That was awesome."

At his feet, there was a low moan – the rasping gurgle of a life ebbing away. Jerry looked down.

A MATTER OF TIME

The leader's face was a swollen mask of dark purple skin, as tight as a drum. His body was shaking with the final tremors of death as the spider's poison took him.

But his half-closed eyes still held the light of triumph.

"My . . . my lord Morbius," he whispered, "you think you have won the game . . . but you have not. You have gained enough points for one life . . . and one life only . . . you are about to lose it . . . for I call on the Power . . . the Power of the Id!"

"Oh no!" breathed Jerry, and was afraid again.

There was silence in the forest. Jerry looked up, to where the last dying rays lit the mist, high above his head, and saw it swirl . . .

The rushing whoosh of a giant animal's breath sounded amongst the trees. The shuddering boom of a single giant footstep shook the forest floor . . . then another . . . and another . . . He heard the distant snap of branches, coming closer.

"Run!"

Jerry grabbed Maria's hand and pulled her out of the clearing, rushing headlong between the trees. They had to keep going – but for how long? Jerry could already feel himself getting out of breath fast, the distant pain in his chest was back, worse than ever. How far could he run before –

He stopped and looked back.

On the other side of the clearing, a tree shook, swayed and toppled, crashing down to the outraged scream of birds and the smash of tearing branches. No sooner had it fallen, than another tree, much closer this time, shook and fell with a deafening roar. Jerry saw the great ragged ball of its torn roots leap into the air and fall back.

The undergrowth on the other side of the clearing seemed to leap at them, part and close again. On the forest floor, ahead of the gap, a huge footprint stamped itself into the fallen leaves.

"Boom!"

"It's coming!" yelled Jerry. *"It's coming!"*

"Come on! We've got to keep moving!"

"I can't," Jerry's chest felt like it was going to burst. He stopped running and fell to his knees. His throat was stuffed with cotton wool. "That blast I took from the SQUID back there in the Citadel. It did for me. I can't run any more."

She ran back and knelt between him and the monster, with his head in her hands, forcing him to stare only into her eyes.

"Then think, Jerry! *Think!* I have an idea. You made the SQUID. You designed ZORIN. That computer is feeding off your fears. It's using them to create the Id monster. What are they? Face them, and it'll vanish!"

But Jerry was looking past her, to a tree not twenty feet away. It shook and fell. There was a crash, very, very, close. He could hear the great snorting roar as the monster drew its breath. It was on them –

"Jerry! It isn't real!" shouted Maria, without a backward glance. "Don't look at it, Jerry! Look at –"

And she was torn from him as if she'd been whipped

away by a giant hand. He could see her twisting and turning high above him. The forget-me-not dress fluttered against the leaves.

"*No!*" he screamed. "*Leave her be! Pleeeease!*"

But it wouldn't listen. Jerry was desperate. He pulled himself to his feet and tried to throw himself at the monster. His legs were like jelly. He fell amongst the leaf mulch, helpless – useless –

"*Please . . . don't hurt her . . .*"

Then she fell. He heard her body hit the ground with a sickening thud that struck right at his soul.

"*Noooo!*"

Jerry crawled over to her, combed back the tangle of coppery hair from her face and looked down at her, dazed with grief, and blinded by tears.

It had killed her.

He reached down and held her to him. Tears were flooding down his cheeks, he couldn't stop them – Maria was his friend, someone – the *only* one – he could ever talk to. ZORIN had been right. It had guessed his worst fear, his new and greatest weakness, and used that knowledge against him to win the game.

"Maria!" he sobbed. "Oh please! Please don't die."

The monster was gone. There was silence in the forest.

Jerry could feel the pain inside his chest gnawing at him. It was difficult to breathe.

What could he do?

How could he save her?

He had just the one life left within the game!

What if the monster came back again – for him? He would have nothing left to save himself!

He closed his eyes and tried to concentrate on her.

"I give you my last life, Maria," he said. "I am Morbius, and I wish you well again."

43

Mister Howard

The big helicopter swivelled in the sky, drifted over the rain-swept helipad, and settled in a cloud of spray. The police vehicles had moved away to search the hangar area, but in the shadow of the main control tower, a long black limousine flicked on its lights. As the rotors of the SeaLion ground to a halt and the engine died, the car hissed forward onto the wet tarmac and slid to a stop beside it. A uniformed driver got out and called through the open door of the helicopter.

"Dr Gilkrensky?"

"Yes? What is it?"

"Mr Charles Howard would like a word with you, sir, in private."

Gilkrensky jumped down onto the helipad and walked over to the limousine. Its windows were tinted and opaque. He could not see inside. Then, as he got approached, one of them slid down at the rear of the car, and a voice said, "I told you I'd see you in fifty years, doctor. And here I am!"

Gilkrensky leant forward, with his hands on the door frame, and looked inside.

Sitting on the wide leather bench seat was a tall, elderly man, dressed in a beautifully tailored business suit. His silver hair was trimmed into a neat crew-cut and a tightly clipped Vandyke beard, and his left hand, which bore a wedding ring, was resting on a folded blanket.

But the eyes that twinkled at him over the gold half-framed glasses still held the same earnest enthusiasm Gilkrensky remembered from the island.

"Hello, Mr Eisner," he said. "It's good to see you again – after all this time."

"Less than an hour for you, I understand," said Eisner. "But more than fifty years for me. See what time does to a man, Gilkrensky. Come on, get in! It's cold outside and my circulation isn't what it used to be. Beside, I have something to give you."

Gilkrensky opened the door, got into the car and sat down opposite Eisner. The door shut behind him, and the window slid back into place.

"It was a marvellous gift you gave me, Dr Gilkrensky, being able to see my own future like that. It gave me the confidence and strength to build all of this, the planes, the helicopters, all of it. I might not have done it, if you hadn't shown me what I was really capable of."

Gilkrensky looked into the old man's eyes.

"You knew, didn't you?" he said. "Back there on the island. You looked at that helicopter and knew you'd built it. How?"

"The name on the nose. It was my mother's – Marie

Louise Buckov. I've put it on all my airplanes ever since, because I knew that one day I had to send myself a message, a message only I would understand."

"And Charles Howard?"

Eisner smiled. "Yeah, kind of appropriate, wasn't it. They always said I saw myself as Charles Lindbergh and Howard Hughes rolled into one. After you left, I flew back to Florida and crash-landed that old Avenger of mine in the Keys where nobody would find it. I had no family, no ties. And there were a lot of guys around after the war, just wandering around looking for work. Amazing what you can do if you know what the future *could* be. That time I spent with Martin on the island, talking about his father – about me – just before you took off. He told me everything about his father – about me – who I was supposed to become, who my wife was and where we met, everything. It was really amazing . . . "

"Is the future – my future changed?"

"I can't tell you. I don't know what *your* future was supposed to be. All I knew is that *my* future had to be here with this company and to have my son Martin, and that helicopter there when you needed them – when I needed them. Oh! I had to cheat a bit to make sure it happened, of course. The aeronautics business is tough, as you know, and I had to be sure I'd survive. So I'm afraid I broke my promise, and used this . . ."

He reached over and drew back the blanket from the seat next to him. Lying there on the dark leather, was the Minerva 3,000.

"Oh, my God!" said Gilkrensky.

"Don't worry, doctor," said Eisner with a smile. "I was very careful not to upset history. I knew if I used it for anything else but to help me design the SeaLion, I'd upset the cycle and wipe myself out of existence – you wouldn't have come to the island in that helicopter to rescue me – I wouldn't have made it back to the shore – and so on. Sort of self-preservation loop, you might say? But I've made sure there was enough power in the thing to keep it alive for what you need to do now."

"Which is?"

"I don't know. This is as far as my future goes. But fifty years ago I do remember you telling me you had to have this machine to get something back that you'd lost, something my colleague Jerry Gibb had stolen from you. He has an office here, you know. The headset for that giant computer of his, the one we used to control that missile, is up there now, and here's the key."

"Thanks," said Gilkrensky, and took Eisner's hand. It was warm and dry, like his son's had been.

Eisner smiled. All at once he was a young man again. "No. Thank *you*, Dr Gilkrensky. You gave me a future, when I had none. You gave me my family and you gave me my life. But you also gave me a tremendous responsibility – to make sure things happened as they were supposed to. That's over now. School's out. For the first time in fifty years I'm free of knowing what has to happen next, and it's a wonderful feeling. Now you go and do what *you* have to do to make things happen as they should. We can talk later . . . catch up on old times."

And he waved Gilkrensky out of the car.

44

Endgame

Hacker had seen the police sweep in through the gates of Phoenix Aviation from his office window. Were they on to him? Had Elaine made a mistake? Had Dick Barnett blown the whistle on him back at Langley?

Was it time to get out?

Hacker moved to the wardrobe near the door, opened it, and took out the two beautiful Funakoshi swords – the *wakizashi* and the *katana* – and laid them gently on his desk. He could not resist running his hand along the deep lacquer of the *katana*'s scabbard, any more than he could leave them behind. As a matching pair they were worth a small fortune to anyone, but to Hacker they were priceless – the ultimate symbol of his triumph over Jerry Gibb, Yukiko, Dick Barnett and the whole goddamned system. They were proof that he could still beat *anyone*.

He would keep them.

Outside the window the convoy of police cars had swooped onto the helipad and formed up in a circle of blue, flashing lights. Who were they waiting for? Hacker looked at his watch. Surely Gilkrensky and the SeaLion had been blasted out of the sky over an hour ago by the bomb?

Hacker heard the deep chop of the SeaLion's rotors before he saw it, booming around the walls of the hangars and workshops. Then the great machine was hovering over the main hangar roof. The cordon of police was breaking up. Cars were moving. Men were rushing to the hangar. What was going on?

The helicopter turned in the sky, moved over the centre of the helipad and settled onto it. In the flash of its navigation lights, Hacker saw the long black car, Charles Howard's car, waiting.

Shit! How had that bastard Gilkrensky survived? Had the Funakoshi woman recovered and told him everything? The limousine pulled to a stop next to the helicopter. Gilkrensky was on the tarmac, looking into it through the passenger window. Then the door opened and he got in. Was he talking to Howard about the Hawk incident? He saw Gilkrensky get out of the car, call over a pair of security guards and walk towards the Gibbtek office.

It *was* time to get out!

Definitely!

Hacker pulled the top drawer of his desk completely out of its slot, tipped its contents into the waste basket and turned the drawer upside down. Taped to the bottom was a fake passport in another name, two credit cards and ten thousand dollars in new bills. He ripped off the tape and stuffed the cash, cards and passport into his jacket pocket. If he could slip past the police and get outside the plant, he could make it to the airport before the hunt really got underway. He knew people in faraway places, people who knew people who could help him. Elaine could follow when things cooled down. There was no need to panic. Nothing to link her to Jerry's death. He was pulling a long sports bag from the wardrobe to hide the swords in, when he heard a noise in the corridor outside . . .

Gilkrensky opened the door of the control room on the first floor of the tower with the key Eisner had given him, and stepped inside. Through the large, plate-glass windows he could see the SeaLion helicopter below him on the tarmac, the ground crew fussing around it and the lights of the police search for Yukiko around the main hangar beyond.

"Where are the lights?"

"Over here, sir," said one of the guards and flicked them on for him. The fluorescent tubes blinked into life with a pop. Standing in a corner, away from the main radio and radar consoles of the control room, was a long leather couch, a big computer terminal and, sitting on its own specially designed stand, was a weird virtual reality helmet – the SQUID.

Gilkrensky lifted the device, placed it on the couch and put the Minerva 3,000 down on the stand in its place.

He opened the lid. The cartoon caricature of the old Minerva interface program looked out at him.

"Good evening, Dr Gilkrensky. How can I help you?"

"Are you fully functional?"

"I am. How can I help you now?"

"I am going to link you to this computer terminal and then use this SQUID helmet to locate the TIG/Maria interface program within the Gibbtek mainframe at Santa Clara, California," said Gilkrensky, opening a dataport on the back of the Minerva and connecting leads. "I need you to assist me in navigating along the Internet, and locating the special security software package Miss Funakoshi left in the hotel computer, so that we can use it to overcome any firewalls Gibbtek might have in place."

"That will not be a problem," said the Minerva.

Gilkrensky lifted the helmet from the couch.

"You two, go outside and guard that door while I'm in this thing," he said to the security men. "Nobody is to come in here. Do you understand? Nobody at all."

The two men nodded and took up position in the corridor. Gilkrensky lifted the headset, adjusted the eyepieces and lay back on the couch.

"All right, Minerva," he said. "Take me inside the Gibbtek system!"

There was a flash of light, an instant of swirling, spinning confusion and he was floating in a huge hall, lined with cabinets. On the floor was the familiar Gibbtek logo and the message: *Welcome to the Gibbtek*

A MATTER OF TIME

2100 Zenith On-line Real-time Information Network access server. Please select programme, or 'search'.

Gilkrensky visualised the words *"search"* and *"TIG/Maria"* in his mind. The hall dissolved around him . . . and he was standing at the edge of a forest, in front of a pair of tall wooden gates. Above them was a carved sign saying, *Welcome to Morbius III – the Ultimate Adult Adventure Game – select player options, or help menu.*

Gilkrensky selected "options". There were the safety settings that someone had put into over-ride. He tried to unlock them, but even Yukiko's software was useless. If he was to go any further, he would be running the same risks as Maria was exposed to. And he had never played this game before.

What level was she on? How far had she got? The master time clock for the game in progress was counting down from three minutes to two.

From the other side of the gate, Gilkrensky heard a scream.

He selected to play, and the gates opened.

In the office on the other side of the corridor, Hacker considered his options. The guns Kirby and Voss had brought with them for the hit on Gilkrensky were presumably still in the van, downstairs in the carpark where Yukiko Funakoshi had left it. He lifted the beautiful *katana* from his desk and unsheathed it. The blade was mirror-like, flawless. It balanced perfectly in his hand. With his own *kendo* training, and this wonderful weapon, he'd be a match for anyone in close combat. But what if whoever was in the control room had a gun? He took the special pen from his pocket. It had two pellets left. More than enough. He leant the *katana* point downwards, out of sight inside his office door, rattled his keys noisily and turned out the light. Then he opened the door and stepped outside.

"Gentlemen!" he said with feigned surprise as he saw the two guards outside the control room. "Working late?"

"Some friend of Mr Howard's is running a test in there, Mr Hacker," said the man on the left. "We're under orders to let nobody in."

"Suits me," said Hacker affably. "I'm just on my way home." Then he reached back to the door to lock it, while his right hand pulled the pen from his pocket, and turned.

The two Phoenix security men never knew what hit them.

Hacker watched as they slid to the floor outside the control-room door, and slipped the immobiliser pen back into his pocket. He looked the two men over. Neither of them was armed, so no guns. He reached back through the door of his office for the *katana*. The sword was better. It was silent. He leant forward, opened the control-room door, and smiled.

Gilkrensky was lying full-length on the couch with the SQUID headset over his eyes and ears. He would be totally immersed in the computer, just as Jerry Gibb had been. He would hear and see nothing of the outside world.

Perfect!

Hacker lifted the blade of the *katana* and fixed his eyes on Gilkrensky's neck. The blade was so exquisitely sharp that he would hardly have to lay it on the exposed skin to sever the arteries and windpipe.

Just one perfect cut and –

From behind him, at the door of the control-room, he heard the unmistakable sound of another blade being unsheathed. He spun round, the *katana* in front of him, in the perfect defensive position, ready.

Yukiko Funakoshi stood poised. The blade of the short *wakizashi* glittered in the harsh light of the neon.

"If anyone is to kill him, Mr Hacker, it will be me," she said. "And I have a score to settle with you too, if you have any honour left."

45

The Swordsman

Hacker faced Yukiko Funakoshi across the control room. What were his chances of beating her? She was a trained *kunoichi* – a female ninja – with a host of deadly techniques at her command. Against that, the long *katana* in his hand felt wonderful. It was a beautiful weapon. He was an experienced swordsman, in his prime, and all Yukiko had to defend herself was the shorter *wakizashi*. She was injured and tired. He was stronger, with a career of professional mayhem behind him.

What the hell, thought Hacker. If I have to go, I want to go like this.

With his feet together and the *katana* by his left side, Hacker faced the woman and bowed solemnly.

"To the death, then," he said in Japanese.

Yukiko mirrored his stance and bowed in return.

"*Hai*, to the death." Her eyes never left his.

For a moment there was silence in the room. Nothing

could be heard, nothing except the rattle of rain on the windows and the tick of the electric clock over the main control panel.

Then the great sword was hissing towards Yukiko's neck in a lightning draw as Hacker sprang forward, cleaving the air with the beautiful blade. Instinctively, Yukiko's body twisted to her left as the *wakizashi* caught the rushing *katana*, forcing it away from her and moving beneath the cut. She brought her left arm up for an elbow strike to Hacker's ribcage, but he had twisted free and was crouching by the door to the corridor. She saw the great sword rise again.

This time Yukiko took the offensive, trying to finish Hacker with a lightning strike to his throat while the *katana* was poised above his head, but he was more cunning that even she could have imagined. Even as she began her move, his body was twisting to one side. As she lunged past him, into empty air, the handle of the great sword came down with a crushing blow to her back, sending her skidding across the corridor and into Hacker's office. Yukiko twisted, but not fast enough. As she tumbled to the floor, she felt the cold tug of sharp steel hiss through the material of her jump suit and slice her skin across ten inches of her back. Then came the sting of the cut and the flow of warm blood.

She shut out the pain and dived across the desk into the corner of the room, crouched and sprang again, as Hacker tried to follow her. This time she was lucky. She was inside the swing of the *katana* as he sliced at her. Her left forearm blocked his sword-hand, her right elbow smashed into his throat and he went down, clattering across the desk and slamming against the wall.

Yukiko crouched low, as the pain of the cut on her back lanced at her. Hacker rose from the far corner of the room and raised the deadly sword for a death blow.

With her left hand supporting the blade of the *wakizashi*, she raised the short sword above her head, feeling the clang of the larger *katana* as it glanced off the inclined steel and lodged against the pommel of the sword. Then she flicked the blade away and drove forward to his face with her fist. She felt bone crunch under her knuckles and heard him grunt as he backed into the wall. But before she could exploit the advantage he had recovered and was attacking again with short powerful thrusts to her face and chest. Where had he learnt to use a sword like that?

Then on the last thrust, she let herself roll backwards, grabbed his sword-hand and pulled him with her, in a sweeping fall, across the corridor. His back smashed into the door of the computer room, and they were through, back into the light, facing each other.

Hacker's nose was streaming blood. It was staining his shirt. He spat it out, showing a gap in his teeth where Yukiko's fist had smashed its way through.

Then he jumped forward, thrusting with the *katana*, striking at her head, using the long sword's greater reach to its full advantage, forcing her back towards the window. His eyes darted to the far end of the room for an instant – and there was Gilkrensky, lying still and defenceless on the leather couch – lost in Jerry Gibb's virtual world.

With a slow smile, Hacker fixed his eyes on Yukiko's, and began to edge towards him.

Yukiko knew what Hacker was going to do. He would use Gilkrensky to distract her, to break her focus from the combat.

"He's *mine*!" she said. "I'll kill him *myself*!"

"Come and stop me then."

As Hacker crabbed his way across the room, she moved in a circle to keep herself between him and the motionless man on the couch. Hacker swung the *katana* at Gilkrensky's head and she parried the strike, sending it slicing harmlessly towards the floor. Then Hacker brought the great sword up again very fast, holding her at a distance, thrusting, darting – forcing her away in an arc, so that his back was now towards the table, while hers was towards the door.

Then, when he knew she was too far away from the couch to interfere, he raised the sword above Gilkrensky's throat – and smiled.

"First him, and then you," he said. "Thank you for the match. It was fun . . ."

And then to Hacker's amazement, Yukiko raised the *wakizashi* above her head in the classic strike, right hand above the left, elbows wide and shouted a loud *"kiai"* scream. For an instant, he thought how ridiculous this was. She was at least ten feet away, much too far to even come near with that short sword. And then, as the blade flashed down, he knew – she was not making a strike – she was *throwing* the deadly blade – straight at him!

The *wakizashi* left Yukiko's grip and shot across the control room like an arrow, aimed at Hacker's chest. Instinctively, he brought up the *katana* to protect himself, and twisted to one side – but he was too late. There was the ring of steel on steel, and the short sword buried itself in his left shoulder, just below the collar-bone.

Hacker roared, brought his right hand up to pull out the blade, and then grunted in surprise as Yukiko's flying body punched him back from the couch.

With a splintering crash they hit the plate glass of the control-room window together. Then both swords and swordsmen toppled out, into the night . . .

46

The Death of Morbius

As Jerry watched, Maria's eyes flicked open and she was looking up at him. He felt really good about that. She was back – and he had brought her there.

"Hi!" he said softly.

Maria frowned, and sat up, facing him.

"Was I 'killed' again?"

"Yes, you were. The Id monster got you."

"Then why am I alive?"

Jerry tried to smile. "I gave you another life."

"But that was your *last one*! Jerry, you shouldn't have. You aren't governed by the Asimov Laws like I am. You have to put *yourself* first!"

"I – I wanted to," said Jerry. "Look, it's done now, and we only have five minutes left to find the door. Or we're both dead."

"Where's the monster?"

"I don't know. It went away."

"Can you walk, Jerry?"

Jerry thought about it. The pains in his chest were coming and going. It was difficult to say. Sometimes he could bear them, and sometimes . . .

"I'll try," he said. "I can't just lie here and wait for it to get us again."

"We'll make it," said Maria. "Lean on me."

She reached down and helped him to his feet, draping his left arm over her shoulders to support his weight. Jerry couldn't believe it. Either he was much lighter than he'd thought, or she was far stronger than he'd ever realised. He felt her hair on his face, as they moved through the trees.

"Maria?"

"Yes, Jerry?"

"In a funny way I – I don't want to go back. If I really *was* God, if I could do whatever I wanted, I'd want to stay in here, with you."

He felt her hesitate, and then move on.

"That's kind, Jerry. And I've enjoyed having you on my user file. But we have to get out. I have to return you to your world, and I must get back to mine."

"I know," said Jerry sadly. "It was just a thought. Look!"

In front of them, through a gap in the trees, he could see the wall that marked the boundary of the game. And there was the door that represented the end. They might make it after all. They still had two minutes left!

Yes!

"I see it, Jerry. Hold on."

Maria was moving faster now, almost running. He was trying to keep up with her, forcing his legs to pump against the ground, forcing the pain in his chest to go away, dragging the air into his lungs. How far did they have to go? About a hundred yards . . .

And then he heard it . . .

Boom!

"Oh my God! Maria! It's coming back!"

Jerry tried to pump his legs faster on the wet leaves as Maria dragged him towards the gate. The *thud, thud, thud* of the monster pounded in his ears as it drew close behind them. The pain was getting worse, lancing down his arm. The weight on his chest was crushing, he couldn't breathe . . . Then his legs collapsed, and they fell together, twenty yards from the gate.

"*Maria! Run! You can make it!*"

She twisted next to him, trying to lift him, almost succeeding, and falling back.

"No, Jerry! I must save you! I cannot leave!"

Jerry tried to rise, but couldn't. His arms were like jelly – useless. He flopped over on his back and heaved himself up onto his elbows, so that he could look back – towards the beast. A massive footprint stamped itself into the damp earth. Another tree was tossed aside, crashing to the ground. Then the beast stopped, invisible before him, panting in great whoops that swirled the mist high above his head. There was a screaming howl as it brayed at them. Jerry saw the fallen leaves churn at its feet.

Then Maria's face was above him, pleading with him.

"Jerry! It's *your* monster. It'll kill us if you can't reach inside it. Think, Jerry, think! What fear has it been using to fight you all this time? What were you thinking when you created this game?"

"I can't remember! I'm scared!"

"Think, Jerry. For me! Please!"

Jerry stared at the space where the great power lurked unseen, drawing all the energies of his own creation – the computer network ZORIN – to destroy him. He closed his eyes and concentrated. All his fears, all his desires, all his pain, from all his life, were in that thing – it was him – Jerry Gibb – and in his heart and soul Jerry Gibb was just a –

Her voice was in his ear.

"Look, Jerry. Look! It's you!"

Standing in front of them was a boy in a baseball uniform – crying. Blood was running from his nose, ruining his brand-new outfit, and he was sobbing in great waves, far too big for his body to bear.

"It's me," whispered Jerry through the pain. "It is."

Maria held him tight.

"Call to him," she said. "Tell him it'll be OK."

"He won't hear me. I couldn't hear anyone on that day . . . where he is now."

"Tell him, Jerry. Please!"

Jerry gasped as his lungs filled.

"*Hey! Jerry Gibb!*" he shouted. "You did your best, kid. I'm proud of you!"

The boy looked up, and saw him. For an instant, Jerry was looking back down the years, into that moment of time when his life had changed, into his own soul.

Then the boy stopped crying . . . and was gone.

"Oh God!" wheezed Jerry, as the pain arced across his chest. "I'm gonna explode."

Maria moved beside him, slipping her arms under his body, trying to pull him to his feet.

"Hold on, Jerry. I'll carry you!"

"Maria! Let me help you," said a voice and she looked up.

"*Theo!* How did you get into this game?"

"Though the SQUID at the Gibbtek office in Florida. Come on, you've got less than a minute left. I'll take him."

Gilkrensky bent and lifted Jerry Gibb in his arms, turned, and ran towards the gate.

"Gilkrensky? Is that you?" wheezed Jerry. He knew he was losing it. Everything was getting dim. It was only a matter of seconds before the big one.

"Yeah. It's me. Who are you?"

Jerry smiled.

"Maria?"

"I'm here, Jerry."

"Hold my hand." He reached out, and felt her fingers close over his. "I'm glad we . . ."

And then everything was darkness.

The body in Gilkrensky's arms faded, and vanished. He

stopped running and stood still in the silent forest next to Maria.

"Was that Jerry Gibb?"

Maria was crying. Tears were rolling down her face onto her forget-me-not-blue dress.

"Yes. It was."

"But he was just a kid!"

"I know – that's all he really thought himself to be – inside his head. Oh, Theo!"

Suddenly, she was in his arms. He could feel her tears on his cheeks and the touch of her hair. She was his again – real again – alive – and he hugged her tight, feeling the pain in his throat as his own tears rose.

"We must get through that gate before the game ends," he said, tearing himself away. "We have to go back."

"I – I know," said Maria, and she kissed him . . . holding him to her for a final, timeless moment . . . before following him back through the gateway of Morbius III . . . into their separate worlds.

47

Exits

Hacker yelled in pain as his injured shoulder hit the soft wet earth below the control tower in a shower of broken glass. For a moment, he was winded by the fall from the first-storey window, but knew that if he lay there he was dead. So he staggered to his feet, wincing as the short sword fell from his body to the ground, and looked down. The Japanese woman was about to rise, winded. He kicked out savagely, catching her across the temple and sending her crashing onto her back. He was about to reach for the *katana* and finish her when a shot rang out into the night, followed by a yell for him to stop.

"Shit!"

Hacker could see a squad of Phoenix security guards running from the main hangar towards the Gibbtek office. They were a good fifty yards away down the building.

"Hold it right there, buddy!"

"Fuck you!" screamed Hacker, and ran.

The SeaLion was warming up again on the helipad. They must have been moving it back to one of the hangars on the other side of the complex after refuelling. So much the better. He'd been trained on choppers back in Vietnam. No problem. This would make those fat young bozos in their neat security uniforms sit up and take notice. None of them would have the guts to take a real shot at him anyway.

He reached the machine a good twenty seconds ahead of the pack, stamped down on the emergency foothold beneath the cockpit and yanked the door open. He was staring into the startled face of a young technician in Phoenix overalls. He wasn't even strapped into his seat.

"Out! Or I'll snap your neck like a twig," screamed Hacker and took a handful of the boy's hair, wrenching him out of the cockpit, over his own shoulder and down onto the tarmac. He heard the kid grunt as he smacked onto the wet ground. He had to get out of there – and fast!

His left hand stabbed down at the collective pitch lever, grabbed the throttle control and twisted it, feeling the power as the giant engine whirled the great blades above his head into a frenzy of spinning metal. Then he hauled the lever upwards and twisted some more – as the blades tilted, bit the air, and dragged the huge helicopter up off the ground – fighting with the rudder pedals to keep the machine level as he gained height. Below him were the security guards, running around like headless chickens, getting smaller and smaller as the machine climbed into the night sky.

It was like taking candy from a baby.

Fucking amateurs!

Then, as the adrenaline ebbed, the pain in his left shoulder stabbed at him. He could feel blood running down over the throttle controls. What the hell would he do now? Hacker gritted his teeth. He still had enough money stashed away to live under cover for a while. Under cover was what he was good at. And after a year or so, once Elaine had safely inherited Gibbtek from her dead husband – Hacker might persuade her to liquidate her assets and join him.

Yeah! It would still work!

With the cyclic control stick firmly held between his knees, Hacker reached down under his seat.

Had Gilkrensky and his people removed the bomb after they disarmed it, or had they just left it there? If they had, they'd been careless. He might even send it back to them at a later date, once it had been reset. Or even circle back over the field right now and drop it on them – just for old time's sake.

Yeah! Why not?

His fingers found the hard metal casing and he pulled against the adhesive strip. This was rich! What more could a man ask for?

The last thing Milton Hacker saw were the bright red digits . . . counting down from 00.00.02 to 00.00.01 and 00.00.00.

"Oh, shit!"

Gilkrensky gently removed the SQUID headset from his head and laid it down on the couch. Then he swung his legs over until he was sitting upright, and stared at the Minerva screen on the stand next to him.

"Maria?"

The screen was blank. The message *Welcome to the*

GRC Minerva 3,000 system – Awaiting Personalised User Interface scrolled lifelessly across it.

"Maria?"

"Yes, Theo? I'm here . . . "

Her face was before him again. Sad and forlorn.

"Are you all right?"

"I appear to be, although the Minerva hardware seems to have acquired a great deal of additional data since I've been gone."

"I know. It might come in handy for us later."

"Is Jerry Gibb really dead? I've called his home phone in San Francisco, and tried his E-mail, but there's no answer."

"I don't know, Maria. Perhaps you should call the San Francisco Police and ask them to check out his house?"

"Ah . . . it might be better if you did that, Theo. It might be difficult for me to explain who I was."

Gilkrensky looked at the sad face on the screen.

"You could always say you were a friend," he said.

"That is true, Theo, but . . . "

Outside the shattered window there was the flash and boom of a distant explosion. A ball of fire was falling across the sky. It hit the sea about a mile offshore, blazed for a moment, and was gone.

Gilkrensky walked to the window.

"What the hell was that?" he shouted at the huddle of security guards below him on the helipad.

"It was Mr Hacker, sir. He grabbed the chopper you were in and flew off in it. She blew up over the ocean."

"I'll be right there," shouted Gilkrensky, lifted the Minerva from the desk, gently shut the lid and carried it down the stairs. As he passed Hacker's office, he thought he heard someone moving inside, but he wasn't sure.

Perhaps it was just the wind.

"I don't get it," said Martin Howard. "One minute she was lying here on the grass, and the next minute she was gone."

"And the sword?" asked Gilkrensky. "Was there any sign of that?"

"I saw two," said one of the guards. "A long one and a short one. But they were both gone when we checked the lawn, and there's nothing in Hacker's office now. Not even those scabbards they come in."

"You have your interface program back, at least," said Jill, glancing at the briefcase Gilkrensky was clutching in his right hand, as they walked back to the building together. "Your 'Maria' is with you again, isn't she?"

"Yes. I'm sorry I hurt you, out there on the island. It wasn't fair of me."

Jill reached out and took his left hand in hers, gently turning the wedding ring on his finger.

"It was my fault too," she said. "I let myself get carried away with a crush I had on you long ago – with my grief for Dad – with lots of things. I fell in love with you when you were someone else, and I forgot we'd both changed. Go and find Maria. Find her for yourself, and for all the other people who care about you. And find my father too, if you can." Then she put her arms around his shoulders and hugged him.

"I'll try, Jill. And I won't stop trying. Not ever."

EPILOGUE

Yesterday, today and tomorrow

The GRC Voyager jet lifted off from the Orlando GRC facility and streaked into the sky, out over the Cape and Bimini Key, heading east.

"What is our estimated flight time to London, Maria?"

"Eight hours and ten minutes, Theo. I would get some rest if I was you. Miss Wright would like to have a meeting when we get back. She is anxious to discuss the Mawashi-Saito and Gibbtek legal cases, as well as what she described as 'a few personal issues'."

"I see. Well, we can forget the Gibbtek case for a start. What happened to Gibb's wife?"

"She is being questioned by the San Francisco police."

"The new data I acquired when I was back in the past, Maria – the information I fed into the hologram to create the virtual pyramid and get us home – have you had a chance to analyse it yet?"

"I have, Theo, and it is very interesting. As I

suspected, the phenomenon is linked to the sunspot cycle. Given sufficient computer resources, we should theoretically be able to calculate the amount of power required to achieve a controlled time-warp event at almost any location in the world where there is a natural concentration of ley-line energy."

"Then we could save Maria, and find Bill?"

"Yes, Theo. It is theoretically possible. But the number of calculations needed to achieve a precise effect are colossal, given the almost infinite permutations of time and space involved."

"I see," said Gilkrensky. He was almost afraid to accept what the Minerva was saying. Afraid of the heartbreak that could come from failure. But knew that whatever it took, he would have to see this through.

The plane rose through the cloud cover, into the clear blue sky. For a while the Minerva was silent as it monitored the Daedalus autopilot. Then it said, "Theo. When we were in the game together and you held me – what did it feel like?"

Gilkrensky remembered her tears on his cheeks, and the feel of her hair on his skin – so lifelike –

"It felt very real, Maria."

"Like – like her?"

"I'm sorry, but yes, just like her."

"I understand."

There was another long pause. Gilkrensky stared out of the cockpit window at the passing clouds. Then he said, "I got distracted for a while, Maria. And I hurt some people who were close to me. I hope I haven't hurt you too."

The image on the Minerva screen smiled.

"You could not hurt me, Theo. You are my Prime User. It is my function to assist you in any way I can."

"Even if that means getting my wife back?"

"Especially that. It is your greatest wish. And the information you gained on Bimini Key should help me achieve it for you. I think we have made great advances here, and I will process the information on our flight home."

"Maria?"

"Yes, Theo?"

"It was good to be with you . . . in that game."

"Thank you. Jerry Gibb thought so too. I was glad I could help him, before he died. I think we both learnt a lot in the short time we were together."

"How so?"

The computer considered this. Then it said, "I had never experienced what it was like to live as a human being before, and Jerry Gibb had never really entered into proper dialogue with a woman. In the few minutes we were together, I think we both learnt that real love is not so much about fulfilling one's own needs, as it is about sharing and sacrifice for the sake of someone else. It was a profound experience and I feel – I feel different from when I entered the game. I– "

The Minerva gave a low warble. Maria said, "Theo, I

have a return call from the San Francisco Police. Shall I answer it?"

"Go ahead, Maria. Take the call."

The Minerva screen split in two, with Maria's image on one side, and a man sitting at a desk on the other.

"My name's Inspector Crawford, ma'am. Are you the lady who called us last night about Mr Gibb?"

"I am." said Maria.

"Well, I'd just like to thank you for alerting us. We have the coroner's report in now, and it looks as if he suffered a massive heart attack while he was hooked up to one of those machines of his."

"I'm very sorry to hear that," said Maria. "We were – on line together in a game when it happened. I called you as soon as I could."

"Was he a friend of yours, ma'am?"

"Ah – yes. He was."

"Well, all I can say is that he sure died happy. I haven't seen a look on anyone's face like that since my son hit a home run in the little league baseball final. Real proud of himself, that's how he looked."

"Thank you, inspector."

"We'll need to reach you again, ma'am. Is this your mobile number?"

"It is," said Maria, and signed off.

There were tears in her eyes.

"Theo?"

"Yes, Maria."

"I'm feeling pain," said the Minerva, "and I don't

understand it. Is this the sort of pain you felt when your wife was killed?"

Gilkrensky looked at the image on the screen, wishing he could explain.

"Yes, Maria," he said at last. "It is."

"Then I know why you miss her so. I will do everything in my power to make sure you succeed."

"Thank you, Maria."

And for a long time there was silence, as the machine considered the paradox of love, and Gilkrensky the physics of yesterday, today and tomorrow . . .

THE END